EMILY DICKINSON:

{GODDESS}
OF THE
{VOLCANO}

A BIOGRAPHICAL NOVEL

by
Despina Lala-Crist

Translated by
Robert L. Crist

Cover painting and sketches by:
Ave George Ioannides

TO
JASON A.R. CRIST
TO
CELEBRATE
OUR
SECRET-SACRED
PLACES

Acknowledgements

My deepest gratitude to my husband Robert for our insightful discussions of the great poet. Special thanks to the Emily Dickinson Museum – the people who help keep her memory alive and have inspired me in my work. I also want to thank Naomi Norwood, Fran Weinberg, and Lance Crist for their editorial aid, as well as many American and Greek friends for their encouragement in the course of the writing. My profound thanks go to the libraries of Dickinson College, Shippensburg University, and Messiah College for granting me access to their valuable collections.

Despina Lala Crist
Carlisle, PA

PRELUDE

Love and Poetry

I reckon – when I count at all –
First – Poets – Then the Sun –
Then Summer – Then the Heaven of God –
And then – the List is done –
(#569)

In the summer session of my senior year, love and poetry burst into my life like a double star, personified in my poetry professor.

He had just received his master's degree at the University of Chicago, while I was a graduating bachelor's student, dreaming of return to my beloved Greece. Three years in America seemed like centuries, and the nearer the time of graduation approached, the greater my nostalgia became. Like a whirlwind, it swept me into a vast ocean of daydreams.

From my dormitory window I viewed the green hill on one side and, on the other, the Kanawha River, which defined the boundary between the campus and the city of Charleston, West Virginia. In my hungry eyes the stream flowed to a vast, glittering sea. Under the bright summer sky, the vessels on the river became Aegean fishing boats floating toward the far horizon, and the rug in my room became sand stroking the soles of my feet. Smiling in bliss, I found myself in Athens, in my home – the garden smelling of jasmine and honeysuckle. I heard the sounds of my neighborhood, the buzzing of bees soothing the ache of homesickness.

Thus I was hurrying to complete graduation requirements, taking courses in summer school – six weeks daily from nine to noon. I held up under the pressure in order to earn my degree at least one semester early.

How little we know our future! We plan, we dream, without suspecting that significant events will steal into our lives, leading us wherever they choose!

The June temperatures were rising, but instead of swimming for relaxation or working to cover expenses, I stayed in my small dorm room on a tight budget, with endless reading. The course was Romantic Poetry: Wordsworth, Coleridge, Keats, Shelley, and Byron. The syllabus was demanding, but it deeply repaid my effort – and I did not know that discussion would finally lead to the incredible world of Emily Dickinson.

The great poets visited the classroom that summer. Their vision poured into my heart as inspiration sprang from the intense voice of the young professor. At once his gaze had circled the class and his eyes rested on the foreign student about whom that week the local paper had featured a flattering article.

"Yesterday, we spoke of you at home," he told me in a warm tone, and I was excited, not by the words but by the way he was looking at me. His avid attention threw me into turmoil. I had dreamed of that gaze from my future husband. When he spoke the two of us alone existed, and my soul responded with all the precious feelings alive in my depths. Surely somewhere, at some time, I had met him and indeed had loved him in all the ways of the heart. Oh, how I had missed him, longing for our reunion.

From the moment we came together, my world was a tender story in which I viewed the hero and heroine, the mentor and the student, with deep feeling and direct interest. The student was wholly vitalized by the meeting. She smiled deeply, never doubting their bond. Her soul flowered in the love she had for him for years, and she felt her heart beat in the powerful rhythm of passion.

For the romantic poets, "The essence of spiritual beauty is love." "The stroke of Death is turned to Victory by love," Emily Dickinson confirmed.

As the course began with Wordsworth, the mind at once formed an image: the figure of a tall man with white hair on a deep-green hill pacing thoughtfully as his lips formed enchanting lines. His brilliant but anguished companion was Coleridge – visionary, poet, and philosopher. Then came Keats, the handsome physician who abandoned medicine for poetry's sake. He passionately hymned ancient Greece and celebrated her ideal beauty. By his side were Shelley and Byron – the three of them friends, poetic giants and philhellenes who declared, "Poetry elicits a feeling of the lofty, the great, the good, and the therapeutic."

Devoted to beauty, they made their lives art, disdaining death, which haunted them. They died in their prime: Keats, who cared for his consumptive mother, departed at the age of twenty-five; Shelley, abandoning his wealthy family for the sake of poetry, drowned in a sailing outing with friends before he was thirty; and Byron, expressing his ideals in action, left this world at Mesolonghi, serving the cause of the Greek revolution. He was thirty-six. They were so young, but their art is so intense, authentic, and innovative. They gave humanity the gift of life-energy, and death triumphantly opened to them the gates of immortality. "Behind Me – dips Eternity – / Before Me – Immortality – / Myself – the Term between" (#721), as Dickinson wrote.

Inspired, the young scholar led the students in probing texts, exploring themes. It was a fertile summer – with revolutionary changes. His eyes never left her, and having confirmed that regulations did not exclude an unattached teacher dating a student, by the end of the second week of classes, he asked her to go out. "My parents want to meet you," he told her, and on the road to the restaurant, they first dropped by his house for her to meet the gracious mother and noted father, who received her with American ease and politeness. Fortunately, she had purchased a print dress with a ruffle at the hem, very fashionable at the time. Having sacrificed her last three dollars at a sale, she felt attractive and comfortable, though no one seemed to pay attention to the skirt or the ruffle. The conversation turned to Hellenic and American education, concluding that the two systems were perfect in their way – so there was no problem. The only problem came up later at the restaurant. Looking at the prices on the menu, the student hesitated. The young man took the initiative, and the orders arrived, first French red wine (not in a bottle, but in two glasses, since the driving code permitted only one drink). It was all in American order, though the young man had a bias for European culture . . . and its products.

A little round table by candlelight, and the two of them dined. The repast held an exotic flavor as he looked into her eyes and repeatedly touched her hand.

"This academic year I will be teaching in Pennsylvania, and then I will return to the University of Chicago for doctoral work," he said before dessert, "and I want to have my life-companion by my side." He looked at her with an eager plea as he meaningfully pressed her palm.

"And how will that come to be?" the student asked in a trembling voice.

"I mean, I will be married. . . ."

"Are you proposing?" she asked in turmoil.

He awaited her answer – not another question, but she went on in a logical fashion, which, however, rang false, even in her own ears:

"But don't you think we need more time. . . ."

He looked at her without responding in words. He just bowed and tenderly kissed her hand.

The professor chose the last day of classes to round out the theory of poetry, citing a definition provided by Emily Dickinson. Standing at the lectern, he gazed at his students a moment before reciting:

I taste a liquor never brewed –
From Tankards scooped in Pearl –
Not all the Vats upon the Rhine

Love and Poetry

Yield such an Alcohol!
(#214)

"And I would define *love* the same way!" the student spontaneously injected. "Love and poetry, the angels of man!" he added, alluding to Baudelaire.

At the end of the term, grades generously assigned, the students, grateful and enriched, left for home, and the campus emptied, while the student remained in her dorm room glued to the window, waiting for his Renault to turn into the parking space and pull up under her window. It was a serene summer night full of stars glittering gently, and the professor got out of the little car, took her by the hand trembling slightly, and with radiant faces they took the path by the riverside and sat down on their bench, silent for some time. Opposite glowed the lights of Charleston. On one side of the river was the college with a few lights in the dormitory windows; on the other, the city shone like a birthday cake with burning candles, above it a discreet, tender moon that gleamed and guessed.

The Professor tenderly captured the Student's hand. "We've gotten to know one another – haven't we?" he murmured. The Student leaned her head on his breast and felt a rainbow of poets summoning her. She soared as she touched with her fingertips the poetic colors of her beloved. Her eyes flowed from deep joy. "I will stay here," she told herself, "– here my whole life, and may it be many years!" When she was able to speak, she whispered, "Yes, we have known each other from long ago!" With that, knowledge of love's nature flashed within her. True love demands more than a long life. Where it truly strikes, it is a continuum from the deep past infinitely into the future. . . .

They were married in Paterson, New Jersey, city of William Carlos Williams, who wrote:

For our wedding, too,
the light was wakened
and shone. The light!

the light stood before us
   waiting!

– and to their catalogue of blessed lines, they added Dickinson's(#491):

Love is like Life – merely longer
Love is like Death, [en]during the Grave
Love is the Fellow of the Resurrection
Scooping up the Dust and chanting "Live"!

Edward Dickinson

Emily Norcross Dickinson

William Austin Dickinson

Emily Dickinson

Lavinia Dickinson

Window on the Past

Come slowly – Eden!
Lips unused to Thee –
Bashful – sip thy Jessamines –
As the fainting Bee -
(#211)

The years filled to the brim and advanced from the time of my first delighted reading of Emily Dickinson. Time flowed for decades on both sides of the Atlantic, with poets and storytellers of the ages ever-present – Emily among them. Fated by deep inward direction, I was led to the street where the goddess of poetry was born.

We were visiting our daughter at the University of Massachusetts, just down the road from the Homestead, and thus I found myself at Emily's door. After a two-hour trip from Boston airport, rounding the square at Amherst center and entering Main Street, my professor-husband parked the car in front of the two-story mansion and playfully challenged me: "Here a master poet was born!" He looked at me as if he were questioning my powers of memory. His eyes, his tone, inquired, "Do you remember who?"

"Ah, Emily! Emily!" I sang out, attempting to control the pounding of my heart. It was that moment at the edge of night when twilight hesitantly steps forward:

The Crickets sang
And set the Sun
And Workmen finished one by one
Their Seam the Day upon

The low Grass loaded with the Dew
The Twilight stood, as Strangers do
With Hat in Hand, polite and new
To stay as if, or go.

A Vastness, as a Neighbor, came,
A Wisdom, without Face, or Name,
A Peace, as Hemispheres at Home
And so the Night became.
(#1104)

I closed the car door and hesitantly entered Emily's garden. My legs were trembling and my eyes were brimming with tears as time dissolved into myriad impressions. Approaching the dark house, I shivered. Faint sounds of voices seemed to be coming from within. Who could it be at such an hour? I leaned my forehead against the window. Bringing my eyes close to the pane and placing my palms left and right, I focused on the interior. The first family of the small town was all there in the dining room. In the light of a lamp set on the buffet, I saw Maggie, long in the Dickinson employ, serving dinner. On one side of the table the girl Emily was seated. Beside her was her sister, Lavinia, nicknamed Vinnie. Opposite was brother Austin, a year older than Emily; and at the head and foot of the table were the imposing father, Edward, and the silent mother, Emily Norcross Dickinson. Taking their leisurely repast, they spoke sedately, aloof to the passing of time. Life was theirs forever – without impatience or restlessness. They did not belong to the category of mortals swept away by daily events, for merely a moment whirling desperately and vanishing through the trap door of time.

Critics – inspired by the encounter – immerse themselves in Emily's work and her epoch, bringing alive not only her life but that of everyone surrounding her. The members of her family come first. They will live in the memory and gratitude of people all over the world because they were blessed by Emily's uniqueness. Next come other relatives, friends, acquaintances, and even those who ony briefly brushed against her. They all enter the story to fill out the puzzle of her life, creating the sense of the historic moment.

Looking at the Dickinson family, I realized that though their lives were but a brief adventure in a small New England town, the art of one of them gave them all a share of immortality. Time and mortality cancel wealth, personal values, countless actions good and ill. Only art rises utterly vital before our astonished eyes. In this house on Main Street, Amherst, Emily Dickinson was born, shut herself away, fashioned her amazing poems, and died, leaving work that will forever stir readers' minds and hearts.

Her fellow villagers – largely oblivious to poetic creation – pursued an existence they never questioned. Misunderstanding and sometimes mocking her way of life, they left basically but a record of their number, three thousand residents in Amherst of that day. Among them, only four stand out significantly. Two became known throughout the world – Emily Dickinson for her singular poetry, and Daniel Webster for his great dictionary. The other two were noted in their day – Webster's granddaughter, Emily Fowler, as a poet, and Emily's friend and classmate, Helen Hunt, known as H.H., as a writer of poetry and prose. The rest of Amherst's people were "extras" – workmen, farmers, teachers, ministers, councilmen, housewives, servants, and owners of large or small shops in the town center near the Dickinson mansion.

The town was small, with a hotel on the corner of Main and Pleasant streets. Next to it was a tavern run by the father of Sue Gilbert, beloved friend and sister-in-law of the poet. Nearby were the bookstore, the pharmacy, the general store, the large stable for shoeing horses, the carriage-making workshop, famous throughout the country, and the milliner's, which brought ladies' hats from Boston each spring. A white brick building housed the Dickinson law office, and nearby was an imposing church with its famous pipe organ and pews dedicated to donors. Services were attended by large congregations two or three times a week. Down the street was the coeducational Academy (the building does not survive today); and shortly before the poet's birth, beginning to spring up were the buildings of Amherst College to whose construction the poet's grandfather was one of the main contributors. The students of the college came from all over Massachusetts and New England. There were a number of foreign students, among them two from Greece, the Rallis brothers from Scion, Corinth, who studied at Amherst from 1825 to 1827. Students from Greece keep coming to Amherst over the years, among them two graduates who were to become prime minister of Greece – Giorgos Papandreou and Antonis Samaras.

In a photograph of nineteenth-century Amherst we find smartly attired students mingling with the gentry in the town's center. The square is clogged with horses and buggies, and as the citizens stroll they pose before the lens of a camera set up along the way. A world of people were flinging their lives to the winds of mortality, but the poetry of one inhabitant sufficed to put Amherst on the spiritual map of the world. Being struck by the brevity of life, I felt deep sorrow. "Had we the least intimation of the Definition of Life, the calmest of us would be lunatics," Emily wrote; and as I pondered the Dickinsons through the dining-room window of the Homestead, I agreed, recalling brief lines by Samuel Menache, which he wrote in seaside sand: *"Pity us / By the sea / In the sand / a moment only. . . ."* Aching with the thought of human transience, I remembered the famous quatrains (#712):

Window on the Past

Because I could not stop for Death –
He kindly stopped for me –
The Carriage held but just Ourselves –
And Immortality.

We slowly drove – He knew no haste
And I had put away
My labor and my leisure too,
For His Civility –

We passed the School, where Children strove
At Recess – in the Ring –
We passed the Fields of Gazing Grain –
We passed the Setting Sun –

Or rather – He passed Us –
The Dews drew quivering and chill –
For only Gossamer, my Gown –
My Tippet – only Tulle –

We paused before a House that seemed
A Swelling of the Ground –
The Roof was scarcely visible –
The Cornice – in the Ground –

Since then – 'tis Centuries – and yet
Feels shorter than the Day
I first surmised the Horses' Heads
Were toward Eternity –

Continuing to view the serene family seated in the dining room, I longed to enter the house, to be near them, to greet them, and – why not? – reach out to touch them. I hurried up the steps to the stoop. Assuming the door was unlocked, I wondered whether I dared to turn the knob. Excitement brought to mind the evocative poem (#609) about revisiting the past:

I Years had been from Home
And now before the Door
I dared not enter, lest a Face
I never saw before

Stare stolid into mine
And ask my Business there –
"My Business but a Life I left
Was such remaining there?"

I leaned upon the Awe –
I lingered with Before –
The Second like an Ocean rolled
And broke against my ear –

I laughed a crumbling Laugh
That I could fear a Door
Who Consternation compassed
And never winced before.

I fitted to the Latch
My Hand, with trembling care
Lest back the awful Door should spring
And leave me in the Floor –

Then moved by Fingers off
As cautiously as Glass
And held my ears, and like a Thief
Fled gasping from the House –

Overcome by emotions, I ran through the yard with tall trees and paused to catch my breath and control my feelings. I asked myself: Did the poem refer to *metempsychosis*? I had to get hold of myself, and I found the proper place to do so by the small plot where Emily had cultivated her rare flowers. Only a few yards away was the street where passers-by would pause to steal a look at the poet in her garden. They wished to glimpse the figure that had become a "myth" as people called her upon her withdrawal from the world.

The more sensitive townspeople honored her desire for solitude, so if they happened upon her in her garden, they at once averted their gaze and crossed to the opposite sidewalk. This was not so, however, with children, who hoisted themselves up on the fence the better to view her. In maturity they would record their childhood impressions. With warmth, admiration, and awe, they recalled a figure attired in white that was like a vision. Kneeling on a small pillow, the lady was caring for her flowers. Looking back, one diarist remembers an exchange with her: ". . . [it was] *a pretty lady dressed in white, with fiery yet gentle brown eyes and a crown of red hair. Never will I forget her voice – clear, low, meloldious. She spoke to me about her flowers, the ones she loved the most; of her fear that bad weather would ruin them. Then she snipped some choice buds and asked me to take them to my mother with her love. For anyone to see Miss Emily was a great event, and I went home with a feeling of a significant experience.*"

Now other hands grow flowers on this spot – regular blooms of the season, not the rare ones planted by the poet. The garden and grounds are carefully tended in her memory. As one faces the Dickinson property from Main Street,

Emily's garden is to the right of her paternal home. To the left, a pathway leads from the Homestead to Evergreens, the residence that Edward Dickinson built for his son, Austin, and his daughter-in-law, Sue. Today the two residences, the property of Amherst College, are maintained as a museum.

Susan Huntington Dickinson

A Strange Encounter

The Poets light but Lamps –
Themselves – go out –
The Wicks they stimulate –
If vital Light

Inhere as do the Suns
Each Age a Lens
Disseminating their
Circumference –
(#883)

As night closed in on the Amherst of our time, alone in the garden, I felt the beloved soil beneath my feet. Eerie echoes of the past took shape slowly and suggestively, and I walked the luminous path the residents had worn between the Homestead and Evergreens – "A path just wide enough for two who love one another," as Emily told Sue. Stirred, I proceeded around a hundred feet and found myself on the doorstep of Sue's abode.

Sealed and dark was the two-story Italianate villa that in the 19th century had hosted personalities of towering stature like Emerson and Dickens. In its drawing room, Emily had surrendered to the tumultuous feelings that possessed her, performing her own inventions on the piano to the delight of those who loved her. "Life is bliss!" exclaimed the poet, enamored with Sue Dickinson and Kate Anthon, thrilled by the starlit night, throbbing with surging life.

In the hushed darkness, I sat by the doorway of Evergreens entranced by the window in the second-floor bedroom opposite where the poet had cloistered herself the final fourteen years of her life. Through that window she looked out on the world. Through that window she lowered the little basket containing cookies – a treat for her nephew Gib and his friends who played in the yard. Through that window she gleaned the excitements and wonders of the times, as well as the great distresses that plunged her loved ones into profound sadness. She was burdened by their distress; its weight broke her and threw her into the coma in which she peacefully awaited her knightly Coachman Death.

I sat on the cold cement of the Evergreens stoop overwhelmed by a host of complex feelings. There was so much light and darkness in the Dickinson history: grandfather Samuel's driving educational vision – its personal and family cost; father Edward's civic leadership and its authoritarian streak; brother Austin's community achievements and his brazen love affair. Emily's loves were taken from her again and again, but she was steadfast in her uncompromising creative drive. In pursuit of her poetic goal, from the age of twenty she began to withdraw from society, and in the final decades of her life she did not leave the confines of her home. She was properly named "the Myth," "the Recluse Queen," and the title she gave herself, "the Queen of Calvary." "Each crucial choice has its costs. Life is not a free festival; there is no wall for protection against the distresses of the world. Through gaps or vulnerable spots life silently and swiftly floods in to bring home the pain that is our lot." These were my thoughts at that moment, and amidst a sigh, a barely discernible sound made me turn toward the door of Evergreens – and there she was!

Standing on the threshold of the doorway, clad in black, bowed by years of calamity, she gazed at me with immense sadness. "Sue . . ." I sighed. Susan Huntington Dickinson – Emily's beloved who married her brother, Austin – stood before me. Seated on the ledge by the stoop, I turned with an impulse to

approach her. Swept away by her dear presence, I longed to greet her affectionately, to enclose her in my arms. I froze for a moment, silently questioning. How
was it that I felt such an overpowering personal tenderness toward a woman of
an era many years before my lifetime?

How did it come about that I found myself before her, my soul brimming
with feelings of affinity? Was this meeting fantasy or reality? Indeed, I had
heard the creaking of the opening of the door, and I had been embarrassed by
the thought that a watchman might appear and challenge my presence after
museum hours. But that moment Sue stepped forth. It was an asstounding
event such as I had not foreseen in the wildest imaginings of my fiction. An
ebony shawl around her shoulders, her hair drawn back in a high bun, her face
dark, her eyes melancholy, she emerged from the house, turned toward me, and
looked at me intensely, as if she recognized me.

I arose, took a step, my arms reaching out; but I did not approach. A gap in
time held me in place. She slowly descended the stoop steps, turned toward
the ledge, sat down, and taking me in a friendly way by the shoulders, drew me
down by her side. We remained silent for a long time. Suddenly the whole area
was illuminated as if day had come and a bright sun were beaming above our
heads. Sue leaned close to me and put her arm around my shoulder. She spoke.
Her voice, low and tender, full of nostalgia, soothed me. "At night she comes to
her window and looks across. There she is – as always from afar yearning for
contact, but it cannot be!"

Raising my gaze toward the house opposite, I saw Emily! Standing squarely
in the middle of the window, she intensely beheld us. She was aglow! Without a
lamp, without a candle, she was herself a great light sending rays that flooded
the yard, passing beyond the little town of Amherst and spreading throughout
the world.

How long did the scene linger? How long did Sue and I sit spellbound?
Perhaps a few seconds. Or was it an eternity? How measure the duration of a
sacred moment? Then – all too suddenly – Emily's figure vanished swiftly as it

had appeared. As if someone had flipped off the switch of our vision, there was no more light, only a feeling of agitation. In a flash the frame of the tall, wide window was vacant. Our breath was cut, and we remained there motionless on the ledge, Sue and I, releasing a sigh of longing.

Sue spoke first, as if she wished to console me. "Often she comes to the window, and we meet that way. I am always here waiting." Thoughtfully, she slipped her hand into the pocket of her dress, bulging with notes and poems that Emily had sent her. She read such lines during the twenty-seven years that she survived after the death of her beloved. She sighed and continued: "I sense that she is about to appear and I come to this spot. I wait and she reaches out to me with her entire being. She has never disappointed me."

Her face glowed with happiness, and as I leaned closer, I sensed her breast rising and falling with passion. Truly love is eternal, I thought, as I waited for the intense sensations to subside. "But who are you, my dear?" She spoke again, perhaps to divert herself from the feelings that ruled her. "Where have you come from?" she asked, and her eyes enclosed me with deep implications. Where did I come from, and who am I? What, precisely did Sue want to know? Could it be the point of our contact through imagination and memory? But what do Memory, Imagination, Time, and Place mean? And something even more important – time-travel, the journeying of the soul? What is the nature of the Mystery that surrounds us? "For the great mystery no one thinks of giving thanks to God," Emily observed, and added: "So I conclude that space and time are things of the body and have little or nothing to do with the self."

Great meetings involve the soul, without our permission or control. The soul always sweeps us away since she is the fundamental cause of our being. She links the visible and the invisible. She dissolves the borders of time; she constitutes and assembles the sum of our eternal essence.

I gazed at Sue with a playful smile. "You ask me where I come from," I said, "but you know that I come from the other side of life – time future. One way or another, it's being together that counts!"

A Strange Encounter

The sound of my voice, strange and hollow, was disturbing, and I fell silent. I took a step backwards, as if I sensed some danger. I feared Sue's touch. I shrank from her as if all this were unnatural; yet, somehow – at the same time – it was a world familiar and unintimidating. The experience was mesmerizing.

By my side, Sue was smiling, and with a piercing gaze, she referred to something I had totally withheld from the world.

"Tell me," she teased. "The mark you have under your right breast, does it have the shape of a heart?"

Astounded, I shot to my feet. Impulsively I held down the edge of my blouse, as if Sue would peek beneath it. My heart was beating wildly. How could she know my secret?

She was very close, eyeing me soberly – apparently awaiting a response. Then, she raised her own blouse and with the other pointed to an identical mark beneath her right breast. By the soft starlight, I saw at precisely the same point on her body, in the same color, the heart-shaped sign like the one that I had shielded from the world from the time of my birth.

"Ah!" I burst out. That moment there was the rattling of a speeding carriage entering from the street. Overcome by feeling, Sue stepped back and hurriedly tucked in her blouse, as her eyes turned toward the vehicle that rocked to a stop outside the stable behind the house.

His red hair waving in the air, body electric with erotic excitement, Austin had been taking the whip to the horse, which was foaming at the mouth. "Austin Dickinson the Great has returned!" Sue sneered. "Every night he comes home soiled by licentiousness and immures himself in his room without shame or even the least token of consideration for me and his children!"

I was alarmed – I had never seen such anguish on a person's face. "Sue," I breathed, reaching out a hand to touch her, but not in time. She had spun and quickly ascended the stairs, entering and slamming the door.

Quiet reigned as the heavy distance of time fell. Drained of feeling I slumped to the stoop, completely alone. Austin and Sue had vanished, but the houses and the trees, the watchmen of time, stood unmoved.

Night sounds of the college town of today wafted into the yard – breaking the flow of imagination, dispersing time past. The world of today revived as I came back – or rather, moved forward – into the present, hearing the whisper of passing cars, distant rock music, and voices from the campus across the street. The Dickinson residences were dark, once more sealed from the pains, joys, loves, conflicts, and hates of the past. I arose wearily from the stoop, and guided by streetlights, I walked to where we had parked. Leaning against the car, my life's companion was gazing toward the Homestead. "You've kept me waiting a century!" he exclaimed, smiling. "What have you been doing all this time in the dark?" he asked. "And tell me – why did you raise your blouse? Did the heat get to you?" I looked at him in confusion. I had no answer or explanation.

"Don't tell me you're at it again?" he grinned. "Will it be your tenth or eleventh novel?"

"Well, it won't be the thirteenth, so there'll be no problem completing it!"

He hugged and kissed me fondly. "Oh, you'll finish it, all right!" he smiled, and added, "Have a wonderful trip!"

"Beginning tomorrow," I returned, "with an important visit!"

family gravestones

Morning at Amherst Cemetery

A Toad, can die of Light –
Death is the Common Right
Of Toads and Men –
Of Earl and Midge
The Privilege –
Why swagger, then?
The Gnat's supremacy is large as Thine –
(#583)

From the Homestead we drove to the square, took a right on Pleasant Street, and immediately turned behind the Mobil station, parking outside the cemetery. I stepped out of the car and gazed at a typical 19th-century burial ground. It was an area large enough for memorials to Amherst's deceased up to the 19th century. Thus I found them: plots side by side, like old friends and acquaintances, with time-blackened headstones throughout and statues here and there. Inscriptions often reflected the Puritan belief in resurrection into a higher world.

No complaints on this ground – there is no reason for arrogance, fuss, pride, or agony. Tranquility reigns as poetry resonates powerfully around Emily's gravesite and the historical mural opposite.

The grave plots varied only slightly. However, at one cross-path a group of graves was enclosed by a wrought-iron fence, and I knew at once that these belonged to the Dickinson family. There were four plaques with names and dates engraved: parents, Edward and Emily Norcross; sisters. Lavinia and Emily.

On the poet's headstone lay a freshly cut rose bud. Her name was chiseled in a semi-circle over the dates of her life span:

DEC. 10, 1830
CALLED BACK
MAY 15, 1886

She was born in the winter and was "called back," as she put it on her death-bed, in spring when the hills were redolent with wildflowers and her garden buzzed with bees. I did not wish to dwell on the day of her funeral – not now; but a moving scene persisted in my mind. Lavinia was at the front door opening for a guest who came to say a final farewell to Emily, lying in her white casket in the middle of the living room. Lavinia opened the door with great care, try-ing to block bees that were attempting to swarm in. Inconsolably, she waved her hands to block the path of the buzzing creatures who seemed intent to approach and hover over the serene, beautiful visage of the departed. I recalled the lines of Emily's poem, which are like a prayer: "I hear the bright bee hum: / Prithee, my brother, / Into my garden come" (#2).

I stood a long time before the family graves, hesitating to leave, but finally intense feelings made me step away. I walked through the cemetery looking for epitaphs of noted personages. A leading clergyman and president of Amherst College, the Reverend Stearns was interred there – nearby the grave of his son, Frazar, the first brave volunteer from Amherst who lost his life in the Civil War. "His great heart was shattered by a small ball," Emily wrote. Looking at the statue of young Frazar, I sensed the grief that Emily and Austin shared in the loss of their classmate and friend. Austin was dazed, incredulous – continually muttering, "Frazar is killed! . . . Frazar is killed. . . ."

How many untold tales did that small cemetery contain? Here lie the noted and the anonymous: civic and religious leaders of singular importance; but also farmers, servants, and former slaves. Buried here are Emily's kinsmen and neighbors. Here lie Sue's family, the Gilberts – but suddenly, I realized, Sue, Austin, and their children were missing. I circled through the cemetery once more. Perhaps I'd overlooked their graves. I was distressed. I felt like calling Sue's name. I was surprised that she had not guided me. Looking up, I caught sight of a thoughtful, dignified gentleman holding a briefcase crammed with papers. "Pardon me, sir," I said, "I can't find Austin and Sue." I used their first names, but he knew.

"They aren't here," he replied. "They are interred in the cemetery outside the town center – Wildwood." He pointed toward the western side of the city. "Of course," I thought, "that is the cemetery planned and established by Austin. He wished to be buried there." "You take Pleasant Street for about three miles," the gentleman continued, "and when you see the sign for a school, you turn right. Across from the school is the cemetery where all the Austin Dickinsons are laid to rest. You will see a boulder on the spot." A shadow crossed his face – he wasn't sure I'd find my way. "You see," he added, "it's a large cemetery." Once more he waved a hand in that direction. Fixed on his pointing hand, my mind and heart precisely grasped the spot. "I'll find it. Thank you, sir," I said, turning to continue my quest.

Soon I arrived at the school. It faced an area with wide lawns and clumps of old-growth trees. I passed by, thinking it was a park. There were two roads. The first – the entrance drive – I passed, paying little heed. At once I came upon the exit drive. Then I realized that indeed it was the cemetery. Turning in, I found myself surrounded by lofty trees under which there were grave plots with markers containing family names. At the head of the individual plots, rectangular tablets were set in the ground, partly covered by grass and leaves. There was no one in sight. It was a true resting place whose peaceful quiet softened the impact of the melancholy plots. The gentle chirping of birds added a serene note to the silence of the morning. Across the road were heard cheery voices of children in the playground.

In this beautiful landscape, only the leaf-obscured bronze plaques with names and dates of entering and exiting life bore witness that it was the place Austin chose for the family's final abode. He knew what he was about when he planned it: a place of wide greenswards and clumps of trees where one would gladly lay himself down to timeless sleep as if he had come on a pleasant excursion.

The car stopped, and my beating heart reached such a pitch that it threatened to burst. I stepped out deeply moved as I stood before the tablets in the ground. They had been cleared of soil and leaves, and a red rose bud had been placed that day in the center of each. Silently, gratefully, I thanked Sue. How could I have arrived directly at this site – what power had led me to the graves of her family – were it not Sue? Trembling I knelt by Sue's bronze memorial, and I recited to her Emily's poem in memory of Elizabeth Barrett Browning (#363):

I went to thank Her –
But She Slept –
Her Bed – a funneled Stone –
With Nosegays at the Head and Foot–
That Travelers – had thrown –

Who went to thank Her –
But She Slept –
T'was Short – to cross the Sea –
To look upon Her like – alive –
But turning back – t'was slow –

Placed about two yards from Sue's gravesite was a large stone memorial erected by the elders of Amherst, succinctly expressing their gratitude for Austin's contribution to the life of the town.

Morning at Amherst Cemetery

In Memory of
William Austin Dickinson
August 1895
Self-forgetting in Service for His Town and College
Resolute in his convictions
At one with Nature
He believed in God and hoped for Immortality

The sizeable memorial rock stands somewhat aside from the tablets for the rest of the family, as does his grave marker. It is simply engraved W.A.D., whereas the others – Sue's first – carry dates and a few words about the beliefs of the departed.

I sat by the edge of Sue's grave and read the brief words etched below the names. Like Emily, Sue was born in the winter and departed in spring:

19 December 1830 - 2 March 1913
There is no Death
What seems so is
Transition

Beside her plot are those of three children – first, to protect her, little Gib:

1 August 1876 – 5 October 1883
The Childe

The simplicity of the inscription – the tender archaic spelling, lending a poetic touch – epitomized the family's devastating grief. This was the little prince who, in his first – and final – eight years of life offered them so much joy and happiness. His death from typhoid fever swept his Aunt Emily into the grave, drove his inconsolable mother into alienation from life, and hurled his father further into an erotic tempest unprecedented in the post-Puritan epoch – at least among such a staid clan as the Dickinsons.

41

The next grave in the row after Gilbert's was the first-born son, Edward – nick-named Ned – who died of heart disease, unmarried at the age of thirty-six:

19 June 1861 - 3 May 1897

Things unseen are eternal

Last came the resting place of Martha Dickinson Bianci, the daughter who left behind two books about her aunt with selections of poetry and letters of the dear friends – her mother and her aunt:

30 November 1866 – 21 December 1943

Risen in Resurrection

Light Immortal Spring

It was a lovely summer day, and the birds warbled as if they were experiencing their first burst of life – such was their joy and intensity. Weighed down by sadness, still seated at Sue's feet, I asked, "Sue, how could you endure such an overwhelming love from both Emily and Austin? And something more – how is it you did not pity Austin after his 'fall', and separated him from your presence, even in death?" I knew how she would answer me: "Just as he expelled us from his life." But I insisted: "Was it his fault alone?" And then I seemed to hear her whisper something like a promise that she would tell me everything.

I sadly contemplated Austin's separate memorial stone. Even in the grave he appears distanced from the family. Delirious in his exultant love, he seems to have paid slight heed to the pain he caused his children and wife during the final thirteen years of his life. His affair with Mabel Loomis Todd – twenty-six years younger than he, and married – was so wildly passionate that it left no margin of concern for anything or anyone else. He died suddenly and unexpectedly of heart failure, as if he could no longer bear his passion, repressed shame, and alienation. I recalled an early letter of his to Sue when soaring love for her still flooded his heart. "Sue, dear, we will grow old together," he wrote; but then the notion seemed to him incredible: "But naturally we will not grow old." A bitter realization possessed me concerning the nature of time and age-ing – above all, the fragility of feelings: "Austin," I breathed, "you did grow old and did pass away, and from the moment that you exchanged one timeless love for another almost two centuries have passed. Rest in peace, knowing that our loves and frailties are beyond our control."

Austin experienced it all: prestige, beauty, wealth, knowledge, pride, love, suffering, and despair. Perhaps he viewed his final pain as disproportionate ret-ribution. How many games life plays with mortals – it disdains feelings, values, aspirations, and pride. What insidious tricks it devises to hurl them crashing to earth!

Emily's Room

Between My Country – and the Others –
There is a Sea –
But Flowers – negotiate between us –
As Ministry.
(#905)

Reading the poem I thought how right she is. Perhaps an ocean did exist between Emily and me – in space, time, and culture – but the precious flowers of her poems retained their freshness and transmitted fragrances beyond time and place. Life had guided me to Amherst, to the residence of one who had lent a portion of her spirit to the mystic core of my soul – and the world's. How wondrous it was to walk in the green precincts of Amherst College, around her house, in the town she frequented as a girl! Here I was on Main Street, in the large property with the two homes of the famous Dickinsons, visiting and studying at my leisure.

Dickinson Children

Emily's mid-60s' Dress

Emily's Room

I mounted the steps of the Homestead stoop, passed the Ionic columns of the portico, and entered the interior with trembling heart. I took several steps in the spacious hall and mounted the stairs to Emily's bedroom on the second floor. As I softly ascended, I sensed the creaking stairs of old, the squeaking of doors opening and closing, the wind brushing against the windows, and echoes in Emily's poems – "There came a Wind like a Bugle" (#1583). In her bedroom, I heard her delicately reciting:

I was the slightest in the House –
I took the smallest Room –
At night my little Lamp, and Book –
And one Geranium – . . .
(#486)

I felt a tug on my heart as I stood in the doorway of the sunny chamber. My vision embraced the space, focusing one-by-one on the objects it contained. My gaze first turned to the fireplace, the only source of heat in the harsh New England winter; then my eye swiftly fell on the little table holding Emily's lamp. In this modest room under the mild glow of that lamp, with singular intellectual powers, Emily Dickinson shaped her immense perceptions, cultivating her unique creative and theoretical powers.

For a long time I viewed with awe the little table with the kerosene lamp, emblem of today's Museum. In this prim, unpretentious chamber, she set down such unprecedented conceptions, such philosophic illuminations, such beauty and truth! In the middle of the eastern wall was her bed, covered by an embroidered white counterpane; and to the left was the small chest of drawers where upon Emily's death Vinnie, her younger sister, discovered 1,775 poems and made it her life's work to see at least a portion of them published. The simple furnishing of the house mirrored the puritan attitudes of Emily's father. Her bedroom held only essential items. On the wall were lithographs of her most beloved literary sisters – Elizabeth Barrett Browning and George Eliot – mounted in simple frames. Nearby, beside the window, hung the little basket in which she lowered treats to her nephew and his friends. Evading the watchful eyes of the guide, I secretively felt the walls and the little writing table; and bending by the bed to tighten a shoelace, I stroked the counterpane.

This was the sacred place in which Emily – at the forefront of poets, both female and male, ancient and modern – expanded her stupendous soul! My spirit overflowed with joy as I shared the passion of Emily's devotees. On critics' pages one senses that while they aim at objectivity they cannot repress their personally felt passion for her. They are carried away by the depth of her verse, the power of her insights, and the nuances of her words. She knew the resonance of syllables that bear profound, arresting perceptions. Her voice – acute, deftly melodious, ever surprising – reaches readers' intuitive depths and entices them into dialogue with her singular spirit. We bond with her instantly, reverently, lovingly. The relationship is vibrant: "My Emily" – one critical title proclaims, reflecting her devotees' universal fervor, the intimacy one shares with a beloved and honored friend. These feelings overflowed as I pressed her little table where she penned her famous letter, which I felt was addressed to me personally, though it spoke as well to a universe of human souls (#441):

This is my letter to the World
That never wrote to Me –
The simple News that Nature told –
With tender Majesty

Her Message is committed
To Hands I cannot see –
For love of Her – Sweet – countrymen –
Judge tenderly – of Me

Emily's Room

In this room was placed the glass case holding the simple but elegant white dress she wore like a uniform of the unique 'society' she personified. How many words have been written about that dress and its significance! What did she express in her withdrawal from social contact of any kind? What did she represent by exclusively wearing this dress – white, with pleats, collar, and buttons reaching down to the waist? Was she a nun without a conventional creed, a bride without a worldly groom, or a blank page without a signifier?

The western window near her writing table faced Evergreens, and I could see Emily in her dark room, her face pressed to the windowpane, imagining the living room opposite where distinguished visitors from Europe and America came for soirees. The following day she relived those evenings though Sue's descriptions.

I lived, too, the famous scene in which Emily rendered wild improvisations on the piano, tossing her head in ecstasy, before her father, rushing down the path between the homes with lighted lantern, came to 'rescue' her.

Evergreens was decorated in accordance with Sue's taste. Curtains were ordered from designers sending goods for the first time to Amherst. The rugs, furniture, and paintings were selected by Austin, each purchase of an artwork becoming an occasion for a celebration with prestigious guests. And something more that was special: there was an indoor W.C. on the second floor, where the children had their rooms, while the Homestead had an outhouse in the yard by the stable. But an environment graced with luxury and refined taste did not suffice to preclude ingrained conflicts. Even in the early years of their marriage, Austin and Sue's voices could be heard raised in argument as their children shrank in fear and covered their ears, until finally the door would slam and Austin would gallop away.

In the other house, silence always reigned. Voices were hushed. There was no purchase of artwork or elegant furniture. Obedience and calm always pervaded the plainly furnished Homestead. In the living room were a simple couch a bookcase, and a piano for Emily. Two armchairs completed the décor.

And life passed, with contentions and silences, with joy, sadness, love, misunderstanding, worry, inspired ideas, dreams, actions good and ill – everything hastily rushing to be done before the heavy hour of mourning arrives, and one-by-one, astonished and unfulfilled, they would fall into eternal sleep. Their existences would all flicker out, disappear, sucked up by the whirl-wind of time. Yet now, as I stood in Emily's room, I felt all of the Dickinsons' presences surrounding me as if we were one, and I was experiencing their histories from the beginning, frame-by-frame, purged of the mysterious and the unexpected – reliving their lives, entire and complete. What an amazing sensation it was to realize the truth of what she wrote – "To die is not to go –"! I glanced into today's yard and watched her 'pilgrims' – from all over the world – in a silent procession, as if in a dream, with pensive smiles on their lips. Certainly it wasn't for the houses and the grounds they had come, but to be with Emily and join their hearts with hers, and to participate with her in tran-scendent experience:

Behind Me – dips Eternity –
Before Me – Immortality –
Myself – the Term between –

Eternity! What does the word really mean? And the other one – immor-tality? In intense analysis of the terms I felt ineffable joy, and a host of feel-ings both clear and intangible gripped me. I tried to locate the place of my beginning and my end. I felt I was on this amazing planet for centuries. I was immersed in innumerable feelings. I caught their quality and signifi-cance – measured their nuances and solidity. What a host of sensations! How describe them but as facets of Eternity – a timeless sphere of measureless moments compacted in the now. The barrier of personal time broke, and the sense of now expanded, possessed by the vital fullness of being. I recognize the moment – each moment – as an eternal and immortal miracle, and cry out with Emily: "Life is a miracle! . . . Life is a spell so exquisite that everything conspires to break it."

I turned my head to look out the window toward the south, where Emily could view two hills, soft and green, which she called her "companions." She climbed them as a child and later was limited to gazing upon them. At night she went to sleep serenely, smiling at the moon, which caressed her through the window. As it passed sliding over the glass, it rested softly on the pane (#629):

I watched the Moon around the House

Until upon a Pane –

She stopped – a Traveller's privilege – for Rest –

Her ears were filled with the murmuring of the brook a few yards away; and as it flowed far from cities, it echoed "the sigh of the Frog" (#1359). She thrilled as she imagined a snake sliding beneath dark bushes, just as she would later picture (#986):

A narrow Fellow in the Grass

Occasionally rides –

You may have met Him – did you not

His notice sudden is –

I leaned against the bedroom wall and tried to imagine how a young woman from the age of twenty-two could gradually withdraw from the social life of her town, limit herself to the immediate environment of the family property, and for the remainder of her days stay sealed within her house, producing poetry that would circulate around the globe – not space enough to contain its grandeur. "Oh what a miracle is man to man!" How deeply I agreed with her words. In this room unfolded the miracle of transcendent verse! I softly whispered with Emily the magnificent lines that so clearly describe the spiritual delight of marvelous hours of inspiration (#1767):

Emily Dickinson: Goddess of the Volcano

Sweet hours have perished here;
This is a mighty room;
Within its precincts hopes have played, –
Now shadows in the tomb.

Back in today's Amherst, in addition to daily visits to libraries, I enjoyed strolling the sidewalks on which she saw Sue and Austin going about their daily affairs. Driving ten miles to South Hadley, the location of famous Mount Holyoke College, I ambled among imposing buildings of Gothic design. In Emily's time there was a single three-story building housing the college to which leading Christian families sent their daughters. On this campus, I felt, above all, a sense of Emily's presence 150 years ago, when she was a student here for less than a year. On the quadrangle, I saw the bust of Mary Lyon, founder and president of the college, who was noted for her puritan convictions and proselytizing spirit.

Seven miles west of Amherst is the little town of Sunderland, where young Austin taught for two years the children of Irish immigrants. Inconsolable in his absence, Emily wrote him daily. The terrain of the area is flat, stretching out to a series of hills where citizens of Amherst came on excursions and during the winter young people drove on sleighs for "sugaring" – a courtship practice in the old days. Sunderland was also frequently a lovers' retreat for middle-aged Austin and much younger Mabel. I could hear the melodic voice of Mabel, who consoled him in his deep mourning over the loss of his son. She – with the cooperation of polite, hesitant Thomas Wentworth Higginson, a noted intellectual of the age – edited the first three collections of Dickinson's verse.

Austin and Mabel went to Sunderland on their trysts. With whom was Mabel's husband, the astronomer, cavorting during those hours? What was whispered in the small town of Amherst, where nothing could be hidden? Austin and Mabel set out in the light of early morning, as if the excursion were innocent and natural. He, in his fifties, took for a drive the twenty-five year old wife of his colleague, while Sue, sealed in the house, mourned the loss of their little son.

I enjoyed driving around Sunderland. The village, unlike Amherst, had not undergone extensive development in recent decades. Many of the residences survived from the 18th and 19th centuries. Everywhere there were small frame houses, and only on the outskirts were there a few apartment buildings buried in the woods occupied for the most part by university students. As if they were still in the 19th century, people seemed to be involved in an easy-going enjoyment of life, smiling and relaxed in manner.

There was a small post office with only one clerk. His right jawbone had been extracted – his sunken, sagging cheek deforming his young face. But he was ever smiling. "Have a nice day!" he warmly bid me good-bye, and responding to his friendly feeling, I confessed, "I'm visiting Amherst because I love Emily Dickinson!" His face glowed and he began to recite (#254):

"Hope" is the thing with feathers –
That perches in the soul –
And sings the tune without the words –
And never stops – at all –

And sweetest – in the Gale – is heard
And sore must be the storm –
That could abash the little Bird
That kept so many warm –

I've heard it in the chilliest land –
And on the strangest Sea –
Yet, never, in Extremity,
It asked a crumb – of Me.

I wanted to hug him for the joy he had given me with such ease, but I limited myself to a smile and said not a word about two other poems Emily had written on the theme of hope—"Hope is a strange invention" (#1392) and "Hope is subtle Glutton" (#1547). Indeed, who but Emily would provide such strange and diverse epithets for hope? *Thing of feathers. Strange invention. Subtle Glutton.* And further, a statement that recalls the Greek writer Kazantzakis: "When I hoped I feared –" (#1181).

The postal clerk with a poetic soul showed me something I had not realized until then – that many of the residents of the area delight in reciting Dickinson poems by memory. My friend Lynn Margolis – pioneering biologist and advocate of the Gaia hypothesis – loved to do so. One unforgettable evening on her porch with a view of the Homestead she lovingly recited Emily late into the night. It was a magical experience, which recurred the following year when Lynn visited us in Greece. With deep feeling she rendered Emily's verse all the way from our home in Lagonissi on the Saronic Gulf – not far from the temple of Poseidon on Cape Sounion, where Bryon carved his name on a column – to our arrival at the sacred precincts of Delphi.

The place where I stayed in Amherst was a small suite whose bedroom looked out on the square. The two streets, which drew my feet by day and entered my dreams by night were Main Street, where Emily was born, and Pleasant Street, where she lived from age three to twenty-five in a house that has not survived. The tragic history of the family's loss of the Homestead, due to the selfless generosity of Emily's grandfather – Samuel Fowler Dickinson – ended when Edward Dickinson eventually bought back the Homestead, and the family resided there again the rest of their lives.

Emily and Austin loved the attractive house on Pleasant Street and always alluded nostalgically to it, as though they had forgotten the funeral processions reflected in five hundred poems like this one (#153):

Emily's Room

Dust is the only Secret –
Death the only One
You cannot find out all about
In his "native town."

Nobody knew "his Father" –
Never was a Boy –
Hadn't any playmates,
Or "Early history" –

Industrious! Laconic!
Punctual! Sedate!
Bold as a Brigand!
Stiller than a Fleet!

Builds like a Bird, too!
Christ robs the nest –
Robin after Robin
Smuggle to Rest!

In the rooms where I was staying, silence throughout the day and night brought a weird somnolence that I attempted to evade by research that carried me to another era. I immersed myself ever more deeply in the lives of the Dickinsons, especially those of Emily and Sue. It was as if I existed under hypnosis with them, in their own time, in their thoughts and actions, joys and calamities. I followed their lives from birth to death, witness to the great mystery called human existence. What an immense revelation is the completed life! Then the essence appears, phantasmagorical and true.

Chapter I

The month of December

Look back on Time, with kindly eyes –
He doubtless did his best –
How softly sinks that trembling sun
In Human Nature's West –
(#1478)

December turned the corner of time, and freezing New England weather set in. Numbing cold swept in from Canada, reached Amherst, cut sixty miles through wooded land, and arrived in the Berkshires – Melville country. There, in a farmhouse near Pittsfield, he completed *Moby Dick*, gazing through his window at a pure-white hill that resembled a whale. The cold steadily moved on to Hawthorne meadow in Lenox, where Hawthorne resided for one and a half years, producing *The House of the Seven Gables*. Freezing, the currents finally reached upstate New York, the region of Irving's Sleepy Hollow.

Like a snake, cold soundlessly and steadily slid into the apartment, and I – wrapped in a blanket – gazed out into the darkness pierced by the headlights of passing automobiles. My eye was drawn by the surrounding leaden clouds that had descended through the afternoon.

Suddenly . . .

–10 December 1830 –

darkness dispersed; a white light appeared outside my window, illuminating my room as if it were dawn. Surprised, I glued my face to the windowpane. Light snow flakes were falling, dancing madly around the street lamp, just lighted by the night watchman, who was bundled up in heavy clothes, a scarf, and thick gloves. He turned, and with slow, soundless steps dissolved into the distance as if his boots did not touch the earth. Mesmerized I gazed as he disappeared – as did I – in a world of dreams, though I was not sleeping, since I could still count the few sleighs as they slid on the snow leaving behind them the delightful tinkle of the bells. Yet at some point I must have fallen asleep because I was jolted awake by a loud sound, and I saw an elegant sleigh turning onto Main Street. I realized that it was the splendid conveyance of physician Isaac Cutler coming to attend on Emily Norcross Dickinson, who was about to give birth. Dr. Isaac Cutler, who had brought over one thousand children into the world, was the first to look upon newborn Emily Dickinson.

The time was just past eleven at night, December 10, 1830, as the doctor's sleigh bells pleasantly heralded his arrival, and I – enthralled by the event – came out into the snow without feeling the cold. I wanted to confirm whether there was an extraordinarily bright star in the sky. I looked up. I felt wonder toward the firmament filled with stars looking tenderly upon the gauzy flakes of snow that swirled in the air. I was searching in awe for the great radiant star, but it was nowhere to be seen. It would rise after her death. It was, in any case, a luminous night – absolutely still! The sky was clear, and the gleaming moon, surrounded by stars, shone upon Amherst. This glorious night Emily Elizabeth Dickinson arrived on planet Earth, and the heaven of poetry opened wide to receive her.

Merchant's Row

America of the Realists and the Idealists

Consider that wee shall be
as a Citty upon a Hill,
the eies of all people are uppon us. . .
John Winthrop
A Model of Christian Charity
(Sermon preached during the
pilgrims' Atlantic crossing,
April, 1630)

E ager to witness Emily's birth, I hurried along Main Street and soon found myself before the famous Homestead, which Emily's grandfather, Samuel, built in 1813. Rather than wood, which was so plentiful in the area, he used brick, constructing the largest house in Amherst.

I walked through the garden to the kitchen porch; and, looking in, I saw Samuel Fowler Dickinson. A muscular, seemingly elderly man, with a thick mustache and a cutting gaze, he was slumped with elbows on the table, his chin resting on his palms. He was silent, and his face held a dour expression. I was shocked, for this was not the personage that had taken shape in my mind from scholars' descriptions of the first distinguished Dickinson in Amherst. He lighted the torch that illuminated the Dickinson name, so when scholars seek a forebear who planted the seed of genius, they seize on grandfather Samuel, whom they describe as a handsome man with red hair, thick mustache, and fiery eyes – his frame filled with energy. It was said that he didn't have the patience to wait for his horse to be saddled but set right out on the seven-mile walk from Amherst to Northampton, where the courthouse was located. He would be the first attorney to arrive, just as he was the first Dickinson to replace farming with a learned profession. He studied at Dartmouth, beginning at the age of sixteen. Noted for his ardor in whatever he pursued, he became one of Amherst's finest lawyers – a tradition sustained by his son, Edward, and grandson, Austin.

Now, however – this December midnight, as the doctor guided the child's entry into the world in the neighboring room – Samuel sat glumly in the kitchen, not participating in the event. The fire in his eyes spent, the nerves of his body slack, slumped in the chair, his face in his hands, elbows supporting his head, he appeared to be an old man, though he was only fifty-five. The cup of tea before him was cold, untouched. While the birth room was illuminated by several kerosene lamps, the only light burning in the kitchen was that of the fire in the stove. In those flickering flames one could discern on Samuel's face deep marks of doubt and despair.

His first-born son, Edward – a young man of twenty-seven, tall and handsome – entered the kitchen with a lighted candle, which he put out, finding the light in the room sufficient. He fed the stove on which the large kettle of water was already beginning to boil in preparation for the birth. Edward turned toward his father and muttered something in a low voice. Not lifting his head, the father remained silent, but Edward insisted, accenting his words syllable-by-syllable, as if the other were resisting their meaning. Edward's gestures and the tenseness of his frame expressed his gravity. He was angry, and Samuel – even more upset – seemed about to lash out against his son, but to avoid this, he sprang to his feet, grabbed his overcoat from the hook on the door, pulled his black wool cap down over his ears, and rushed out of the kitchen to the stable at the rear of the house. He lighted a lamp, seized a brush, and set to currying the mare with fierce strokes. The stable cats cocked their heads and looked with curiosity at the angry, nervous man present at such an hour. Their eyes also fell on the horse that, whinnying with pleasure, was lightly tapping the stall floor with her right forefoot. Their interest quickly satisfied, they curled up once more in a ball and fell asleep.

When Edward saw the dim light in the stable and heard the sounds of the horse, he realized that Samuel had not taken to the road in such nasty weather at so late an hour. Breathing a sigh of relief, he sat down at the kitchen table and sought to purge his feelings against his father, riveting his attention on what was happening in the living room. Deep moans of birth pangs reached his ears, along with the voice of his mother, who spoke curtly to his wife. Edward was deeply thoughtful, clearly sad. They had been almost two years in this house and his mother had never spoken considerately to his wife. Even now, in this tense moment, his mother was telling her daughter-in-law that she was timid, incapable of being a good wife and steadfastly giving birth. The first month of his marriage, his mother had told him, "It was a hard bargain, wasn't it?" And the truth was that Edward – a Yale graduate, brilliant lawyer, and eventually outstanding Massachusetts congressman – had great difficulty in persuading Emily Norcross, from the neighboring town of Monson, twenty miles away, to accept his marriage proposal. By nature she was a very quiet girl. He had made her acquaintance at a meeting of college graduates, and it seems that he fell in love at once, though he never confessed his passion even to himself, for such a feeling was not acceptable to one with puritan inclinations. In any case, in accordance with the practices of the time, he proposed to her. The answer was a long time in coming, but since his elected bride had not refused, the young attorney was certain that she was of a mind to accept. Thus, he had continued to write to her daily and to send her books, hoping to whet her spiritual interest and break her silence. He was absolutely certain that he had found the woman of his life.

He wrote daily – without the passion that flamed in his son's missives to Sue Gilbert a generation later. Though such control would usually be difficult for a youthful lover, this was not the case with Edward. He systematically informed

Emily Norcross about himself, his success in civic and legal affairs, his ambitions and dreams, his plans and how he would go about realizing them. He told her what he envisioned in life and marriage. He analyzed his own personality and hers, asking her to confirm his conceptions; but the prospective bride, sluggish and taciturn, replied rarely and vaguely to his letters. He received no concrete responses, even when he wrote spiritedly, for example, about the revolt of the Greeks in 1821, referring to the splendor of ancient Greece—"a place of beauty and refinement"; a glorious nation with gods and goddesses – concluding the letter, "In short, the name of Greece alone fills the mind with all things lovely and perfect" – the place where "Homer sang, Plato taught, and Demosthenes spoke."

In one instance, however, Emily Norcross was not delinquent in responding. Two students from Greece were studying at Amherst and had rooms in Samuel Dickinson's house. The brothers, Pandias and Konstantinos Rallis, went to visit another Greek student, Nicolaos Petrokokinos, at Monson College during the latter's illness, and Edward sent his letter with them. Emily Norcross at once wrote to Edward, praising Konstantinos's gracious help.

It took months, however, for Emily Norcross to respond to his marriage proposal, telling him to present it to her father, which Edward most earnestly did. Unfortunately, from the well-to-do farm owner of Monson he did not receive an immediate reply. Edward then insisted all the more to her: "I tell you, my dear, that I find in you exactly what I have always been searching for – a true lady to make my own. . . .You will determine the date of marriage." After some time, Emily Norcross finally accepted the proposal, provided Edward did not rush the time of the wedding date. Already two years had passed.

Emily Norcross was the most beautiful creature Edward had ever met. She was a serious young lady – a devout believer. Her qualities were highly desirable to him, and he paid no heed to her silence, just as he ignored talk of the Norcross children dying young from consumption. First it had struck the girls, and then time changed the object of the attack – the boys of the family passed away; but time did not change Emily Norcross's silence.

Finally, the couple were married and settled down in the house he had rented and furnished. When Edward had asked her to look the place over, she had sent her younger sister Lavinia. Edward acquiesced. A year later, 1829, their first offspring arrived. He was named William Austin, a traditional name in the Norcross family. Now they awaited the arrival of their second child.

Voices from the birth room continued as Edward sat in the kitchen wondering whether he had made the right decision in moving into his father's house. When the economic situation of his father, who had eight offspring living with him, had become difficult, Edward, eager to help, moved in with them. He purchased half of the property, added two rooms on the east side of the house, and worked in his father's law office. The situation would have been workable, had his father improved his handling of money. Though Samuel's extreme generosity – imprinted in his nature – won him an outstanding name, it contributed to the great tragedy of his life. "The success of the individual springs from the educational institutions of the place where he lives," Samuel declared, and according to this principle, he invested all his efforts and personal earnings in education in Amherst. Thus, the one-room schoolhouse for the boys of the area became in 1814 the Academy of Amherst, a primary and secondary school for boys and girls. From that school Emily and her two siblings graduated. On its establishment rested the reputation of Samuel Dickinson and the distinguished Dickinson line.

"So far – so good," thought Edward, "but what need is there for a college in such a small place, particularly since there is an excellent university just a few miles away."

The kitchen door slammed open, and Samuel, flushed with moral indignation, confronted his son. "Great cities must be founded on the mountain top, so that all the world can see them!" he thundered, adding with a mixture of bitterness and pride, "And my personal finances are secondary!"

Edward turned toward his father, but his attention was distracted by the faint crying of an infant. "At last the babe has arrived!" he exclaimed, rushing in to greet the child and the mother. A moment later he stuck his head through the doorway to announce to his father, "A daughter – her name Emily Elizabeth Dickinson, born just before midnight!"

Samuel heard the word *daughter* without being able to grasp its import. For him, the city on the hill was the great event. It did not enter his mind – not the least shadow of a thought – that his dream had been realized in this birth. The city of imagination would be built very high indeed, and it would be a beacon for the world's poetry.

I tiptoed into the birth room. The mother was slumped exhausted in an armchair while her mother-in-law hastily gathered the soaked, ensanguined sheets from the bed. The babe, in a small cradle at her feet, slept peacefully. Grandmother Lucrecia forcefully gathered the sheets, grumbling, "If these are not washed at once, the blood will leave a stain, and I do not waste sheets!" The name of this angry woman, who raised nine children and died alone, abandoned, far from Amherst, distanced from her children and the mansion built by her husband, was Lucrecia Gunn Dickinson – Emily's grandmother and Samuels's wife. A poem of Emily's comes to mind whose seed may have been sown during a stay at her grandmother's house –"My life had stood – a Loaded Gun"(#754). Indeed the image of the grandmother who was standing this moment over the babe's cradle was that of a charged, threatening weapon.

The mother lay down in the freshly made bed with the child beside her. Before alleviating weariness by sleep, the mother looked curiously at the child's tiny face, the little shock of hair that held a reddish tint under the lamp, the upper lip that was like a circumflex. The nose, however, was regular, like the white smooth skin. The babe did not appear conventionally beautiful, but she had elegant features, and her radiant expression held a special quality. The mother did not know how to describe it, but the child's features brought a flood of delight. The child will take my name – Emily – she thought. Emily Elizabeth, she added, and dreamed of their becoming close friends and her daughter's supporting her in old age. Peaceful and content, having endured the enormous trial of birthing, she gazed upon the baby's eyes until they both fell asleep.

Forefathers

As the door opened noiselessly, I witnessed visitors pausing on the threshold. They were the forefathers, who had come to bless and counsel the child. In the lead, entering hesitantly, quietly, was Nathaniel – the first settler of the family. He was wearing a severe black suit whose long coat was buttoned to the chin. The britches were tied below the knee, with gray stockings above the high, broad-buckled, pointed shoes. On his head was a tall black hat bearing witness to English Puritan origins. Holding himself stiffly, with marked pride, he gazed at the child, and with an air of giving thanks for her presence, he leaned over and placed a small book by her pillow. It was a collection of the sermons of the first governor of Massachusetts, John Winthrop. They had arrived together in 1630 on the *Mayflower*, and Winthrop's teachings had shaped Nathaniel Dickinson's life. He addressed the child gravely, formally: "Emily Elizabeth Dickinson, I come to say that two hundred years ago, to this day, I reached the shores of this blessed land. I left my home country so that I could worship as I saw fit. I earned my bread from the hallowed ground I cultivated and loved, with the Lord ever my protector. I attended good governor Winthrop's sermons, and his inspiration guided me. The spirit of God informed my experience and my life, and I communicated that to my children. You too, child, shall follow that light." Turning to leave, he quickly added with emphasis: "Never forget that we are immigrants from England and the elect of the Lord!"

Though the infant's eyes flickered open, she appeared unreceptive to his words and tone. You could say that she was relieved to see the tall, black-clad personage depart. Then her gaze was drawn to the next two figures who entered and greeted Nathaniel Dickinson. One was his first-born son, Samuel, and the other, Ebenezer, son of the latter. Wearing worn, simple clothes, high boots, and wide-brimmed hats for protection against storm and sun, the men diffidently approached the cradle. They gazed for some time at the child and then showed her their calloused hands. Their faces hard, lined, worn by toil and conflict in a hostile environment, they told a tale brutal, unvarnished, brief. Samuel spoke. "Look at our hands. . . These hands held the plow, cultivated the earth, and devastated her enemies. The redskins fell by these same hands that reaped the blessings of Him who guided us to this fertile land. The Bible, the Plow, and the Musket were the instruments of our survival." The visitors had nothing more to say. Having summed up their lives, in three words, they swallowed and departed, making way for two more forebears – Nathan, the elder, and Nathan, the younger. Exhausted but proud, father and son told the same tale: they worked the soil, cared for the animals, and fought in war, with God ever their support. The one followed the other, narrating heroic acts. They had fought "for the American cause" in the French and Indian War and the War for Independence. With God's help, their cohorts were victorious, but with great casualties. As the elder spoke, the younger nodded his head in agreement, since from the time of childhood harsh memories of war had burdened him. When the other concluded, he spoke up concerning events in the new world: "I took part in the farmers' uprising in Massachusetts. When we defeated the English landholders and claimed the colony as our own, we also had to defeat powerful local merchants. That we did, and at that time the Dickinson properties in Amherst extended over the hill to the area beyond. That whole stretch of land belonged to our family."

It was an extensive holding with creeks, deer, frogs, snakes, various furry critters, farmland, and woods. That land had been held by four generations of Dickinson men and their families of eight to ten children. Edward alone had only three offspring, as did his son, Austin, whose progeny turned out to be the last generation.

Forefathers

The forebears exited the room as grandfather Samuel shouldered his way in. A vigorous man of fiery temperament, it was as if the birth had revitalized his spirit. His reddish hair reflected that of the newborn. With feeling he was barely able to master, he placed a bible by the child, saying "May your deeds be conducted high on a hill where the world may behold them!" The baby's eyes remained closed, but we can imagine these lines potential in her spirit (#288):

I'm Nobody! Who are you?
Are you – Nobody – Too?
Then there's a pair of us!
Don't tell! they'd advertise – you know!

How dreary – to be – Somebody!
How public – like a Frog –
To tell one's name –the livelong June –
To an admiring Bog!

The eight lines – like a damp sponge – wiped away grandiose assumptions of puritans and forebears, erasing ephemeral commonplaces of American history and society. The poet could not abide conventional thoughts and values. She held that "The soul's Superior Instants / Occur to Herself alone" (#306). All ideas would be assessed by her own incisive intellect, and her spirit would elaborate those of choicest intellectual hue. These insights – tied to deep intuitive testing – she would shape into poetry, so they would convey the essence of mankind. For that purpose she chose withdrawal, silence, and contemplation, seizing countless "Superior Instants."

Now, a few moments aftermidnight, on December 11, 1830, falling asleep, the babe prepared to set forth on the quest of her life.

Soul Sister

Happy the one who meets the sister soul, the love of one's life . . .

Nine days after Emily's birth (December 19, 1830) Emily's sister soul came to earth in Deerfield, not far north of Amherst. Susan Huntington Gilbert – whom Emily would affectionately call Sue, Susie, or Dolly – was the seventh child of Thomas and Harriet Gilbert, her father being the owner of the large tavern one street over from the Homestead. Thomas Gilbert was the sole citizen of Amherst who wandered the streets of the town when he'd taken one drop too many, and Sue, who was the great love of Emily's life, was the only one in town who truly recognized the quality of Emily's poetry. "Sue, you are my imagination," Emily wrote; "Sue, you are my universe."

The Childhood Years

The period of childhood – sunk in memory, timeless, all-powerful – accompanies us the rest of our life. It appears in illuminated patches or shadowy, twisted scenes that the selective self studiously garners. Placed in the channels of the mind, these scenes shape thoughts and affect decisions. Piercing the heart, they bring wounds and joys.

Like swarms of wasps, problems buzzed in Emily's house. The Homestead would soon be lost; the bank threatened foreclosure. Surpassing in zeal the contributions to the college's development by fellow townsmen Daniel Webster and Luke Sweetzer, Samuel Dickinson did not hesitate to put up the house for collateral. He had always insisted on believing in miracles to achieve his dreams, on setting out on new ventures, but his unharnessed generosity sank him deeper in debt and despair. He no longer proudly walked the streets. Going by closed carriage, shrinking back in the corner of the seat, seeing and greeting no one, bitter and angry, he moved through town. Eventually, his difficulties led to a decline in his faith, and he retreated into the kitchen many hours daily, head in his hands. Banks daily clamored at the door. Lucrecia Gunn faced down the messengers in her own way; the sons were angry; the daughters were embarrassed, and Edward doubled his hours of work at the law office. Emily Norcross Dickinson, mother of the poet, alone in the house with two children, sealed herself in the eastern wing, attempted to turn a deaf ear, and prayed, but nothing could block her suffering. Piercing voices echoed in every room of the house. The young wife trembled at the thought of what would take place at every meal when the families would meet, and she did not know what to say or do. Her mother-in-law's bitter observations, fiery gaze, and acid outbursts corrected her every word and action.

Emily, a child of three, shielded herself behind her older brother, Austin, four, who hid behind his mother, and she behind a deafening silence, wild as midnight alarm bells. The children absorbed her melancholy through open pores. Wordlessly, she communicated dark thoughts and feelings that were to impact Emily's poems (#216):

Safe in their Alabaster Chambers –
Untouched by Morning –
And untouched by Noon –
Lie the meek members of the Resurrection –
Rafter of Satin – and Roof of Stone!

Grand go the Years – in the Crescent – above them –
Worlds scoop their Arcs –
And Firmaments – row –
Diadems – drop – and Doges – surrender –
Soundless as dots – on a Disc of Snow –

Impressions of a Journey

All smiles, the young woman bustled into the disturbed house, embraced the mother, her elder sister, took the children in her arms and waltzed them around the living room with a vigor and joy that the darkness in the house could not dampen. Aunt Lavinia, a youthful nineteen years of age, had come from Monson to pick up young Emily. Emily Norcross Dickinson, soon to give birth to her third child, could not deal with her lively daughter, but well-behaved Austin would remain at home with his mother.

Emily's suitcase had already been prepared, since they had to depart early for the strenuous journey of over twenty miles, which would take a full day. The paired horses pulling the carriage were handsome and spirited, as was Aunt Lavinia's cousin, Loring, who had come along to accompany them on the trip. A handsome twenty-year-old, he laughed spiritedly, expressing his enthusiasm as he looked into Lavinia's eyes. He leaned toward her, lightly touching her, and Lavinia turned toward him laughing. Their faces gleamed. Their young bodies trembled with flowering love, and their delight overflowed and spread!

Emily saw and felt it all. She was inoculated with that feeling which is the most delicious and most characteristic of the human heart. At that moment she did not know what it is called. She learned the word later. It was *love*, or what the Greeks call *eros*. People spoke the word in warm, vibrant tones. In this case, being in love caused a great to-do because Loring was Lavinia's first cousin. But love is love, Emily later realized, and Lavinia was Lavinia – her life was her own. It belonged to her; she had no reason to heed the attitudes of others. Thus, in spite of opposition, the couple wed. They had children – the most beloved cousins of the poet, Louisa and Frances, who corresponded with Emily throughout their lives. When the hour arrived, Aunt Lavinia died, and immediately after, inconsolable, Loring also passed away. Emily wrote her orphaned cousins: "Since I cannot pray for my beloved aunt let me sing," and as her own death approached, she wrote them as an announcement without complaint, "Called back"; and she went back; and they wept bitterly, for they adored that rare creature, and their names, like their dearest aunt's, were inscribed in the records of Emily's admirers.

Now, on the trip to Monson, nothing in the future was on the minds of those in the carriage. They felt immune to time. The idea of their own death had not struck them. Their only concern that day was the distance of twenty-two miles, a day's – not a lifetime's – journey. At home, family were anxiously waiting, so the travelers had to hurry.

Emily – between Aunt Lavinia and Loring as they leaned to touch each other – was pressed in a warm double-embrace, inducing a delicious feeling of euphoria. She smiled continually, wishing that the journey would never end. Midway in the trip, in the middle of nowhere, a storm broke out. "There, there, dear little thing!" Aunt Lavinia murmured, wrapping Emily in a blanket. The sky was capped by a leaden cover, which every so often opened, releasing yellow streaks which furiously slashed the clouds in two as stormy bugles blared. The bushes shuddered; the trees leaned and branches swayed like limbs of animals in agonizing pain. The little child's heart quaked, but in her aunt's close, comforting embrace, lines like these, in eleven storm poems, were taking shape in her mind (#824):

The Wind begun to knead the Grass –
As Women do a Dough –
He flung a Hand full at the Plain –
A Hand full at the Sky –
The Leaves unhooked themselves from Trees –
And started all abroad –
The Dust did scoop itself like Hands –
And throw away the Road –
The Wagons quickened on the Street –
The Thunders gossiped low –
The Lightning showed a Yellow Head –
And then a livid Toe –
The Birds put up the Bars to Nests –
The Cattle flung to Barns –
Then came one drop of Giant Rain –
And then, as if the Hands
That held the Dams – had parted hold –
The Waters Wrecked the Sky –

But overlooked my Father's House –
Just Quartering a Tree –

The theme of love, too, brought hundreds of poems. Love stirred her. She felt it bursting from the breasts of those young travelers, and it filled her soul. It overflowed and sealed the feeling within her, energizing her poetry and her life. "... Love is Immortality, / Nay, it is Deity. ... Love reforms Vitality / Into Divinity" (#809). She loved intensely, flinging passionate adoration upon fellow souls, male and female, classmates and mentors, teachers and select clergymen; and she never hesitated to offer the theme of love, as she did her life, to the divinity of poetry. Throughout her life, her love of Susan, her sister-in-law, was unchanging: "Sue, you are my sun's avalanche," she wrote in a letter. She penned, in turn, the following lines in which the original *her* of the first line was switched to *his* after the poet's death.

What would I give to see his face?
I'd give – I'd give my life – of course –
But that is not enough!

Stop just a minute – let me think!
I'd give my biggest Bobolink!
That makes two – Him – and Life!
You know who "June" is –
I'd give her –
Roses a day from Zanzibar –
And Lily tubes – like Wells –
Bees – by the furlong –
Straits of Blue
Navies of Butterflies – sailed thro' –
And dappled Cowslip Dells –

Then I have "shares" in Primrose "Banks" –
Daffodil Dowries – spicy "Stocks" –
Dominions – broad as Dew –
Bags of Doubloons – adventurous Bees
Brought me – from firmamental seas -
And Purple – from Peru –

Now – have I bought it –
"Shylock"? Say!
Sign me the Bond!
I vow to pay
To Her – who pledges this –
One hour – of her Sovereign's "face"!
Ecstatic Contract!
Niggard Grace!
My Kingdom's worth of Bliss!
(#247)

The travelers arrived in Monson late at night, and weary Emily was carried into the house in Loring's arms and laid down in grandfather Joel's bed. Grandfather, an affluent farmer whose property expanded as his family shrank, looked at Emily with love and tenderly kissed her on the forehead. She blissfully sank into sleep. Emily stayed three months in her mother's paternal home, in which death had nested. Grandmother had passed away just three years before, shortly after the birth of Austin. Emily's mother mourned her loss at a distance and was faced with the problem of relating to the woman whom her father shortly married. The oldest son died a year later, leaving behind in his father's care a sick wife with their two little children. They played with Emily in an area adjacent to the room where their mother was failing from the same illness that had taken their father. At Mount Holyoke Emily would be classmate of the elder cousin – also named Emily – who died young, followed by her brother. Consumption was the scourge that laid waste the Norcross family. Emily did not comprehend death, but an abstract fear seemed to encompass her, and in the middle of games with her cousins, she appeared sad. Aunt Lavinia rushed to embrace her. The little girl, sighing, asked, "What can dear Austin be doing now?" Of the entire family, it was Austin alone that she missed, and it would always be Austin who was her favorite. Emily did not ask about her mother and father, nor did she inquire about her newborn sister who was delivered with great difficulty, risking her mother's life. It seems that this final childbirth determined the erotic life of the Dickinson parents, since they did not have another child during a period when numerous offspring were the norm.

At Monson, Austin was continually in Emily's thoughts. She always loved him so much that years later she encouraged him to marry Sue, though she held her in the dearest region of her heart.

Return to the Homestead

Emily returned home after the three month stay in Monson. Angry storms of financial ruin had left their mark on the faces of the family members. Emily's uncles and aunts, hearing hard times knock on the door, were flung east and west. Only the youngest son remained as head of the Homestead household.

Samuel and his wife, sad and humiliated, remained in the western wing of the house, while the eastern wing was allotted to Emily, Austin, their parents, and the infant, Vinnie. The mother – exhausted and fearful from the tribulation of childbirth – was battered by Lucrecia's bitter words. Echoes of a storm swirling in her mind like volcanic sparks blurred her feelings, and she took refuge in numb silence. The father, Edward, a representative in the Massachusetts legislature, was absent most of the week. On weekends he was home, where the family gathered in the living room to study scripture and gain counsel for the trials of human life. Painful silence and the drone of anguish sank deeply into the child's consciousness.

Humbled and poor – his faith shaken – Samuel Dickinson would sit in the kitchen awaiting foreclosure on the eastern part of the house. In his presence, Emily always tiptoed quietly by, while on meeting grandmother she would shrink back against the wall with closed eyes.

The time arrived for grandfather and grandmother to depart from the Homestead – an event that came after Grandfather's old friend, the pastor, informed him of an opportunity that had arisen. Hastily entering the house, the pastor took him by the shoulders, and shook him.

"Friend Samuel, God has answered my prayer," he announced, trembling with feeling. "Come with me to Ohio, where I am joining a college faculty. You will oversee a building project on campus."

Samuel's body grew erect; his eyes gleamed. Once again he had a chance to prove what it meant to be a Dickinson. Within a few days, Samuel and Lucrecia found themselves in Ohio, far from their beloved town – far from their children, friends, and colleagues, in an unknown place, among unknown people. Most trying, however, was the challenge Samuel once more faced in monetary affairs. He had enormous responsibilities in handling building funds. He worked intensely for five years, exceeding the budget as well as his physical and spiritual powers. His rampant decline was irreversible, and thus the generous idealist Samuel gave up his life to the Lord, whom he no longer trusted.

Grandmother Lucrecia – alone and penniless in a strange place – yearned for return to Amherst. She wrote: "My life is at an end; I am weak and failing"; and in another letter—"I know I am full of imperfections. My only happiness is to be with my children." Nevertheless, Edward's first concern was his spouse. His mother's presence would exacerbate her withdrawal and depression. He could not give in to sentiment; after all, he was not an only child. So, Lucrecia plunged into silence, and a year after her husband's death, abandoned and despondent, she surrendered to the fate of her spouse. Her realistic first-born son arranged for her remains to be transported to Amherst.

The Childhood Years

Thirty years later (August 30, 1871) an Amherst newspaper published an article entitled "A Beautiful Event." The anonymous writer noted: "In my walks about this beautiful town on the morning of the late Jubilee of Amherst College, I was attracted to the Cemetery. There I observed a family gathering about the grave of the Hon. S.F. Dickinson. . . . All the daughters from their city homes with their husbands and children, and of friend Hon. E. Dickinson, were there. They came loaded with flowers. . .". Forty-five Dickinsons had come from throughout the nation to honor the eminent patrician of the clan, though he had fallen into poverty and humiliation. Thirty years were needed to heal wounds, to set aside personal interests, so that all the Dickinsons could view with pride and gratitude Samuel's creative drives and spiritual extremes. Observing the years that had passed, hearts overflowed with nostalgia, fierce scenes of conflict were downplayed, and the piercing jibes of grandmother Lucrecia became jokes that the grandchildren mimicked in their games.

Edward – saddened by the death of his parents, and plagued with regrets – strove to find a workable solution for his anxiety. One portion of the house having already been given up for debt, he sold the east section, which he had purchased from his father, and made a purchase on Pleasant Street. It was a fine residence. The large yard, with neat lawn and cheerful flowerbeds, faced the busy street and bordered the cemetery. From behind the fence around the yard during summer, and from the living-room window during winter, the children viewed funeral processions. Groups of mourners clad in black slowly filed into the cemetery, and horse-drawn hearses bore hither their heavy burden. These moments of grief in the air intensely affected the children. Images of death and pain were planted in the soul of the child and would flower in five hundred poems of varied form and rich meaning. Still, Emily and Austin loved the house. It was a dwelling untroubled by the whispering and tensions of the paternal home. In letters to friends decades later, the Dickinson siblings allude with pleasure to charades in which they enacted roles they were to repeat throughout their lives: Austin was the lord of the manor, Emily the lady, and little Lavinia their trusty lady-in-waiting. Other characters in the play were mother as the wordless queen withdrawn into her room with a headache, and father as the king absent on state affairs.

The silence in the house was very real. Mother, prone to headaches, would retreat to her room, and Emily accordingly wrote: "I never had a mother. I suppose a mother is one to whom you hurry when you are troubled. . . . I always ran Home to Awe when a child, if anything befell me. He was an awful Mother, but I liked him better than none." Always alone, the three children focused their attention and love on one another, and they remained close to one another to the end of their lives. Edward, as a politician, was absent in Boston or Washington, and when in Amherst he spent hours in his law offices. "I think of my father in his lonely life and even more lonely death," Emily noted sadly at the time of his passing.

Life on Pleasant street was indeed pleasant, but for Edward it was of paramount importance that the Homestead be recovered. The house belonged to the Dickinsons – they had to get it back. Stubbornly, insistently – and with years of hard work – he achieved his goal in 1855. With terrible memories of Lucrecia's sharp words, which also influenced the children, Emily Norcross followed her husband back to the "brick house," as she called it without enthusiasm. Emily must have felt that again they had returned to "their Alabaster Chambers."

School – the Stirring of Feelings

School is a challenging entrance into a jungle of feelings. They all start here; seeds sprout that develop incessantly: love, envy, competition, fear, pride, loneliness, emptiness, intellectual delight.

Sophia Holland

Is there more than Love and Death?
Please, tell me its name . . .
(E.D., in a letter)

"Emily, it's time to go to school," mother called at the foot of the stairs, and Emily thought of the bother they were imposing upon her for no reason. In 1839, at nine years of age, she could read and write. Why should she go to the Academy and be away from home so many hours daily? No, she had decided; she would not go to school unless her sister, Vinnie, three years younger, would come with her!

So it was that the two girls set out, hand in hand, mother giving advice from the stoop: "Watch out for carriages in the street, listen carefully to your teacher, and don't forget your recess apple." Emily hurried to arrive – to see for herself what they called school and spoke of with such respect. Vinnie was proud to be accompanying her older sister, though she was out of breath as Emily pulled

85

her along Main Street. The Academy, just off Pleasant Street, was not very far. The school yard was overflowing with students and mothers. The two little girls had had the same thought: "Why had mother not come with us?" Though this saddened Emily, Vinnie, gaily looking around, caught sight of her cousin, and immediately called, "Sophia! Sophia!"

The girl responded, running to Emily's side. They looked at one another with yearning for security and the warmth of friendship. "That's what school means," Emily thought, and she instantly loved Sophie, all of her schoolmates, and the teacher as well, who patted the children gently on the head. She also loved the books and the lessons, just as she was infatuated with the young men on the faculty. Most of all she loved the music of the mind as it vibrated with the sounds of newly formed strings. The teachers lovingly opened the paths of the mind, and she through imagination extended them to high roads.

Sophia, a distant relative, was Emily's first friend – the first step in the life with others, the first tender experience, a strange happiness because she did not know or even imagine that the powerful feelings of friendship could cause pain that might last a lifetime. Beloved and inseparable, Emily and Sophia one lovely day in spring went on a school outing. They were already fourteen, still walking hand-in-hand, laughing and carefree – Emily red-haired and alert; Sophia, blond with laughing blue eyes. Sophia urged Emily to avoid the crowd of classmates and enjoy the time together in the magic of the woods. If they hurried, they would reach the brook on the other side of the meadow. They did not hesitate. They plunged through the meadow and into the woods, and before reaching the clearing – where the stream flowed in the distance – they were dazzled by the spectacle that arose before their eyes: having just been released from cocoons, a wave of small white butterflies playfully billowed in the breeze. The darting creatures swirled in the first dance of their lives, and the girls sat for a long time quietly admiring the splendor of the sight. Changing shapes of color and movement formed a perfect harmony, awakening the senses. As if hypnotized, Sophia released her companion's hand. "I want to fly!" she cried, spinning amidst the cloud of butterflies. She reached out to touch the butterflies darting about her, their wings brushing her beatific face. Mesmerized, Emily felt that this creature – her friend Sophia – belonged to the ranks of the angels. Her eyes brimmed with tears of love. "We'd better hurry!" she cried, "They may have gone back already!" The girls raced down a hill to the road and rushed perspired into class, their eyes filled with awe and their hearts with delight in existence. They sat at their desks with lowered heads, and the teacher smiled, saying not a word about their tardiness, though her eyes widened in anxiety when Sophia began to cough. Persistent, dry – it was the cough of terror.

Death, the tyrannous monarch, had chosen his next victim. A week sufficed to claim his prey. Every afternoon on the way home from school, Emily – her heart in her mouth, her books under her arm – stopped for a few moments outside Sophie's door to take a deep breath and whisper a wish: "May she be well today, waiting for me!" For a week she found her friend motionless in bed, pale, lost in the white sheets, as parents, siblings, and close relatives stood frozen in dread. At her bedside, Emily murmured heartfelt words, incapable of imagining what was to come. Now it was Saturday, and Emily knocked urgently at Sophia's door. After a long wait, someone opened, and on seeing her at once slammed the door. At first she futilely pounded and pushed, but then her thoughts flashed to the back door, which was probably open. Racing around the house, she swung the kitchen door and tremblingly removed her shoes. A heavy silence reigned within. With swift soundless steps she mounted the stairs and squeezed in among the relatives who stood numbly outside Sophia's room. The doctor spotted her, took her by the arm. "No, Emily, no," he whispered sternly, "you cannot go in." Emily refused to listen, attempting to pull away, and the doctor relented, though he kept his hand on her arm. "From here at the doorway, dear, you may see her and say good-bye. She is dying." Emily could not hear the last word – she did not want to hear.

From the doorway Emily gazed at Sophia: "Peaceful and beautiful as if untouched by sickness, her pale features illuminated by an other-worldly smile," her friend turned her weak glance towards Emily, her lips opened to utter a word that was not audible, and Emily understood. She could see clearly; Sophia was leaving – no one could hold her back. She was departing ... her breath shallow in small puffs . . . labored . . . halting . . . returning: a deep heave in the air . . . spent . . . . it was her last. Sophia departed. "She was too lovely for earth, and she was transplanted from earth to heaven," was Emily's first thought, and she was immediately seized by panic. How could Sophia find the road to paradise in that vast sky? She despaired at this thought. With the eyes of her mind she saw Sophia utterly alone, searching, wandering in strange regions. Searching for . . . whom . . . what? Confused, Emily stared at the door of Death, whose threshold her friend had crossed. Emily searched. With gaping eyes, she was looking for some sort of explanation. She was seeking in those around her assurance – an answer to the great question that had frozen the working of her mind and had blocked the channels of her heart – but what words could dispel the question that weighed on her bosom? She opened her mouth and only a hollow moan emerged. The doctor, who was still holding her, drew her out of the room, through the hall, and down the stairs. Finally, he took her out to the street, and she – victim of the question – followed him without resistance, and there at that juncture of despair, she heard him say, "Emily, go home – go home to your mother." And she took the road to her house – barefooted, as her shoes remained by Sophia's back steps by the kitchen door. With eyes cloudy and frightened, drowned in sensations, she mounted the stoop, without tears, without words, because what she had seen was so enormous that it could not be expressed in language or tears or thoughts; not even in the heart, which – sunk empty and immobilized within her – had no power to protest.

She arrived outside their back door. Her mother opened and gently drew her in. She said nothing – not even asking about her bare feet. She simply sat her down at the table, offering her a glass of warm milk. She could not drink or speak. Vinnie entered and embraced her, and took her to her room. She was continually thinking of her shoes, wondering why her mother had not asked about them. Once when she was a little girl, she had stepped into the brook and her boot had stuck in the mud. Mother had noticed the missing boot at once and had chastised her. Now she had said not a word about the shoes, or about her being silent for days, barely touching her food, and not going to school. Seated by the window in daylight, she faced outward without seeing. At night half-awake she would be trapped in whirling chaos. The blackness would suck her in, and she would sink into a well of anguish.

One night, however, as she fell asleep, a glorious vision came to her. She found herself surrounded by dazzling light. She was walking on a luminous path. Sophia was beside her. She felt her hand, weightless as a feather. She could not make out her face or the rest of her body. Nothing showed – everything was covered by radiance. They were moving without bodies. It was as if they were playing. Carefree, they were swimming, not in water, but in the air in an unknown place. Suddenly there was a cloud of many-colored butterflies dancing around them and blanketing them, and with swift movements the young friends slid away from their touch. Suddenly Sophia vanished, and it all disappeared. Emily was no longer swimming in air, but fell heavily to the stony ground. Her body pinned where she had fallen, she began to cry, "Sophia! Sophia!" "Here! Here!" came a laughing reply; but she could not be seen, and the sound kept fading farther and farther away. Emily saw a swaying, glowing cloud like a rainbow. It was not on the horizon, but on the road right in front of her. Moving with a pleasant slide, the glowing cloud left no light behind it – only an empty, deserted place. Alone, Emily cried out in desperation, and the cry of fear awoke her in darkness. Soaked in sweat, she strove to discover where she was, but night dragged on and on. She was so frightened, she could not get up. She only felt Vinnie's hand nudging her as she lay down by her side and engulfed her in a calming hug.

In the morning she awoke with a powerful drop of knowledge. The realization of human fate had distilled deep within her. Silence was the sole question and the sole reply. The family gazed at her with anxious eyes, and as her silence continued, they prepared the carriage, a few clothes, and two or three books, and with Austin and handy-man Joseph, sent her to Boston.

There, on the stoop of the house to which they had moved years before, was Aunt Lavinia waiting with open arms, her two little girls by her side. Emily threw herself into her warm embrace and burst into tears. Aunt Lavinia stroked her head, held her tightly, "There . . . there. . . my soul . . . ," she kept saying.

At the end of the month she returned to Amherst and her schoolwork. Dormant in her soul, years later (1862) a poem took shape, recalling *The Kimomeni* (the "Sleeping Girl"), a memorial by Greek sculptor, Jannis Halepas (#369):

She lay as if at play
Her life had leaped away –
Intended to return –
But not so soon–

Her Merry Arms, half dropt –
As if for lull of sport –
An instant had forgot –
The Trick to start –

Her dancing Eyes – ajar –
As if their Owner were
Still Sparkling through
For Fun – at you –
Her Morning at the door –
Devising, I am sure –
To force her sleep –
So light – yet so deep –

The image of Sophia on her deathbed, indelibly imprinted on Emily's mind, appeared intense and clear whenever associations sharply evoked memories. Years later, when she was twenty-six, she confided to her friend and classmate Abiah Root: "I write to you tonight because it is cool and quiet, and I can forget the toil and care of the feverish day, and then I am *selfish* too because I am feeling lonely; some of my friends are gone, and some of my friends are sleeping – sleeping the churchyard sleep – the hour of evening is sad. The tears come and I cannot brush them away."

Time was passing, and as Death circled the town with ease – friends, acquaintances, neighbors and relatives fell and disappeared – the event became knowledge with many shades and feelings, and the tragic dimensions of the first shock lessened. The delights of youth holding the reins of life pulled her into its natural path. Love acted powerfully upon her and drew her into experiences of joy.

The Many Faces of Love

Love – thou art Veiled –
A few – behold thee –
Smile – and alter – and prattle – and die –
Bliss – were an Oddity – without thee –
Nicknamed by God –
Eternity –
(#453)

Susan Huntington Gilbert

The school year was a festival. Emily was sixteen – her last year at the Academy, and her being, filled with joy, overflowed and spilled out. A flood was the laughter, joking, teasing – and passionate feelings began to gallop in the heart. The moment arrived when Emily's spirit demanded dynamic sensations, and then she focused on the person (classmate, boy or girl, young teacher, friend) before her, who would become the erotic idol that sprang from her passion for life.

A daily joy was the savoring of life at the Academy, where all Emily's friends from the neighborhood were students: Susan Phelps, Mary Warner, Abiah Root, who was a dear friend with whom she corresponded for years, Abby Wood, who eight years later founded with her husband the American University of Beirut, and Helen Fiske, a well known author with the pen name Helen Hunt who recognized the stature of Emily's poetry. There was also Emily Fowler (Noah Webster's granddaughter), four years her senior, a poet who never recognized the significance of Emily's work.

At the Academy fate knocked at the door, and Emily opened it wide and kept it wide-open throughout her life. In her last school year she met Susan, Sue as she called her – her most beloved friend, who at once grasped the rare worth of her poetry. Their friendship was the underlying, inspiring, but tormenting theme of Emily's existence.

The day was rainy. Vinnie was staying home with a cold, and Emily, holding her jacket over her head, descended the front stairs. From the doorway, mother called, "Don't get wet! Watch the mud!" but Emily, eager to see her friends again, excitedly breathed in the aroma of the moist earth. Saturated, the atmosphere brought pleasurable shivers, as tiny drops of rain wet her cheeks. It was such a splendid day, and the warm delightful shower that had remained from the earlier downpour had created a misty, magic creek which steamed above the asphalt, forming two channels – one of shallow water, and above it, one of white mist. The students jumped as they crossed. Emily – walking carefree in a delightful dream – stepped into the water with eyes closed, wet feet, and face moist from mist and rain.

She did not see the young, raven-haired student, and bumping into her, she opened her eyes to see a joyful face gazing smilingly at her. Water dripped from the girl's uncovered head onto her face, ran across her cheek, turned down her chin, dropped to her neck, and took the road to her breast. She made not the slightest move to wipe away the water or shield herself from the rain. Emily spontaneously raised her jacket and covered their heads. The girl, smiling, extended her hand, took Emily around the waist to bring her closer, and thus embraced, their heads touching, they ran, tripping against one another, tittering, and exchanging glances. The bodily touch and the freshness of the rain on a warm day elicited in the girls for the first time tender excitement and laughter from the heart. It was an exotic meeting! Side-by-side they raced through the tall doorway into the Academy. They stood in the vestibule shaking water from their locks and giggling with delight.

"I adore fall showers," the girl declared, "and today's my lucky day – my first day at the Academy." She added joyfully, "You'll see, Emily – the shower's a sign of blessing." She looked deeply into Emily's eyes, and Emily blushed, lowering her gaze, surprised by her name on the girl's lips. It was the first time they met and of course she didn't know her name. Looking, however, into Emily's eyes as if they were friends for years, the girl raced on: "I love the rain, but today I may have overdone it! My hair is soaked!" She tossed her hair to throw off the water, but it continued to run down her cheeks onto her neck. She freed her blouse to dry her face. Emily offered her scarf, and the girl patted her neck and hair, returning the scarf with a humorous handshake. "I am delighted finally to meet you," she said spiritedly. "I am Susan Gilbert," she added, lowering her voice in the surname, which was hardly audible.

Before Emily stood the loveliest girl imaginable, with deep brown eyes and ebony locks, slim and somewhat taller than she. She admired her handsome dark features, the gleam in her eye, and the deep smile on her lips – touched, perhaps, with hint of irony. Nothing escaped Emily's keen eye – neither her new friend's pert breasts, nor her alert posture. Bold and confident, she made her presence felt in a charming way. Holding her hand, Emily felt Sue's fingers, one-by-one, pressing hers, and tenderness flowed within her. She held the hand for so long that Susan felt strange and pulled her hand away with a small, awkward laugh. Experiencing a pang of hunger that she had never felt before, Emily thought, "Tenderness is like bread – you don't ask for it till you experience hunger." Out loud she said, "You know me, Susan, how is that? Where are you from? When did you come to Amherst?" The questions numerous, the answers brief, the unforeseen destiny of the two girls was fated to be, drawing Austin into the path of their relationship.

In the classroom they sat side-by-side. "What joy, what joy – what poverty have they who do not feel it!" Emily whispered to herself of the friendship, as she gazed at her new companion.

Susan Huntington Dickinson

Leonard Humphre

Leonard Humphrey

A lively young man of twenty-two and a distinguished Amherst alumnus, Leonard Humphrey stepped through the door and at once a hush of admiration descended on the classroom. Handsome and tall, he brought energy that heightened the town's life and stirred students' spirits. The favorite of all the schoolgirls, Humphrey charged their minds with whispered secrets, brought blushes to their cheeks, and made their hearts pound in crazed rhythms. The inseparable companions Emily and Sue passionately adored the young academician. What a delightful theme of their everyday talk he was, as they strolled arm-in-arm and bent close to whisper fanciful thoughts about the dashing scholar! "What would you do if he tried to kiss you?" one of them would ask, and the other, voicing outrage at such boldness, would invent numerous means of evasion. "But what if he truly took you by surprise – stealing a kiss out of the clear blue sky?" And the question became a swift act: the one placed a stolen kiss on the other's cheek, who at once returned it. "Are you really talking about such a little kiss?" Emily asked, giving it again. "You refer to this?" Sue repeated the example. So, the two repeatedly exchanged kisses, continually laughing.

Eventually, Humphrey showed his preference for a young woman older than the two, and thus Emily and Sue stopped their favorite game. But the great mystery of the erotic continued to titillate them. Humphrey remained at the center of their lives as he was in the life of the town. Church elders and town leaders hailed him as "a young man of rare talents and great promise," believing that he would put Amherst on the national map with his sermons whose visions, unfortunately, he never fulfilled.

Now, however, the world drew on his inborn enthusiasm and the knowledge gleaned in his fervent studies. He established a literary club in which young people gathered to discuss lyric poetry and Shakespeare or participated in social events involving conversation and dancing. Emily and Sue were ever present. On cold winter days young people from greater Amherst absorbed ideas that, like the endless snows of New England, fell constantly and softly, leading the spirit with thoughts and questions. "Ideas inform poetic language," said Sue, Emily adding, "And ideas demand princely words to feed the poem!" She continued, "The poet must shape words that are like a foreign language yet are at the same time familiar."

The artistic young teacher directed his students' attention to their inner world and informed it with a passion for life. He inoculated the two friends with the literary word, and they excitedly discovered the world of images and ideas, filling their lives with the poetry of Robert and Elizabeth Browning, Tennyson and Shakespeare, Wordsworth, Keats, Shelley and Byron, and the work of great figures of their own age, Hawthorne, Austen, the Bronte sisters, Poe, and Melville. They recited poems and wept reading the works of Jane Austen and the Bronte sisters. As intellectuals they revered the work of the great philosopher and poet Emerson, whom Sue was to meet as Susan Dickinson. She was to tell Emily, "As the moon sailed the sky of Amherst, I took Emerson's arm and my soul soared. We conversed, and he turned his gentle philosophic face towards me waiting upon my commonplaces with such expectant quiet gravity, that I became painfully conscious that I was I and he was he, the great Emerson, and I shut up like a spent flower;" and Emily responded: "As if he had come from where dreams are born." At the time – keeping to the space she had prescribed for herself – Emily did not meet Emerson after his address at Amherst when he was staying overnight at Evergreens.

As Christmas recess at the Academy approached and the literary club would not meet for several weeks, the members decided to have a farewell party to celebrate the season before parting for the holidays, in spite of the snow that continually fell in the area.

Austin winked at Emily. "The old folks are leaving tomorrow for Monson..." he declared meaningfully, and the news spread at once. "There will be dancing at the Dickinsons' house tomorrow." The whole literary club gathered, as well as youth from Amherst neighborhoods. Leonard took charge of the dancing, Emily played the piano, and Vinnie and Sue offered refreshments as the couples, dressed in their best, whirled. Mattie, Sue's younger sister, came, met Austin, and they danced often that night. New friendships, with vibrant talk, were a great event. In small groups, they discussed the future of their country, maintaining that America would progress because the nation had divine sanction. "God Bless America" was the motto of the epoch. Others, however, insisted that religious faith was not sufficient; economic opportunity and enlightened human relations played crucial roles. Emily maintained that poetry was the spiritual lever that could lift the nation to the highest plane. The debate was endless, the voices intense, and Leonard called for louder music. They danced once more. The large rug was removed from the living room and taken to the hall, and the hours passed with laughter, flirting, and tenderly pressed hands. Very late, the celebrants reluctantly departed with a joy that would persist decades in their hearts. The leader of the event was last to leave. He wished to assure Emily that she was entirely correct about poetry. "The poets are the great resource of every country; they provide the intellectual drive and spiritual foundation of culture. Poetry is the soul of the nation," he whispered. Bending near, he added, "I trust that you will become the soul of Massachusetts, and that from here the spirit will pervade the land."

Emily's heart beat with excitement toward creativity. Every confirmation of her poetic talent brought inspiring emotion and encouragement that such hopes would be vindicated. These feelings were bound to those of love. She loved Leonard with all her heart. She did not suspect – how could she? – that this was the final dance organized by the handsome teacher.

The next day her parents returned, and her mother's eye fell on the rug. "What happened?" she asked, "The tiger's tail was always turned toward the window; now it's turned toward the door!"

With soothing voice Emily explained to mother, "Some friends came and we danced a while. We put the rug in the hall, and when we brought it back, we spread it backwards. Please, don't say anything to father!"

Mother breathed, "It will be our secret!" and she kept her word.

Unfortunately, the talented youth left nothing behind but his image in Emily's heart and a brief visit to Mount Holyoke the following fall. Delighted by the honor, she wrote to her friend Abiah, "Leonard came! Leonard visited me!" And indeed he visited her, bringing along his lady friend – which did not distress Emily. She loved him, and thus she received flashes of inspiration. He, however, was not destined to remain many years in this world; his roots were elsewhere. He had no chance to savor Emily's poetry. His destiny was not a missionary's, nor a teacher's, nor the chosen one of the great poet – as scholars conjecture he might have been, immortalizing his name and photograph in their monographs. Ever-present death, however, claimed him and swiftly snatched him from family and friends.

Phosphorescent Knowledge

Emily pulled Sue along. "Today Professor Edward Hitchcock, my favorite, is teaching! He's so inspiring!" They sat at the same desk, and with the excitement that brings delighted expectation to the heart and a glow to the face, they awaited the arrival of the brilliant teacher. President of Amherst Academy and internationally famous in the field of Geology, Edward Hitchcock brought the minute wonders of nature to his tongue and articulated them in all their glory as a reflection of God's nature. Listening to him, Emily saw the woods as a magic realm where lights, shadows, wild flowers, plants, and animals became an image of paradise. With closed eyes she absorbed his "phosphorescent knowledge," as she described it, and felt the presence of the divine not in ecclesiastic dogma but in the beauty of the world, expressed in countless poems on the theme (#668):

"Nature" is what we see –
The Hill – the Afternoon –
Squirrel – Eclipse – the Bumble bee –
Nay – Nature is Heaven –

Nature is what we hear –
The Bobolink – the Sea –
Thunder – the Cricket –
Nay – Nature is Harmony –
Nature is what we know –
Yet have no art to say –
So impotent Our Wisdom is
To her Simplicity.

So great was her love of nature that she read her teacher's book to gain comfort when in winter her flowers withered and bent to the ground with sadness and complaint, as if they were dying. He wrote that they lived, awaiting the spring to bloom once more and delight in life. She then knew that in truth "they were alive," and "without lips, they have speech." With them she received her guests: ". . . Flowers negotiate between us" (#905). She sent Sue flowers, identifying with them and adopting the nickname Daisy (from "Day's Eye," mirroring E.D. and recalling, in small, Blake's sunflower):

I hide myself within my flower,
That fading from your Vase,
You, unsuspecting, feel for me –
Almost a loneliness.
(#903)

At the edge of the small creek, under the trees, looking upward, Emily whistled an invitation to the birds. Sue watched, surprised by their instant response. They flew so near that the girls could touch them. "How do you chirp to them – tell me, show me!" she exclaimed ardently. "Once I was a bird!" she replied, laughing. She grew serious and silently wondered, "What sort of bird was I? And what does it mean for one to be a bird?" Turning to Sue, she answered, "Dearest Sue, nature is alive – breathes, moves, withers, and regenerates. Be still; listen to the quiet whispering of the garden. Come and see the buds – how they open their eyes to welcome the sun, to greet the new day. Listen, the secret joys whisper." Nature was her great love and inspiration, becoming her prayer (# 18): "In the name of the Bee – / And the Butterfly – / And of the Breeze – Amen!"

But Emily did not limit herself to the gentler side of nature. For example, she begins her poem about meeting a bird by humorously noting a shocking reality (#328):

A Bird came down the Walk –
He did not know I saw –
He bit an Angleworm in halves
And ate the fellow, raw .

The years in the Academy constituted the most pleasant period of her life. In 1846 she graduated, moving on to the initial creative phase of her career. In 1894 Daniel Taggard Fiske, principal of the Academy, looked back over the decades to Emily as a student:

I would say that I have very distinct and pleasant impressions of Emily Dickinson, who was a pupil of mine in Amherst Academy in 1842-43. I remember her as a very bright but rather delicate and frail looking girl; an excellent scholar, of exemplary deportment, faithful in all school duties; but somewhat shy and nervous. Her compositions were strikingly original; and in both thought and style seemed beyond her years, and always attracted much attention in the school and, I am afraid, excited not a little envy.

Mount Holyoke

"Emily," Edward Dickinson announced sternly, "I have enrolled you at Mount Holyoke. The semester begins at the end of August." His decisions regarding his children were a *fait accompli.* Resistance was out of the question. Emily dared not refuse or utter a word of commentary either about beliefs taught at the college and advocated by its founder-president Mary Lyon, or about its location in South Hadley, seven miles from Amherst. Emily did not open her mouth to express her anxiety concerning the homesickness that awaited her, since she was the only student from Amherst to attend Mount Holyoke at the time. She simply awaited the day classes would begin.

Austin, driving the large family carriage, accompanied his sister to the college. It took close to two hours to cover the distance, and it seemed an endless trip without the high spirits that they usually shared. Throughout the journey, the older brother, a student at Amherst, spoke in praise of the college in order to break the silence. He alluded to his research under distinguished professors, while Emily – apprehensive about the upcoming experience – held her silence and from time to time touched Austin's hand to confirm his support. She was disturbed by the idea of being away from home virtually an entire year among new faces, harnessed to a curriculum imposed by others. The new situation, determined by her father, appeared in black letters in her mind. The horses galloped or trotted ever more distant from the family home. The carriage entered the Hadley woods from whose thick foliage emerged the smell of moldy leaves, while from the high branches was heard the warbling of innumerable birds. It was as if she were immersed in the world of children's fairy tales, headed toward a land of witches in the garb of the professors assembled in Mount Holyoke hall. At the clearing at the center of town stood the large, white, three-story building. The only large building in the area at the time, it no longer exists. Now the college is housed in extensive facilities of imposing Gothic style.

Viewing the massive building, Emily felt her heart sink and her legs tremble. Now she fully realized how lonely she would feel among the 240 girls from all over Massachusetts under the tutelage of Mary Lyon, widely esteemed for her puritan zeal.

Emily Dickinson: Goddess of the Volcano

Fully aware of Emily's apprehension, Austin strove to calm her as best he could. On reaching their destination, he helped her step out of the carriage, took her little suitcase, and set it down on the polished floor of the common room. At once his eye gleamed with the sight of attractive students who were beginning to arrive from points throughout the region. Smiling and glancing in all directions, he embraced Emily and kissed her on the cheek. "You'll be with cousin Emily," he comforted her, but his sister was deaf to his words, numbly watching him descend the stairs, cross to the carriage, and set off for Amherst. Only her awareness of her classmates checked her impulse to dash after him and clamber into the carriage for the trip back to the Homestead. With tear-filled eyes, she carried her suitcase to her room, where she found cousin Emily whom she had not seen since the age of three. Then they had played together when she stayed in Monson for three months, but the only thing that remained fondly in her memory and her heart from that period was Aunt Lavinia, not cousin Emily, then six years old – a terrified dry little girl who had lost her father to consumption and whose mother then lay dying of the same malady in the room the children were forbidden to enter.

With a timid smile, Cousin Emily, dressed in her best clothes, was waiting for her seated on the edge of her bed. Emily spread her arms to hug her, but the cousin remained hesitant, and Emily realized that she was still that terrified dry little girl.

At six in the morning the school bell jolted Emily. She had hardly slept at all, reliving the events of the first day throughout the night. Alarmed, she opened her eyes to face an image of utter despair. Totally rigid, cousin Emily was standing in the middle of the room, already fully dressed, well-groomed, with arms crossed – the personification of duteousness – gazing at her with righteous patience. This was the first sight of the day, which would lead to the second – the towering presence of Mary Lyon. A short but imposing figure with a voice that was melodious yet resonant enough to fill the large auditorium, President Mary Lyon delivered her first address of the term to the student body. The

theme was "The First Parting" from parents – a necessary presupposition, as the speaker explained, for the students' coming of age and assuming their own place in society. As spouses of ministers and missionaries, they would become mothers and raise children with Christian convictions. These words chilled Emily with the thought of leaving her parents, growing up, marrying, childbearing, and – above all – being forever separated from the life of the Homestead. In the second portion of her talk, Mary Lyon celebrated the splendor of these young ladies' salvation through the spirit of their Savior Christ, their guide and protector. Prayer and conversion were the fundamental priorities of life at the college. Group prayer and revival sessions were a primary activity, just as meditation was performed by every student two and a half hours daily in her room.

Pious Mary Lyon was determined to lead each and every member of the student body to salvation through meetings that included prayer, hymn singing, and fiery sermons. Each girl was called upon to publically declare her conversion – her acceptance of the Lord who had sacrificed Himself for her salvation. In professing faith, the student had to abandon resistance and egotism – the cause of spiritual ruination – and faithfully follow the Lord's commands.

On the second day of the term, again sleepless and lost in her own thoughts, Emily attended the first revival meeting. Wearing severe dresses and proper smiles, the professors were all seated on the stage before the student body. The service began with emotional hymns to arouse the feelings and stir the consciences of "wayward" students, guiding them to inspiration in their leader's spiritual charge. The students, who were familiar with the hymns, joined their young voices to those of the faculty, and the auditorium reverberated with rousing harmonies. Then the president, leader of the chorus, launched into her sermon. In varied persuasive tones her voice stirred the hearts of the young students, her words spurs to salvation. To those susceptible to fear, she quietly expressed immense sadness that they were facing death defenseless, but her voice soared with the thought that salvation was as yet attainable. Their Savior was reaching out to embrace those in need. In contrast, her tone took a sharp edge toward the listeners whose egotism was so extreme that it did not permit them to accept the love of Him who gave his life for their sake. She intensely portrayed the unspeakable fate that awaited the unrepentant after death. Finally, she triumphantly lifted her voice addressing that other portion of the assembly who were redeemed by steadfast faith.

Mary Lyon's appeal was periodically punctuated by "Hallelujahs" and "Amens" from professors and student body alike. As the sermon approached its end, girls overcome by feeling leapt from their seats shouting "Praise the Lord!" and knelt before their preceptor. She, taking their heads in her hands, lifted her eyes to heaven, on the one hand thanking God who had accepted his trusting lambs into the company who possessed "Trust in Salvation" and, on the other, referring to those souls not as yet blessed by healing faith and thus "without hope." At the end of the service the congregation prayed in unison, expressing thanks to God for those who received His forgiveness and beseeching His intervention for those who remained lost in darkness.

The curriculum at the college included mathematics and chemistry, taught by Mary Lyon, as well as instruction by other professors in geography, botany, astronomy, music, and literature, including Milton and Pope. But the state of the students' souls remained the central concern. In a condition of numbness, students who had not been "saved" attended classes and then at the hour of meditation prayed for the miracle of repentance whereby they would prepare their souls for Jesus, who had invited them through the prayerful and often commanding voice of their leader. Emily eagerly attended the services of awakening regularly scheduled during the ensuing weeks. She listened attentively to the sermons and prayed intensely with Mary Lyon. While she strove to set out on the road to redemption, it was useless. Her heart remained closed, and her mind rejected every pompous word of the fiery speaker. Nonetheless, she jealously witnessed her classmates uttering fervent prayers announcing their withdrawal from worldly belief and devotion to heavenly life. Alone in her room for over two hours daily, Emily prayed and meditated, yearning to feel the need for Christ – but without results. Her love of life was too great to permit her to "stray" into the region of the reborn. As she wrote to Abiah: "I am afraid to stray into something about which I am not as yet certain." Thus, she remained "without hope of salvation."

Daily devotions, however, revealed to her a precious faculty which she cultivated to the full. In moments of prayer and meditation, the endless energy of her spirit led her to subjects that intensely concerned her. These were "Flood Subjects," as she put it, which came to her during the hours of solitude and deep contemplation, and the practice of meditation became a way of life. These personal thoughts plunged her into contact with great concepts: Life, Death, God, Sin, Eternity, Eternal Life, Love, Ecstasy. These stood out during those meditative moments and rooted deeply within her, later to be transformed into personal poetic imagery.

Nevertheless, the struggle to embrace faith was real, as was the daily prayer for her salvation by teachers, fellow students, and, of course, Mary Lyon herself. Though she was divided within herself under the enormous psychological pressure exerted upon her, Emily did not progress toward belief, but remained true to her personal thoughts and feelings, though she harbored doubts regarding her decision, as she later wrote to her friend Abiah: "I regret missing the golden opportunity to give myself and become Christian. I have postponed the decision." She confessed that "evil voices whisper in my ears." These voices of evil later became "sirens" and "beautiful tempters" who carried her away into isolation from all forms of social contact and enabled her to write the 1775 poems that raised her to the height of the "finest poet of the West in the last 400 years," as Harold Bloom would put it.

As the semester progressed, a cold spell arrived, along with great impatience for the arrival of the Thanksgiving holiday. More than most students Emily yearned for the comfort of home. Each evening she crossed out with black ink the date of the day that had passed. The third Thursday of November approached with agonizing slowness yet still each day was a step in the direction of Amherst and the warmth of her home.

It had begun to snow, and a layer of white spread over the ground. Standing by her window Emily eagerly watched for the arrival of the Dickinson horse and carriage among the many that arrived at the college early that morning. Finally she saw it, with the familiar plaid blanket over the horse's back. Stepping down from the driver's seat, Austin gave the horse a pat of gratitude and turned toward the school. Dressed for the trip and carrying an overnight bag with clothing and a few books, Emily met Austin, gave him a hug, and hustled him toward the door. He held back, returning the smiles of girls who had stepped into the hall to catch a glimpse of the handsome red-headed son of the honorable Edward Dickinson. Emily interrupted the flirting. "None of them can hold a candle to the girls of Amherst," she exclaimed to him, pulling him through the door toward the carriage. She climbed into her seat first, followed by Austin, who took the reins, still smiling back at the enticing faces.

They set off at once, and Emily spoke of everything that was going on at school. Raising not a single complaint, she went on and on about her courses, the professors, and her classmates. All the while, she was stretching her arm to touch the light snowflakes which whirled about the carriage. She laughed seeing the horse tossing his head and waving his tail to rid himself of the dust of snow. "It's going to stick – it's going to stick!" she shouted, but the snow turned to heavy rain, making the trip home more difficult. The cold season in New England was setting in. Soon, weighted with ice, the tree limbs would bow to the ground. Around her head the wool scarf sent by her mother, Emily talked smilingly, delighted by the chance to spend a short holiday at the Homestead.

They arrived, and everyone was there with their noses touching the pane, surveying the road, and the moment they saw the carriage, they rushed out to greet Emily, help her step down, and touch her. How tender they were, and how much they had missed her! Mother, wrapped in her shawl, dried her tears of joy, constantly talking; father, dressed in his best, gazed at her in tender pride;

Vinnie enclosed her in her warm hug. They all ran their hands over her, injecting little compliments. Even Vinnie's cat dared to come out into the street, ignoring the freezing rain just to touch her and to rub up against her leg. "Vinnie's cat was anxious to appear as dainty as her dignity permitted," as Emily put it. Blissfully Emily climbed the steps, whispering to herself: "My beloved home . . . Home is a name for God . . . a portion of Paradise."

The next evening they were guests at the home of Emily's beloved teacher at the Academy, President Hitchcock. The menu was stuffed turkey, sweet potatoes, corn, apple pie, and several other specialties of the season's cuisine; and a number of family friends were there lovingly fussing over Emily. She embraced them with her eyes and heart, enjoying the tenderness of those whom she had known from her childhood. She especially valued Professor Hitchcock's praise of his outstanding former student, Mary Lyon.

That evening, meditating within the "Flood Subject," she reached a final conclusion – Amherst was the great love of her life, her paternal home, her great security, and Thanksgiving the supreme holiday of the year.

On Monday she returned with a heavy heart to school – as yet one of those "without hope" entering the second round of Mary Lyon's regimen. The dedicated president was determined to multiply her efforts toward the salvation of the thirty students who had remained outside the fold. She doubled the number of group prayer meetings and meditation hours. When she understood that these measures were not sufficient, she took another step. The week of Christmas she announced that there would be no holiday recess. Those students 'without hope' had to be saved. These holy days would be spent in devotional study and prayer. The students took a grip on themselves, and on Christmas eve came the next decree: Christmas would be a day of fasting and prayer. In order for President Lyon to be sure that the gravity of her ruling was understood, she requested that the students stand up as a confirmation of their agreement. All the girls leapt to their feet except two. President Lyon could not believe her eyes. It was a painful shock, though she managed to conceal her feelings as she continued to discuss the rationale of her ruling. Once more she elicited the students' understanding and cooperation. "If anyone disagrees with the program, she will stand up for everyone in the school to see." To her amazement, Mary Lyon saw that of the two who had earlier remained seated, the one – the most petite and sensitive student – rose to her feet before the astonished gaze of two hundred and thirty-nine classmates. Upright, Emily looked the president steadily in the eye. At that moment she did not realize the full weight of her stand in opposition to the puritan establishment.

Her withdrawal had begun.

To her fellow students she later explained: "If I had accepted the ruling, I would not have been sincere." Moreover, if that were a difficult act for this sensitive student – that was not the end of the matter. On Christmas eve she acted on the conviction that the arbitrary rule of holiday fasting – which had deprived students of their favorite dessert, ice cream – had to be opposed. Without hesitation or fear, she dared to spirit the confection away from the pantry to her room as a treat, at least for those classmates who had been stigmatized "without hope".

Recalcitrant behavior occurred again two months later, in February, when Mary Lyon ordered that the girls neither send nor receive Valentine's Day greeting cards. The rebellion, however, had already begun. In one way or another, including tips to the postman, students received and sent cards with satirical as well as romantic messages. Emily produced what would be one of her longest poems (#1, forty-five lines), a witty piece sent to a middle-aged colleague of her father, who had remained a bachelor, though many a lady longed to be – as the poem says – taken down by him from the apple tree, like the six girls to whom the poem alludes, among them *Susan* and *Emeline*. The poem was published anonymously, but the identity of the author spread quickly, surprising classmates who did not expect from shy Emily such devilish wit.

The admiring eyes of Emily's fellow students had been turned upon her because of her strange ideas and her lively metaphorical language which demanded keen thought for comprehension. The petite, idiosyncratic student had begun to attract attention. It was not her classroom performance that set her apart, but her unique use of words, as well as the quality and seriousness of her thought. Her style of expression bore no resemblance to that of fellow students or teachers. Emily's words were like rare or exotic flowers. She also treated like precious flowers the individuals she chose to bring into her life.

Though she had not won her battle for Emily's soul, President Mary Lyon was influential in many respects. She stressed careful choice in regard to both friends and words. "Never set down," she said, "a trivial thing in a letter or any piece of writing"; and Emily writes in # 1261: "A word dropped careless on a Page... Infection in the sentence breeds." The poet also reflected Mary Lyon's sardonic assessment of shallow prettiness: "My soul," Mrs. Lyon said, "is pained by this empty gentility, this genteel nothingness"; and Emily recognized this insight as a shrewd observation about feminine affectation and lack of substance, writing with acid humor, "What Soft – Cherubic Creatures – / These Gentlewomen are" (# 401).

Among her experiences with her fellow students, one of the most memorable was an image of tranquility and beauty. One spring afternoon when she was contemplating the stigma "without hope," she was surprised to receive a tap on her door, which opened before she could say "come in." The face of a classmate "with hope" appeared. With a timid smile and arms outstretched, she invited Emily to go for a walk. Willingly, Emily arose with laughter, and holding hands, the friends crossed the courtyard and turned toward a small hill. At the top of the rise, benches were positioned so viewers could enjoy the sight of the meadow that spread into the distance to a dark, mysterious wood.

They chose to sit on the grass, and with smiles surveyed the peaceful landscape at the radiant hour of sunset, which painted the trees a scarlet hue. They felt a warmth within that stirred their spirits, filling them with joy. The girls spontaneously began to sing familiar hymns. They raised their tender melodious voices as the dark shades of evening slowly approached. The stars, like the lights of a distant city, gradually began to glow, bringing an ecstasy they wished would never end. The supper bell interrupted them when they had already exhausted their hymn repertory, just as the formal studies of Emily Dickinson would soon be over.

Toward the end of the term, word of Emily's cold had reached Amherst by way of Monson in a letter from cousin Emily to her grandmother. "Emily's cough has persisted for weeks." To her great surprise one morning Emily found she was facing a smiling but determined Austin. "Father says you are coming home, and mother sends you this." It was a coverlet to keep her warm during the return trip. Emily was sad, but she was powerless to refuse. Her father's decision was based on the thought that a cold might presage consumption, and the fear sufficed to curtail further formal education. Life held nothing more precious than his daughter. It was also obvious to him now that his dream of Emily's conversion at Mount Holyoke was illusory.

Emily gathered her few clothes and books, packed her suitcase, climbed into the carriage, and silently turned her eyes upon the road to Amherst. College education was over for Emily, but at once serious studies began in her esoteric university. Alone in her room, she would plunge into contemplation, studying the Bible, Shakespeare, Keats, Carlyle, Ruskin, and whatever great book fell into her hands. She would grasp insights vitally within her inner world, unblemished by conventional teaching.

The horses slowly drew the carriage toward the familiar streets. Her joy swept her away, and she sighed with delight. As they pulled into the Homestead driveway, Austin gazed at her and, smiling, mentioned in conspiratorial tones, "I forgot to tell you. Someone's very eager to see you."

Emily burst out: "Susan . . . my Sue! When did she come back to Amherst?"

"No, not Sue," he replied in a voice with lively irony. "It's someone better."

"There's no one better," she protested. But he, leaning toward her, chuckled meaningfully:

"His name is Benjamin Franklin Newton – father's assistant and my close friend!"

"So what?" Emily shot back with a grin, shrugging her shoulders. Then, smiling slyly, she asked, "Is he handsome?"

"Let The Touch Of Love Be Lightning"

Benjamin Franklin Newton

Experiment to me
Is everyone I meet
(#1073)

Indeed the young law clerk, Benjamin Newton, was handsome! Emily set eyes on him as he entered the living room at the beginning of the new academic year. It was August, and the Homestead glittered, as did Edward Dickinson's two daughters welcoming the many guests and aiding Maggie, the maid, with refreshments.

Every August the Dickinson family had the honor of receiving entering students and upperclassmen, as well as distinguished citizens of Amherst and the surrounding area. It was the most splendid celebration of the little town, so dazzling that on leaving the guests saluted one another, "May we be well and meet here again in next year's gathering!"

Benjamin Newton, tall, slim, elegantly attired, with hat in hand, appeared in the living room and solemnly took Emily's hand. Looking into her eyes, he announced, "It is a great honor! From the moment you returned from Mount Holyoke, I've been hoping to meet you!" Emily smiled awkwardly, unable to understand why her heart was beating so irregularly from a mere handshake with the young law clerk.

"I hear that you love poetry," he said, "and I have requested repeatedly from your honored father permission to accompany you to a lecture by the remarkable Emerson."

"O, what a mistake!" Emily exclaimed.

"How so, my dear Miss Dickinson?" Newton returned. "Emerson is among the masters of American poetry and thought!"

"Sir, that was not my meaning. I was referring not to Emerson's greatness but to my father, who looks down on poetry," she confided, bending close to him as she felt her father's burning gaze from across the room.

At night in her bed, Emily recalled every detail about the young attorney. She concentrated on his eyes: "How sad they are!" she perceived and felt anguish for her new friend. She pondered word-by-word their conversation and the way he expressed every phrase. "His knowledge of poetry is so marvelous. Would that I had read as many books as he," she thought with a touch of jealousy. "How crystal his every utterance!"

Benjamin Newton had a deep affinity with words and their nuances; furthermore, he honored great poets and their work. To be with him was so stimulating and comforting! He never tossed off superfluous phrases but expressed his precious knowledge in modest tones, discussing literary giants without display. His voice became hushed and affectionate as if they were his close companions. How superb were his tributes to lofty art – and he said something else to her! How did he say it and why did he say it? "Before I die, I want to see you receive your due as a poet!" As yet warm, his syllables found their mark in her mind and heart. "He views me as a poet!" she thought, and before the excitement of pride swelled, she felt the weight of sadness in her bosom. "He wants me to come into my own as a poet – *before his death*, as he says. What does he mean? He's so young, tall, distinguished! He adores poetry and believes in my gift! What does death have to do with him? No! Death's shadow cannot fall upon him!" she concluded, and suddenly Benjamin was at her side. He bent tenderly and brushed her eyelids with his lips.

Sleep chanted melodies, as she heard the night sounds of her neighborhood, gentle and familiar. Horses pulling carriages outside her window lent feelings of security. In the brook frogs croaked in soft rhythm, accompanying her imagination; the breeze whispering in the trees was like a stream bearing her to unknown lands. She heard something more: the boy! Late in the evening, the boy always passed by under her window whistling. How melodious! His lips expressed to perfection the moving beauty of music.

What a joy was beloved Amherst! How peaceful night could be when it was enclosed by gentle whispers that captivate the mind with rare syllables and precious blessings! "I want to see you receive your due as a poet!"

A Poet! What a glorious, inebriating title! The thought lifted her to heights bordering on the divine. She felt a soft embrace enclose her, and ecstatic joy swept her away. Someone was holding her hand and aiding her in ascending a slope. It must have been the hill nearby, yet it seemed so different, like enchanted territory. As she passed by them, the trees recognized her and bowed to greet her, rustling their leaves. The water in the little brook slowed in order to view her better, and many-colored birds hovered so close she could touch them. She and her companion mounted with ease and reached the crest but did not stop. Everything seemed like an incandescent vision, not at all like faded ordinary life. She and her companion, aglow, swept down the other side of the hill, as if they were flying. Before them the sea poured out like a broad silver veil unfurled, spreading to the horizon. With awe they beheld its shimmer. On its sands as yet stood clusters of dissolving foam, bearing witness to the exultation that had overflowed – an immense wave from the sea's depths. Smooth and tranquil now, the sea invited them.

Emily, her white dress lifted to her knees, and Benjamin, his trouser cuffs rolled up, dashed madly along the shore. As they splashed the cool water up to their waists, soaking their clothing, Emily thought of her father. What would he say when he saw her soaked dress? She tried to turn away from the sea, but greedy pleasure held her there, the moisture caressing her. At the edge of the shore, Sue suddenly appeared – her face sad, her hands outstretched. Emily released her companion's hand and ran to her friend, embracing her longingly. "Look, Sue – Benjamin!" As she pointed to the young man, her voice turned into a cry of agony, seeing the swell buffet him; losing his balance, he fell and the water greedily engulfed him. Its currents dragged him as if he were bereft of flesh and bone, and Sue kept saying, "Come along, my darling – come along!" But Emily in terror screamed, "Benjamin! Benjamin!" As Sue held her close, she turned her face from the sea so she could not see her friend pounded by the waves.

She awoke with confused feelings. She could still see dear Benjamin gazing at her sadly, but Sue's embrace, warm and familiar, brought comfort and delight. Erotic sensations vibrated in her body, and at that moment the boy passed below her window whistling. She sat up, focusing all of her attention on the sound . . . It faded at the turn of the road . . . . It dissolved. For the first time Emily realized that the boy was whistling from fear. He feared the mystery of love; he feared death – they weighed on his spirit. Because of those fears, he whistled, and in his ears the beautiful, bold sound reassured him. "Love and Death – is there anything else? Please tell me!" thought Emily, and the gravity of the question overcame her. She sighed as she could not whistle. The thought of death was heavy; the thought of love exciting, and that of the sea, exotic. For the first time she faced the ocean! The hues and the glittering made her tremble, and when she thought of the power of water, she let the surge of the tide carry her away and relieve her body. All morning in bed, Emily was happy and joyful as images became a poem (#520):

I started Early – Took my Dog –
And visited the Sea –
The Mermaids in the Basement
Came out to look at me –

And Frigates – in the Upper Floor
Extended Hempen Hands –
Presuming Me to be a Mouse –
Aground – upon the Sands –

But no Man moved Me – till the Tide
Went past my simple Shoe –
And past my Apron – and my Belt
And past by Bodice – too –

And made as He would eat me up –
As wholly as a Dew
Upon a Dandelion's Sleeve –
And then I started – too –

And He – He followed – close behind –
I felt His Silver Heel
Upon my Ankle – Then my Shoes
Would overflow with Pearl –

Until We met the Solid Town –
No One He seemed to know –
And bowing – with a Mighty look –
At me – The Sea withdrew –

The Departure of Benjamin Newton

Edward Dickinson, reading of the influence of Adams and Jefferson, exclaimed: "How I envy their fame! How marvelous to foster the happiness of a million citizens whose number keeps increasing!" He said this never suspecting that such a creative force was under his very roof.

The night following the important reception, Edward could not sleep, thinking of the unseemly behavior of his nineteen-year-old daughter. The next morning at bible study hour, the sisters at once noticed their father's cloudy expression. Emily threw a sardonic glance toward Austin, mouthing, "Vesuvius is about to erupt!" Vinnie cowered behind her mother's back where she had seated herself humbly at the table. Edward's voice rose like a "trumpet of God," making souls tremble and Emily think: "father is addressing an Eclipse . . . in marshal tones."

Accordingly she turned to her own thoughts, which she found more fascinating than the biblical allusions father never ceased to mouth. The daily reading of the Bible did not stimulate or awe her. Vinnie, however, listened obediently, knowing that father was right. The fear of God's punishment nested in her soul. On the other hand, Austin ostensibly looked in his father's direction without seeing or hearing him. Mother lowered her head, remaining silent inside and out.

Edward pressed forward in his tirade. The 'voice of God' was not enough; he had to add the father's voice regarding his daughter's Christian duty and her obligations as a young lady of her circle. There was no need whatsoever for worldly invitations, get-togethers, and wayward talk. She should look to home duties and the companionship of modest girls of her acquaintance. As for her volumes of verse, which she read so hungrily – they should be replaced with sober tomes, for poetry had nothing to do with urgent realities of life.

Emily – her soul sinking – found relief by the window through which she viewed each morning and evening Benjamin going to and from her father's office. She recognized his silhouette from afar. Tall, wearing a hat, he differed from all the other youth of Amherst. His sight, though faint, gave her fulfilling delight, sustaining her through the loneliness of the entire day. Lonesomeness in Amherst was very real, particularly from the day Sue left to visit her aunt. The place was empty without her friend being there to talk with, to analyze, and make events real. Alone, Emily was limited to writing letters: "Oh, my adorable

Sue – if only you were here to meet my friend, Benjamin. He knows you so well. I have told him so much about you, and how much he wants to meet you . . . . If you were here, even father would be more bearable. How much I miss you, my dear Sue. . .".

There was a knock on the front door and Emily rushed to open. Surprised, she faced her friend, his hat in his hand and a smile on his face.

"Your esteemed father has just departed for Northampton, and I have brought you a book by Emerson. It came out just this week," he told her conspiringly.

She happily gazed into his eyes, which laughed with a glow of happiness as they carried her image to the center of his heart. Emily responded timidly while she noticed that his hands were empty. Benjamin turned his head toward the bushes by the stoop, and she – following his gaze – saw a small package between the branches. It was the book. Yes! Benjamin had brought her yet another wonderful literary work.

"Thank you! Thank you!" she murmured.

"Dear Emily, I did not know you would come to the door. Whenever I come upon something good, I'll hide it in that bush!"

It was the only way they could communicate, since her father had ruled out any invitation or meeting. Thus, they only saw one another briefly and occasionally. Even at that, Emily was happy.

It was a summer night at supper time when father remarked coolly and decisively, "Today Benjamin Newton, after two years' work in my office, tendered his resignation and left Amherst."

The fork dropped from Emily's hand. She looked at her father with shocked eyes, and the question escaped her lips more loudly than she intended. "Why?" A heavy cloud of silence enveloped those present. Father hastily swallowed a bite, looked at her in amazement, and responded as logically as he could, though anger was choking him.

"I don't know! I didn't ask! It's not my concern!" He thundered the last words.

Emily arose, murmured an apology, and fled up the stairs to her room. They watched her wordlessly, knowing that the tears would flow unendingly once she found herself alone. Austin looked dour; Vinnie sighed sadly; mother bent her head almost to her plate; and father coolly continued his repast.

Emily's precious friend left the town before she had time to bid him farewell. He sped to Worcester, a larger city some distance from Amherst. She sat dully by the window in the morning and evening, her eyes turned on the road at the point where she had always followed his slim silhouette turning the corner. Now she could discern nothing – no hint of his presence. Benjamin Newton, her first mentor, had indeed departed from Amherst, and that spot at the corner was as blank as her poetic inspiration.

Austin opened the letter with controlled enthusiasm. At last his friend had written, though months had passed since his resignation and departure. His smile, however, vanished at the final line of the letter, which – though sunny and friendly, describing the progress of his law office and the pleasantness of the town – in closing added three words like a post script referring to a third person: "Benjamin Newton married."

"What does he say – what?" Emily blurted, seeing the smile vanish from Austin's face. Not wishing to pronounce the words himself, he handed her the letter.

"Read it," he said dryly.

She read slowly, carefully; her spirit filled with distress and her eyes with tears. Emily did not know where in her mind or heart to place this abrupt statement about the marriage of her precious friend. If only Sue were there to discuss it, she could perhaps understand the situation; but Sue, far away, had left her alone, deserted. Harsh complaints swelled to anguish.

In the evening she mournfully dragged herself down to dinner, and father looked at her baffled: this daughter of so many moods was his hidden pain. At times she was joyful and could not stop babbling; at times her deep silence weighed on them all. Yet who can do the least about the joys and sorrows of others? He observed her, hardly able to touch her food, swallowing with difficulty, while Austin gabbed continually about trivialities. One moment he abruptly announced, "Ah, I forgot to tell you." His voice took on an informative tone. "I received a letter from Benjamin. He has opened a law office, and it's doing well." All eyes were on him. "And something more," he pressed on, "He got married."

Father, without raising his eyes from his plate, added matter-of-factly, "He married a woman much older than he."

They turned toward him in surprise, and he added almost angrily, "He has consumption. . .".

The awful word struck them breathless, and a frozen silence ensued, because father's words obliterated Benjamin's existence.

Emily's spirit felt empty and weak. She ceased watching the street. Her mentor was no longer around any corner, but he was lodged in a corner of her heart where he would remain forever.

She continued to receive collections of poetry mailed from Worcester without the name or address of the sender, and at night by candlelight she greedily drank them in as letters for her. Those nights, sadness engulfed her until daybreak, when liberating sleep brought relief.

A year had passed when another letter arrived, and it was a puzzle for her mind and soul. It was his last.

The Aurora Borealis and Poetry

Struck, was I, and not yet by lightning.
(#925)

Father knocked on Emily's door. "What would my daughter fancy doing today?" he asked, and before she opened her mouth, he announced, "We're going on a drive to the big river. Hurry up. Mother is ready and I bet that Vinnie is already waiting in the carriage."

"I'll be right down!" she chirped. She slipped her book under the pillow, grabbed her bonnet and dashed outside. In the driveway she jumped into the carriage beside Vinnie. "What put this into his head?" she asked with a playful nudge. "I've no idea," came the answer, "but I like it!" Then, seeing Emily tie her bonnet, Vinnie remembered hers. "Wait a second," she blurted to her parents, who were just about to close the front door. In a few moments the family – riding in the town's finest horse and carriage, dressed in their Sunday best – were moving along Main Street with their heads high and smiles glowing on their faces. They had not as yet left town when Emily abruptly stood up and blurted, "Stop! Stop!" She had seen Sue, carrying a baby in her arms. She jumped out of the carriage and spread her arms wide to enfold Sue and the baby, and with a joy that was impossible to contain, she complained. "When did you return, my darling? Why didn't you write? Why didn't you come to see me?" Emily's embrace squeezed the child, and it began to cry.

Softly pushing Emily back and soothing the child, Sue spoke in low hesitant tones. "I returned two days ago; my sister asked me to come because the baby was not feeling well . . . . I would have dropped by to see you – you know I would, Emily – but I had too much to do. Now, I'm on my way to the apothecary." Throwing a self-conscious glance in the direction of the honorable Edward Dickinson, his fancy equipage and elegantly attired family, she whispered to herself a line from *Wuthering Heights* – "What do you, a rich girl, know about heaven and hell?"

Emily gently rested her hands on her friend's cheeks. Dancing on the spot, she insisted, "Promise you'll come! Say you'll come right away – tomorrow! Promise! Promise!"

With a veiled look toward Mr. Dickinson, Sue hastily promised.

"Yes, Emily, I will! I'll come tomorrow for sure!"

"How wonderful! How wonderful, Sue!" Emily exclaimed, giving her friend a peck on the cheek and heading back to the carriage without observing the shadow on Sue's face. Before climbing into her seat, Emily called out, "Sue, dear – tomorrow afternoon. Early. All right?"

"What a nice girl!" mother said. "A wonderful girl!" Vinnie added, and father, nodding affirmatively, lifted his hand, and touched the brim of his hat to Miss Gilbert as the horses fell into a trot.

Two days later – an enchanting summer afternoon – the two sisters seated on the Homestead porch listened sadly to Sue's complaint. "I'm happy only when I'm with my aunt in Geneva! She has been like a mother to me, since I was so young when mother died. I was only five, and I don't remember my mother, Emily. I don't remember her face. It's as if I never had a mother."

"Me, too, Sue. It's as if I too didn't have a mother!" Emily comfortingly embraced her friend.

"Mother is always sick, and tomorrow father is again going to Washington," Vinnie said sadly. "But he promised that this time he would take us along! We'll see the capital, meet congressmen, and see the White House... We'll..." Vinnie's voice warbled as she looked at Emily, thinking "What does she mean by 'I never had a mother'?"

"I'm not going anywhere!" Emily snapped, and then, looking at her friend, she asked, "Will you come stay with me while they're away?" It was both a question and an invitation. "Do say you'll come!" she burst out with radiant feeling expressed on her face and a deep appeal in her voice. Sue's face shone. "As if you needed to ask! I'll escape the eyes of my brother-in-law, who counts each bite I eat!" She lowered her head and continued very softly, "When my father was alive, things were better."

The girls were struck silent by the reference to her father. The image of the town drunkard was embarrassing, and Emily swiftly changed the subject. "Tell me – what did you read when you were in Geneva?"

"Emerson, naturally! By the way, Emily, I brought you his last book,"

"I have it. Benjamin sent it. Emerson's wonderful! Benjamin says that he's the finest poet and thinker that America has to offer!"

"Whitman's marvelous, too!" Sue said.

"I don't know about Whitman," Emily responded hesitantly. "I've heard a lot about him that puts me off."

"But Emily – his poetry . . ." Sue continued to speak, but Vinnie abruptly interrupted.

"What are all these words about?" Vinnie blurted. "They're always babbling about poetry," she thought. For her the subject held no interest. "Poets and writers," she said, "are not relevant to life. That's what daddy says – that none of them know the realities of the world. Life has to do with keeping the house in order so you're ready to receive visitors and gentleman callers who will escort you on a drive in their carriage." Her mind went to the young man who had recently taken her for a drive. This was the fledgling lawyer, Joseph Lyman, whom she had known since childhood. He had studied in the south. Now he had returned, purchased a carriage, and driven up before the Homestead. "Come with me on a ride," he urged, and with a big smile she had at once grabbed her bonnet and jumped into his carriage. She would always remember that after-noon and his leaning over and pressing his lips to hers! She sighed deep in her heart, and called up in memory the thrilling taste of that kiss . . . .

"One day Joseph Lyman will be more famous than that poet you're talking about – Whi . . . Whi . . . – whatever his name is!" She spoke sharply, and then continued mildly, "I'd better go to see if mother needs anything."

"Dear, lovely Sue!" Emily murmured, once they were alone, and as they were seated side-by-side, she put her arm around her waist. She leaned on her shoulder and pressed her head tenderly against her face. Sue gave her a quick spontaneous kiss, lowered her head, and sighed with strange internal confu-sion. "She loves me," Emily thought, "but not as much as I love her."

Their friendship gave them an intense, unique joy. It thrilled them through and through. Each touch was a spiritual but also an erotic caress. Every exchange of words brought an arousal of thought that demanded further analysis and a more intense effort to achieve full realization of an idea. How deep was their bond! These two were the only girls in their community who could endlessly discuss serious issues that were central to their lives. Even Emily Fowler, who was raised in such a learned environment and was already considered a poet, since she had published poetry in Boston, was incapable of such flights, and she avoided the themes that entranced Emily and Sue.

"Poetry! That is supreme joy!" Emily exclaimed, and that moment the whole atmosphere changed color – changed dimensions. The boundaries of the town swelled as a cataract of light poured down and spread about them, as if a piece of the sun broke off and poured down in thousands of vertical shafts, covering the town with a dust of colors, transforming the environment into a rare terrestrial work of art!

And it happened so suddenly!

The light, heavenly energy in countless serpentines of color, exploded in the sky, creating a primal stroke of magic. Bronze, scarlet, orange, ochre, green, violet, glowing white, in countless variations, in exquisite forms, lent bewitching tones to everything within view. The town of Amherst was transmuted into a collage of precious beauty. The muddy street in front of the house was blanketed with a layer of gleaming particles that erased footprints and horse droppings. Bushes became exotic flowers that swayed in delight as multi-hued light gently washed every leaf and twig. The tree near the house – which to this day stands witness to the past – lifted its head like a masterwork of the Divine Artist.

Ecstatic, the two girls embraced in celebration of the incredible spectacle. The wondrous beauty took their breath away, and their hearts pounded wildly. It was as if they no longer found themselves in Amherst, or anywhere on earth. They were soaring to the height of another sphere of splendid loveliness that lent feelings of indefinable delight. Transcendence they called this precious feeling; and Emily felt her heart of hearts brimming with love for everything she touched, saw, felt, and experienced in that sacred moment. "Surprise evokes the feeling of wonder, excitement, divine inebriation." Like a ray of light the thought flashed in Emily's mind. And that moment, as by a miracle, she heard the heavenly tolling of bells. The girls as yet could not comprehend what was happening. Even when they heard the familiar voice, they could not believe it was Edward Dickinson's – but it was; they saw him as he dashed through the streets, repeatedly pausing to shout.

"People of Amherst! Fellow townspeople! Come outdoors! The aurora borealis has come to Amherst for the first time! Come outside! Behold this stupendous natural miracle! Witness God's presence with your own eyes!"

His voice swelled with feeling as he reiterated the proclamation like a crazed town crier. He raced through lanes and streets. Returning to the church, he pulled the rope of the church bell, which responded joyously, urgently. He – the congressman, the representative of the people of Massachusetts, the staid and famous Edward Dickinson – as if he were the humblest civil servant of Amherst, rang the bell summoning the people of the town to come out and share the miracle, and they kept coming out.

Emily looked with wonder on the unforeseeable stance of a human being in the presence of the remarkable. "Just as the essence of nature appears in so many strange forms, so does man." It was the first time she beheld her father so rapturous, so spontaneous, so inspired, so humble! What curious creatures humans are! How many forms they assume!

Truly, who was this man who was her father? To this question – at this moment with everything around her transformed – she added ultimate issues: "What is man? What moves him? What motivates him? What tames him? What sweeps him to lofty thought? What makes him mindless and violent? What humbles him?"

Just three days before, who was that man, her father, in relation to the horse? It was a scene she attempted to escape, to erase from her memory. Her father had gone on his morning drive, and the sisters knew that he was racing against Mr. Luke Sweetser, church elder and prominent businessman. Emily imagined their neighbor dressed in his flowery vest, wielding the reins of his splendid horses – on his face an ironic smile directed toward the Honorable Congressmen, whom he had left far behind in the dust.

Outraged, Edward Dickinson, galloped the carriage into the stable yard, leapt from the driver's seat, took his whip, and set to pounding the animal's flank. Ruthlessly and wordlessly he flailed, oblivious to Vinnie's screaming from the kitchen doorway and to Emily's intervention between horse and driver, shouting, "What are you doing? What possesses you, father?" Only when she shoved him did he hear and understand. Ashamed, he cast off the whip, low-ered his head, and retreated into the kitchen.

Emily threw her arms around the neck of the horse, which was swaying its head to and fro and whinnying in protest to such behavior from its master whom it honored and obeyed. Meanwhile the little lady hanging on its neck stroked and wet its muzzle with her tears. That evening the family sat silent at the table. Gloomy and penitent, Edward went to put a bite in his mouth and noticed his chipped plate. "I'm fed up with meals food served on such worn plates," he complained, and Emily – the afternoon's incident fresh in her mind – snatched the plate and dumped the food back into the pot, dripping sauce on the stove's surface. Ignoring this detail, she went out by the stable, smashed the plate with a stone, and hurled the pieces into the bushes. Back inside, she snapped "You won't be served again on such a plate, father!" Mother and Vinnie trembled in fear of father's reaction, but not a word came from his mouth.

Now, however, humbled by the immense event, in the presence of "God's spectacular display," his voice filled with emotion; he pointed heavenward and intoned, "Oh glory! – Oh glory!"

That was the good, kind father as Emily had witnessed the winter before in another incident. She had been in the kitchen, and she heard him drawing water from the well near the stable. The snow was almost a foot deep, and father was hastily pulling up the bucket as the chill air pierced him to the bone. Emily expected that any minute he would come through the door, but there was a delay. She bent and looked through the window. She saw that he was crouched by a corner of the stable – motionless, to avoid disturbing the hungry sparrows that were pecking at what might be bits of food on the crust of the snow. Gazing with a delighted smile at the diminutive creatures, he did not rush to seek the warmth of the house.

How much she loved her father when he was in this phase of his being! His pride was absent; cancelled were the arrogance and the severity that could swell to the bounds of harshness. These other qualities had no place in the kind, caring side of his personality. The phantasmagoric aurora borealis had to the greatest extent summoned his finer self. Small, humble, overwhelmed with gratitude, he bowed in awe before nature's powers.

The spectacle of splendid colors – and, even more, the response of viewers – was a revelation for Emily. She would study the deep impact of the optical experience in order to grasp one of the secrets – not of her father or her neighbors in this particular situation – but of humanity in the presence of lofty art. In her father's reaction she perceived the great miracle that takes place when human beings encounter consummate beauty, when they can perceive and realize miraculous loveliness shaped by God or man. Thus, Emily told herself, "What a miracle is man to Man!" Turning to Sue she spoke breathlessly: "We are witness to the response to the sublime – like that brought by great Art – the astonishment born of awe! Dear Sue, we mount to Paradise on the Stairway of Surprise."

Stirred to the depths, Sue focused her attention on what Emily was about to say. Emily paused, attempting to put the thought into words. She gripped Sue's shoulders as if she wished to shake her. "Sue, look at the people around us! Do you see how their faces glow? They are no longer the neighbors we knew. They are elevated by the rare glory of the event. Likewise," she burst out, as if she could not contain her feeling, "the word shaped by Poetry must strike us like 'a bolt of Melody'! Poetry must evoke surprise and awe!"

As she watched the ever-shifting shapes in the sky whose colors faded and then disappeared, Sue excitedly embraced her friend and she, too, spoke ecstatically: "Such an image of creation, though you meet it but a moment, will remain before you a lifetime as the manifestation of God."

"Poetry should be a similar manifestation in artistic form," Emily repeated, and the two young women remained speechless for a moment to define "creation-image-perception-poetry."

Sue spoke in quiet awe. "Emily, you perceive divine truth and beauty! You create with such sacred power! You reflect the saying that the Poet embodies the image of God!" Emily reacted powerfully. "No, Sue. No. God is the wellspring of creation. Poets cannot touch the divine center, only the circumference, and from that perspective, with consciousness of the cosmos, they transmit transcendence." She felt the nature of poetic creativity flowering within her. "The word must lead to surprise, its content to awe! It is such poetry that I wish to create." Ten years later she wrote the famous poem about the aurora borealis in which she conveyed the elevated spirit infused with "Taints of Majesty."

That moment the word *circumference* rang strangely in her ears, but the idea took root like a seed within her, bloomed, and became the definition of her poetry. The poet must be bold, surpass his limits, burst his circumference, break free of all restrictions. Imagination guides him to extremes; it distances him from his habitual beliefs, and he boldly faces chaos of thought and feeling. Only then can he create. The recognition of the extraordinary was planted within her. Time would determine when this insight would be expressed in poetry, as in #290, based on the experience of the aurora borealis:

Of Bronze – and Blaze –
The North – Tonight –
So adequate – it forms –
So preconcerted with itself –
So distant – to alarms –
An Unconcern so sovereign
To Universe, or me –

Infects my simple spirit
With Taints of Majesty –
Till I take vaster attitudes –
And strut upon my stem –
Disdaining Men, and Oxygen,
For Arrogance of them –

My Splendors, are Menagerie –
But their Competeless Show
Will entertain the Centuries
When I, am long ago,
An Island in dishonored Grass –
Whom none but Beetles – know.

"Struck, was I, not yet by Lightning" (#925) is another poem expressing the enormous impact of that afternoon.

The term *circumference,* in turn, is defined in lyric #633:

When Bells stop ringing – Church – begins –
The Positive – of Bells –
When Cogs – stop – that's Circumference –
The Ultimate – of Wheels.

George Gould

For each ecstatic instant
We must an anguish pay
In keen and quivering ratio
To the ecstasy.

For each beloved hour
Sharp pittances of years –
Bitter contested farthings –
And Coffers heaped with Tears!
(#125)

Alone at home, Emily longed for an object of love as prospectors avidly sought precious ore in California streams. The memory of the journey at the age of three seated between two lovers in a storm laced with lightning had sealed in her heart knowledge of love's property – an electrical charge burning her being, a thunderbolt in the festival of existence.

It was long in coming, but she was ever eager. It is said that George Gould appeared unexpectedly on the road. The story goes like this.

One Sunday after church the Dickinson family were going for a drive. On leave from his congressional duties, Edward Dickinson frequently took his lively daughters and his melancholy wife on excursions. "A brisk ride in the great outdoors can never do any harm!" he boomed. After all, didn't he keep the finest horses in his stable? Emily loved outings and she was quick to agree.

George Gould

They could not have been very far from Amherst when they caught sight of a young man, knapsack on his back, trudging wearily toward town. Raising his gaze, he saw Emily looking intently at him. As he touched the brim of his hat to greet the family, his quick eye caressed her cheek, producing an excitement that radiated through her body. Her face must have flushed deep red, for Vinnie gave her a peculiar look.

As Edward snapped the reins and the vehicle moved past the hiker, Emily turned, kneeling on the seat. She longed for him, too, to turn – but in vain. He kept walking, eyes ahead.

"I've never seen such a tall fellow!" Vinnie burst out.

"And so arrogant!" Emily added, disheartened.

"His clothes are from the Monson Sewing Circle," mother noted unexpectedly, turning to look at the figure of the youth that was already very far away. "When I was a girl, I was a member of the club, and that was the style of clothing we sewed for needy students at the Academy." Her voice was filled with pride.

The information was not of interest to Edward. He made no comment, for the entire appearance of the weary traveler neither impressed nor concerned him. The young fellow continued to trudge in the opposite direction, increasingly angry at the unexpected encounter. Two days on the road from Monson, and he had met no one. Now, one hour from his destination, he had met precisely those he had dreaded seeing him under such circumstances. Why should they know that he had to come on foot from Monson? Of course he recognized the Dickinsons. Who did not know the famous congressman? In fact, in his jacket pocket he had a letter of recommendation to Edward Dickinson from Joel Norcross, Mrs. Dickinson's father, asking for assistance in case he needed a job or a place to stay.

Joel Norcross, Emily's grandfather, who had contributed to the founding of Monson Academy, never failed to aid a deserving graduate. Such alumni, "the nation's future leaders in thought and action," as he called them – were his primary concern. They would create the country's spiritual power. His letter was a paean to the gifts of this young graduate. Norcross believed that one day George Gould would become the greatest orator of Massachusetts, surpassing even his great relative on his mother's side, Patrick Henry, whose words had inspired countless young volunteers in the war of independence and whose fellow citizens had gratefully elected him the first governor of Virginia. Such were the ancestors of this penniless young graduate!

With the recommendation letter in his pocket and pride in his heart, George Gould did not rush to seek help, especially from the Dickinsons, though they were – after all – distant relatives. His family, too, had originated in England and had ties to the Montague family, who were relatives of Patrick Henry. Young Gould could not endure the thought of exposing his situation to the proud Dickinsons. These thoughts were in his mind as he lifted his head and resumed his route to Amherst.

The following Sunday, the same youth, with the same suit and the same thoughts, crossed the threshold of the Homestead as a guest of Austin. Joel Norcross's letter of recommendation, hidden at the back of a drawer in his dormitory room, never was delivered to its intended recipient, the Honorable Edward Dickinson. Emily – fired by her brother's enthusiasm toward his classmate – welcomed him with great warmth, while Vinnie, her thoughts as always quickened by new acquaintances, closely inspected all his features. First of all, gauging his stature, she found it impressively tall. Then she examined his face and she diagnosed enormous sadness. Beneath his outward show of family pride, there was deep melancholy. Many said it was due to his poverty, which appeared early in his life and as he grew older became a source of pain and agony. Thus, his expression altered between pride and sadness. Indeed some of his friends suggested that sadness had a negative influence on his health, which later as a successful minister with adequate funds, he tried to restore on journeys to exotic islands whose names were mentioned in their correspondence and appeared in Emily's poetry.

The young man crossed the threshold hesitantly, while Emily's mother embraced him warmly as a person from her home town, inquiring with deep interest as to his health and long trip. Her questions revolved around his sleeping arrangements during his walk from Monson and how tiring it was to trudge so far. He responded awkwardly with feigned willingness, praising farmers along the way who had generously given him food and a decent place to sleep in their clean barns. Edward examined him with a piercing gaze and foresaw his future – a pastor with no permanent appointment who was never adequately paid, and worse, never claimed his deserts. It was obvious, moreover, that the young theological student was involved in poetry and rhetoric. What could come of such interests?

Enthusiastic about George's literary insights, as Austin described them, Emily explored with him the subject of verse about which the visitor was knowledgeable. Indeed, he was an acute critic. "Poetry must be exquisite," he said; "otherwise, it is superfluous." He then boldly proceeded to challenge the verse of Longfellow, the most popular poet of the age, and to praise Tennyson, whom too few people knew in depth. He used all of his rhetorical skill to celebrate the poetry and philosophy of Emerson. Emily was thrilled.

Austin brought the discussion around to the upcoming competition among students who would present lectures before the student body at the end of the academic year. The competitors prepared for months. The event was a challenge for their rhetorical skills as well as a launching for their professional careers, and they competed with zeal. The young host gracefully expressed the hope that the winner would be George Gould, whom he characterized as the best speaker of the year. Truly he was, and Austin's wishes were realized. George Gould was the choice of the judges – even above Austin himself, whom everyone expected to be the main speaker of 1850. This information was to confirm Edward Dickinson's feelings about young Gould – that he was nothing but a rhetorician with poetic tendencies without promise of a successful future.

Everyone at the dinner that Sunday – except Edward – tried his best to make the occasion as pleasant as possible. Only Emily, however, grasped the guest's extended discussion of poetry. She listened with passionate interest to his intuitions and theories, while the others remained unable to hear, imprisoned in their personal assumptions. The visit passed swiftly, no one imagining the part that the promising young man would play in the romantic legend that would link his name and Emily's. Not even Vinnie, who was to foster the myth, foresaw such fulfillment.

The July moon, bright and carefree, passed over Amherst, stooped a moment above the Homestead and caressed the affectionate couple seated on the stoop wordlessly savoring their mutual tenderness and admiration.

Their flirtation, which had begun timidly, was expressed more openly on Saint Valentine's day when Emily wrote a letter to George as editor of the student publication, *Indicator*, in which she passionately proclaimed, "I am Judith the heroine of the Apocrypha and you the orator of Ephesus." Their feeling for one another had deepened that spring, and perhaps that summer the young man would dare to confess it.

How wondrous an evening can become when there is no need for words to express feelings, which become a chiming of bells from a gentle touch! They were holding hands and gazing toward the stars when suddenly the door behind them opened and the father stood there stiffly with a lantern in his hand, the moonbeams ironically cancelling its light. With a harsh voice he ordered the young man to leave and Emily to come inside immediately.

That had never occurred before.

Clenching his teeth without uttering a word, the youth – head held high – hastily departed from the congressman's presence, while Emily, deeply upset, at once went inside, shouting more loudly than he, "If you do not trust me, I shall never leave the house again!" She rushed up the stairs and slammed the door, rattling windows, as Vinnie and mother, clutched in one another's arms, dared not cast their eyes on the angry father who entered the kitchen yelling fiercely and slammed the lantern onto the table. He sat in his chair, shaken to his core.

That, too, had never happened before.

The thought that his daughter was capable of carrying out her threat particularly disturbed him. Anything could be expected from that unruly creature! Her reading, her behavior, her words, her silences – all declared that his authority was threatened, just as the whole world was crumbling about him and another world was dawning with new concepts and ideas about the grand nation that he avidly supported in congress. Everything was under examination and revision; even – was it possible? – the role that up to now had been played by the church. Youth in the universities even dared to speak of the liberation of the slaves of the south, which is to say that the state would interfere with private property! They even wished to liberate women – to change legal control of men over women – for them to be in charge of their own property, as if they were capable! In other words, women would not be guided and protected by their husbands. What did women know about money and marital assets? And something else – they wanted to give women social rights and even the vote! Madness! That was their benighted state of mind! Everything was to change, including the conservative function of religion. They wanted to challenge it in agreement with Emerson. In accordance with a day-dreaming poet! God forbid! The boldest – or rather, the maddest – idea, was improvement of the condition in prisons! In other words – to waste hard-earned money on convicted criminals! Such were the demands of liberation, though Edward and colleagues in the congress worked hard to pass laws holding back the tide. But the most tragic of all was that his older daughter admired such thinkers, celebrated their books, and was influenced by them to such a degree as to forget her place as a woman and a Dickinson. For example, take tonight's incident. Who was this young upstart to sit close to her on the Homestead doorstep? And what if he got hold of a carriage! The thought that his daughter would be driven to Sunderland for sugaring made Edward Dickinson grow faint. He was somewhat relieved, however, by the realization that the needy young student would never have a carriage, and his daughter would always be sealed and secure behind closed doors. But what were those words of hers all about – staying inside if I didn't trust her? If she stayed at home, never paid visits, didn't even attend church, what would people say and how would he deal with it? He feared her temperament, for as a Dickinson, once she got an idea in her head she would carry it through, and the family would become the object of gossip and smears.

"Emily is so hot-headed!" Edward sighed, thinking about what had taken place the Sunday before. Shortly before church he had simply announced that within five minutes all of them must be outside. It was obvious that the family would be late for church, since Emily and Austin were inside as yet casually conversing. He had just said "In five minutes you will be out the door!" Perhaps his tone was a bit abrupt, but after all he was the head of the house. Five minutes went by, and Austin was on the stoop, Vinnie two steps down, and mother was already in the street; but Emily was nowhere to be seen. Angrily he hurriedly mounted the stairs and looked into Emily's room. She wasn't there. He went throughout the house – still his elder daughter was nowhere to be found. He then joined the rest, and they entered church after the service had begun, drawing looks from the worshippers. The family sat in their pew, avoiding the gaze of the congregation. They directed their eyes only to the pastor, all attention; and after service they at once returned home. They knew they would be asked about Emily – How is Emily? Is she ill? At the Homestead, Edward pretended that nothing was amiss. He did not ask about Emily, whom Vinnie had discovered on the back porch reading a book. To Vinnie's question as to her not hearing father, she answered calmly, "Of course I heard him, and I obeyed. In five minutes I was outside the house!"

Indeed she was a whimsical creature who required special treatment he had yet to fathom. It appeared that while his paternal authority was threatened, if he insisted on the obedience and respect owed him, everything would be all right. He had solved so many family problems – would he not solve this one?

It only required careful thought. He pondered and concluded that he would accept Christ in the next revival meeting. Providence would rule.

That evening Emily breathlessly took refuge in her room with her back against the door to hold it closed, though she knew that moment no one would dare seek contact with her – Vinnie and mother from fear, and father from anger. Austin – the only one who openly supported her – was away teaching in Sunderland. Emily was angry and her eyes overflowed with tears of resentment and outrage. Father had humiliated her for no reason. She thought of George – he must be deeply hurt. Wiping her eyes with the back of her hand, she rushed to the window and searched in the moonlight to see whether her friend was standing nearby. Her gaze swept up and down the road, piercing even into shadows under trees, by bushes, or by the single house opposite, but her young friend was nowhere to be seen. She searched for some time, hoping. Suddenly she realized that his pride ruled out a confrontation with her father. Her friend was not possessed by a passion that would arm him to claim his prize, as in the case with Robert Browning on fire with love for Elizabeth Barrett. No – George Gould could only stand up in the name of his distinguished ancestry.

Emily felt her legs collapse and her heart emptying. She sat on the edge of the bed and dried her eyes. Her gaze fell on the picture of Elizabeth Barrett Browning on the wall opposite smiling at her as if nothing had happened that was so tragic. She turned to the other wall holding the proud visage of George Eliot. She too was smiling. Observing the expression of the two, Emily understood for the first time how happy those two famous women had been. Their personal histories were a declaration of victory. On her desk, their books bore witness to their struggle against all forms of oppression. They had broken the bonds in which the world had confined them. No power could have held them prisoner within the community's concept of the woman's place and the manner in which she was supposed to write. They did not permit a father figure or establishment concept to block them from expressing their creative gifts.

Emily Dickinson: Goddess of the Volcano

Emily arose from the bed, stood by her writing table, and tenderly touched their books. Her soul overflowed with joy. "My companions. With you my hunger is satisfied," she whispered. She approached the corner between the two portraits, reached out and caressed the faces. She grew calm. "Women now! Queens now!"

She thought of her father. A strange, alien being appeared in her mind, and it seemed that she heard his voice hoarse and distant. As she wrote to her friend, Joseph Lyman, "Father . . . when he forgets the barrister & lapses into the man, says that his life has been passed in a wilderness or on an island. . . . I hear his voice and methinks it comes from afar & and has a sea tone & there is a hum of hoarseness about [it] & a suggestion of remoteness as far as the isle of Juan Fernandez." "And my mother," she asked herself, "In what mental desert does she find herself?" She felt deep pain for her mother – the same that she felt for her distant father. Austin was away in Sunderland, and her only support was the devoted but timid Vinnie. "I am alone and in rebellion," she thought and withdrew into remote sadness. For the first time the thought came to her that she should escape from that prison – that she would flee that instant. She got a small suitcase, tossed in a few clothes, and hurried down the steps. The house was totally dark and silent. With determination she moved to the front door and seized the doorknob. Then she froze. She could not turn it – it was impossible to open the door. Her feet were cut out from under her. Her breath came in agonized pants, and in panic her mind commanded her to return to her room.

Legs trembling, she mounted the stairs and shut her bedroom door behind her. She curled up on her bed and longed for her companion Sue, who was away at her aunt's home in Geneva. "Oh, how I've missed you, Sue!" she breathed, feeling the power of love. "My friends are my wealth!" She nestled under the coverlet and gave herself to the embrace of those she loved.

The moon, a luminous traveler, touched her window pane and invited her on a walk, and she – closing her eyes – slipped out of the house and wandered the streets of Amherst.

"Let The Touch Of Love Be Lightning"

Suddenly she found herself in a desert. A landscape unknown and harsh – dirt and rocks. Alone, she was walking barefoot, and dryness like a rash extended from the terrain into her body. The sun – was it before rising or after setting? Its faded light etched a leaden deathly land. She, utterly alone, was walking, and dryness like a blight arose from the landscape and struck her body. She felt her skin stretch and split. Her mouth was without saliva. Her throat down to her gut entirely drained; her loins dead. Thirst obliterated her. She wanted to immerse in a lake, in a river – but everything was dry, stony. No hope for water anywhere. She was stricken by a hunger that wrenched her stomach, but there was not a single crust, only the horror of deprivation and loneliness slowly slithering like a snake next to her. It followed her very close, threatening her with a sly wiggling slide. Every now and then, it would touch her naked feet. She fearfully turned her gaze and saw dry snakes under and above the stones eyeing her insistently; and she violently seized one, but it slipped out of her grasp, slid away, and vanished in the empty light. With horror she then realized that its skin was left in her outstretched hand, the thin, dry coat about to split. She tossed it away in disgust, and then she saw the tree out of the corner of her eye. She rushed to it and found herself before a high trunk like a bare column. It had neither leaves nor the least trace of a limb. It was a just a stark trunk with dried strips of bark. Her hands were pricked and bloody as she climbed with difficulty. Every so often the stumps of limbs she grabbed trembled, broke, and fell to the ground. She heard their dry thump and did not bend to look down.

As she reached the top exhausted, pain knifed her body and pierced her mind. Her hands, feet, and body were red with bleeding cuts. Here and there her body was patched with bits of bark which had pierced through to her insides. She looked at her belly and touched it delicately. It was wrinkled, lifeless – stained by the color of the dead tree. She was shocked with grief toward her body – a grief without tears, drenched with sorrow and pain. Her heart was rent, and when she could no longer endure it, she turned to her soul.

Her soul, in a different sphere of existence, was still smiling.

"Look around you," it encouraged her, and then she found herself in a lush meadow. There was water and flowering life around her, and as far as the eye could see it was like a sea planted with diversely hued flowers where birds were twittering – bees and butterflies flying. "In the name of the Bee, / And of the butterfly," she thought, filled with awe, and the miracle of the dream was complete. The dry trunk transformed before her eyes into a tree of rare freshness – branches and greenery, with blossoms and exotic fruit. She sighed with contentment, and when a gentle wind came, she breathed, "And of the Breeze – Amen!"(#18) Feeling the delight of ecstasy, carried away by beauty, she cried out and her powerful voice woke her up. "Poetry! Poetry!" she sang out. The word was full of promises. "Sue, my love," she murmured, "they pushed us into prose, but you and I belong to poetry." She spoke to her as if she were there with her in her soul, sharing every moment of the day and every thought. She embraced her and sighed with relief.

Sun poured into her room; everything was aglow from the inexplicable joy that had come with the sunrise. It was a splendid day in the presence of God. Emily prepared to communicate the shades of wonder with gratitude and joy. "Life is power!" she burst out and leapt out of bed. Walking around her room, she stroked a red geranium in a pot on her writing table, scanned the titles of books, and touched the open dictionary, feeling each word injecting her with energy, dispersing in the room and arousing her. "The soul is the best friend of the self," she told herself smiling, prepared to deliver her spirit to writing.

That moment she did not know that her dream was prophetic; she had no need to analyze. She was living each instant with awareness, seeking in her senses, intuition, and language from moment to moment. She savored the light and it did not concern her that night would fall and pitch her into despair. She saw that throughout life's journey we live between the poles – rising to joy and ecstasy, falling to anguish and doubt.

The night that George Gould was expelled from the Homestead, he stamped out of Emily's yard without looking back even once. Deeply hurt, he reached the dormitory shedding tears of wounded pride. He would later confide to his diary his need for revenge against the man who insulted him. As for his life's work, he confessed to his wife at the time of his death, "Life has disappointed me." He had not realized that life had not failed him. Rather, he had failed life.

Alone in Rebellion

Very early in the morning Edward noisily went up and down the stairs opening and closing doors. For him it was a deeply significant day. Everyone had to be up to dress in their best and accompany him to church. He was to deliver his heart and mind to Christ, traveling God's straight path like the majority of Amherst citizens. His conversion had been long delayed in contrast to many relatives, who prayed for the event. The same was true of his family. His wife and his daughter Vinnie had given their faith to Christ years before. He had held back, and that fact may have influenced his older daughter and son. Now everything would change. He would join the faith, not as a nominal believer but as an authentically reborn Christian; and he hoped his example would spur Emily and Austin to Christ. He feared Emily would not get up on time – that she would not go to church, even today for her father's sake. After all, her behavior had motivated him. Also her dear companion Sue and other friends, that day dedicating themselves to Christ, would take their place in the fold. The year 1850 was the year of Awakening in Amherst; the number of her reborn would surpass that of the Great Revival of 1849 in Northampton.

He was right to make so much noise, since his fears for Emily were very real. "Emily has to wake up and join me!" he told himself with sinking heart. In fact, she did wake up, open her eyes, only to turn over at once and go back to sleep.

A few days before Austin had taken to Emily a letter from Vinnie, who was so keen for the two of them to join the awakening. Vinnie had written: "How beautiful if we three could all believe in Christ, how much higher an object should we have in living! . . . Does Emily think of these things at all? Oh! that she might!" Emily responded with that personal smile of sadness and irony. "Oh, if I had ever thought of it! If only she knew how many times I have struggled with the idea; in fact, for a short time, I felt I had found my savior. I never enjoyed such perfect peace and happiness. But when doubts seized me, I was saved from that peace and I began to pick Satan's flowers and to sing songs with the bad angels, as our pastor characterized both Austin and me."

"I could not live my life without the sense of sin," she said to Austin, who had also refused to assume the yoke of faith. "I don't care about the joy of pardon, the holy strength, the happiness, as our friend Emily Fowler writes – commonplaces copied from the pastors." She raised her voice as if it were his fault for reading her the letters from Vinnie and their friend, Emily Fowler. "I stand alone in rebellion. The ark of safety is not for me !" Angrily she threw down the letter. Her voice changed and she spoke calmly to Austin, smiling, "Remain unbelieving by my side, and let us burn in hell, as our pastor said in his sermon looking at us." She gave a melancholy laugh. "I felt sorry for poor Vinnie. She believed him, and how much she suffered for us!" Then she smiled brightly. "The feeling of sin, the feeling of forgiveness, the power of happiness – every thing will come, dear Austin, in time. . . in time."

The service began, and Edward, dressed in an elegant new suit – grave, inspired, though embittered by Emily's absence – knelt in the presence of the congregation. Though he was mindful of his professional and political status – the main benefactor of Amherst – he humbly knelt and avowed that he was lost without the aid of a higher power.

The church packed, the converts with eyes lowered confessed their faith in Christ as their savior. Sue – humble before the lord and proud beside the chief citizen of the town – accepted the minister's blessings with tear-filled eyes and trembling lips.

As he knelt, the proud state representative must have thought, "This is what happens to parents who have children like Emily!" In any case, confessing his devotion to Christ, he felt peace and happiness and he forgot the episode with

George Gould, who as assistant pastor that significant day recorded in his diary, "While Hon. E.D. of Amherst was converted – who had been long under conviction – his pastor said to him in his study – 'You want to come to Christ as a *lawyer* – but you must come to him as a *poor sinner* – Get down on your knees and let me pray for you, and then pray for yourself.'"

Two Swimmers in a Raging Sea

To own a Susan of my own
Is of itself a Bliss –
Whatever Realm I forfeit, Lord,
Continue me in this!
(#1401)

The coach pulled up in front of the Homestead, and the Dickinsons' Irish servant, Joseph, hastened to load the ladies' luggage. With deep respect the driver offered a hand to help them into the carriage, and the two, after embracing Emily and Sue, took their seats.

Emily Norcross Dickinson and daughter Lavinia were departing for the nation's capital. Congressman Edward Dickinson had engaged the very finest coach and swiftest horses; and he had, in turn, planned for many events in the capital that would please his beloved wife and daughter. It was a shame that Emily had refused to make it a trio. The next time, he told himself, he would insist on her going. If she would ever make the trip, she would appreciate his significant associates in the House of Representatives, just as she would gauge the respect that numerous members of that body bore him.

The travelers sent kisses from above to Emily and Sue, who were standing on the curb, and the mother delivered final words of advice with extreme severity – that Emily should eat properly, dress against the cold, and enjoy the company of her friend. Her last words were repeated in a sad tone expressing how sorry she was that Emily was not coming along, just as Vinnie exclaimed in disappointment, "A pity you're missing out!"

"Next time, Vinnie dear – next time!" Emily returned.

With mixed feelings mother and daughters waved good-bye, as the horses shivered in restlessness. With the first tug of the harness, they set off, and in a moment the coach had turned the corner. Emily joyfully squeezed Sue, exclaiming "At last! We'll be alone to talk and spend hours together! To read, eat, sleep, enjoy ourselves as we like – free of the eyes, ears, advice, and carping of others. Hoorah for freedom!"

Sue was laughing! No other young lady in Amherst applauded freedom as she did. Her life with her sister Harriet, the conformist, and her brother-in-law Cutler, who deemed the female a flawed creation, was so humiliating that she was ashamed openly to voice her sense of enslavement. What she supremely valued in Emily was that she shared these feelings without the need to put them into words. For Sue, anyhow, freedom would mean not to be continuously forced to care for her sister's sickly child, to tolerate the miserable lives of people with a poverty of ideas, and – most difficult of all – to express her gratitude to them! How humiliating, especially for an individual like Sue, who was known for her boldness and sharp tongue. When Sue was angry, her words cut like daggers, as Emily wrote: "There is a word / Which bears a sword / Can pierce an armed man – / It hurls its barbed syllables" (#8).

Sue's world after the death of her parents was that of her scattered siblings. She lived with her aunt in Geneva, New York, but she was hustled to Harriet in Amherst according to the dictates of the moment. Maria, older than Sue, was married at a distance from Amherst, and Mattie, a year younger, went with her. Her two older brothers had left home to establish themselves in the west. Sue admired her brothers and envied their freedom and wealth, while she despised her drunkard father even after his passing, respected Maria, simply tolerated Harriet, hated her brother-in-law, and adored soft-spoken Mattie.

"Let The Touch Of Love Be Lightning"

Among all the siblings, Mattie stood out. Relatives always contrasted the two, saying "Sue's not gentle, like Mattie," but Emily made another distinction – "Mattie's not an intellectual like Sue." Anyhow, the neighbors, who gossiped about the relationships of the two Gilbert girls, suspected that Austin had eyes for Mattie and that the Gilberts hoped one fine day to become in-laws of the Dickinsons.

Emily and Sue went into the house and sat laughing on the couch, erasing from their minds the list that Mrs. Dickinson had placed in their hands. Their priorities were different. The enjoyment of their friendship was linked to endless discussion of books and literary artists.

"Sue, did you keep the list of the chores mother asked of us?" Emily inquired in a very serious tone.

"Of course," Sue answered, putting her hand in her pocket to reach the paper supposedly there.

"Oh, my mother! My mother!" Emily sighed, and then began to laugh. "I can see her in Washington as the blabbermouth of the evening." Emily bent a little and mimicked the dulcet tones of her mother, beginning, "What would you like for dessert? An apple? Or would you prefer a slice of apple pie? I baked it with my own hands! Would you like a throw-rug to warm your toes, or would you prefer my rendering of the national anthem, or better, the constitutional amendments?" Emily clapped her hands, and the girls joined in raucous laughter.

"I love Ik Marvel's *Reveries of a Bachelor*!" Sue exclaimed to curtail Emily's hyperboles.

"Splendid!" Emily returned. "Love scorns arrangements and conventions. And Austin brought me Longfellow's *Cavenaugh*."

"I want it!" begged Sue."

"As soon as I finish it," Emily said. "But you know, my dear, that father forbids such books, so I keep them hidden by day and read by candle-light. I can't even risk a lamp."

"But it's worth the candle!" Sue added.

"Poor father," said Emily, "he buys me books yet begs me to be wary even of his approved titles, because he says literary works can trouble my mind." The two of them once more burst into giggles. Serious again, Emily noted, "Father's library is full of old classics. He says they don't write now as they did when he was young, and he always keeps his eye on what Austin and I are reading."

"One of my favorites," said Sue enthusiastically, "is Lydia Maria Child's *Letters from New York!*"

"Truly, that's a real book!" Emily returned, "But there are so many more," she sighed, adding "Ben Newton sent it to me, Sue. I miss him so much. You didn't get a chance to meet him but I told him so much about you.... He was my tutor," she breathed nostalgically.

"And I gave you Jane Austen. What does that tell you? Am I not your tutor too?"

"I adore her, as I adore the sisters Bronte!" Emily said. "And poetry! Poetry! It gives me such a thrill!" She danced around the room chanting "Po-et-ry, po-et-ry, po-et-ry! Keats's nightingale – Shelley's skylark!"

Sue leapt to her feet, raised her hands, and making quick spins imitating Emily, ecstatically intoned: "Shakespeare! Shakespeare ! Hail the bard!"

"Shakespeare – yes, yes! Elizabeth Barrett Browning – yes!"

"And Robert Browning – yes!" Sue concluded, still laughing.

"Hail their freedom and love!" Emily chanted once more.

It was past noon; they were hungry, but they didn't want to break the flow of their talk. Only when they heard steps on the kitchen porch did they rise and open the door. Cousin John – as Emily called John Graves, a relative on her Grandmother Lucrecia's side and a student at Amherst – appeared with his broad grin.

"Girls!" he announced jocularly – unable to remain serious about the duty he had been assigned – "Uncle Edward has asked me to stay overnight with you." The girls clapped their hands, joyously welcoming the company of the handsome young fellow. "Expect me after classes – around five."

"Be prepared to have the most delectable meal you've ever eaten!" they piped.

"Don't put any arsenic in the soup – it's the only thing I don't care for!"

"No, no, Mr. Socrates!" the laughter continued.

It was past five and Cousin John had not appeared, though the table was set. The girls decided to play hide-and-seek. Emily – head lowered and eyes closed – was at the kitchen table. She counted slowly to twenty and announced, "Ready or not, here I come!" Dashing into the living room, she glanced behind the sofa and the arm chair. "Lovely Sue, where can you be?" she chirped, stepping into the dining room, looking under the table and beside the buffet. "Darling, where are you?" she whispered, but Sue wasn't there. She raced upstairs and looked under her bed, panic mounting. It was as if Sue had vanished from her life forever. With a premonition of disaster, she sped down the steps, scanned the dining room once more, and entered the hallway into the kitchen. There, behind the door of the nook under the steps, she at last found Sue in the darkest corner of the hideaway, standing against the wall, silent with closed eyes, holding her breath.

"Sue! Sue, dearest," she cried. Achingly, longingly, she embraced her and kissed her passionately on the lips. "I found you! I finally found you!" she chanted as her body trembled and her eyes overflowed with tears.

Sue smiled awkwardly. "But of course you found me!" she blushed. "I wouldn't go and leave you alone! After all – I promised to stay with you tonight!"

"That wasn't what frightened me," Emily returned, looking deep into her eyes. "Sue, my love . . ." she murmured in a velvet voice.

That moment came the sound of Cousin John's deep greeting at the kitchen door. "Is supper ready, girls? I could eat a horse!"

Emily took Sue's hand. "Come, let's feed hungry Cousin John!" she urged playfully and they appeared smiling in the kitchen.

The evening progressed and the three gazed at one another somewhat exhausted by the talk. Sue was on the couch and John was in an armchair, while Emily was still on her feet speaking so emphatically that the other two were uncomfortable. The conversation had reached a difficult point for John and Sue. John had his eyes half closed in order to hide his reactions to Emily's piercing gaze, while Sue was shifting restlessly on the couch. The subject was intense and obvious. Emily was speaking of Elizabeth Barrett's father, whose name was Edward (what a coincidence!). The man had such anxiety about his daughter, such "concern" for her health and honor that he never let her out of his sight. "Elizabeth's great happiness, and our good fortune, was that a man with greater passion than her father's obsession was found to claim her," Emily said with burning outrage. She applauded the decision of the lovers to elope, disdaining the consent of the father, who never spoke to them again. The tone of Emily's voice – in the pride of her second name, identifying her with the great poet – had risen to the point that the two friends realized Emily was not referring to the famous poet's father but her own. Emily's companions were upset. Sue especially revered the congressman. She disagreed with her friend, squirming in her seat, not knowing what to add or subtract from her words. Emily, standing tall and scarlet with anger, hurled the father of the great poet into a bottomless abyss and praised the lovers, exalting their passion. "Love is the core of cre-ation. God was in love with beauty and passionately created the world. Look at its glory! Its wisdom and loveliness! Elizabeth and Robert were in love! Read their poetry! The father was blind to the miracle of love!"

Listening to her censure, John was stymied since his wit was insufficient to support Uncle Edward against Emily's onslaught. Further, he had the feel-ing that in some way he had betrayed him by listening to Emily, for Edward Dickinson had aided young relatives attending the college – especially John himself, among many who cherished great gratitude toward him. That moment, hearing the cuckoo clock sound the hour of nine, Cousin John stood up and – contriving a carefree expression on his pleasant face – announced with mock severity,

"Nine o'clock. Young ladies, as protector of the delicate female constitution, I remind you that it is late. Therefore, to your beds immediately!"

Sue was relieved by this solution. She seized the opportunity and slowly proceeded toward the stairs forcing a great yawn, a clear sign of exhaustion and sleepiness. Emily, thunderstruck – a string of complaints issuing from her lips – watched them climbing the staircase toward the dark hall. Seizing a lamp and raising it high, she followed them silently, went first into Vinnie's room, given to Sue, and lighted the lamp there. Then she proceeded to the eastern wing, where John would sleep. Lighting his lamp, she turned on her heel without a word of good night. Enraged, she entered her room and locked the door.

Sue woke suddenly when she heard her door opening. In the moonlight shining through the window she saw that it was John who was bending over her and gently shaking her shoulder. "Sue, Sue," he whispered, "come downstairs."

Silently, barefoot, with pounding heart, Sue followed John the length of the dark hall that pulsed with the notes of the piano from below, and with infinite quietness went behind him down the stairs. They stood at the entrance to the lighted living room and looked in at Emily who, dressed in a long white nightgown, was improvising a piece on the piano. Her face glowed as her fingers moved with esoteric knowledge over the keys. The notes, entwined with the pulsing of her heart, were shooting up and pouring down, a fountain wild, burning, exalted. The passionate music had transformed her face and even her frame, which seemed to soar. She appeared strange and powerful. Open-mouthed, Sue perceived that Emily was no longer the girl who was her friend and classmate; she was no longer even the person she knew and loved, but instead a fierce primal goddess that had burst from the entrails of the earth. She gazed thunderstruck, heart bursting, and suddenly realized that this goddess would determine her fate, while John, hypnotized, backed away and tiptoed to his room.

Dawn arrived. The first faint illumination showed in the living room windows, and only then did Emily's fingers – indeed her entire body – feel exhausted.

Trembling, she stood up, put out the lamp, and climbed the half-lighted stairs to her room. At her bed she heard deep breathing. Sighing deeply, she lifted the covers and placed her trembling body next to Sue's, warm, moist, and soft.

Emily was awakened late by the noise of a carriage pulling up in front of the house. Jumping out of bed, she saw Sue climb into the passenger's seat. "Sue! Sue!" she cried, tapping on the window, but Sue did not turn to look at her, and in wild distress Emily raced barefoot down the stairs and onto the stoop, managing to catch just a glimpse of the carriage as it moved in the distance down Main Street. She felt a frigid blast knife her. She closed the door and went up to her room. Her body was numb and her heart in turmoil, but her mind, the ruler of her being, recognized her inmost feelings. It saw and recognized the activated volcano, the lava boiling within her core.

She searched her feelings and painted them with words. She wrote seven poems on the volcano theme. In #1677, the volcano is burning within but its sides are covered with tender grass:

On my volcano grows the Grass
A meditative spot –
An acre for the Bird to choose
Would be the General thought –

How red the Fire rocks below –
How insecure the sod
Did I disclose
Would populate with awe my solitude.

Of Sue she also wrote passionately a poem that nineteenth century editors refused to include in the early editions. It was published in the 1951 edition and later set to music by her admirers. I heard it on May 16, 2009, sung to guitar accompaniment at her graveside on the anniversary of her death (#249):

Wild Nights – Wild Nights!
Were I with thee
Wild Nights should be
Our Luxury!

Futile – the Winds –
To a Heart in port –
Done with the Compass –
Done with the Chart!

Rowing in Eden –
Ah, the Sea!
Might I but moor – Tonight –
In Thee!

Equally revealing was the image of a miraculous moment of love. Was it in heaven or on earth (#518)?

Her sweet Weight on my Heart a Night
Had scarcely deigned to lie –
When, stirring, for Belief's delight,
My Bride had slipped away –

If 'twas a Dream – made solid – just
The Heaven to confirm –
Or if Myself were dreamed of Her –
The power to presume –

With Him remain – who unto Me –
Gave – even as to All –

Emily Dickinson: Goddess of the Volcano

A Fiction superseding Faith –
By so much – as 'twas real –

My decision as a writer was to learn the truth from Sue – to learn details about their relationship that eluded me and could not be found in any book, in any library. Straight-laced commentators could not answer my questions. They did not recognize such love. If they suspected it, they were not willing to put it down on paper and indelibly expose themselves.

In search of Sue, I went up and down the streets from Harriet's house to the pharmacy, from the bookstore to the town center, frequenting corners she often passed. I visited the most unlikely spots and pursued the slightest hint where I might find her. For a week, I criss-crossed the town center without success.

Then, hoping against hope, I suddenly caught sight of her walking down the street with Harriet's baby in her arms! "Sue!" I shouted joyfully. She turned her head and looked, and I was sure she recognized me, but pretending that she neither saw nor heard me, she walked on. I ran after her and eagerly asked what I needed to know. "Sue, I want you to speak of Emily – of the feelings you shared, and why you left her side." I insisted, but for some time she evaded my question. Touching her on the shoulder, I urged, "Sue, I beg of you!" Then she looked at me with a gaze that seemed to come from very far away. Finally, she spoke, and her words reached my ears, not with syllables or sound, but as if a warm breeze were blowing from somewhere. She spoke a long time, but I understood only her last words, more through reading her lips than from the sound of speech. "Geniuses are strange people!" she cried. "They demand your soul. I have to disappear from her life, if I want to be saved . . .". Mumbling, she added, "but I can't." She lowered her head and hastily dried her eyes. I was shocked by the tone of her voice. Accented at a high pitch, it expressed the terrible struggle that was going on inside her, and her eyes showed total panic. I continued my probing calmly, insisting on a specific answer. "Sue, do you love her – and how?" I reached out to touch her, but my hand remained suspended.

Sue disappeared before my eyes, and once more I was standing in the town of today. Later I learned from Emily's letters that this was the time that Sue had left Amherst for Baltimore to teach mathematics at a school for girls.

I once more immersed myself in books about Emily's life which cast light on every member of her family, including Cousin John, whose daughter years after his death was asked about his relationship with Emily. She smiled and sighed with relief as if she were glad finally to have an opportunity to speak. "When my father spoke of Emily Dickinson, his expression changed. His eyes showed tender nostalgia, his face glowed brightly, and his spirits soared, brimming with joy – he loved her so much! 'She was different. Emily Dick [*sic*] had the greatest charm of anyone I ever knew,' he would say with a deep sigh."

The Trials of the Soul

Winter dragged though New England. The cold kept doors closed and visits rare. Each day became darker and more oppressive. The residents of Amherst, withdrawn in their homes before roaring fires, wrapped in woolen blankets, maintained that such a harsh winter had not occurred within recent memory. Edward, who had been marooned in a station near Amherst for almost two days, agreed. He arrived at home feverish but refused to admit it, since he found Emily coughing, and his fears of consumption were renewed. He had to take care of Emily, for she was susceptible to colds and recovered with difficulty. He had been away, and Austin, too, was absent, teaching at Sunderland. The three women were alone. Who would bring in wood, light the fire, do the shopping, and draw water from the well? The three alone – and only one, Vinnie, practical! Edward went to the newspaper office and placed an advertisement:

WANTED – Highly recommended woman capable of undertaking household needs of a small family – permanent employment with good pay.

Thus Margret Maher – nick-named Maggie – entered the Dickinsons' lives. The Irish potato famine of 1845 drove the needy like a flood throughout the globe. Among them was Maggie, who was with the Dickinsons for years, and whenever they needed help on the property brought close relatives and friends. She was energetic, dependable, and affectionate toward her employers, who returned her feelings and enjoyed her services. Illiterate Maggie, listening to the speech of Emily and Vinnie, attempted to adopt it, to the great amusement of all. Her phrase, with a smile, when a visitor appeared asking for Emily was, "We are out."

During the long winter, Emily nervously paced the rooms and slammed the doors in passing. Mother was afraid to say a word, and Vinnie preferred to stay in her room rather than face her older sister. Maggie sadly nodded, saying, "Miss Emily, ah, Miss Emily!" and often recalled the event: "She stepped on a nail, our little Miss Emily, and I pulled it out, and all night she was awake, but she don't complain. She just whispers, 'Listen, Maggie – listen to the nightingale. It's singing to ease the pain in my foot.' But now, angry, she slams doors."

Winter, and the loneliness in the house was torturous. Doors, windows sealed; colors drab; shivers down the spine; the silence deafening. Not even the sound of tree limbs as they were tossed wildly in the air. Only their aggressive movement could be discerned through the window, as if they wished to disperse the absolute silence in the house. It was so silent that Emily began to wish for visits even from her aunts, uncles, and their families. When they came and stayed for a week, she would be irritated and angry. She could not stand their noise. "Austin," she wrote him in Sunderland, "they are not like us." Now, however – in such bleak moments – she needed them. She spent her time sending letters and poems to friends, according to impulse: "A Day! Help! Help! Another Day! / Your prayers, oh Passer by!" (#42) And through the window of her room, she searched the road for the postman. Even he avoided being outside in such weather. Deliveries were delayed.

This dark, cold year Emily slowly and laboriously learned to live in solitude. Her only outside contact was correspondence with loved ones or those with whom she shared some interest. Two and a half thousand individuals are on the list of people to whom she wrote. During the day by the window, and at night by lamplight, she wrote letters, read, and studied the dynamics of poetry that burst out in the ground-breaking innovations of her style.

This verse, which lifts the soul of the reader and hones the intellect, evoked ecstasy in its creator; it taught her to embrace a fertile solitude that produced an exhaustless source of profundity, wit, and sensuality – in short, ecstasy, the sea of the spirit:

Exultation is the going
Of an inland soul to sea,
Past the houses – past the headlands –
Into deep Eternity –

Bred as we, among the mountains,
Can the sailor understand
The divine intoxication
Of the first league out from land?
(#76)

Death the Omnipresent

Spring arrived and everything bloomed; houses and souls lighted up. Hearts breathed with the joy of youth, finding delight in each little thought, each walk, each shared moment with friends. The literary club was also flowering. Emily gaily went out to attend every single meeting.

"Fortunately, we have the club," Emily thought. "Only there do we share vital thoughts," she happily told friends, musing, "Life is so dazzling that death is necessary to provide balance." Then she spontaneously added, "'Tis so appalling, it exhilarates," and no sooner had she completed the thought than Death arrogantly and callously appeared before her.

There was a knock at the door and Emily called down from above, "Maggie, I'll open!" She ran down the stairs and found two handsome faces, unsmiling, looking at her in sadness. Cousin John, with his close younger friend Emmons, attempted to smile, but their news blocked their efforts. John reached out his hand and touched Emily gently. "Emily," he said, hesitating to continue. He searched for words. Unable to find a gentle phrase, he blurted out what was on his mind harshly and decisively, "Leonard died yesterday morning." Emily shuddered as if she had plunged into an icy lake. With open mouth she looked at them, wanting to scream. Turning her back, she ran to hide in her room. There she inconsolably wept for her friend.

Her philosophic conclusion was established: "All but death can be adjusted."

Just a week before, the weather had been beautiful and students in the literary club at the academy had gathered to wish their teacher a pleasant journey. Leonard would be spending a week visiting his father a few miles from Amherst. In good spirits he received his students' best wishes. When he arrived at his destination on Saturday evening, he was feeling mild discomfort and a slight headache. He paid no heed, attributing the condition to the difficulties of the journey; however, as the hours passed, the pain became unbearable. On Sunday morning young Leonard Humphrey, twenty-six years old, was dead. His students were shattered by his terrible fate, and his loss blighted the community as a whole. Club activities, dances, literary and poetry discussion groups, were suspended. Never again were things as they had been with the presence of the young pastor and teacher, the thought of whose loss chilled the hearts of his students. Swift and unforeseen, death in the 19th century struck down people of all ages and social backgrounds, and worst of all – no sooner had one death occurred than people were shocked by the announcement of another.

The following March, as loneliness dripped softly within her (her loved ones, Austin and Sue, were away), she received a letter from Benjamin Newton. She took it tenderly, slid it into her pocket and stroked it. She savored the letter before opening it. She had to go upstairs to be alone and enjoy it in her own space. She finished kneading the bread (her sole chore) and impatiently, eyes glistening with joy, mounted the stairs. She sat down at the little table and with great care opened Benjamin's delayed news. Her beloved teacher had not written in two years, and finally he sent her a page virtually blank – with but two terse sentences. She was shaken as she read what her friend had written: "If I don't die, I will come to Amherst to see you. And if I die, I certainly will." One week later the story appeared in the press. Benjamin Newton, her companion and tutor, was dead. Consumption had cut off life and friendship, but Benjamin's memory remained "a nail in the breast" for years. In the evening Emily sent word to Austin, who was in Boston. Her letter was pleasant till she reached the salutation, "Love from all of us," adding a postscript, "Monday noon. Oh, Austin, Newton is dead. The first of my own friends. Pace." It was an enormous trial for Emily. Nine months later she carefully wrote a long letter to Benjamin's pastor in Worcester. She wanted to learn if Benjamin "was willing to die, [and] if you think him in his heavenly home." The letter raises the idea of the believer of the age that one must be willing to "go home" in death. The pastor did not reply, but there was an article in the *Daily News* with details regarding the history and passing of her friend. It praised the ideals of the young man and, concerning last things, stated "He did not show any fear, and something more, just before his death he greeted all his friends and loved ones." This inspiring thought was slight comfort for Emily, whose memory of Benjamin twenty years later was still intense. She wrote to Higginson about her "friend who taught me Immortality – but venturing too near himself – he never returned."

For Emily, death appeared an absolute power that suddenly intervenes and seems to conquer life. The theme became a compulsive element in her studies, as she sought to learn: What is death? Why does it exist? How is it for one to die? Can one indeed be willing to die? She wanted to know *how* and *why*, but finally she submitted to inescapable ignorance about this most significant theme. In one poem she stated:

I shall know why – when Time is over –
And I have ceased to wonder why –
Christ will explain each separate anguish
In the fair schoolroom of the sky –

He will tell me what "Peter" promised –
And I – for wonder at his woe –
I shall forget the drop of Anguish
That scalds me now – that scalds me now!
(#193)

The Tragic Triangle

Eros the Teaser

With all its might, the ponderous New England winter again descended upon Amherst. Emily cleared the condensation from the kitchen window and looked out into her domain. She could hear the little hearts of her flowers quake as the ice of the night before bowed their stems and blocked their breath. There was a deep cold which – though it was expected – came with astounding force. She sighed and looked out toward the street as if in expectation. Her attention was drawn to a carriage making its way cautiously so it would not slide into the ditch. Then she was surprised to see it pull up before the door of the Homestead. "Who can it be who is visiting us in such weather?" she wondered, hoping that good news might be involved. Opening the door, she found a stranger. Holding his hat in his hand, he kept his eyes on the hall floor, waiting for the lady of the house to speak the first word. "Oh no – this man is not bringing glad tidings!" Emily thought, striving to calm the beating of her heart.

With Vinnie beside her, encircling her waist with her arm, she asked abruptly, "Who are you and what do you want?" Lifting his head, the man gazed sadly at them and spoke in quiet stumbling tones: "Miss Sue sent me with the message that today at dawn her sister Maria died in childbirth and the baby as well – the birth was difficult and the doctor could do nothing." All this was uttered in one breath in an Irish brogue, bearing witness to the servant's recent arrival on their shores. Speechless, the two girls looked at the messenger who, having done his duty, bowed respectfully and returned to the carriage. Emily had gone pale, her legs trembling. Vinnie supported her back to the kitchen, easing her into a chair. Emily rested her head on the tabletop and burst into tears. Vinnie stroked her hair as her tears joined Emily's.

"Oh, Sue! Oh, Sue," she moaned with bowed head, and the waves of her love became a tide of sadness, as she wrote in a letter of consolation:

You must let me
go first, Sue, because
I live in the Sea
always and know
the Road –
I would have drowned
Twice to save
you sinking, dear,
If I could only
Have covered your
Eyes so you wouldn't
have seen the Water –
(letter – lines in verse form,
from Hart and Smith)

That evening Austin heard the news and his heart ached for his dear friend Sue. Up to that fatal moment – Sue's dark hour – his attention had been fixed on her younger sister, Mattie. Mattie was of easy-going temperament, without lofty ambitions, elaborate dreams or a strong sense of feminine independence. She was simply a young lady who knew her place. She wanted to marry, have a family, and be a good wife. Anything more challenging she left to Sue, whom she admired and adored. As for the charming young patrician – oh that he would confess he loved her and that she was the wife of his dreams! She did not preclude the event. They talked and laughed endlessly; that is, he did most of the talking and she most of the laughing. That evening when the parents were absent they had danced continuously, and in her bed she thought of him tenderly. Austin's heart was lifted by thoughts of her, too, and he frequently wrote in friendly and tender ways. However, the news of Sue's unbearable pain, brought home by Emily's tears, awakened in Austin a sudden feeling of love for their fiery friend Sue. The image of Mattie, which for months had preoccupied him, suddenly faded, while that of Sue spread throughout his being.

Perhaps that is the way eros tricks a human being. He finds him vulnerable – without grounded thoughts and purposes – and leads him in a direction that had been long in the making. That chilly night as the three young Dickinsons sat in the kitchen, the warmest room in that large house, and mourned the sorrow that had struck the Gilberts, they did not suspect that very moment would tellingly impact the course of their lives. They were not mainly thinking of Maria, who so young had lost her life in the blow that struck so many women of the nineteenth century. Rather, it was the fiery, determined Sue who filled Emily and Austin with charged feelings, as if the attitudes of the one confirmed those of the other, making feelings more insistent and intense.

What unconscious need drove the siblings to react with such intensity toward the same person? Was it love they felt toward one another, or was it competition that – in spite of mutual affection and admiration – was unconsciously present throughout their lives? The father's weakness for his precious son, whom he considered unmatchable, even in the poetry he once attempted to write, did not go unobserved by Emily. One Sunday afternoon when the family had completed a delicious meal prepared by Maggie, Austin jumped up, took a paper from his pocket, and announced he had written a poem. Father pushed his plate away, used his napkin, and – glowing with pride – waited in hushed expectation. The pleasant expression on his face did not escape the notice of Emily, who awaited Austin's poem with curiosity. Its singsong lines, bland wording, and naïve themes tickled her. She held back her giggles as Edward Dickinson pontificated about 'significant' verse. Without a word, she smiled awaiting the moment when the two of them would be alone, and then launched into spirited teasing: "Out of the way, Pegasus, Olympus enough 'to him', and just say to those 'nine muses' that we have done with them! We raised a living muse ourselves, worth the whole nine of them. Up, off, tramp!" She looked at her brother roaring, continuing to tease him. Though he dared to hold that her joke was stupid, he never wrote poetry again. In his passionate letters to Sue and years later in his erotic correspondence with suave Mabel Loomis Todd, he did not dare to pen a single line of verse, but overflowed with purple prose.

Now – in 1852 – young Austin felt heartbreak for Sue and fell in love with all the power of his youthful passions. As for Emily, she had intense physical and intellectual passion for Sue from the first day of their meeting. Such a love, however, always permitted an additional object of affection. In any case, for Sue she had feelings never experienced in relation to any other friend. In a letter she writes:

Susan knows
she is a Siren –
and that at a
word from her,
Emily would
forfeit Righteousness –
Please excuse
the grossness
of this Morning –
I was for a
moment disarmed –
This is the
World that opens
and shuts, like
the Eye of the
Wax Doll –
(from Hart and Smith)

Vinnie – distanced and objective – feared this emotional dependence of Emily's: "Sue will shorten her days," she always said, and frowned on her.

Did Sue share Emily's feelings?

There are many indications that their relationship may have consisted of the affection the Victorian age permitted young girls to share – a tender relationship that brought delicious erotic excitement. Emily had such a feeling toward her friends Abiah, Emily Fowler, and even Mrs. Holland. The reader finds the feeling in her correspondence. However, if the feeling were initially that sublimated Victorian mode of affection, from the time Emily began her voluntary withdrawal, the affection became a passion. In the 128 letters and 201 poems that Emily sent Sue during their life time (and which Sue kept as a precious treasure to the end of her days), most would express erotic attachment, including hurt feelings of jealousy and misunderstandings. It was always Emily who capitulated at once, begging love and attention. This bond did not preclude other loves, or fleeting relationships interpreted as such by critics – even wedding plans, as in the case of Judge Otis Lord, friend of Emily's father.

"Love and death – does anything else exist?" she said, and throughout her life she found herself in a situation of unfulfilled love in which Sue was supreme. "Sue, you are my imagination," she wrote to her, recognizing that love for Sue was the most vital element in her poetry and her life. From on high at her window, she followed Sue's life and through it supplemented her own – "Vesuvius at home."

For Austin, the crucial turn occurred that evening. Love for Sue took him like a maelstrom, sweeping him into a narrow, rocky path of marriage in which her behavior would be dubious from the beginning. Austin describes his feelings as he courted Sue, writing to her: "I am overwhelmed with my emotions. I can't write. I haven't slept. All the night has a crowd of strange, tumultuous feelings made wild riot in my heart. The excess of my joy is very pain."

Austin's wooing of Sue, however, was not the matchless adventure he envisioned. He had wished to become like a storied knight who rode into Sue's life, sweeping her away from pain and death into a world of ecstasy. The two of them would live in an erotic delight that other couples could never imagine. They would be the pioneers of a rare happiness – which finally he would seek thirty years later, when he was approaching sixty, with an enchantress of twenty-five. Now, at the beginning of his life, he was determined at any cost to bring happiness to his beloved Sue. He wished to fulfill her visions, her dreams – to complete every facet of her being. He wrote to her: "I want you to feel free – to come and go – and see and do when and who and what you will and have no fear that it will displease me." How little the young man of twenty-three knew about a life of "wine and roses." He believed that his life was the guarantee of a marriage of harmony and happiness. "I love you, Sue, most fondly and tenderly – but you seem so pure and so good and so generous. I feel today as if I committed almost a sacrilege in holding your love for my own. If I could only be sure you knew just who I am."

How little Austin knew of women's feelings, or how idiosyncratic Sue would be, or even that she might be in love with another – and even worse that she might respond to Emily's plea for "a bit of Sue," as she wrote to her: "Suzie – when he takes you from me to live in his new home, may I have *some* of you. I am sincere." What impact would this have on Austin's life? On all their lives? The cost would be great for all three in this strange trio.

Letters to Sue

In her Baltimore room, Sue gently touched the two unopened letters in the drawer of her desk, one from Emily and one from Austin. Beside them were a set of student exercises that she had to mark for the following day. She sighed, feeling jealousy knife her: "That rich pair of Dickinsons write to me because they have time to spare!" she whispered in her mind. Then her heart softened: "But they care about me and I care, too!" She touched the letters tenderly, pressed them to her lips, and once more carefully placed them in the drawer. "I will read them tonight at my leisure." She caressed them in her thoughts and turned her full attention to grading.

She slipped under the covers, nested between the pillows, and made herself as comfortable as possible. Closing her eyes, she shuffled the letters several times and then raised her lids to find the one that ended up on top. She smiled. It was Austin's. His figure sprang sharply to mind – tall, slim, and red-haired, with cultivated features. "He has an air about him, all right," she whispered. "But," she sneered, "everything was handed to him on a silver platter!" Sue realized how readily she was irritated by certain thoughts. It was as if she could not forgive the material privileges enjoyed by the brother and sister. She strove to control her resentment. "Nobody as yet knows, but one day I may become a Dickinson," she thought, and felt a heaviness weighing on her heart. Suddenly, without her willing it, she saw in her mind's eye the young gentlemen who had flirted with her, none of them winning out. She hesitantly opened the envelope, finding a three-page letter including detailed features of Austin's family life and values, suggesting that he and Sue would face any eventuality in the spirit of his upbringing. He was certain that she shared his conception that this was the only way for a couple to live. Sue acknowledged his great need to share his views with his future spouse, but she could not suppress amusement at the style of the letter. With literary flourishes, the writer alluded to Narcissus who perished in the anguished effort to grasp the image that appeared to him in the pool, which for Austin represented the "transparent soul" of Sue. The missive concluded with affirmation of great love: "I Love you, Sue, up to the very highest strain my nature can bear – the least tension would snap my life threads – as brittle glass – more you could not ask – more man could not give – Love me Sue – love me – for it's my life. Austin."

Sue was exhausted. She sighed and closed her eyes, thinking, "The other letter can wait till tomorrow morning or, perhaps, evening." She was overcome by weariness brought on by a conflict she saw no way to escape. She changed the position of the pillows. She patted them. She leaned back. They seemed softer. She stretched out, sat up again, and tried to improve their arrangement. But they gave her no comfort, no matter how she tried. "Oh, Austin. . . Emily. . . Amherst," she thought, as restful sleep refused to come. A memory came to mind that kept her awake most of the night.

She had gone to the railroad station in Amherst to join the crowd celebrating the service that had been established through the efforts of their representative, Edward Dickinson. Approaching the location, she heard an uproar and saw people – mainly men – shouting and laughing as they ran toward the station. She, too, ran, and the smile was wiped from her face when she was confronted by the spectacle that was exciting the citizens of the small town. A mob was holding a young man in its grip. Naked, hands bound behind his back, he was coated with tar and feathers. With jeers, roared taunts, and raucous songs, the young men of the mob were dragging their victim toward the station platform to await the train whose belching smoke was seen in the distance. Terror and panic clearly branded on his face, the victim did not open his mouth to utter a single word, but his heaving breath and glaring eyes broadcast extreme pain and humiliation. He was at the mercy of the mob, who were deriding his trespasses as they dragged him from their spotless city. Behind the youthful crowd, a group of older men egged them on, reciting pious phrases concerning sinners who polluted their respectable town. Such a one was this young outsider who had seduced a naïve farm girl. Getting wind of what had happened, they were determined to punish him in spite of his honorable proposal of marriage, appealing to the girl's father. The townspeople of Amherst – determined to give him a stern moral lesson – had condemned him to tar-and-feathers, a widespread practice of the time.

As the train approached, Sue watched the crowd pitch the captive on the station platform like a sack of garbage. She turned her head and fled from the station. She wanted to see neither the train nor the townspeople endowed with such lofty ethical standards. The scene was painfully etched in her memory, and she was powerless to distance or erase it. As a young girl, her view of the victim's private parts plastered with tarred feathers had hit her in the stomach, bringing a nausea and uneasiness she had never experienced before. She had often wondered how many times she would once more view such a scene, and thus she had decided "Oh, I must take my distance from this horrible town!"

Austin's erotic siege, with the promise of a socially prestigious marriage, made her wonder, "Very well, assuming he's the right man for me – could I stand living in Amherst?" The thought tormented her as she pondered the two letters. Slowly, wearily, she returned the suitor's message to the envelope and placed it on the bedside table. Then she gazed at Emily's letter. She touched it gently, and trembling spread over her body. She pressed it to her heart, then raising it to the light to see if she could see the writing through the envelope. She could not. She slipped it under the pillow and closed her eyes in an effort to sleep. She felt a chill descending on the room – not from the fall weather but from her thoughts. She tossed and turned in bed, seeking comfort. She adjusted the sheets, pounded the pillow, and kept heaving sighs until at last she slipped into the realm of dreams.

She found herself in a dark space on her hands and knees. Something soft and cold touched her, and she shivered, seeing it was a fat little worm that seemed to love her and want to creep onto her. She felt sympathy, or rather pity, for the little crawler, but still she did not wish to let it climb onto the bed, so she looped a string around its head and secured it to the bedpost. Since it could not move and bother her, she was relieved and went to sleep. Emily woke her up. "How about taking it for a walk?" she asked. She took it by the leash and was walking away. Sue looked down and saw that now the worm had stretched into a snake with stripes and bright colors [imagery from #1670]. It whistled and moved pertly and proudly, crying "I scare you! I scare you!" "Not so!" Emily answered it, and Sue cried out, "No, No! Don't take it along on our walk! Don't!" but Emily walked off leading the snake as Sue's heart was pounding wildly.

Sue awoke before dawn. At once she reached for Emily's letter, lighted the lamp, and read:

Dear Sue,

It's of no use to write to you – Far better to bring dew to my thimble to quench the endless fire – my love for those I love – not many – not very many, but don't I love them so!

The letter ended with a poem (#4):

On this wondrous sea
Sailing silently,
Ho! Pilot, ho!
Knowst thou the shore
Where no breakers roar –
Where the storm is o'er?

In the peaceful west
Many the sails at rest –
The anchors fast –
Thither I pilot thee –
Land Ho! Eternity!
Ashore at last!

Sue repeatedly read the letter, and then she arose, trembling. Suddenly bodily excitement rose from sunken flames of forbidden thoughts that shot up and then almost flickered out, yet still endured as bold impulses. Sue, however, forcefully held them off. She arose from bed, paced the room, felt very thirsty but drinking did not quench her thirst. She shrugged, asserting, "It's impossible! Such feelings for her are out of the question! The church forbids them!" Her mind shifted back to Austin: "Dear Austin, help me! Rescue me from your sister's siege!" Before going to class, she wrote him an erotic letter, which received an immediate reply: "My wonderful Sue, join me in Boston on your return to Amherst! Do you wish it! Can you do it! I plead to you!"

In Amherst Emily kept pacing up and down, slamming doors in rage over Sue's delayed response to her letters. The days passed as she kept writing and waiting. Harried by loneliness and doubt, she wrote to Sue of the anguish she felt in her absence. There was no response, and her next letter complained –

> I love you as dearly, Susie, as when love first began, on the step at the front door . . . and it breaks my heart sometimes, because I do not hear from you. . . . . I miss you, mourn for you and walk the streets alone – often at night, beside. I fall asleep in tears for your dear face, yet not one word comes back to me from that silent West. If it is finished tell me, and I will raise the lid to my box of Phantoms, and lay one more love in, but if it *lives* and *beats* still, still lives and beats for *me* then say me *so* and I will strike the strings to one more strain of happiness before I die.

Sue, overflowing with memories, wrote a tender letter, perhaps asking for more love, and Emily – wild with love – responded:

> But what can I do towards you? dearer you can not be, for I love you so already, that it almost breaks my heart – perhaps I can love you anew, every day of my life, every morning and evening – oh, if you will let me how happy I shall be.

The next letter from Sue also brought Emily happiness, but doubt did not cease to torture her. Thus her answer to Sue was the following poem, expressing her fears (#156):

You love me – you are sure –
I shall not fear mistake –
I shall not cheated wake –
Some grinning morn –
To find the Sunrise left –
And Orchards – unbereft –
And Dollie – gone! . . .

Time, like Hermes the winged god, with quick, lithe hops bounded over the days, the months, and the desired hour of her return approached:

> I meet the glad July – and have you in my arms – Oh Susie you shall come
> – . . . Oh my darling one, how long you wander from me; how weary I
> grow of waiting and looking and calling for you, sometimes I shut my
> eyes, and shut my heart towards you, and try hard to forget you because
> you grieve me so, but you will never go away, oh you never will.

Vinnie tapped on Emily's door and hesitantly peeked in. "Emily, dear, I need you to do something for me . . .". "Yes, Vinnie, anything you need!" joyful Emily warmly replied. "For us to go to Washington together!" Vinnie whispered, and seeing the change on her sister's face, she continued in a quick voice, breathless. "You know how much father wants it – and I even more; it was so wonderful when I went before: high society and all those monuments and grand boulevards – you can't imagine! And now to be together there! Oh, come with me, Emily – please!"

The elder sister gave her a look of wide-eyed consternation: "Why, Vinnie – you know that Sue is coming back!" "Sue will always be here," Vinnie returned, "but this chance won't come again! Father wants both of us! I beg of you!" Virtually on her knees, she gazed at Emily with tear-filled eyes. She knew that father would insist on Emily's coming, and there would be an argument. Father had seen Emily falling into the grips of melancholy, and he believed that a change of scene – the sight of the splendid capital – would do her good, as it had when she was younger, mourning the loss of her friend, and her grief was relieved by a trip to Boston. Edward knew, however, that Emily might resist a father's wishes, and that only Austin might persuade her to go. Austin, however, was away at Harvard, and a letter from him would take some time. It only remained for obedient Vinnie to persuade Emily.

Thus Emily came face-to-face with Vinnie, who when asking for something that was resisted, became so distressed and insistent that she overcame all opposition. Thus, Emily felt that resistance was impossible and she accepted accompanying Vinnie to Washington.

Sunday, before they began preparations for the trip, which would last over a month away from Amherst and Sue, Emily wrote another letter:

> Sunday afternoon, so sweet and still, and Thee, Oh Susie, what need I more to make my heaven whole? Sweet Hour, blessed Hour . . . .

The Rev. Charles Wadsworth

Monday morning the sisters would be leaving for Washington where, in addition to sightseeing, they would hear Edward Dickinson address the House of Representatives. That was of slight interest to Emily. In any case, for Vinnie's sake, Emily headed for the capital, while her heart was focused on Sue's return to Amherst.

Contemplating his dear daughters in a hotel room near the center of Washington, Edward Dickinson breathed a sigh of relief. He was pleased with the expression on his gifted daughter's face – his plan was a success! Emily appeared ready to enjoy the stimulation of the capital and get-togethers with colleagues' families. It seemed that everything would work out at a distance from the melancholy and conflict that so often ruled at the Homestead. How magnificent – three weeks in America's splendid first city!

At dinner parties with distinguished families Emily's spirited wit brought a proud smile to Edward's face. He did not know, however, that though his elder daughter appeared carefree, her thoughts were in Amherst and her heart was fixed on Sue and Mattie, to whom she wrote:

> Sweet and soft as summer, Darlings, maple trees in bloom and grass green in sunny places. It hardly seems possible this is winter still; and it makes the grass spring in this heart of mine and each linnet sing to think that you have come . . . Dear children – Mattie – Sue, for one look at you, for your gentle voices I'd exchange it for all The pomp – the court – the etiquette – they of the earth will not enter Heaven . . . Will you write me . . . This is not forever, you know, this mortal life of ours. Which had you rather I wrote you – What I am doing here or who I am loving there? I am coming every hour to your chamber door. I am thinking when I wake, how sweet if you were with me and as I fall asleep, to talk with you will be sweeter still . . . .

Three weeks later, Edward sent the girls on a two-week stay with their Coleman relatives in Philadelphia. In her book about her Aunt Emily, Martha Bianchi, wrote: "[In Philadelphia] Emily met the man of her life," thus focusing attention upon the person with whom Emily established a tie during her visit there – the renowned Charles Wadsworth, the pastor of Arch Street Presbyterian Church, with whom she was to correspond until his death.

Sunday morning at the Coleman's, the three girls began the day with laughter and teasing. They slept in the same room – Emily and Vinnie in one bed and cousin Eliza in the other. They awoke at dawn to the delighted warbling of their young hearts. Eliza, carefree, babbled and giggled as if the joy of life – arrested

Rev. Charles Wadsworth

within her for a year following her sister Olivia's death – had suddenly burst out of the prison of pain and was playfully soaring in an endless flow of words.

"Oh, what a day! It will be a sermon the like of which you've never heard before," Eliza confided smiling, as Emily looked at her beautiful face, thinking, "The shadow of death is a mask fastened to her face. No sermon, no enjoyment, can swiftly eradicate its blackness. Only time can disperse it, if meanwhile it does not become blacker from other deaths and miseries." As she was concluding her thoughts, and they laughed gaily, tears of grief suddenly poured down Eliza's lovely cheeks. Emily hugged her, patted her on the back, and said, "Hush, darling, hush," while into her mind came Poe's poem "Annabelle Lee," expressing the belief that the death of a lovely innocent girl is the most powerful and moving of all themes. "The truth is otherwise, Mr. Poe," Emily whispered within herself. "Death is a personal struggle with the unknown without angels for support and comfort. Death has no explanatory face or voice in our world but it only whispers of nothingness to the one facing it." And she continued her thought sarcastically, "Mr. Poe, Death is not poetic or beautiful; it is only a slashing steel truth. It splits existence asunder."

Vinnie came running with a glass of water for her cousin, and seeing Emily she returned to the kitchen for a second glass. The girls dried their eyes and attempted to cheer up; and Emily, to relieve the emotional intensity, feigned deep interest: "Well, tell me about this minister; I have heard that he is a superb speaker – but tell me, is he striking and idealistic? Is he poetic? A pastor must be poetic. Poetry and the divine are closely linked. Tell me, is he poetic?" Eliza laughingly replied, "He writes poetry but is not a worshipper of Tennyson whom his wife adores." "Ah, at last a poetic pastor, though not a Tennysonian. I'm delighted that he is a devotee of verse!" Emily exclaimed, giving her cousin a big kiss.

"Did you hear what I said: *his wife* . . . . Stop, Emily – stop! Don't fall in love with him – he's married. He does have an assistant, unmarried, whom I *won't* introduce to you. That's out of the question." Blushing, she lowered her voice. "I believe he is going to propose to me."

The cousins danced with joy, and the young assistant pastor did marry Eliza; indeed, as nasty gossip had it, she advanced the date of the marriage and avoided all contact with Emily Dickinson during the engagement period. It was a beautiful wedding. The years allotted to them were happy, but their union was terminated by Eliza's consumption.

Regarding the Reverend Charles Wadsworth, Dickinson scholars have had much to guess at and disagree upon. In any case, it was a grand day in the lives of the three girls. With no thought of the future – only of hurrying that moment to church to see the renowned preacher – they gaily donned their Sunday dresses and best hats. Brimming with health and bright smiles – virtually running from the house to Arch Street church – they arrived a half hour before the beginning of the sermon, finding themselves in a spacious, packed hall of worship. Such an event Emily had never experienced. The sanctuary was crammed, the pews over-flowing, and standing worshippers also lined the walls. Even in the courtyard, people joined the crowd, pushing to get in. Squeezed together in the family pew, the cousins admired the marble work of the church, which is in operation to this day. Breathlessly, they awaited the coming of the celebrated minister.

Suddenly at the pulpit was a charismatic figure clad in a white ecclesiastic robe. He was of medium height, with black hair – a gentle smile reflected in his glowing eyes. Instantly, as if on cue, absolute quiet fell on the congregation, though there were still attempts of late worshippers to push their way in. All eyes were fastened on the minister who somewhat haltingly began to speak. His phrasing, at first faint, tentative, gradually built to lofty rhythms. His eloquent gestures and deep conviction spoke to the depths of the soul.

Throughout the sermon the drop of a pin would have exploded like a shot – so hushed was the silence. The vibrant voice alone rolled through the beautiful sanctuary and pierced the heart – a sacred melody that told the drama of God's incarnation, the glory of his spirit, the anguish of his loneliness and suffering. The offspring of God, yet with human mind and heart, Christ raised a prayer to the Father for the awakening of man's spirit. Breaking with emotion or soaring to lyrical heights, the pastor's voice surpassed the bounds of the soul's capacity to endure inspiration; it touched and "fumbled at the soul," as Emily would put it. Spellbound, Emily was enchanted by the sacred syllables and the profound meaning they evoked. The speaker touched a sense of the divine in accord with her intuition. Mesmerized, she gazed at the minister, who suddenly fell silent and vanished. For a few moments the congregation – as yet dazzled – remained seated; then they thoughtfully filed out through the main door of the church. Emily moved forward assuming that she would meet the pastor at the exit to greet him with a handshake and for him to inquire as to the worshipper's health, as all the Amherst ministers did. To her great surprise, the minister was not in the doorway. With a smile Eliza was quick to whisper that the pastor had vanished down a hidden stairway behind the pulpit that had been built according to his design, and Emily should not expect to greet him – at least not at that time. "But, Eliza," Emily pled, "I must meet him!" Her voice was charged with deep feeling. "All my life I have been seeking a man of God who struggles in the name of faith yet at the same time lives in doubt, as I do – such a minister, far from my neighborhood, parish, and Amherst, I seek. If this minister is such a one, I sorely need him as a spiritual counselor. We must meet!" She tossed her arms in desperation and stressed each word so as to induce Eliza to do all she could. "To such a pastor I could confide my most hidden thoughts with the certainty that he would not judge me, regardless of anything I said." She seemed about to burst into tears.

Eliza at once firmly assured Emily right there in the church courtyard that she would certainly make arrangements. She would convey the request to the Reverend Wadsworth's assistant, who would make an appointment. "Don't worry!" she reassured Emily, and that moment, her father appeared. "Hurry girls!" he said with a smile, "the carriage is waiting!"

Avoiding greetings to friends and neighbors, the three hastened to take their seats in the carriage. Eliza and Vinnie were laughing and tossing off pleasant comments about passers-by on their Sunday promenade, while Emily remained quiet and self-absorbed. Eliza's parents took the seat opposite the cousins, and the driver set off for home. Halfway there, Emily suddenly felt a tremor from head to toe. She felt a chill and she was short of breath. As her sight turned inward, she relived the tragic scene that had taken place the year before in this very carriage. Eliza's older sister, Olivia – attired in an airy spring dress and flowery hat – was laughing gaily when she was seized by a persistent cough. The blood of death ran from the mouth that a moment before held the laughter of life, and alarmed everyone, who bent over her asking, "How do you feel? Olivia! Olivia!" and Emily imagined Olivia slumping back in the seat, eyes closed, the horses galloping on, passing along familiar streets, by the school, the cemetery; and the driver – a chivalrous Knight – did not look back but only gazed forward toward Eternity, as the young girl ceased coughing and her lovely head collapsed on her ensanguined breast, her eyes closed in a deep, eternal sleep. The scene was stamped forever within Emily – forever etched in words: "Because I could not stop for death / He kindly stopped for me."

Olivia's noble escort wore the mask of forever, and she – stunned – accepted the journey into the unknown. Emily bid Olivia farewell in her heart as not long before she had said good-bye to Cousin Emily, who had been with her at Mount Holyoke and she, too, had left life behind. Consumption claimed the young girls – Cousin Emily twenty-six, Olivia nineteen. "Nineteen, and I twenty-three!" Emily told herself, and the desire to see the Reverend Wadsworth became a life-or-death need. "I absolutely must speak with the pastor," she said, interrupting her silence. Taking her hand Eliza knowingly whispered as they entered the house, "Everything is arranged – you'll see him in two days." "Thank you, Eliza!" Emily sighed with relief.

Late in the afternoon, she came out of the church. Her face held the absent look of a person who is contemplating the serious concerns of existence. They troubled her but at the same time elicited spiritual euphoria, a divine inebriation. She was soaring in an unknown, mysterious sphere. Vinnie and Eliza, who were waiting breathlessly in the church courtyard, viewed her emerge with radiant eyes and a blissful expression of gleaming thoughts. Seizing her hands, they avidly questioned, "What did you say all this time? What did you talk about? Why did you take so long?" These queries were put to an Emily who was not present – her mind and heart had remained in the small antechamber by the sanctuary, where the pastor and she had sat and talked. Her spirit had overflowed with sacred feelings, ethereal ideas. Her face glowed with a personal ecstasy that could not be expressed in words but was etched deep in her being – transcendent perceptions, which would later emerge in her poems.

She had, at long last, met the man of her life. Equals in thought and expression, they had spoken of earthly and heavenly things in the same idiom of the soul. They had felt such a tender rapport that the minister had not hesitated to confide in her, "My life is filled with dark secrets." This confidence stirred her heart with a love that dwelt in the realm of holy things. The girls looked at Emily, questioned, pleaded, insisted; but she did not hear them. She was thinking (#315):

He fumbles at your Soul
As Players at the Keys
Before they drop full Music on –
He stuns you by degrees –
Prepares your brittle Nature
For the Ethereal Blow
By fainter Hammers – further heard –
Then nearer – Then so slow
Your Breath has time to straighten –
Your Brain – to bubble Cool –
Deals – One – imperial – Thunderbolt –
That scalps your naked Soul –

The Tragic Triangle

When Winds take Forests in their Paws –
The Universe – is still –

A second Sunday they witnessed the glory of his service, and the middle of the following week, with leaden heart, Emily took her seat in the train, and Vinnie anxiously attempted to dispel the melancholy that was spreading over the angelic countenance of her sister. "What a wonderful time we had – eh, Emily? You enjoyed it, didn't you?" Emily did not voice the least satisfaction, and Vinnie, unabashed, strove to retrieve moments, faces, conversations, scenes, and significant politicians invited to dinner, but Emily remained mute. Only at the mention of the word significant did Emily seem to hear Vinnie. She turned toward her and exploded. "The only significant personage whom I met during this visit is the Reverend Wadsworth! Oh, Vinnie, I will never forget that meeting!" Her eyes filled with tears. "If only I could express how his words inspired me! What deep analysis of theology! Ah, would that he were in Amherst, so I could have a spiritual counselor whom I could trust – to whom I could confess the doubts that plague me! Only to an aware pastor could I express my spiritual anguish and purge my mind, so I would not be troubled night and day." The tears overflowed and she wiped them away with a white handkerchief that she drew now and then from her little purse. "You could write him. Correspondence is your delight! Write him, Emily – write him!" Vinnie said to her sister with the confidence of one who has found the solution.

Leaning close, Emily whispered in a child-like voice, "Oh, Vinnie, he's such a handsome man! A very handsome man, but married!" The tears overflowed. "He's married, I tell you!"

The other – wide-eyed, taken aback – did not reply.

The wooden seats of the train seemed even narrower, even harder; and the continuous rocking of the coach made the long return to Massachusetts trying. Exhausted, the sisters leaned against one another, attempting to find relief in sleep; but their rest was interrupted by the blast of train's whistle, the thumping of the wheels, and the restlessness of their fellow passengers. When dawn finally came and light outlined the shapes of houses and trees, Vinnie took Emily's hand and she responded with a faint smile. Slowly crossing the Connecticut valley and reaching Amherst, the train arrived at the station near the Homestead, and Emily viewed the neighborhood as the coaches jerked to a stop. There, near the platform by a tree, she saw the silhouettes of her two beloved friends. Her soul filled with delight. She seized Vinnie's hand and hurried toward the door shouting, "Sue and Mattie have come to welcome us – though it's so early in the morning!" Pushing past Joseph, who had come to take their bags, and gently replying to his greeting, she hastened to step down to the platform. Her friends stood near the coach steps, and she jumped into their arms with little delighted outbursts. She held Sue close, who whispered a complaint. "You haven't written me during the last two weeks, and I missed you so much!"

"I have so much to tell you!" Emily burst out, and the two laughed, holding one another in a warm loving hug.

Sue also had much to tell Emily, but she said not a word about stopping over in Boston, as if it had never happened.

Boston Stopover

The end of the term arrived, the school year complete, and Sue reluctantly prepared her suitcase for the return trip to the dark precincts of Amherst. The thought of the town alone was enough to make her heart sink. Should she, or she should not, go on living in such a town? There were so many painful memories. Only the presence of her sister Mattie and her friendship with Emily lifted her spirit. Mattie was waiting for her with open arms, but the other – her friend – had chosen this time for a trip to Washington. To do what? And from there she would be travelling to Philadelphia. When, then, would she return? Sue proceeded toward the station disturbed by unpleasant thoughts, which made her steps weary and hesitant. Sighing as she entered the coach, she took a seat. The thought that she had hitherto managed to avoid – Austin's invitation to a rendezvous in Boston – pulsed in her mind. "How much I yearn to see you, my love," Austin had written to her, and in an impulsive moment she had said yes. Truly she wanted to see him. That the train would be going through Boston provided an excuse. Yes, it would only delay her return for a few hours. She would see Austin, they would talk for a while, and she would catch the next train to Amherst.

Exhausted to the core, she stepped down onto the platform in Boston. Gingerly she descended from the coach. Her knees felt watery and she swayed as her feet touched the platform. A light rain and damp fog clung to her face and dimmed her sight. Wiping the dampness from her cheeks, she strained to discern the handsome figure of the young man who claimed to love her passionately. She saw him dashing toward her, and then she grasped her great mistake. What if an acquaintance caught sight of them? That moment out of the corner of her eye she thought she saw a young Dickinson neighbor who studied at Harvard. However, as the youth was bending over, his hat turned against the rain, she did not see his face clearly. She was not sure it was he; but the suspicion froze her. Her feet did not support a hasty retreat, and that moment Austin's hand tenderly touched her arm. Without even greeting him, she indicated with a shift of her gaze the young man who was disappearing among the crowd. The carelessness of their encounter weighed upon the moment, and her face remained tense, unsmiling. She prayed for invisibility and resolved to make the visit short so that everything would turn out well. Austin's fingers moved around her arm, and she trembled as if she felt a chilling breeze, though the temperature was pleasant. Looking at her companion, she permitted an urgent thought to form in a sigh: "Shouldn't I get back on the train and at once continue on to Amherst?"

Austin bent toward her and the scent of his damp hair brought her an intense memory that made her heart throb. His wet face, his smell, his eyes looking at her intensely, brought to mind Emily when as girls they had met that rainy day near the Academy. As they took one another by the hand, they were sprinkled by a sudden spring shower. They had felt such a great inexplicable joy . . . . That same ineffable joy swept her away as she looked at her beau – the beloved brother of her friend. Austin took her gently by the arm and she smiled. "My darling, my darling!" he whispered with yearning, as he bent to take her bag. "Welcome, my love; it's so wonderful you've come," he said softly so as not to be overheard and nodded toward the exit they would take. "Only a block away I have secured a room. It isn't far. You look exhausted, my poor dear . . .".

Sue was indeed totally worn out; she had traveled twenty hours seated on a narrow wooden bench. During the night the coach was filled with disturbances. Sounds of conversation, babies crying, arrivals at stations, and changes of trains had not permitted her to catch a wink of sleep. Moreover, the final days in Baltimore with academic duties and preparations for the trip had hardly been easy. She had arrived at Boston drained of energy, but that wasn't the source of the problem. What truly wearied her, body-and-soul, were her feelings toward Austin. She wanted to see him – that was why she had agreed to get together in Boston; but precisely what did the rendezvous mean? Did she really love him truly as her future husband? Did she honor him as a wife who would stand by his side in joy and pride? And would this Boston stopover itself be decisive? Or, feeling uncertain, should she hastily withdraw? True – in a moment of weakness she had given in to the impulse to meet him; perhaps it would show her that she loved him. Here they were together, yet her quandary was not resolved! She was by his side, but her heart did not quiver with delight. He was, as always, a truly dashing gentleman – but what of that? Love also demanded other less worldly feelings.

She responded to the situation with a strained smile. As Austin gazed at her weary eyes, he wanted to smother her in kisses, to prevent her sloshing in the chilly puddles by carrying her in his arms. "My love – my heart – a nice warm room and comfy bed await you, so you can relax, sleep, and recover. You will see!" he told her. Oh, how he yearned to touch her tenderly, but he dared not do so, lest the eye of an acquaintance witness the intimate gesture.

She awoke in a dim red light late in the afternoon lying in a soft bed, and sitting close was the young patrician passionately gazing at her, without the velvet waistcoat and silk foulard that were carelessly flung aside. Austin's immaculate white shirt was open to the waist and his sinewy thighs were outlined in his tight, fashionably cut trousers. His feet were bare – his arms reaching toward her this vital moment of her refreshed awakening. Weak rays of light penetrated the red curtains, casting crimson on the floor, the bed, and her reclined figure. Her eyes were open as if she were awake, but she found herself enclosed in another enthralling dream. She stretched her body in a slow, soft movement. The moisture that poured through her steeped her in an arousal such as she had never experienced before. Her gaze united with the yearning eyes of her companion. For a moment he as yet held back; then his feline desire surged and drove him. His hands touched her, galvanizing her desire. Their bodies quaked without words. There were only heavy, slow, panting breaths exchanging agreements and pledges of love. They felt indescribable harmony. Slowly Austin pressed his length upon her. Sue closed her eyes, parted her lips, and he breathlessly, hoarsely whispered her name. His lips trembled upon hers and his fiery breath joined hers. Mesmerized, she melted into him like one wave joined to another in a heaving sea. One of her arms was locked around his slim waist and the fingers of her other hand were plunged into his thick scarlet locks.

The Price

Whistling regularly at crossings, the train moved steadily along, stopping every so often to release and take on passengers. Seated by the coach window, Sue stared at the forested countryside. Her numb brain was incapable of setting even one thought in order. From the moment that the train had powerfully, rhythmically, set out, a poem of Emily's kept repeating itself in her head and whispering on her lips, entirely beyond her control. Her mind absolutely rejected any review or assessment – any coherent memory – of the erotic explosion in the hotel room with Austin. Emily's childlike lines alone kept running on and on *(#585):*

I like to see it lap the Miles –
And lick the Valleys up –
Then stop to feed itself at Tanks –
And then – prodigious step

Around a Pile of Mountains –
And supercilious peer
In Shanties – by the sides of Roads –
And then a Quarry pare

To fit its Ribs
And crawl between
Complaining all the while
In horrid-hooting stanza –
Then chase itself down Hill –

And neigh like Boanerges –
Then – punctual as a Star
Stop – docile and omnipotent
At its own stable door –

Mattie was waiting for her with a smile on the platform of Amherst station. Calmness filled Sue's heart. She lifted her suitcase and rushed to the door of the coach so as to be the first off the train. She embraced her dear younger sister and without knowing that it was coming on, burst into a rain of tears. As Mattie's eyes also overflowed, she tenderly patted Sue on the back, both of them laughing and using handkerchiefs.

"I don't know what has come over me!" Sue exclaimed, and Mattie replied, "Don't ever go away again! Never again!"

Arm-in-arm they set out for home. When they were about to turn the corner to the house, Mattie suddenly stopped Sue, drew her close, and gazed intensely into her eyes. Alarmed, Sue felt her knees tremble as a suspicion burned in her mind.

"Is it known?" she asked. Mattie nodded her head affirmatively. "Does Harriet know?" Sue asked in alarm.

"Yes," Mattie returned, "and your brother-in-law knows, too. Be prepared for a storm. But I beg of you, Sue – be patient, don't make things worse . . .".

Sue remained silent, walking quickly – virtually running – to the house she disdained. Without knocking, she opened the door and found older sister Harriet standing stiff with rage in the parlor. Her arms across her chest, she was glaring with disapproval. Sue glared back and without a greeting carried her suitcase upstairs to her bedroom.

In her cramped room she weighed for the first time the Boston episode – the deed and the cost. It was terribly great! She was overcome – she could not justify her action. A wave of rage against Austin seized her and sank her in despair. "It's his fault. He forced me to stop over, and he didn't shield my honor. He's unmanly, dishonorable, disgusting, and crude! To take advantage of a helpless, innocent creature!" These were the first words to spring to her mind regarding the man she had respected. Now she realized he was not exempt from a "man's requirements," as she and Emily called them. "He was slovenly, bestial, monstrous," she summed it up. All that was left for her to do was to dismiss him from her mind – to turn her thoughts toward healing calm, but the monster Austin permeated her brain; confusion reigned in her heart.

Sue was back again at the same point in her life – in that dark miserable room in her sister's house. Soon William Cutler would be at it again with snide, sarcastic remarks. For her brother-in-law, Sue was not the picture of what a "proper lady" should be, and he did everything he could to humiliate her.

Admittedly, life in the house was no longer as exhausting as it had been before the sad loss of the baby, who had made great demands on her energy. Still, it was a hostile environment. She had to hold the others at a distance as best she could, and this kept her in a continual state of tension. Her nerves were always on edge, making her prone to foolish outbursts. Austin dominated her mind; it was as he had a grip on her brain. She thought of him day and night, her feelings continually shifting. In logical moments doubt was dominant. Her mind was riddled with questions that she could not answer – the main one being, *how did she really feel about the young patrician?* Indeed, she had stopped in Boston to find an answer to that very question, yet now she was more than ever uncertain of the answer. Was he the right choice for her husband? Was he the life-long companion of her soul? She shrugged her shoulders. As for the key issue – *did she love him?* – that immediately led to the more precise query: *Would she* come *to love him?* In the meantime the irreparable act had taken place, which meant that the answer to the question was irrelevant. She was in a terrible quandary – her situation could not have been worse. Moreover, Emily was away in Philadelphia and would not be back for two weeks. And if Emily had heard about Boston – then things would go from bad to worse! The only blessed presence she could now rely on was Mattie, whose steady good will and gentleness were shown in every action. For Mattie the tie between Sue and Austin was truly fortunate. She spoke to Sue warmly of Austin and the great rewards that awaited her, and for the first time Sue realized the deep affection Mattie felt toward him. Her every word was praise for his gentility and beauty of spirit. She characterized him with silken phrases, showing not a trace of jealousy on her part. On the contrary, she was overjoyed with her beloved sister's success. The realization of Mattie's deep affection for Austin was painful to Sue, for Austin had once preferred her to Sue; but events had taken their course, and nothing could be done to erase the pang in Sue's conscience.

Back in the routine of Amherst life, Sue found an outlet in correspondence. Her first letter was to a young man with whom her relationship had been more intense than mere friendship. To Edward Hitchcock, son of the headmaster of Amherst Academy, she wrote: "I hope a snowstorm will give new life to the town, for we are as quiet as if the Plague had ravaged the streets." She wrote to her friends, the Bartletts (she was particularly impressed by Mr. Bartlett's perceptiveness): "[I am] making all sorts of attempts to seem happy, when in fact I am really homesick for you all." To her brother she wrote: "... As for me – I sew – make all the pies and cakes – sweep and dust – do errands – try a little to make others happy – and be rather useful – [actually I'm] rather ornamental – rather superfluous. Congratulate me that I have found someone who by and by is going to encumber himself with me."

Sarcasm and bitterness poured out with particular force toward Austin, who wrote passionately to her of the love she had granted him, her caresses, her wondrous body, her pure soul. He was striving to be worthy of her, impatiently awaiting the moment they would be united in bliss. Then he received her return letter ...

It was as if he had been struck by a bolt of lightning on the sunniest day of his life. Numbed, he placed the letter on top of his law books and nervously paced around his desk in the dormitory, eyeing the acid missive from afar, not daring to touch it, unable to acknowledge the attitude it expressed, hoping that the text books on justice on which the letter lay would transform the meaning and tone of its words. Finally he ceased pacing and carefully took the sheet in hand, praying that the first reading was faulty – she had intended to say something else! There was a misunderstanding that he would be able to disentangle; he would find the proper solution.

He read vigilantly, excavating the words, searching for redeeming nuances – but the sentences remained the same, bursting with exasperation, anger, and recriminations, calling him a "monster." He was hurled into an abyss of disappointment and confusion. Sue was so gentle and pure! Where could those words about him have come from? Was he really an ogre whose only thought was to exploit her helplessness and trust in him? With sinking heart he shut the poisonous message in a drawer and turned once more to circling the room. The space was too cramped to ease his sadness, so he decided though it was late to take a walk by the river. He did not, however, linger long but rushed back to his room, perused the letter anew, and burst into tears. After some time he grew calm and wrote to Sue, expressing his love and distress, promising her that he would fulfill "every desire of her soul, every need of her spirit, and every aspiration of her existence." Maybe she was right to blame his behavior; in any case, she would never have cause to doubt him again. He proposed that they marry at once so that eternal love would seal the happiness she deserved, ending the letter with the complaint of a little boy: "I want to go to Amherst, see my sisters and parents, look them in the face, and from their eyes tell if I am really the monster you say I am."

In her reply, Sue affirmed that he was indeed a monster and it had all come about because "You have not given yourself to Jesus, and on account of that your acts are sinful." Austin admitted it was true that he had not confessed belief and hastened to promise that as soon as he got back to Amherst he would rush to the minister and make a pledge of faith. What he could not accept, however, was her doubt about her love for him, which she had expressed at the end of her letter. He at once wrote to her: "No, my precious Sue, we cannot marry unless you are absolutely certain that you love me, or can come to love me. I adore you so much that it is enough for both of us, but you must be absolutely certain about our marriage – only then will you be happy. I worship you and will wait for you." The word *marriage* shook Sue, for though she was somewhat softened by his words of love, the thought of marriage frightened her and she discovered one reason after another to point out the weaknesses of his personality, especially the fact that he wanted to remain in Amherst though the West held greater promise for the younger generation. Why should they not build a life on the frontier? Austin hastened to agree that they would leave their small town and go to Illinois, Michigan, or anywhere else they determined.

In the meantime, life had become unbearable not only with her brother-in-law but also with her sister Harriet, both of whom were increasingly petty and demanding about Sue's behavior at home and in town. Harriet insisted, for example, that Sue continue to wear black in memory of their tragically lost sister, Maria, and that she limit her visits to the Dickinsons. Furthermore, her economic situation, which had always been difficult, was worsening. She found herself on a dry, barren path; she had to make a decision about marriage. The truth was that Austin was coming closer to fulfilling her needs, and she felt better about the relationship. He was responding to her demands: they would have a life together in the distant west; he would be a husband who accepted Jesus; she would have social and economic independence. She would be the daughter-in-law of Edward Dickinson, whom she deeply respected, and of Emily Norcross, whom she could tolerate. Vinnie – simple minded, cunning, unread – she could easily ignore. Austin's dear sister, Emily, however, was the great, as yet unwritten, chapter in Sue's life. If she remained in Amherst, what would their relationship be? Or, how would Emily react to their moving away, thus depriving her of both herself and her dear brother Austin? How would the whole family react to their departure? Her life with Austin would be pleasant enough, provided she could find peace with him in her heart by obeying logic. Yet her heart – disturbed, unreceptive – refused to say yes. The road to the future as yet seemed tortured and uncertain. Two weeks passed with a disheartening exchange of letters with Austin, involving accusations and excuses. The thought of Emily alone was enough to evoke a variety of feelings and a wild beating in her breast, as the moment of the return of the sisters from Philadelphia was upon her. Sue, with her sister, hurried to the station to meet her friend and future sister-in-law.

Sue and Emily met in the alcove under the stairs, the "Northwest Passage" as they called it – in that hideaway far from everyone's eyes. They hugged and kissed without uttering a word. Her arms about Emily, Sue thought, "I will build a nest in her embrace, not she in mine." She recalled lines from a poem by Emily: "For me this nest is a home built with love." She pressed against her friend wiping her eyes as they both thought, "What a miraculous comfort to the soul are the arms of a friend!"

Alone in Boston, Austin was under intense pressure from his studies, and his inability to concentrate in spite of his efforts was deeply disturbing. His frequent correspondence with Sue continued in the same spirit with which it had begun. Though he had promised to accept Christ, his situation for Sue was evident – the atrocious sin of continuing distance from faith. Poor Austin knew this was no fault of his. He was true to his promise of attending services two times a week. He had made every effort to listen to sermons that would inspire his soul, guide his spirit to the proper path, and amend his character. But his heart went untouched, and the time and effort went for nothing. He was unable to listen to scripture readings to the end, follow the whole sermon, and ponder application of its teachings. As finals approached, exhausted by weeks of mental effort, continually worried by the loss of valuable time, he found himself in a panic because there was no time left to complete the material. Thus, in the midst of services, his eyes would grow heavy, but he learned to go into a near sleep with his eyes open, so he would not draw the attention of the congregation. Back in the dormitory, anguishing over his failures, he missed meals. At his desk, he was increasingly unsuccessful in his studies and he thought of the one person who might be able to help him. Without going into detail, he wrote to Emily about his lonely situation. She at once replied, suggesting that he immediately come home for two or three days in order to rest. As for loneliness, she had a different view, which she added at the end of her letter: "Loneliness is the great university of the self. When you do not converse with another, you concentrate on thoughts that are bright and golden . . . . The continual contact with friends impoverishes ideas and feelings; . . . the completion of perceptions is lost."

She wrote this without a full picture of Austin's situation, and only when he appeared at the kitchen door with his small knapsack did she understand. Mother gave him a tender hug – something she hadn't done in years. "Why so melancholy, my boy – why?" she kept saying, comforting him. "Don't go on, mother," he returned, gripping Sue's last warm letter in his pocket. "It's just an awful exam period, but it will soon be over and everything will be all right – you'll see! Just bring me one of your wonderful meals, and I'll be fit as a fiddle!"

Emily looked at Austin with deep concern. She adored her brother. Whatever slips he might make did not matter – only his happiness and health were important. She was even willing to give up Sue for his sake, though her own heart would bleed. "Sue is coming over this afternoon," she hastened to say in order to please him. "We planned to surprise you, but I had to tell you now. We talk only of you. Oh, Austin, she loves you so much, and I am happy too; Henry Emmons calls on me often, and we go on drives to Sunderland."

Austin was dazed. He couldn't believe all might finally be well. He had been in despair, yet Emily, who always understood what was going on, confirmed that Sue did love him! And it was so wonderful that Emily had a serious gentleman caller. But wait a minute – hadn't he heard that Henry Emmons, a sophomore at Amherst, was engaged to a friend of Emily's?

Austin was enjoying the moment as Emily warbled about the splendid visits she and Vinnie had in Washington and Philadelphia. That moment the door burst open and Vinnie entered the kitchen in a rage. As usual, she was trailed by her cats, who also attempted to enter, but with her foot she forcefully kept them outside as she closed the door. Emily and Austin looked at Vinnie in surprise, for she had never done that before. Since Vinnie adored her pets and always treated them gently, such behavior showed that she was truly beside herself.

As Vinnie hugged Austin and gave him a perfunctory kiss, she looked at him with a sharp question in her eyes.

"What is going on, Vinnie?" Emily demanded.

"Don't worry," Vinnie barked, "I put them in their place. I told them to mind their own business!"

That moment, there was a knock on the door, and Mattie entered, Sue following her. They meekly entered the kitchen and hugged Austin, who was trembling, his heart pounding as if it would burst. Kissing him on the cheek, they smiled and tried to appear gay until they felt Vinnie glaring at them with a mouth full of the words she had in her mind. Without a greeting, she poured out, "In this town people don't have anything better to do than stick their noses into other people's affairs! Do you know what Jane dared to ask me, though we've been friends for years? 'When was Austin engaged but you kept me in the dark?' she asked me. She has always dreamed of having Austin for herself. 'And where,' I asked her, 'did you hear of such a thing?' though I knew very well it was probably Mrs. Sweetser, who's behind all the gossip about what's going on in the Homestead. 'Don't play innocent with me!' Jane answered. 'What was Sue doing in *Boston* last week, if not meeting Austin?'"

Emily froze, her gaze going back and forth between Sue and her brother. Ready to burst into tears, Sue blurted, "I stopped in Boston to visit my ophthalmologist and just happened to run into Austin!" "That's right," Austin swiftly confirmed, addressing Vinnie, while he was thinking of Emily's reaction. "We ran into each other at a tea parlor, and we talked a while before she caught the train for Amherst."

A frozen silence descended. The tension in Sue's voice and Austin's ill-disguised nervousness told the story. Emily understood, and a paleness came over her face as if her heart had stopped pumping. Very slowly and wearily, without uttering a syllable, she arose from the chair, left the kitchen, and went through the hallway. All eyes were on her as she disappeared down the hall. Then came the sound of her steps on the stairs, the closing of her door, and the turning of the key in the lock.

A pall fell over them all. Life had taken a turn, and from that crucial moment their relationships would change forever. The figure of Emily had disappeared from their sight. Her door had shut – not violently or noisily, but with a decisive pull. The sound of the turning key had been deeply unsettling. They all foresaw the changes their future held. A ghastly silence weighed on their hearts. They sat with bowed heads. Vinnie longed to have swallowed her words, Austin repented coming to Amherst, and Sue trembled uncontrollably. Mattie wordlessly dried her eyes, her habitual smile erased. She took her sister by the arm and pulled her to her feet, saying to Austin in a low voice, "I'm glad you are engaged. You will be happy together. All will be well." Austin gratefully kissed Mattie on the forehead. He reached out and held Sue by the shoulders. "I love you, Sue – I swear!" The Gilbert sisters opened the door, and Vinnie's cats scrambled freely into the kitchen as the sisters went out the door and across the lawn toward the street.

To change our lives takes time and painful effort, but when life changes by itself, an instant suffices for an utter transformation.

That moment Emily knew her life had changed forever. Through her window she watched Sue and Mattie cross the yard, the one walking unsteadily and the other holding her tightly. Emily felt weak and hollow. With misty eyes she followed the two silhouettes partially hidden by the trees. She stood on the tips of her toes, though her legs were trembling slightly, stretched her neck, and saw the tips of their heads as the girls moved into the distance, reached the corner, and disappeared.

The road was deserted, empty – like her life. Now there was no one. Everyone had left her. One-by-one her friends had taken husbands, had children, vanished from her life. Now it was Sue's turn – her most beloved . . . "Why, Sue, why? How could you shove aside the tenderness I feel for you?" That moment she perceived that the relationship she desired could not be realized (#84):

Her breast is fit for pearls,
But I was not a "Diver" –
Her brow is fit for thrones
But I have not a crest.
Her heart is fit for home-
I – a Sparrow – build there
Sweet of twigs and twine
My perennial nest.

She saw even the nest being torn down and her life at a disastrous cross-road. Her precious friend was taking the heavily trodden road: she would marry, have children, and take a distance from her life; but what road would she take?

Disheartened Loneliness, arm-in-arm with angry Agony, noiselessly crossed Emily's threshold and with the ease of familiar companions took a seat on her bed. Emily collapsed to the floor.

She felt profound anger – or rather, outrage. The knife of betrayal had slashed her open, and she knew that from this wound her life would drain. How dare they lie so shamelessly! If Sue had simply run into Austin by chance and passed some time together, it would have been the first thing she would have told Emily. The shielding of the truth was evident, and Austin's sadness was the proof of failure of the meeting, which was their concern. Hers was that the two people whom she loved more than anyone else on earth – these precious friends – had betrayed her, had left her uninvolved in the great decision affecting all of their lives.

They had acted together selfishly and shoved her aside!

Sadness, an angry sea, had struck and obliterated the dream of her life. Those two – in spite of the great love she had given them – had cheated her, had abandoned her. It was all over! Neighborhood people may be crude – crudeness is the prerogative of the ignorant. But their judgment was correct: Austin was engaged without informing the family; he had to marry Sue. She – Emily – was outside their life. What role could she play, and what would her life be without the absolute devotion of Sue? "Ah, if only we were children, living as children forever!" She broke into great sobs and refused to answer the knocking at her door. She did not want to talk to Austin or Vinnie, or whoever wanted to enter. She had to think, or rather, to weep – to weep for the huge portion of her self that was dead. She had to mourn its loss and bury it – but how could she manage that? How could she bury the thought of Sue? It would be like burying also her own mind, heart, and soul. What would be left? She was thrown into emptiness, consigned to nothingness. Joy was gone forever. What remained was only a blank resulting from the demise of ineffable joy, of all delightful thoughts, of every deep feeling – those things that lead to glorious inspiration. Inspiration was her life. Now there was nothing. Austin and Sue gone, her own joys and desires defeated. Sue was a member of her family but never again the object of her passion.

Emily understood that while many facets of life may be transient, if passion ceases, the very capacity to continue living is negated. There is only anguish for lost ecstasy – insurmountable mourning. Moreover, the higher one has mounted in happiness, the lower one falls. From now on her life would proceed with two all-encompassing companions – Loneliness and Agony! Could she endure?

She turned to look at the two figures seated on the edge of her bed. Loneliness was a melancholy girl, plunged into meditative silence. There was something appealing about this figure. It reflected her soul. The other person, Agony, was advanced in age with a countenance strangely etched. Her features, deformed, conveyed the indelible mark of decline. Her right cheek and eye were sketched with wild fear: her left held vast rage. *"Can I live with Agony?"* she tearfully asked. She sat by Loneliness, embraced her, and looked Agony straight in the eye (#241):

I like a look of Agony,
Because I know it's true –
Men do not sham Convulsion,
Nor simulate, a Throe –

The Eyes glaze once – and that is Death –
Impossible to feign
The Beads upon the Forehead
By homely Anguish strung.

Shutting herself in her small room, Sue understood her insuperable situation. Fate had brought her to this infernal pass, and of course it was not her own fault but Emily's. Astray, she lived afar from Jesus, as did her brother, and that would bring her unhappiness which she truly did not deserve. Sue wrote her a letter, which Vinnie in great anger burned, but we have Emily's intense response, sent that Tuesday morning:

> Sue – you can go or stay – There is but one alternative – We differ often lately, and this must be the last . . .
>
> You need fear no more to leave me, lest I should be alone, for I often part with things I fancy I have loved, – sometimes in the grave, and sometimes to an oblivion rather bitterer than death – thus my heart bleeds so frequently that I shant mind the hemorrhage, and I only add an agony to several previous ones, and at the end of day remark – a bubble burst . . .
>
> It is the lingering emblem of the Heaven I once dreamed, and though if this be taken, I shall remain alone, and though in that last day, the Jesus Christ you love, remark he doesn't know me – there is a darker spirit will not disown its child . . .
>
> We have walked very pleasantly – Perhaps this is the point at which our paths diverge – then pass on singing Sue, and up the distant hill I journey on.
>
> Emily

The decision was made. She would continue the journey of her life alone, with a personal chest in her room into which she would consign, as if they were ghosts, friends, relatives, the entire town, and she would never look at them again.

A third time Vinnie mounted the stairs. The game played by the two friends infuriated her. "Emily!" she nervously burst out the moment she opened the door, "Sue is here and says that she is not about to leave if you do not come down and talk to her. She even threatens to go out in the yard and stay there as long as necessary night and day, until you come down and see her." And she emphasized coldly, "She's crying broken heartedly, but do as you please! I'm going to my room and won't climb these stairs one more time!"

Vinnie slammed the door. Without haste, Emily arose and descended the stairs. Shrinking in her familiar corner, Sue was leaning her head against the wall, her eyes closed and swollen. Emily came to her, reached out and gently stroked her face, and Sue opened her glazed, blood-shot eyes and moaned in a stricken voice, "I beg you, Emily, accept me as your sister. Love me," she murmured, "love me! How can I go on living without your tenderness?"

Emily said not a word – she just put her arm around Sue's waist, and thus the two held one another, sobbing. "Yes, Sue, you are my sister," Emily whispered. The tears subsided, and Sue knew she would soon receive a loving poem (#14).

One Sister have I in our house,
And one, a hedge away.
There's only one recorded,
But both belong to me.

One came the road that I came –
And wore my last year's gown –
The other, as a bird her nest,
Builded our hearts among.

She did not sing as we did –
It was a different tune –
Herself to her a music
As Bumble bee of June.

Today is far from Childhood –
But up and down the hills
I held her hand the tighter –
Which shortened all the miles –

And still her hum
The years among,
Deceives the Butterfly;
Still in her Eye
The Violets lie
Mouldered this many May.

I spilt the dew –
But took the morn –
I chose this single star
From out the wide night's numbers –
Sue – forevermore!

On Sue's face a smile returned, which Emily joined. Sue kissed Emily tenderly and left with an air of content. As Emily watched her depart, tears of bitterness and anger burst from her eyes. "Why Sue – why were you so fearful?" she questioned. "Why did you hesitate?"   (# 446)

I showed her Heights she never saw –
"Would'st Climb," I said?
She said – "Not so" –
"With me –" I said – With me?
I showed her Secrets – Morning's nest –
The Rope the Nights were put across –

And now – *"Would'st you have me for a Guest"?*
She could not find her Yes –
And then, I brake my life – And Lo,
A Light, for her, did solemn glow,
The larger, as her face withdrew –
And could she, further, "No"?

In her anguish, where could she seek solace? Tearfully she sat down at her little desk and penned a letter to the Reverend Wadsworth. A reply came at once:

My Dear Miss Dickenson [*sic*]:

I am distressed beyond measure at your note received this moment, – I can only imagine the Affliction which has befallen, or is now befalling you.

Believe me, be what it may, you have all my sympathy, and my constant earnest prayers.

I am very, very anxious to learn more definitely of your trial. And though I have no right to intrude on your sorrow, yet I beg you to write me, though it be but a word.

In great haste,
Sincerely and most
Affectionately yours –
Charles Wadsworth

We do not have her letter to her friend, but it appears she had written to him of her distress, her "Affliction," in general terms. She did, however, express her pain – her sorrow, as Wadsworth put it. He responded with deep sympathy, with a slip in the spelling of her name, and thus began the correspondence that lasted until his death.

Henry Vaughan Emmons

In this short Life
That only lasts an hour
How much – how little – is
Within our power
(# 1287)

Henry Vaughan Emmons

Emily Dickinson: Goddess of the Volcano

Fiery young Henry Vaughan Emmons frequently dropped by in his buggy at Emily's door. He knew that usually Emily would find an excuse not to come with him, but when she did accept his invitation and went on a ride to Sunderland, it was the "sugaring" of his spirit and soul. The time he spent with her was like an electrical charge; it energized precious thoughts and analysis. Emily was the only person who could truly fire his heart and mind. She nudged him deeper into every perception and inspired his articulation of extraordinary ideas. From the moment Cousin John introduced him to Emily, he had been distinguishing himself in his studies. Though his fiancée, Susan Phelps, was a fine, beautiful girl who loved him as he loved her, she was not drawn to deep thought, while from boyhood thought had determined the direction of Emmons's life.

At the age of fifteen, he left his home in Northampton and the rule of his pious father, a judge. Life there had not granted him what he thirsted for, and he had to act. He went to Amherst where friends took him into their house. He enrolled in Amherst Academy, and that was the beginning of his development. Later, as a student at Amherst College, he met Emily, a few years older than he, who became the great inspiration of his life. She shared with him a sense of the mystery of language, the expressiveness of style, the great power of metaphor, the splendor of verse. Every time he received one of her letters, he trembled with delight reading it and analyzing its import, syllable-by-syllable. A missive of hers never contained a mundane thought or commonplace locution, and exegesis of her strange metaphors was his supreme delight.

Vinnie hastily climbed the stairs whispering, "Thank God – thank God!" She believed Emmons was the answer to her prayers. It was especially auspicious that the sun was shining with delight after the morning rain. All the clouds had cleared; the sun stood sole master in the skies. Everything was so joyous that it seemed the Lord himself was conspiring to bring Emmons to Emily's door. Vinnie, heart bursting with excitement, entered the room and gazed at her sister. "Emily," she said gently, but also firmly, "Come at once – Emmons has come calling. He is dressed in his best and has a book – surely it's Wordsworth! Come, go with him to take the air and sunlight!" Emily stood with an inward expression, as if she did not hear her sister. "Emily! – either go for a ride with that fine young man, or at least personally inform him you can't go out today." Vinnie took her by the arm, drew her from the room, and led her down to the living room where her handsome friend was waiting. At once he sprang from the armchair and with a deep smile reached out to her. Emily responded as if she were awakening from a trance. "I won't keep you long, Emily," he said eagerly, "I want to discuss with you a lecture I'm writing. Please . . .". Emmons's pleading eyes expressed much more than he dared to say, even to himself.

"Very well, let's go," Emily replied, smiling. Vinnie was already holding Emily's light white jacket and broad-brimmed hat. With his restless ideas and intellectual ambitions, Henry Emmons was the most talked about student at the college. He had revived the literary magazine for which Emily had occasionally written anonymous articles, and on his initiative students wore black armbands for a month upon the death in Amherst on October 24, 1852, of Daniel Webster.

Now, seated by Emily in the carriage, Emmons overflowed with words about the lecture he was preparing – "The Sources of Originality" – which he would present in the speech competition before the student body. As Henry's features glowed with excitement, he looked meaningfully into her eyes. Her gaze was a mirror of her thoughts, and he followed their reflection as he presented his ideas on the subject of deep interest to Emily. Her eyes gleamed when his thoughts were precise and clear, but her expression darkened when his analysis was faulty or incomplete. In such a case, he revised his statement or provided a more apt example. When he concluded, Emily smiled, and then the young student joyfully knew that in the final academic event of the semester he would win the blue ribbon.

The buggy small and the horse – at the peak of its power, seeming to know that his passengers were precious – danced forward like the words, thoughts, feelings, and spirited laughter of the passengers. In Sunderland, Emily and Henry strolled under tall walnut trees. They breathed deeply the fresh moist air, which punctuated for a moment the flow of their thoughts. Deeply grateful that life had blessed him with this wondrous intense companion, Henry impulsively seized her hand and brought it to his lips – the kiss burning, his gaze passionate. His simple words of gratitude could not mask ardent feelings.

"It's time to return, Henry," Emily said, shaken.

As they approached Amherst, Emily came to grips with a dilemma. The relationship was beautiful, but the time away from her writing had been damaging. During the drive, the goddess of inspiration had come to her, but she could not reconstruct the inspired lines that had flashed in her mind that moment. The call of creativity was commanding and did not tolerate postponement; she must always be present when it came! "This outing must be the last," she thought. In her room, sighing, she laid away the phantom of Henry Vaughan Emmons in the chest of forgetfulness. After midnight she awoke with the thought of Sue. She arose from bed, lighted the lamp, and wrote throughout the night:

How sick – to wait – in any place – but thine –
I knew last night – when someone tried to twine –
Thinking – perhaps – that I looked tired – or alone –
Or breaking – almost – with unspoken pain –

And I turned – ducal –
That *right – was thine –*
One port *suffices – for a Brig – like* mine –

Ours be the tossing – wild though the sea –
Rather than a Mooring – unshared by thee.
Ours be the Cargo – unladen – here –
Rather than the "spicy isles –"
And thou – not there –
(#368)

The Malay – took the Pearl

Williiam Austin Dickinson, Harvard graduate and licensed attorney, with his prestigious name a ticket to travel the high road laid down by his father and grandfather, had triumphantly set out. With soaring pride and absolute certainty, he was treading in their footsteps. His future held glittering promise: titles, affluence, respect, the love and honor of all his fellows in the thriving town of Amherst. It went without saying that the intelligence, vitality, and good looks in his line played their role. In sum, he was the most sought after bachelor in the area, but his heart and mind belonged only to precious Sue. Yet whenever they met, his soul was plunged into doubt. Indefinable fears and suspicions plagued him. Sue and he kept their meetings brief and hidden from Harriet. Austin longed to hold her close as he had in Boston – to feel the pulse of her body against his and receive kisses that would erase ugly thoughts and disturbing suspicions. After each fleeting rendezvous, he was smitten by the blows of her ill-concealed aversion, her coolness and indifference to his erotic fire. It shamed him and at the same time fueled his passion. It reinforced desire and maddened him. The only reward for his love was a cool parting kiss – erotic fulfillment a dim promise for the future. The final solution was marriage, but she kept revising the vague date, failing to respond either to his logical appeals or his anguished pleas.

So it went: Austin steadfastly persisted while she stubbornly refused. Months passed thus. Meetings became ever more trying. However, one glorious evening capricious Sue finally gave in and accepted him. Wearing his finest smile and fashionable graduation suit, Austin responded to the invitation from

William and Harriet Cutler. The great day had arrived – he would formally ask for the hand of his beloved in marriage! His phrasing was honed to perfection. The Cutlers were duly impressed by the blend of legal terminology and language of the heart, but nothing could touch Sue. Austin's words were replaced in her mind by the sardonic turns of phrase that she and Emily laughingly used regarding men's feelings when their "requirements" were clothed in flowery words.

Thus, with serious thoughts and satiric words one spring day in 1855 Sue, twenty-four, acquired the title of fiancée of the twenty-six year old aristocrat, William Austin Dickinson

Austin was soaring in the clouds, while his fiancée labored on the ground bowed down by the weight of the new phase in her life – the formal engagement. Each day the demand for setting the wedding date sank deeper within her, provoking uncontrollable nervousness. Smiles vanished from her lips. The bitterness in her heart and confusion in her mind made her feel in every slight bodily discomfort the threat of death. She felt besieged by demands on all sides. Sue strove to counter Harriet's sneer – "That simple-minded aristocrat is blind to what he's getting into!" Sue stubbornly wanted to prove to her sister exactly the opposite, but merely the thought of marriage made her tremble. The thought of carrying and bearing a child was frightening, but how could she back out? Austin, Harriet, the neighbors, the church elders – the whole world – hinted or even demanded that she decide the date. The noose tightened, and Sue was once more in the prison of the town, its words and demands crushing her.

Sue was harried by the voices of Harriet and her brother-in-law, who reminded her daily that the issue of her life as a woman had to be faced. It was her decision. Would she become a fashionable married woman of the time or remain an old maid at the beck and call of her brothers. She was also pressured by Austin who, visiting her daily with ardent caresses and pledges, hymned their future happiness, including a beautiful large family and distinguished position in society. His dream was her nightmare. Her sister, Maria, who died in childbirth, appeared in her dreams with a knowing smile that terrified her. There was no one whom she could seek for support or counsel. Her envied life as Austin Dickinson's fiancée seemed anything but paradise. Her thoughts kept returning to her life in Baltimore – her smiling students, her freedoms and responsibilities as a teacher. Her entire former life appeared blissful – the antithesis of what was taking shape in Amherst. If she could only share with Emily her doubts about a future in the town! But Emily lived in a creative world of her own. Even her beloved sister, Mattie, would not understand. Mattie's vision was simply having a husband and children – the place they lived, Amherst or the west, did not matter.

The necessity to set the wedding date was pressing upon Sue. Time became a vise mercilessly closing. The passing hours and days smothered her, irritated her, sickened her soul, and she desperately sought a solution. As always, from the time of the death of her mother whom she still mourned in her dreams, she found a way to evade the soaring pressures. She fell sick with a high fever that lasted for weeks. "Nervous fever," the doctors called it, and thus Sue had a valid excuse to postpone the wedding. With enormous relief she left Amherst and went for a stay in the home of her aunt in Geneva, some distance from her betrothed. In Amherst everyone breathlessly awaited her recovery. Emily corresponded with her and Austin visited her. Released from daily pressure about the marriage date, Sue paid attention to her aunt's common-sense counsel about the advantages of such a marriage, and let her heart overflow with love for Emily and favorable feelings about Austin, Edward Dickinson, and even Emily Norcross Dickinson. The only person from whom she felt a great distance was Vinnie, because Vinnie alone saw stubbornness, wrong-headedness, and arrogance in Sue's behavior. Moreover, she had never approved of Vinnie and her cats, for she did not consider her intelligent enough to be a true Dickinson.

The weeks passed swiftly and Sue, completely recovered, returned to the asphyxiating town. Its life limited mainly to the activities of the college, Amherst did not satisfy Sue's communal needs. She dreamed of a place for her and her husband in a distant cosmopolitan center – far from the town's narrow-minded busybodies and their demands for conformity. Their happiness was to be found in the West where freedom was dawning, together with affluence and bold new ideas. She discussed her dreams with Austin whose passion led him to agree but whose family concerns were deep. The thought of moving away from the Homestead and especially Emily made his heart ache. Nevertheless, if a change would finally win Sue, he would leave it all behind.

Edward Dickinson listened to his son sing the praises of opportunities on the frontier, but he discerned that Austin's words masked hesitation. It would hardly be easy for him to part from the family, historic ties to Amherst, professional security, the delightful environment of the college, and intellectual inspiration from faculty as well as influential friends in the area.

"Austin." Edward tapped his son on the shoulder. "Drop by the office in the morning for a chat. I'll expect you around ten."

On his stroll to his father's law offices, Austin rehearsed his response to the objections Edward Dickinson might raise against his departure. His words were chosen deftly and decisively in support of his decision to set out on a new life. He would sway his stern father with the stirring slogan that had thrilled thousands of avid youth – "Go West, Young Man, Go West." It was a five-minute walk, and along the way he met neighbors and friends who gave him greetings and congratulations on his graduation from law school. He entered the building with a broad smile on his face and perfected arguments pounding in his mind. Mounting the stairs, he was determined this would finally be a man-to-man meeting between him and his powerful parent.

It was a clear, bright day, and sunlight poured through the large windows of the offices facing the street. In the roomy working areas the shelves were lined with ranks of gleaming leather-bound law books. As he entered, Austin's eye rested with pride on the shiny brass plate on the door:

The Malay _ took the Pearl

EDWARD DICKINSON, Esquire

WILLIAM AUSTIN DICKINSON, Esquire

Attorneys at Law

Austin's heart pounded with excitement. It had been but a few months since his graduation, but he was already licensed in his profession. The conscientious, dedicated Austin Dickinson was the partner and son of the distinguished lawyer, the Honorable Edward Dickinson, Treasurer of Amherst College, and grandson of Samuel Dickinson, its great benefactor.

He took a deep breath and pushed open the door. Entering the polished surroundings, he found his office door bravely marked: WILLIAM AUSTIN DICKINSON, ESQUIRE, Graduate Harvard Law School. Austin's mood soared. Yes – this moment he was a lawyer and colleague of the famous Edward Dickinson, prepared to undertake major cases and make his name known from Springfield to the great metropolis of Boston.

He took a firm step inside, seated himself in his own luxurious armchair, and relaxed. The idea of departure suddenly faded. Why should he wrestle with the task of building a new life in the West or the East? Here in the town of his birth, his background guaranteed exceptional success, tuned to the benefit of his family, the law and society. At that moment there was a knock on the door; it swung open and his father entered. Soberly and formally, he shook Austin's hand. "Congratulations, dear boy. This is for you." He set a small velvet box on the massive walnut desk. The young lawyer, deeply moved, opened it with trembling fingers. It contained an heirloom – Samuel Dickinson's etched gold pocket-watch and chain. On the back was inscribed his name and title. Recognizing the family treasure, the handsome grandson was moved to tears, but his father left no margin for display of feelings. "You are now my partner, and shortly you will hold the position of College Treasurer – a demanding job, major honor, and great responsibility!"

Overcome, Austin waited for his father to conclude, so he could convey his gratitude, but Edward was poised to say a great deal more. His tone changed.

He had become the practical father. Still standing by his son's desk, he rested a folder on its surface and spread its contents before Austin's surprised gaze. "These are the blueprints of the house that will go up on the other side of our lot. The title is in your name. Study the plans and tell me if you approve. We are naming the house Evergreens." Thunderstruck, Austin lovingly fingered the blueprints, while Edward pulled out his watch and exclaimed anxiously, "Ah – I see it's grown late." He hastily added, "I have a case to present. Take a look around the premises at your leisure. I'm looking forward to your beginning work within a fortnight." Saying good-bye with, "I'll see you in the evening at home," father opened the door and slipped out.

Dazed, Austin sank into the comfortable desk-chair with his hand resting on the folder – his body pulsing with joy. Laughter exploded inside him. He could no longer stay in that enclosed space. He had to share this triumph with his Susie. He slipped the folder of blueprints into his black briefcase and took the watch from the antique velvet box. He ceremoniously draped the chain across his new waist-coat and bounded down the stairs. With grand strides he reached the Homestead and asked Joseph to prepare the big carriage. He was eager to pick up Susie from Harriet's. Before leaving his room, he gazed in the mirror. The chain hung graciously and the stem gleamed above the top of the watch pocket. He studied his appearance with admiration, confirming that everything about him epitomized the image of a young gentleman. He was the third Squire Dickinson.

For the first time Sue encountered *this* Austin. He appeared taller, strikingly masculine, with his bold top hat, colorful foulard, ornate watch-chain, and gleaming leather boots. At the curb the horse whinnied impatiently, behind it the fine carriage beckoning her with its soft velvet upholstery. Austin stood at the door. No, he would not enter. Such a residence was too small to contain his immense happiness. "Dear Susie, let us take the air in Sunderland! I want to talk to you!" It was a resonant command, and Sue did not hesitate. In her bonnet and shawl, she quickly stepped into the carriage. Throughout the trip she held her head high, gazing into the distance. Amherst smiled beneath the rays of the spring sun. The roads were broad and clean, and the trees on the hillsides seemed to wave to her in greeting. The few townspeople they met on the way left Sue indifferent, while Austin every so often doffed his hat and politely greeted them.

A gentle breeze wafted in Sue's spirit. "I will become Mrs. Dickinson!" echoed in her heart as they drove through the countryside. For the first time so seized by joy, she felt no anxiety for what Austin might have to say. They reached the first park outside town, and – unable to hold back any longer – Austin pulled the carriage up under a maple tree, and without a moment's hesitation embraced Sue, kissing her fiercely on the lips. For a time Sue bore his outpouring of feeling, and then, pushing him gently away, she asked, "What do you have to tell me?"

"Nothing! I want to *show* you our house!" he exclaimed, unrolling the blueprints in her lap. Looking at the design, Sue viewed a residence that she could never have dreamed of owning. It was a European-style villa unique to the town of Amherst. She looked around the town in her mind's eye and found nothing so elegant. She judged it even more splendid than the Homestead. "Here the aristocrats – the intelligentsia – will congregate!" she thought. She smiled and loaded her spirit with an arrogance that she bore the rest of her life. This same load was bestowed years later on the shoulders of her daughter, Martha Dickinson Bianchi.

The Wedding of Austin and Sue

At daybreak of July 1, 1856, Austin – alone, dressed in his best suit – left the Homestead, walked two hundred yards to the railroad station, and took the train for Geneva, New York, where Sue and her sisters were waiting. It was the wedding day, and the young patrician – deeply saddened – was going to the wedding all by himself. Not a single family member accompanied him.

Strangely, it was that very day that Mabel Loomis Todd – who would come to be his adored mistress – came into the world in a difficult birth taking place in Washington, D.C.

During his journey, Austin pondered the year that had passed from the time the wedding date was set. During that period he had eagerly performed his duties in the law office, observed his father's court appearances, and supervised the construction of Evergreens, urging the workers to complete the job within a year. The villa was ready in precisely twelve months' time. In the meantime, Austin realized that his union with Sue did not promise the bliss he had once envisioned, and his hope and passion plummeted. "It was as if I was going to my execution," sixty-year-old Austin is said to have confided to his beloved Mabel.

The ceremony took place early in the morning at the home of Sue's aunt. Only very close relatives of Sue were present. There was no elaborate reception; simple refreshments of ice cream and cake were served. No description of the wedding day by the participants survives – only absent Harriet's catty remark, frequently noted by commentators. She gazed into Mattie's eyes and whispered: "That young patrician will grow up fast. He'll learn the difference between the complacent and the sharp tongue of a woman!"

Why did no one from the Dickinson family attend the wedding of their cherished Austin? We know that Emily Norcross Dickinson was in a period of such deep melancholy that she could not be left alone. However, Vinnie, who did not care about Sue, could have taken Emily's place at her mother's bedside. If Emily did not attend the wedding because of her habitual shyness and immobility as well as her conflicting feelings about the match, what about Edward Dickinson? Could it be that the family's absence was due to something yet to be suggested by commentators?

The Possibility

Sue's attitude kept me at my desk for weeks. I had to uncover why she behaved so harshly towards Austin. The word *monster* and her concern that Austin had not accepted Christ were grave issues that led me to serious inquiry.

What had happened in Boston? What was the result of the couple's rendez-vous? What course did their relationship take? Hours in the library brought me no answers. The thoughts of scholars – that the family's absence from the wedding was due to Sue's not being of their class and that her behavior was over-bearing – did not explain developments. I could not identify with the opinions of others; they were not satisfactory. Nor could I accept facile statements about Sue, whose intellect was so deeply respected by Emily. Sue's anger, the utter silence of the Dickinson family, their absence from the wedding, Sue's alleged sickness ("nervous exhaustion"), Mabel Loomis Todd's claim in her diary that the couple had no erotic contact for months after the wedding, and Austin 's statement that on the wedding day he "was going to the gallows," and his seri-ous comment, "Sue forced me to marry her," made me suspect that the result of their meeting in Boston might have been pregnancy. In turn, Sue could have miscarried – perhaps by her own intervention; or the baby could have died at birth.

If this were actually the case, Sue had undergone a deeply traumatic expe-rience, and the fault was Austin's. In Puritan times, the code of sexual conduct was addressed to the man, not the woman. The man should strictly control his sexual conduct before and after the marriage. Woman – especially the unmar-ried – were held to be desireless, a conception paralleled by the notion that lacking sexual desire, women did not possess the creative drive. In art as in society, the woman remained untouched. Given the questionable circumstances of the marriage, the puritanical Dickinson family, though they adored their son, may well have distanced themselves from the marriage ceremony. Moreover, Emily's witty poem about the "lover bee" and "the Earl" may well refer to Sue's loss of virginity (and possible pregnancy), since "the Earl" is her repeated met-aphor for Austin (#213):

Did the Harebell loose her girdle
To the lover Bee

Emily Dickinson: Goddess of the Volcano

Would the Bee the Harebell hallow
Much as formerly?

Did the "Paradise" –persuaded –
Yield her moat of pearl –
Would the Eden be an Eden,
Or the Earl – an Earl?

Emily, eyes red from weeping, heard Austin preparing for the trip to Geneva. She got out of bed and with her ear to the door followed his movements. He took his small suitcase and went down the stairs to the kitchen. Father was waiting. They silently ate breakfast, and a few moments later Emily heard the kitchen door opening and Austin's footsteps heading for the station. She hurried to the window and saw him in his wedding suit, strangely stooped as he proceeded down the street. He did not resemble a happy groom. He seemed leaden, moody, strained.

Her eyes cloudy, she attempted to penetrate the dawn haze, but everything was covered by a gray veil mirroring her emotional state. The parting was a knife in her heart. Her life would change drastically without the presence of Austin, who had shared with her so much humor, wit, and vitality. Dominant now – aside from her own creative drive – would be the silence of her mother, the Puritanism of her father, and the practical ways of Vinnie.

She heard Austin's footsteps fading down the street and vanishing around the corner to the station, and in this total silence, she once more burst into tears. In the next room Vinnie turned over in her sleep. Edward continued to drink tea in the kitchen. Mother sighed deeply.

The image of Sue in Emily's mind and the agony of her loss were an arrow of love that pierced her. "My beloved is gone," she groaned.

The Malay – took the Pearl –
Not – I – the Earl –
I – feared the Sea – too much
Unsanctified – to touch –

Praying that I might be
Worthy – the Destiny –
The Swarthy fellow swam –
And bore my Jewel – Home –

Home to the Hut! What lot
Had I – the Jewel – got –
Borne on a Dusky Breast –
I had not deemed a Vest
Of Amber – fit –

The Negro never knew
I – wooed it – too –
To gain, or be undone –
Alike to Him – One –
(#452)

At the end of the week, the couple arrived in Amherst prepared to take the "flower strewn road" of their marriage. They established themselves in the pristine residence decorated with the finest furniture from New York City and a library packed with excellent volumes, all from the $5,000 gift of Sue's brother in Chicago, who also did not attend the wedding. The setting appeared filled with promise, but what about their hearts?

Sue at Evergreens

The young husband, sprucely dressed, a leather portfolio under his arm, threw a swift glance around his handsome home, smiled, gave his wife a peck on the cheek, and whistling a spritely melody, stepped into the street. Sue remained on the stoop watching Austin walk toward the town center at a quick pace.

In the house of her dreams, her gaze scanning the luxurious carpets, Sue wearily climbed the stairs to the second floor to wake up Austin's two little cousins in order to prepare them for school. That task complete, she went to the sitting room with its new furnishings. The furniture was perfect, but she felt the arrangement should change. She shifted armchairs and a table, setting a comfortable chair by the window through which she could view the garden. She raised her eyes to Emily's window. She saw a profile behind the glass. It was her friend! Her armchair would remain here.

She sat back as comfortably as she could and pondered her life – from poverty to material comfort, from the shameful name of a drunken father to the title of Esquire, from the company of common people to discussions with the intelligentsia. Friendship with faculty members, conversations with dinner guests, talk until midnight – and sometimes dawn – without sleepiness or effort, offered her the greatest spiritual stimulation she had ever experienced.

She rose from the armchair and sat on the couch. Her heart had throbbed with excitement the day the furniture had arrived from New York. It was three months after the wedding. She – with the air of the mistress of the house – directed the movers in the placing of the furniture. If it did not please her, she would say, "Not there – here, please... a little further over ... and the chair: bring it forward ...". She stepped back, and gauged the aesthetics of the arrangement. Tired, but eager to please her, the movers worked patiently to fulfill her every whim. What a joy – what a great joy!

In the afternoon Austin had arrived with flowers. They arranged them in vases, stood in the doorway, looked, were pleased, and sat down on the couch;

he put his arm around her shoulders and held her tight. "Oh, Sue – oh my angelic Sue!" he told her, pressing her to him. He loosened her blouse, and before they realized it, the act of love on the new couch was complete. It was the first time after their wedding. They laughed, kissed, and felt the pleasure of the union flooding mind and heart. How much her very own was this handsome man! And how important in her life!

Then it was not long before something went awry. How had the change come about? For Austin and her, the months began to drag by in the same routine: the same phrases, the same morning and evening kiss. It seemed that their gazes were following diverging paths, other thoughts; and every little difficulty became an issue. The longer it went on, each problem became more of a dead end. Sue wondered: When did Austin stop seeming so handsome and desirable? When had he become insignificant – unworthy of her attention? What a great mystery human feelings are! What a labyrinth their nuances! How is love's path lost? How can you live the daily hours that have suddenly become slack and boring?

The situation was sealed by the arrival of Austin's two little cousins. Her father-in-law had set terms after the couple had moved into Evergreens. Edward Dickinson's father had built the house using the funds his late brother had left in his care for the upbringing and dowry of his two orphaned daughters. Edward's terms were that the children's room and board would be Austin and Sue's responsibility, while their dowry would be his. Sue had no objection to the children's support, but she felt absolutely no affection toward the little girls seven and ten years old, who occupied the second floor and were always present around the couple.

Sue lost the enjoyment of the exclusiveness of her space, and Austin became an ever more routine partner. His interests had turned entirely toward his professional activities combined with the excitement of success, and his marriage was a situation of decreasing interest. The little girls were a constant distraction and a drain on Sue's energy.

Emily – who could have been her finest companion – was preoccupied with the problems of her mother's increasing melancholy. From the day of the family's return to the Homestead, Emily Norcross Dickinson's memories of the first years of marriage worsened her situation. In 1856 her nervous condition intensified and she spent a number of days at Northampton hospital, mainly for thermal baths.

Given Emily's support of her mother and her own withdrawal from social life, her communication with others was limited to correspondence. The servants Joseph and Maggie went back and forth between the Homestead and Evergreens bearing Emily's letters, flowers, and poems for Sue. At the same time, she corresponded with "my friend from Philadelphia," as she called the Reverend Wadsworth. The marriage of Austin and Sue was a center of suffering for Emily that bled scarlet ink as she daily penned anguished masterpieces, Thus, life in both houses was stamped by feelings and decisions chosen by each of them. As the road to happiness narrowed for all of them, only the road to poetry widened and shone.

Joseph Lyman

Vinnie was busy as she could be as guardian of affairs around the house and witness of goings-on in the town: courtships, alliances, marriages, births, families moving away, departures and arrivals of faculty members. Her cats had increased to more than ten out in the yard and stable, and three more favorites – soft balls of gleaming fur – that had the run of the house. Everything was going smoothly – life appeared normal – yet something was bothering her. Gradually she came to realize what it was: all her friends and classmates from the Academy had married and left town, which made her wonder about her own future. When would her blessed day arrive? Yet her eye never left Emily, who – silent and obscure – was her continual concern. Only in her bed at night alone, before sleeping, did Vinnie have time to think of Joseph and imagine him deliciously slipping under the sheets by her side.

Joseph Bartwell Lyman

Emily Dickinson: Goddess of the Volcano

How many years had she known Joseph, and how much she loved him! He was from a needy family of the area – a widowed mother and her eight offspring. Opposing the burden of hardship, Joseph was a top student at the Academy – with "his bow in his hand," as Emily put it. On a fellowship he attended Harvard Law with Austin. Then he sought opportunities in Amherst, but none arose. He lived some distance from the town center, but when he came in, he frequently visited the Dickinsons. He was well received. For Vinnie he was the man of her life. He was the one she loved! He had touched her lips. They went sugaring in Sunderland and on longer group excursions with no concern for the neighborhood gossip. How wonderful was that spring evening when they were together on the back porch! Joseph was sitting in the armchair and she on a pillow at his feet – her right arm lying on his thigh, the left hand lifted to touch his chest, and her head titled back, her eyes intensely meeting his, exactly like the drawing she'd seen in a magazine. How her heart raced with his words and throbbed even faster as he leaned down, placed his hands on her cheeks, gazed a long, long time, and very seriously – almost formally – united his lips with hers.

How blissful a kiss can be – what a great event! However, she did not know that this first kiss would also turn out to be the last – nothing but an aching memory. Joseph kept coming, and his visits became more frequent when he discovered Emily's vivacity. They spent hours in conversation. Vinnie observed them and savored the change in the spirit and attitude of her friend. As he alertly attended Emily's words, he seemed to grow taller, and his countenance glittered with a strange sheen as if mirroring the aura of an exotic land. As the two of them spoke, their words were like birds with lovely feathers flying back and forth between them, beating, now wildly, now softly, their brightly hued wings. Like a little child, Joseph delighted in Emily's turn of phrase, agreeing to "a simple life with lofty thought." He relished what she said concerning words, and he later wrote in his memoirs Emily's every word: "I used to think, Joseph, that words were cheap and weak. Now I don't know of anything so mighty. I lift my hat when I see them sitting prince-like among their peers on the page.

Sometimes I write one, and look at its image on the page till it glows as hot as sapphire. How delightful is the great cunning of words!"

Joseph wished that his life would become a wave of words washing over Amherst, but to no avail, and he departed, taking with him phrases, impressions, notes, and perceptions from conversations with Emily that he tellingly recalled in a slim volume, *The Papers of Joseph Lyman*, with detailed references to Emily's observations on her father, her mother, and herself. Whatever he could carry with him from the Dickinson family he took with him to the South – except Vinnie's dreams. He had cast away her hopes, but he could not take away her memories of him, which she kept like a talisman close to her heart over the years as she lay down to sleep.

Joseph Lyman went South with the promise of returning but became enamored of the region, embraced its ideas, advocated the plantation culture, and decided to establish himself there. Time became barren for Vinnie; there were no dates to be stamped on her life. The months slipped away leaving only the indefinable sadness of emptiness. But then, out of the clear, blue sky, she received a message from her dear old friend. It came at a time when she was more than ever caught up and pressured in Emily's dark orbit, and she was shocked. It was not a letter beginning "My Dear Friend"; it was a wedding invitation! Joseph had given his heart to another – a southern belle. What could Vinnie do? What could she say, except what she felt that instant: "Oh, Joseph, how much I wish I could see you again, if only for a moment." Holding back tears, she climbed the stairs to see if Emily was ready for dinner or wanted to go out into the garden for a breath of air.

It was Emily who was Vinne's life concern. Joseph had vanished from their lives; and he would have remained unknown to the world, had he not drawn the attention of scholars, since he felt the need to write of the Dickinson sisters. Grateful for the information, commentators were wont to sympathize with his fondness for words, which he loved so much they became melodramatic. Amidst his lines were confidences the sisters had shared with him in conversations and letters. Some scholars no doubt accepted his use of a word in regard to Emily – a word that stood out in his vocabulary, for he used it also in relation to his southern fiancée. In that case, it went unobserved, but it became a label in regard to Emily that had some influence. The word was "morbid." Thus Joseph Lyman characterized Emily Dickinson. So little was Emily's spirit understood by Joseph Lyman, who considered himself a ladies' man and significant writer.

"I wish you happiness, Joseph," stunned Vinnie hastily continued in her letter, and at once her attention turned ever more closely to her sister. There was nothing and nobody that could compare to such a sister! "Emily enchants everyone she meets with her magical language!" she would say. Nailing Sue with her gaze she would sigh, "Sue will be her early death!" With that, she intensified her protectiveness. Emily should want for nothing, and nothing should distress or frighten her.

One summer a devastating fire broke out on Pleasant Street. Alarm bells rang, the fire brigade sped to the scene, and people raced shouting through the streets. Vinnie reassured Emily, who anxiously watched from her window, "It's the Fourth of July, Emily! That's why there's so much excitement and ringing of bells! Don't be afraid, Emily." "Thanks for telling me, dear Vinnie," Emily feigned credulity, sensitive to Vinnie's concern for her peace of mind. How wonderful their rapport was! When the fire was extinguished she wrote the Norcross cousins, "The conflagration was so immense that from my window that night I could discern a caterpillar crossing a leaf in the garden."

Samuel Bowles

It was August and Edward Dickinson was in his element. The doors of the Homestead were opened wide, and the three ladies of the house – now four, including daughter-in-law Susan Gilbert Dickinson – attired in the finest dresses of the season, would receive the most select and significant personages of the town and the region.

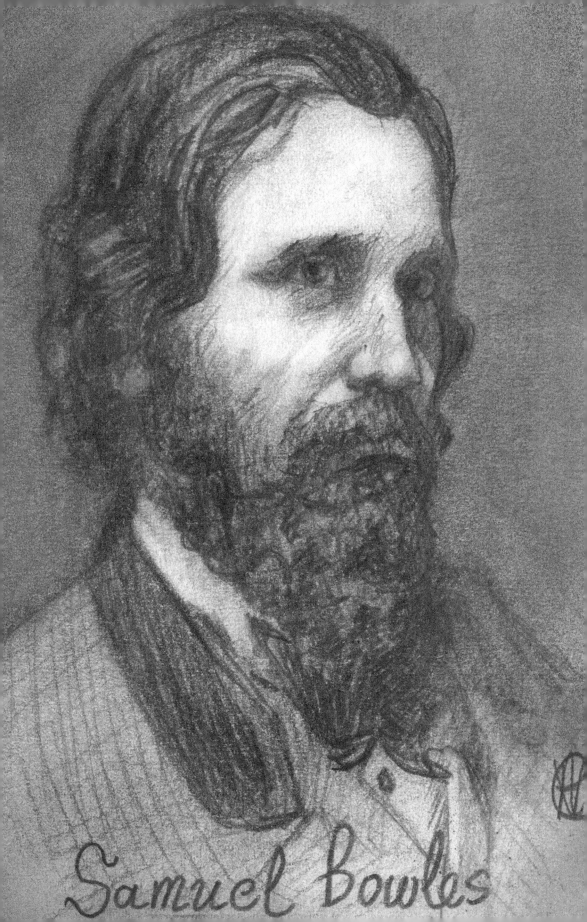

Samuel Bowles

Edward had invited Samuel Bowles, the editor of the Springfield *Daily Republican*, the newspaper of largest circulation in the area, who not only with great pleasure accepted the invitation, but also requested that he be accompanied by his assistant editor, Dr. Holland, who would write a feature article about the annual party at the beginning of the fall semester. Thus, Samuel Bowles formally entered the Dickinson circle and became a close friend.

With timid steps Emily left her room, freezing mid-way down the stairway as she saw groups of visitors entering the living room. She felt light-headed; there were so many impressive guests. Among them she distinguished the two handsome gentlemen whose articles she daily read in the newspaper. She took a deep breath, and for a moment remained undecided whether to join the celebration or retreat to her room.

With closed eyes she contemplated her next step, when suddenly she felt a warm hand on her arm. With a sigh of relief she found Sue before her smiling, a shrewd gleam in her eye. "Come down at once, Emily – Mr. Holland is unmarried. The other one, Samuel Bowles – cross him off the list; he's married, bound hand and foot."

Recovered, with heart beating normally, Emily went on Sue's arm as quietly as possible down the stairs. In the living room Vinnie received her with the splendid smile she reserved for special occasions. "Come Emily," she said, unable to mask her excitement, "I want to introduce you to Mr. Samuel Bowles."

"Miss Dickinson, I have heard so much about you, and have been so eager to make your acquaintance! May I say this is the happiest moment of my life!" He laughed so as to lighten the hyperbole, but at the same time held Emily's hands, initiating a close friendship.

"I admire your boldness, sir, not only in the written word but in speech! How did my name chance to fall upon your ears?" Emily asked flirtatiously.

"Why, how else but through your two avid supporters and admiring critics, your brother and sister-in-law. I already have a poem of yours, ready for publication – *Safe in their Alabaster Chambers* – sent to me by a person who says I have permission to publish it. I thank you in advance on this great success for my newspaper, and I trust that our future collaboration." "Thank you, sir, for the honor," Emily cut him short. She made no attempt to mask her irritation toward Sue's submitting the poem without her permission. What concerned her at the moment – what she hoped for beyond hope – was that the newspaper would publish the poem in the precise form that she had written it. But that did not take place. The poem was heavily revised so as "to be understood" by readers of the time, who preferred conventional full rhyme.

Charming and effusive, Bowles kept her hand in his for some time as he commented on the poems he had read. Though his words were flattering, they did not express a true grasp of the subtleties of Emily's work. The comments derived from pleasure in meeting the poet but did not reveal a precise estimate of the mastery of her lines. Furthermore, he could not overlook the fact that she was the daughter of a refined family writing poetry that disregarded the conventions regarding how a woman should write. Naturally, as one of the finest journalists of his time, he had eyes not only for current events but also for the cultural life of the day. He read and admired the verse of all the well-known poets of his era, but he did not have time to probe Emily's complicated texts.

As Emily carefully listened to Bowles's words, nothing escaped her in his mirroring conventional attitudes – especially those of clever, fashionable people. It was evident that Mr. Bowles was in the dark about the great themes and techniques of verse. She felt the effect of his charming presence, but protecting her poetry was her main concern.

That moment – the last Sunday of August, 1857 – Emily determined, without anxiety or bitterness, that her father's receptions bore no relationship to her life. The great fall festival, which belonged to her father, was her last. As for her poetry – she would determine what it was for herself; she would define it personally, give it her stamp, and refuse to publish because she firmly believed that publication meant selling out her values and compromising her creativity: "Publication – is the Auction / Of the Mind of Man –" (# 709). She was convinced that "The great enemy of Literature is the commercial success of a book. The spirit is lowered to the standards of the market." All Emily wanted was to have time alone with her thoughts and feelings to achieve absolute collaboration with the Goddess Inspiration who enraptures the spirit. Inspiration for Emily was the "subtle seed that either springs from the divine plan or simply happens," as if a spirit silently approaches the door of one's being and instills its precious power. Body and soul are then filled with a vast erotic euphoria. The mind is captivated by turns that the artist laboriously selects to express a web of myriad meanings and carefully puts them down in a unique form so that their nuances may play in readers' minds and provoke the spiritual excitement of creativity. For this complex creative process to unfold, solitude and uncompromising labor were imperative.

Before leaving, the honored guests Bowles and Holland asked Emily with flattering smiles to contribute to the arts section of the newspaper, regularly sending them selections of her poetry. To their great surprise she refused in serious tones as gently as she could. The guests departed with the impression that she would change her mind, though the matter would not greatly affect the circulation numbers of their paper.

The splendid reception ended, the guests of honor departed deeply pleased, and only the young students remained conversing in small groups. They spoke spiritedly about current events, especially the issue of slavery which divided the nation.

Emily felt free to leave and she had not yet reached the top of the stairs when she heard steps behind her. Sue joined her saying, "Let's leave the straightening up to those who like it!" Maggie, Emily's mother, and Vinnie got right to work, while Sue and Emily undertook commentary on everybody and everything.

In Emily's room, the two of them – Sue flopping down on the bed and Emily perched on the chair by the desk – sharpened their tongues on the events and personages of the evening. Their remarks were filled with giggling and mimicry, but when they arrived at the theme of Samuel Bowles, Sue took the floor. Her earlier sarcasm gave way to boundless admiration. With a deep blush on her cheeks, her tongue went rampant with praise. She was unable to separate her enthusiasm from the reality of everything she so intensely described. Emily gazed silently at her friend, surprised at the intensity of her tone, which Sue then understood and reigned in her hyperbole. However, she could not drop the subject that burned in her thoughts and on her tongue, but turned in a different tone to gossip that was in the air. "You wouldn't believe it, Emily. Our neighbors claim that he has a mistress," she giggled, and her excitement once more carried her away, as she attacked the vulgar gossipers, at the same time excusing the flamboyant editor, even in the event that the gossip was accurate. For Sue, Bowles was justified, for his wife lacked the intellectual refinement of the alleged mistress, Maria Whitney, whose brother was a professor at Harvard; and she herself was an outstanding member of the community – a cousin of Bowles's wife, Maria, who suffered from depression from losing three children in childbirth; and Maria Whitney had helped her by living with the Bowles's, but she had misinterpreted her husband's graciousness toward her helper; and Maria Bowles's complaint to her spouse deeply offended Maria Whitney, who threatened to leave the house at once if she did not receive an apology, which was not forthcoming; so she left immediately, and now Mr. Bowles frequently went to Northampton where said lady resided; and he also took therapeutic baths for overwork and melancholy at the town's large hospital, on which occasions he and said person would have long conversations and openly take buggy rides before the eyes of offended observers; and when he was in Amherst, he never failed to drop by at Sue's and Austin's for advice . . . .

"And do you know, Emily, what he is trying to do?" Sue continued breathlessly, "Mr. Bowles is planning something completely new – his paper coming out on Sundays." There would be no paper on Monday, but it would circulate on Sundays – a serious problem for upset church elders and other town authorities. Bowles sought the counsel of Austin, requesting that he appease the elders.

Austin promised he would do so, suggesting to church authorities that pious readers be instructed to read the Sunday edition on Monday, a matter in which Austin succeeded.

"Of course," Sue told Emily, "I know that you do not observe the Sabbath, and I fear you will read of worldly affairs on Sunday; but I will never do so!"

Sue fell silent a moment, sighing deeply. Once again she felt her superiority as she contrasted her zeal in the faith to Austin and Emily's attitudes about religion. And at the same she expressed her admiration for gifted minds like Bowles's, since she had no reason to judge their morality, because at that moment she could not imagine that the same situation – a mistress . . . carriage rides . . . vulgar gossipers – would recur with protagonists, not Bowles and his wife Maria, but Austin and his wife Sue. And how could such an event occur, since Sue was an intellectual while Mabel Loomis Todd played the intellectual, but it did happen – as the saying goes, "Don't count your chickens"– because irony, for good or ill, floods the world, and is woven into the fabric called life, including intellectuals and non-intellectuals alike.

Emily grasped all the events – both those she heard about from Sue and those she perceived in the excitement on her face. She realized that the situation at Evergreens was not rosy. Her heart began to beat irregularly, an indication that withdrawal, even from the house opposite, was possible – a horrifying thought which she hastened to repress, for if the major part of her essential life was poetry, the rest was her two loved ones, Sue and Austin.

Having exhausted her themes and feelings, Sue turned and gazed at her friend. She saw, understood, and at once fell silent. She felt humiliated and repentant about everything she had blurted with such enthusiasm. She wanted to leave, vanish from Emily's presence, but she did not know how. Abruptly, she took Emily's hands, pressed them warmly to her lips, and rushed from the room.

Erotic Melodies

Exhilaration – is within –
There can no Outer Wine
So royally intoxicate
As that diviner Brand
(#383)

From the niche under the stairs in the Homestead – the Northwest Passage – Sue called out: "Emily! Emily! Come down!" She would not go up to Emily because what she had to say was so wonderful she wanted to share it in their secret place. Emily descended, a forced smile on her face. She was hard at work. Time was always wanting, the poem demanding, and the least interruption of feeling and thought was distressing.

She stood before Sue, questioning, waiting. "Kate Scott Anthon is coming!" Sue excitedly announced. "We are expecting you for dinner at six! Don't refuse! Isn't it wonderful! Don't refuse, dear." She was so excited by the coming of her friend that she did not wait for a reply, but – blowing Emily a kiss – dashed gaily off, as Emily continued to concentrate on the word she was seeking.

It was a gentle spring afternoon, and soft reddish-yellow sunlight permeated the parks and gardens of Amherst. At dinnertime she was at Sue's door wearing the new dress that her father had brought from Washington. She knocked and entered at once, finding herself in a celebrative atmosphere. Sue had filled the living room with flowers. Dressed in her finest clothes, she was standing by a tall, striking young woman whom she enthusiastically brought forward. "Here's our dear Emily!" she exclaimed, "And here's my good friend and class-mate, Kate Anthon!" The two women looked at one another. Their observations, keen and quick, spun through their minds. "What a beautiful woman!" Emily thought. "What a spiritual presence!" Kate perceived. Spontaneously the two embraced and kissed, and the three of them began to laugh conspiratorially.

They could have shouted, "Hail feminine genius! Hail women's emancipation!" but they controlled themselves. While such sentiments circulated boldly at the universities and salons of Boston, informed women of Amherst impatiently awaited developments without pounding loudly on the drums of liberation. Nonetheless, these women enjoyed a freedom that was denied the women of most classes. Thanks to their affluence and free thought, they eschewed social conventions – especially those rife with religiosity – and laid down the path of their lives through personal choice.

Like a heroine from the pages of Henry James, Kate had declared her freedom by frequent trips to Europe. She always visited only the capitals, her aim knowledge of European culture and the enjoyment of select company. She took long vacations in luxurious hotels, going to museums, visiting galleries, and attending theatrical productions without concern for expenses or social disapproval. She had inherited much at the cost of great pain from the death of her husband, her brother and beloved sister. Death had marched through her life, but now life belonged to her, and she compensated for the absence of loved ones through close ties to friends like Sue and acquaintances in Europe. Whenever she returned to her home city of Albany, sixty miles from Amherst, she was sure to visit Evergreens.

The life style at Evergreens excelled that of the Homestead on all occasions. "Blissful!" was the word that guests used to describe the ambience of Sue's home. The Austin Dickinsons' table rivaled the finest restaurants in Europe and the United States, and their aesthetics were equally refined. The residence glowed from the décor. A splendid staircase led to the second floor, while the entrance hall and the living room walls were embellished by a collection of valuable paintings, to which Austin added annually. On the left as one entered the house was the spacious living room with luxurious furniture, drapes, paintings, and a marble fireplace, which drew the visitor's eye. To one side was the fine spinet on which Emily loved to perform. In the neighboring dining room were a large mahogany table that sat twelve and a massive buffet topped by dinnerware imported from England. The carved-wood ceiling was the gift of a noted architect.

Across the spacious hall from the living room was the library, its shelves filled with leather-bound volumes. After the poet's death, her niece named it the *Emily Dickinson Room,* where manuscripts and documents were collected before a number were donated to the Harvard library. Another chamber on the first floor was the couple's bedroom, while on the second floor were rooms for the children and servants. Sue had grasped the aesthetics of life and she applied them most dexterously.

In this environment the select company that evening began their menu with special appetizers – caviar, lobster, and shrimp. They continued with beef or trout, and a green salad from Sue's garden, and they concluded with ice cream with strawberries, also from the garden. It was a dinner of exquisite flavors.

The women arose from the table, having already drunk two glasses of red wine. Carrying a third, they proceeded to the living room flushed with pleasure that flowed from their deep affinity. Austin's tie to Sue and Emily was deep, but he was unable to participate fully in the excitement of the evening. Emily sat down at the piano and played a medley of old-time favorites, as the light of sunset which had tinted the room in gentle pink-orange modulated to dark purple, leading the hosts to light the lamps in the house.

Suddenly Emily stepped to the lamp on the small table by the piano and blew out the flame. Before she could get to the lamp on the table by the wall, Sue had blown it out, laughing in a tone filled with significance as a thought took her breath away, "Now Kate will understand what 'Goddess of the Volcano' means!"

Lighting candles throughout the room, Austin sank into a comfortable arm-chair as far as he could get from the trio. Kate chose a seat on the piano bench very close to Emily and, mesmerized, she watched the suggestion of a smile play on her dimly lit face. As Emily's long fingers stroked the keys like a caress, with quick pants Kate breathed the rising notes.

The soft waves of a gentle sea drenched their faces and refreshed their bodies. They shivered with deep feeling as the fingers continued to dance in a special way, sometimes with a powerful thrust, and sometimes barely skimming the keys in singing waves that induced a stirring excitement. Each note added to the feeling as the ripples of music suddenly shot into the air and then fell on bodies with a powerful splash that penetrated the soul and flesh with delicious poignancy.

The candle light danced quickly in the ecstasy of sound and grew calm as the notes soothed. Emily added her voice to the melody. Filled with erotic joy, arpeggios mounted higher and higher, wrapping her spirit in velvet; her insatiable soul kept expanding. Time was cancelled, place was erased, her friends transformed, absorbed into the throbbing unity of the moment. Erotic vitality, splendid within her, raised Emily high in intense personal joy. It elevated her to the ecstasy of the highest order.

Transcendence – that matchless ineffable sensation – had seized her!

With a life of their own, her fingers deftly ranged the keys. Her notes and those of the instrument, like sparkling fireworks, lifted her and delivered her to sublime colors – scarlet, indigo, and azure streaked with yellow. In her own world, body throbbing in volcanic explosions, she beheld flames made of notes, and within her she felt the quaking of the eruption, syllables flashing like fire and crescendos burning fountains of ecstasy. Incredible intensity reigned. The words, the notes, were exhaustless within her. The volcano erupted and lava dissolved, melting all ties to mundane things.

The others – souls and bodies magnetized – could not endure the intensity. First, Austin sprang to his feet and fled up the stairs. Kate was trembling. The primal journey had enmeshed her in exotic folds of desire, and panting she remained fixed to the piano bench beside the shooting flames. Sue, who had experienced such moments before, breathlessly imbibed her wine, drinking in the rare moment of liberation and joy, unable to extricate herself from the rule of the Goddess of the Volcano, who mercilessly swept her to matchless heights and pushed her to terrifying limits. Fearing she had reached the breaking point, she turned her head toward the window and glimpsed a figure rushing toward Evergreens' door. She breathed a sigh of relief.

With a lantern to light his way on the path, Emily's anxious father was coming to rescue her. Sue gratefully slipped into the hall, opened the door, briefly greeted her father-in-law with relief, and with head lowered stepped to Emily's side. "Emily," she whispered, "your father . . ." – and then, more loudly, "Your father, Emily!"

Though she was jolted, Emily's voice lingered in the melody and her fingers dwelt a moment on the keys. Unable to grasp what the words meant – or what relation they bore to the region in which she found herself – she remained suspended, and then she felt the grip of a hand on her arm, the fingers tightening. Her mind as yet distant, she neither heeded the irrelevant contact, nor recognized the voice that insisted, "Your mother wants you, Emily." The voice repeated, "Emily, your mother wants you," as the hand guided her out of the living room, into the hall, and down the stairs. She lifted her eyes to the star-filled sky and saw the stars beholding her with wonder, but before she had time to react, her father shouted, "Let's go home, now, Emily!" and Emily suddenly crumbled. The moment of ecstasy was shattered, joy scattered to the winds, and the weight of her flesh dragged her into an alien, absurd place that shook her spirit and wrenched her body.

She heard the thump of her soul falling, and sensed the hand of the man called father on her arm. He had pulled her away from the piano, away from the living room, away from ecstasy, saying in a caring voice, "Watch your step, Emily!" as he raised the lantern to light the way that she knew with her eyes shut. It was the familiar path she had taken time and time again, but now she saw the whole scene from far above – her father's long arm, his fingers tense on her arm. He was guiding her in a peculiar manner that was a blend of authority, protectiveness, and tenderness. The lantern cast a dim light on his face, which was dour, determined, filled with sadness and concern for her welfare – and she saw that his was an arrested, automatized being: rigid, distant, completely alone, he was wasting his life on an idol he fashioned in his mind imposed on himself and others. Himself its slave, he called it "responsibility," and it led his entire family to the dark, narrow path of his making.

What irony, what a lie, what a trap! Who could throw off such a yoke of 'protection'? Emily beheld her mother, Vinnie, herself, and Austin – who had such promise of glowing life – swept round in the orbit of an extinguished sun. Terrified, Emily was seized by knowledge she had always possessed but had been unable to drag to light. Now, however, the thought rose and lay bare the world as it was. She saw the ways of mankind, especially when it came to belief – how they imprisoned God and kept Jesus nailed on the cross, replacing spiritual enlightenment with empty words. It was a sudden and terrible revelation for Emily: imprisoned by words, people laid down the path of their fate and followed it blindly. There was a flaw in human perception that distorted the natural world, society, the family, and even what was called the Divine! That was the original sin, which had marked human existence over the ages and had waylaid even the ecstasy of love.

Weighed down by sadness, Emily climbed the stairs one-by-one to her bedroom thinking, "Nevertheless, my father is a good man who always desires our welfare. His heart is pure and terrible and I think no other like it exists." She felt the despair of a dead-end. In her room, she leaned her forehead on the window pane and gazed at the path through the trees by her house toward the home of her beloved Sue and Austin. The moon, ignoring the clouds that passed before it, illuminated the path that she had fashioned from the love that soared in her heart. She suddenly froze. Like an ill spirit the shadow of Sue appeared before her eyes at moment she had shouted, "Emily, your father! Your father, Emily!" She asked herself, "Could it be there was relief in her voice, and triumph in her eyes?" She set the thought aside and wrote (#340):

Is Bliss then, such Abyss,
I must not put my foot amiss
For fear I spoil my shoe?

I'd rather suit my foot
Than save my Boot –
For yet to buy another Pair
Is possible,
At any store –

But Bliss, is sold just once.
The Patent lost
None buy it any more –
Say, Foot, decide the point –
The Lady cross, or not!
Verdict for Boot!

The boot, indifferent, waited for the lady to take command – an event that had already begun to take shape.

Weeks had passed and still thoughts of Sue's party brought an erotic shiver. Kate, a hallowed memory, was already on the other side of the Atlantic. Resuming her partying, she neglected writing to Emily. Yet Emily still felt the embrace of her fiery farewell. She still tasted her burning kiss.

The day after the party, right after twelve noon, Emily had gone to Evergreens to be with Sue and Kate. They had said nothing about the evening before – the vibrant piano, the intense singing, Edward Dickinson's rushing to the scene. Not a word of all that – just a few hints and looks filled with significance. They had thrown themselves into conversation of the kind that fills the heart with affection and encloses the body in an avid embrace.

They were talking and laughing, when suddenly Emily looked out of the window and saw the pastor of their church, with his pious air, stepping though the gate. A moment later there was a knock at the door. Emily took Kate's hand whispering, "Come quickly!" and controlling their laughter, they hastily took the stairs to the second floor. As Sue opened the door to the formal visitor, the two girls slipped into the first bedroom at hand and threw themselves prone behind the bed. It was as if the minister were about to ascend the steps and they wished to be hidden from his view. Hugging, they giggled scandalously. In the meantime, the pastor – who on entering had seen the two girls going upstairs – sat down patiently in the living room expecting that they would be coming back down to greet him as was proper. He spoke with Sue for some time, not daring to utter the name of Emily or Kate, who, dizzy with erotic feelings, were holding hands oblivious to the outer world as they released a stream of words about their lives. Kate told of her European adventures – the flirtations, concerts, galleries – and Emily visualized it all in detail, recalling then the recital she had attended in Northampton with her father – how much she had adored Jenny Lind and her fiancé, Otto Goldschmidt. The couple's divine love, Jenny's heavenly voice, and her splendid gown had sealed a radiant image in Emily's heart: "Her heavenly eyebrows, her plaintive notes, wild and commanding, the panther and the dove, each so innocent."

Thus Emily described the couple she had viewed that unforgettable night. Recalling Jenny and looking at Kate, she said, "But you are even more beautiful!" As she tenderly caressed Kate's cheek, the trembling of her hand was transferred to her friend. It was a moment of overpowering emotion, and as Kate bent and pressed her face against Emily's deeply flushed cheek, the door opened and Sue entered glaring in anger. "Is that a way for proper young ladies to behave – to rush away from a visitor? Emily, your brother is beside himself!" Her voice was stern, her face frowning. "You must beg the pastor's pardon. He left affronted by your contemptuous behavior!"

Emily assumed an attitude of childlike remorse, though her blush of deep excitement refused to go away. "Of course I will ask his pardon," she breathed. Still glaring, Sue spoke no more. She turned on her heel and exited, slamming the door, and Kate – as if she had impatiently awaited Sue's departure – hugged Emily and joined in a warm kiss. It was then that she promised she would keep in touch, and Emily waited months that stretched beyond a year. Kate was continually in Emily's thoughts but she grew weary of writing and awaiting a response that never arrived. Her last letter contained a poem with the lines, "Why Katie, Treason has a Voice – / But mine – dispels – in Tears" (#1410). She received news of her from Sue, who often wrote to Kate. When memories of faces and experiences had faded in the past and Kate was still alive, questioned about her times in Amherst, she answered excitedly, as if she were reliving beautiful moments: "O-O-O-O-O-Oh! – those blissful days at Sue's. O-O-O-O-O-Oh! – the joys of life and the memories they leave!"

Sue, angry, had limited her contact with Emily, and the weeks had passed in dark silence full of agony. But her jealousy, as usual, dissolved, and subliminal erotic feelings were restored. The episode with Kate was erased from Sue's memory, just as Emily's had erased Sue's sarcastic smile that evening and her whispered words, "Your father, Emily . . . your father!" Also expunged was her anger toward father, who had become another person. After that night, he was kind and polite. As if he were seeking forgiveness, he performed little services for her, and everything would have returned to normal, had not knowledge been entrenched within her: *People can betray you without a warning.* She suddenly experienced a strange exhaustion that plunged her into the Existential Abyss.

Romance – Puritan Style

Emily heard the welcome sound of a large carriage pulling up at Evergreens, followed by enthusiastic greetings and laughter. Samuel Bowles had arrived next door, and Emily's heart surged. How marvelous! Bowles, with his charming smile and suave compliments, had come early to spend an enjoyable day at Sue's. Yet Emily did not want to leave her room. Though Bowles's presence was certainly an incentive, she had no appetite for talk. Sunlight poured through the window. It was her beloved hour of noon. Late into the night before, she had labored over ideas and images. With trembling hands, she picked up the sheet of paper and closely reread the lines several times, revising a number of words. The midnight labor had been productive indeed. "There's some evidence here that I'm a poet!" The thought came to her, and it was frightening. The responsibility was great – for the highest poetic art demanded a supreme commitment. Was she ready? How much of her being was she prepared to place on the altar of the Goddess of Poetry?

Refusing to complete the thought, she folded the paper and slipped it into the drawer. She sighed. Yes, she would send the poem to Sue later, perhaps to Bowles also, when the excitement of the visit receded. Sue's comments were helpful, if not absolutely necessary. She got up, went to the window, and looked out. In her garden, Sue was showing her blooming flowers as she was gazing with irrepressible admiration at their dear friend. She had sent a servant to Austin's office to inform him, and the enjoyment of the friends would begin, as usual, as the three of them would sit relaxed in the living room with a drink in their hand discussing the slavery issue; they would criticize and revise Lincoln's every word, congratulating themselves on the way they had grasped the significance of the Union, confirming that civil war was the only solution. Satisfied, they would drink in the polish of their statements and perceptions. They were truly a splendid intellectual trio savoring two great values – spiritual and material. The aesthetics of the house were perfect, the upcoming meal superb, as was the embrace of their friendship. Bowles commented that Evergreens was truly Paradise on Earth and the hostess the spirit of the house at the side of the distinguished William Austin Dickinson. As for Emily, she was indeed the withdrawn Recluse Queen as he called her, whom he loved like a little sister. He honored her intellect almost as much as that of brilliant Sue! Regarding her poetry, there were some problems, but he read her verse with interest.

Emily was once more at her little desk with the poem on a slip of paper on which she had jotted down alternative words. There was a knock at the door, and Maggie entered with a glass of milk on a tray and a gleam in her eye, announcing "Mr. Bowles asks to see you now." "Not today," Emily returned, surprising Maggie, for it was clear that not only did Emily admire the newspaperman but she flirted with him as much as Mrs. Sue did. Emily's staying in her room was a puzzle for Maggie to solve, perhaps with the aid of her sister after Sunday services. Certainly it was a delicious mystery, for everyone knew Emily's special admiration for Bowles. All the women in the Dickinson family sought his companionship, and when the three ladies were together they spoke even more about Bowles than about the heroes of novels – even those of Jane Austen.

Maggie and her sister were not alone in conjecture about Bowles's importance in Emily's life. Her neighbors discussed it; and a number of future scholars would identify Samuel Bowles as the much discussed "Master" whom Emily addressed in three letters left amidst her poems. Other commentators would assign that identity to the Reverend Charles Wadsworth. None would comment, however, that erotic feeling is a necessary precondition in the life of the artist, the spark that ignites the fire of poetry.

Emily might well have been preoccupied with such a vibrant figure as Bowles – especially in her small dark room at night engaged in thoughts and dreams, but not in daylight with a poem in progress demanding the intense task of revision. The words glowed on the paper, and Emily touched them with the tip of her tongue, whispering them to test for metaphor, music, and the surprise they would evoke in the reader, when she suddenly felt the jolt of the voice of her dear friend from the bottom of the stairs. "You rascal, come down!" The strange invitation was accompanied by affectionate laugher that pierced her heart. She leapt excitedly from her chair.

Yes! Bowles, the master of her erotic inspiration, had commanded her, and she would go down, go to the house opposite, and give him a poem; she would offer him a basket of apples from her garden; she would bake the bread he loved; and she would propose the name of his fourth child – *Robert*, after the great poet; she would send a poem to Bowles's wife, Maria; she loved them all – his mistress Maria also. Her heart filled with love for everyone in his family. She lost her breath as a great weight of shame fell on her spirit. She felt humiliated by the naïve love she had spontaneously granted. "Life with others becomes so difficult, so confused," she thought sadly; "people don't understand me. When I say something, men reply 'What?'"

She prepared to descend and cross to Evergreens, yet at the same time she felt the impulse to lock her door, draw the curtains, and remain in her room writing by candlelight. However, she told herself firmly, "I'll go! I'll go!" She drank the milk in a single swallow, and with a timid girlish smile descended the stairs.

Her heart pounded with infatuation for the handsome man as he stood before her with a broad smile and open arms. She cuddled in the warm nest, blood racing, as he rested his lips in her hair. He laughed heartily like a brother while he squeezed her slyly, forgiving her all her childish games.

Emily was grateful for his attention, as Sue – soberly and rather strictly – took her by the hand and drew her into the living room. "Come," she said, "you've interrupted at the most important point of our conversation."

Emily at once understood the theme of their talk. Recovering from the magic of erotic sensations, she sat down in her armchair somewhat dispirited. Once more she had to listen to the same bombastic phrases concerning the necessity of war, details of battle, and feats of heroism. All that left her unmoved, immobile, silent. One statement sufficed to express her perception of war: "War brought chaos and Death without reference to the soul of man. Chaos and life are criminally joined in times of war." The company's fancy phrases repulsed her. Austin, who agreed with her views but had stopped voicing them out loud, lowered his eyes and avoided her gaze. Sue was smiling knowingly, while Bowles commented that Emily's concepts were utopian – but that was understandable, since she lived in the ethereal world of poetry, not the prosaic but challenging realm of history.

That beautiful spring day in 1861, as they were seated in comfortable armchairs with refreshing drinks in their hands and freshly cut flowers in vases around the room, the political talk was winding down. Historic developments were in progress, and their conversation had reached a pitch when – that key moment – church bells began to toll in tones of mourning. The company moved uneasily in their chairs and nervously gazed out into the street, hoping that the tolling would cease, but it went on and on, and Austin rushed to Town Hall, returning at once.

Pale, with trembling lips and breaking voice he announced in hollow tones: "Oh, Frazar is dead … Frazar is dead!" Tragedy had struck and blasted all notions of the glory of war. The idea of war took on shocking dimensions, since this death was unthinkable. The young man was the son of the college president, a recent graduate of Harvard, and also a dear friend of Austin's! He too could have paid three hundred dollars as Austin did to avoid conscription, but he had not. Frazar's death was a smear on their beautiful and brave words, and they shifted uncomfortably in their seats. Bowles, clearing his throat, remarked that sacrifices were meaningful in a struggle for justice and ideals. But his words rang hollow, since Frazar's loss was horrible and immediate. After all, Frazar was their friend, and they had grown up together. Carefully chosen words stimulating for the mind with so many significant arguments could not speak to their hearts, which had sunk in the blackness of events. Not only was the slaughter of their young friend inscribed on the roll of their spirits but also that of a host of young men as yet to fall in countless battles as the war continued ruthless and insatiable. The number of the dead was mounting with incredible speed, spreading to every state, to every town, to every neighborhood. The cause had created a huge number of gallant volunteers, fanatic patriots, who thrust themselves under fire and fell to the ground they had not long before plowed, planted, and harvested.

Emily arose from her chair and abruptly left the gathering. No one dared to keep her there. Her heart fixed on the young man falling on the battlefield, she wrote (#409):

Frazar Stearns.

They dropped like Flakes –
They dropped like Stars –
Like Petals from a Rose –
When suddenly across the June
A wind with fingers – goes –

They perished in the Seamless Grass –
No eye could find the place –
But God can summon every face
On his Repealless [sic]*– List.*

Her mounting pain confirmed the conviction that truly she did not belong to this world. The farther away from society's words and actions, the better for the spirit. She ceased to attend church services in which ministers always found pompous words to arouse students who rushed to enlist; by the hundreds ardent college students signed up to serve – indeed four southern students at Amherst, moved by ministers' appeals, hastened to their home states to join the opposing camp. College enrollment dwindled, casualties mounted, church bells tolled mourning. As leaders spoke eloquently, the citizens of Amherst stood silently outside town hall awaiting the latest addition to the expanding casualty list. Emily grew sadder and more distant, referring to the Civil War in only four poems (# 409, 426, 444, and 596), without acknowledging anything necessary or justifiable in that conflict or any other.

Austin fell silent about the war, while Bowles penned fiery articles for his newspaper. Reading them, Sue realized that the sacrifice of the body of man on the altar of eloquent ideology not only ignored the soul, as Emily said, but also transformed the delight of the soul in joy into arrogance. What was the proper stance toward life? She opposed the war, proclaiming life a glorious celebration that must be honored. She organized gatherings of distinguished advocates of poetry and ideas; and she arranged the party that was to be Emily's last. It was unforgettable, not only for the poet but for all her commentators.

CHAPTER II

The Soul At Its Limits

In silence we meet
the inexplicable area
of existence.
Rainer Maria Rilke

Time was racing at a speed that it alone can take, with a force that it alone can choose, indifferent and unbending toward human efforts to control and tame it. As Emily felt time's boot coming down upon her, she resisted by composing poems. She felt the knowledge of human behavior more and more deeply; it chilled her and made her shrink from human contact. Each day she probed more deeply into her soul, not for salvation in the Calvinist grain, but for in-depth understanding of experience. She studied the great principle *Know Thyself*, striving to catch the texture of life – to refine ideas and feelings. The hours were filled with reading and meditation, and when "flood subjects" surged within her, she shaped her lines, selecting words – metaphorical, symbolic, evocative, arcane – to create images dense with meaning, while deftly maintaining a unique rhythm and tone that mounted to surprise and awe.

Inspiration and crafting of images demanded extended periods of time, and sealed in her room the poet withdrew step-by-step from the community and the family establishment. She left the housework to Vinnie, who undertook it without hesitation or complaint as Emily curled up with her dictionary, her "best friend." The great effort to distance herself from social surroundings, "to surpass the world," as Bowles put it, demanded great sacrifices and enormous endurance. Emily avoided numerous relationships – even those the small community deemed women's obligations. With her dog Carlo, a gift from her father, she took long walks around the extensive Dickinson properties, though on meeting someone she slipped behind a bush until that person went off into the distance. Just as church was no longer a part of her life, visits to friends' homes ceased. She even curtailed visits to Evergreens. From the day that she had stopped meeting Bowles, his requests to see her left her cold, though she still felt bitter toward Sue for her attempts to undermine her relationship with him, as in the case of the article about literature.

Sue had appeared at the door of her room early one morning. Strangely disturbed, she was holding something behind her back that appeared to be the reason she had come. "Girl, did you read the newspaper today?" she asked, striving to appear casual.

"Not yet – I don't know where it is. Maybe Vinnie has it," Emily returned, feeling a surge of joy. She had recently sent Bowles a poem. It was one of her favorites, and she was hoping that he would give it the close attention it deserved. In fact, the poem related to him, and if he read it closely he would find it flattering. Above the poem was a playful salutation: "I can't explain it, Mr. Bowles."

Two swimmers wrestled on the spar –
Until the morning sun –
When One – turned smiling to the land –
Oh God! the other One!

The stray ships – passing –
Spied a face –
Upon the waters borne –
With eyes in death – still begging, raised –
And hands – beseeching – thrown!
(#201)

She had openly challenged Bowles by confessing that two friends were fighting over him, and having chosen the one, he had abandoned the other to perish in agony.

"Has something been published?" Emily anxiously inquired, extending a hand. Nodding in confirmation, Sue handed her the paper folded on the page in question. There was an article, written by their dear friend, entitled, "The Literature of Misery." Emily's expression sobered. She swiftly surveyed the lines, and – growing pale – let the paper slip from her hands.

"There is . . . a kind of writing," the article stated, "only too common, appealing to the sympathies of the reader. . . . It may be called the literature of misery. The writers are chiefly women, gifted women maybe, full of thought and feeling and fancy, but poor, lonely and unhappy. Also that suffering is so seldom healthful. . . . [I]t too often clouds, withers, distorts. It is so difficult to see objects distinctly through a mist of tears."

Emily was frozen, stripped of any response. Sue commented on the article, justifying the writer's stance and assuring Emily that their good friend could never consider Emily such a case. Sue's words were wasted, for Emily saw that Sue actually wanted Emily denigrated and the field open for her own benefit. Emily cut her short with hasty agreement. She was thinking that Bowles rarely published a poem of hers, which led her to think that he was incapable of penetrating her work. It was evident that he hadn't even a hint of its depth, although she had sent him many poems.

Emily Dickinson: Goddess of the Volcano

Emily went to the window facing west and told herself, "One more ghost in the trunk of forgetfulness." Just so – she would never see Bowles again. The bitter thought brought burning tears to her eyes. Wiping away the tears and continuing to gaze outside, she felt Sue's comforting touch. Sue pressed against her and they remained so for a few moments. Then Sue leaned and silently left a kiss on her neck. Emily heard her footsteps on the stairs, and it was the first time that she felt relief on their parting. The friends no longer lived the powerful bond that had united them for years.

Emily was withdrawing. Day to day she was ever more intensely engaged in shaping her poetry. When the need for maternal comfort became imperative, she visited Mrs. Dwight, a smiling church elder over fifty, with blue eyes and an ever-welcoming embrace. Emily nested in her arms and for a moment drank in that "milk of human kindness" which she never tasted as a child.

When friends came on winter afternoons for tea and pleasant talk, Vinnie chirped and laughed. Out of habit, Emily hesitantly descended from her room to greet the visitors and confirm that "People talk loudly and foolishly of God and embarrass my dog." She always swiftly retreated. Above all, she wished to avoid the maddening visits of relatives, who stayed for over a week. There was the fuss of "Uncle Elizabeth," as Emily called her father's sister, who made a great to-do of reciting satirical verses. Some moments were amusing, but the situation soon became unbearable. Uncle Elizabeth's pounding of her heels as she went up and down the stairs countless times a day and the regal purple of her dress maddened Emily – though not to the degree of her younger sister Aunt Catherine's lugubrious disquisitions on "the God of Wrath." Her all-knowing ways and insufferable self-righteousness offended Emily's sensibility – and perhaps even that of her husband, who one summer day in New York, where they resided, announced that he was going down the street for cigarettes and never returned. That day a clipper ship had set sail from New York to London.

"They are not like us," Emily told her brother; yet she felt reluctant tenderness for all the relatives. In any case, when the length of their visits approached insufferable duration, Emily would withdraw to her room and firmly shut the door, though even then their babble reached her ears and shook her concentration.

In her room, she was free! Poetry was her sole companion and delight. Only at her desk did she feel alive. She had begun poetry from an early age. At twenty-five it became somewhat more serious, but at twenty-eight she launched into conscious creativity, and it suddenly came upon her that the poems she had written on whatever scrap of paper fell into her hands had formed a sizable package. Holding the package tenderly, she felt the pulse of the poems harmonizing with the pulse of her soul. Deep emotion ran through her body as she touched each of the lyrics. She caressed them with her eyes and the tips of her fingers. As she read them slowly one-by-one, tasting them, their flavor produced a sensation of strange delight. The poems powerfully nourished her life. This was a delight she had never felt before, and there was no other thing or person in life could offer such indescribable joy, a raising of the soul without pride, a lifting of the body as if her feet did not touch the ground, her movement becoming weightless flying. It was as if a spirit had led her to a chamber of an exotic castle and placed her on a throne of honor, crowning her with bays and proclaiming her a monarch. "I'm saying every day / 'If I should be a Queen tomorrow', I'd do it this way," (#373), she wrote, feeling a surge of creativity sweep her into the heavens.

"I am a poet!" she confirmed; "but am I wholly fresh and new?" she wondered. "My verse must be special, or it's not worth the effort!" She would accept nothing less than unique creativity, just as it had been with the piano. When she heard a virtuoso perform, she realized: "That is the art of the pianist!" She returned home, closed the keyboard cover, and never played again." "Art is inviolably sacred," she said. "It must bring the choicest ecstasy, like the feeling of supreme love."

Relations with people brought disappointment, sadness, and agony – at best, they were a waste of precious time. Writing poetry, on the other hand, produced the experience of ceaseless fulfillment. The number of poems in her drawer mounted. In 1859 she wrote ninety-four – almost two per week, most of them bearing the uniqueness she strove to achieve. She gathered them in packets (fascicles), kissed them, and placed them reverently in her bureau drawer. "The Goddess of Poetry has knocked on my door! May I be worthy of the title Poet!"

She ceased receiving visitors and going out to see the world – without concern for the effect on her mind and body. Months on end shut in her room, she studied her feelings. She turned her eyes inward, observed, felt, wrote.

Winter passed, and spring came slowly with rain and persistent cold. In the middle of a dreary day, Vinnie anxiously mounted the stairs two-by-two, opened Emily's door without knocking, and spoke breathlessly:

"That man with the deep voice is downstairs asking for you!"

Emily sprang up and rushed past her sister, who at once dashed to Evergreens calling out – "Sue! Sue! That man has come, and father and mother are not at home. I fear that Emily will go away with him!"

Bursting into the sitting room, Emily found herself facing the person who had fumbled with her soul – had profoundly inspired her, contributing to the development of her poetry from the time they met in Philadelphia.

Seated on the sofa staring at his hands, Charles Wadsworth tensely awaited her. At once Emily's eyes fell on the mourning band sewn on his left sleeve. In agony before the display of grief, Emily wanted to ask, "Did Mrs. Wadsworth pass away?" but she did not dare. She simply whispered, "You are in mourning, sir?" Her eyes rested upon him. He took her hands, and a tender shiver passed through her.

"I have lost my mother . . .". He spoke tremulously.

Emily took hold of herself, self-conscious concerning her earlier feelings about new possibilities. She breathed, "Was she very dear to you?"

"Very much," he murmured; then he said, "I leave Philadelphia. I go to Calvary Church in San Francisco. I came to speak to you. I want to – . . .".

That moment Sue rushed into the room, Vinnie behind her. Sue's eyes shot flames, but before her tongue could issue wounding bolts, Charles Wadsworth greeted her with complete composure. Quickly turning back to Emily, he enfolded her hands in his, bowed, and placed a formal kiss. "Having come to consult with my counselor, Dr. Clark, in Northampton, I could not fail to pay you a visit, Miss Dickinson – Emily . . ."

"Why did you not tell me you were coming, so I could have it to hope for?" Emily asked in trembling tones.

She did not permit her voice to reveal distress. In any case, the visitor had already stepped through the hall and out the front door. Emily collapsed on the couch, and Sue sat by her side, giving her a comforting hug.

"Oh, Sue!" Emily moaned. "My inspiration has flown! I can write no more!" Sobbing choked her, and Sue held her even more tenderly, whispering, "No, no, dearest one! Great poets do not depend on others, for they have unfailing inspiration within. It always stays with them in their vital thought and imagination – so they write unendingly, Emily darling!"

Vinnie observed Sue with relief. "Fortunately I thought of running to fetch her! What would we have done if that man begged her to go with him to San Francisco and she was unable to resist!" Vinnie nodded her head in satisfaction and for the first time in her life felt gratitude toward her sister-in-law. "Only Sue could have stopped her!"

Clinging to Sue's shoulder, Emily continued to shudder. "I am the Queen of Calvary," she sobbed, ". . . the Queen of Calvary!" Her heart recognized more fully than ever that love, tragedy, and inspiration are inseparably bound to one another.

The Word from the Sea

What is the poet?
A creature whose heart is
filled with secret pain.

His lips are so strangely formed
that his sighs and tears sound
like beautiful music.

Soren Kierkegaard

A poet is someone
Who can pour Light into a spoon,
Then raise it
To nourish
Your beautiful parched, holy mouth.

Hafiz

Autumn galloped with ill omens of the coming winter. The days were heavy, dark. The clouds sank low, and lightning strokes on the horizon were the clawing of wild beasts. Somewhere in the distance rain fell in deluges and the dampness showed that downpours would soon reach Amherst. With repeated wheelbarrow loads of wood, Irish workmen trod back and forth on paths to the woods, split the logs, and stacked cords in back yards. Seated on the stoop of Emily's house, with frozen fingers I dip my pen in the inky sky, striving to pursue my narrative. The storm in Emily's life is coming, and I am so moved by inconsolable sighs and weeping coming from the floor above that it seems impossible to write. Abandoned and alone, Emily is sobbing.

Yet a few months before, everything was normal, relatively smooth and bearable. Visits were rare. Uninterrupted writing nourished the racing days, and the hours slipped rapidly by. She would awake Monday morning and it seemed that Friday had already come. Perturbed, she realized the expending of her life: "I have no Life but this – To lead it here" (#1398). Indeed, how does one consciously *lead* one's life?

Thoughts and endless questions mounted in her mind, battering her mercilessly. She felt bodily and spiritual weariness. She dragged herself around the room, seeking relief from strong emotions, contradictory feelings, claims on her attention from visitors below, conflicts with her family, insomnia at night, tremblings during the day. She sought a means of comfort: not speaking, not eating – just sitting abstracted by the window. She simply felt like doing this day after day, in spite of demands from her mother and Vinnie. She could not define exactly what they wanted, but they insisted on drawing her into their lives, while she was swept into different spaces, in the infinite flow of her mind.

Many times she peacefully passed the day, but when evening came a shadow fell upon her; it perturbed her, and the echoes of faint sobs came slowly and insistently from somewhere inside her. They shook her profoundly. Standing by the window she watched the sun turning westward, the hills dripping sunset, the light descending on the church, reddening the bell-tower. Moving above the town, it fell upon trees and bushes and spread a curtain of fire over the streets, reached her window, pierced through the glass, embraced her with a warm, gentle glow, and she melted – became one with the light. Her body and soul surrendered to the beauty of the sunset and her heart vibrated with a plaintive melody. These moments calmed her, but when dusk descended and darkness surrounded her, the feeling of strangeness intensified, and she was unable to describe what was happening to her. An ever lurking, indefinable longing attacked her, wrapping her in feelings of desire, and words – a jumble of sensations – enclosed her. She sought inspiration to describe and define experience.

As the words overflowed, she inscribed a poem that caught the ecstasy and pain of the moment of transcendence as it comes and goes (#258):

There's a certain Slant of light,
Winter Afternoons –
That oppresses, like the Heft
Of Cathedral Tunes –

Heavenly Hurt, it gives us –
We can find no scar,
But internal difference,
Where the Meanings, are –

None can teach it – Any –
'Tis the Seal Despair –
An imperial affliction
Sent us of the Air –

When it comes the Landscape listens –
Shadows – hold their breath –
When it goes, 'tis like the Distance
On the look of Death –

The Deprivation of Love

Time passed in blankness, inertia. As the days became months and the months painted the landscape the colors of the seasons, Emily entered more deeply the domain of solitude. Visitors dwindled and vanished, even from her thoughts. It was enough to view Sue's life through the window, letting the days slip by indifferently while the poignant light of melancholy tinged the gray clouds over Amherst, covering Emily with numbing silence. Her soul hemorrhaged with agony, and only ecstatic creativity brought moments of escape before she once more plummeted into darkness (#512):

The Soul has Bandaged moments –
When too appalled to stir –
She feels some ghastly Fright come up
And stop to look at her –

The Soul At Its Limits

Salute her – with long fingers –
Caress her freezing hair –
Sip, Goblin, from the very lips
The Lover – hovered – o'er –
Unworthy, that a thought so mean
Accost a Theme - so – fair –

The soul has moments of Escape –
When bursting all the doors –
She dances like a Bomb, abroad,
And swings upon the Hours,

As do the Bee – delirious borne –
Long Dungeon from his Rose –
Touch Liberty – then know no more,
But Noon and Paradise –

The Soul's retaken moments –
When, Felon led along,
With shackles on the plumed feet,
And staples, in the Song,

The Horror welcomes her, again,
These, are not brayed of Tongue –

Vinnie climbed the stairs, lighted Emily's lamp, and speaking calmly, so as not to disturb or upset her sister, placed the dinner tray on the small table and quietly insisted that she take a bite before retiring. Emily absent-mindedly obeyed and ate sparely, paying no heed to the food. She only listened to the words as they exploded inside her, punctuating her darkness.

Lying in bed one morning, she thought she heard a sound coming from outside on the lawn. She got up and peered through the window. A winter dawn of rare brightness made the area between the houses seem to glow with happiness, and Emily's eyes devoured the figures in the scene. The couple she loved so much formed a beautiful image by the door of Evergreens. Their bodies spoke to her of life as their velvet silhouettes confirmed a moment of precious fulfillment. Their arms were linked as was their gaze, and Austin bowed very near Sue's face, kissed her, and seemed to whisper a magic phrase. Their countenances glowed as he slowly descended the steps, approached the horse, which was restlessly tapping its hoof, and affectionately patted its snout. As the horse tossed its head in the proud knowledge of its master's love, Sue gazed smiling and trembling from the stoop, her body confessing the bliss of intimacy.

Emily saw and felt. A wave of deep emotion swept over her and she released a mute sob of deprivation.

She heard the whinnying of the horse like a trumpet of departure. For a long time she imagined the carriage passing through town, seeing it even when the sound had ceased. Sue entered the house and locked the door. The scene was fading, but precious words of longing continued to echo in Emily's heart. "Oh, Sue," she groaned deep within.

The seed of pain fell upon the aching ground of her heart. The yearning for love wrenched her. Bowles had betrayed her; Wadsworth had withdrawn far, far away. What a deprivation of intimacy, of sharing – what an affront to her helpless spirit!

From the very beginning of her life she had been deprived and affronted. There had been a poverty of closeness from her brooding mother and busy, distant father. Her youth had lacked the tenderness and awareness all souls need. In her existence there had been such a pervading lack of feeling and affection!

She thought of Vinnie. Ever patient, supportive, uncomplaining, even she one time exploded with resentment. Upon returning from Washington, she had thrown her arms around Emily and in a voice trembling with emotion said, "I met two girls, daughters of a congressman. One evening when I was in their room, their father came in and spoke sensitively to them. Before leaving, he hugged and kissed them, saying, 'Good night, my special girls!' They laughed in delight and told him that they were expecting him to accompany them and their guest around town the next morning. They had the boldness to make demands upon their father! And when I asked them about the kiss, they told me that each and every night he gave them a tender kiss at bedtime. And, Emily, they told me this as if it were the most ordinary thing in the world! But our father never kissed us goodnight in his life! He would have died for us, but he also would have died before he'd expose his feelings!"

The warm touch of the security that Emily lacked as a child remained in her maturity like a neglected seed demanding to burst into flower. Her repressed complaint became ingrained sadness, and the dream of love became an idol ever beyond reach. Her need informed tones of lament:

God gave a Loaf to every Bird –
But just a Crumb – to Me –
I dare not eat it – tho' I starve –
(#791)

***

It would have starved a Gnat –
To live so small as I –
And yet I was a living Child –
With Food's necessity
(#612)

Poetry would offer her precious crumbs of fulfillment. She rooted herself in its syllables. The words flowed, the rhythm mounted, and she lived through its vitality.

Emily did not hear Sue's voice calling to her near the "Northwest Passage" under the stairs. She was deeply immersed in writing, and Sue left angrily. This was the second time that Emily refused to see her. The first time, Emily wrote her a note: "Sue forgive me for not seeing you. Be Sue and I am Emily – Be next – what you have ever been Infinitely. Yet I must wait a few days before seeing you. You are too momentous. But remember it is idolatry, not indifference." Sue, enraged, thought, "Before I forgave her but not now." She now felt the anger choking her and stubbornly drew her curtains shut. She could not permit Emily to go on doing just as she pleased. "Let Emily remain glued to her window watching for a sign of me," she vengefully thought.

Every morning Emily eagerly watched Austin leaving, and every evening with the same eagerness awaited the quick hoof-beats of his return. She watched him standing in the carriage, his red hair waving in the wind as he pulled up before the stable. He was always looking toward her window and raising his hand in loving greeting, while the curtains of Evergreens remained drawn shut and Sue never in view. The curtains did not permit even the shadow of her beloved to appear.

Solitude occupied her heart. The Queen of Calvary was alone – all, all alone – she confirmed, and the quiet tears of melancholy swelled to inconsolable terror and panic. She felt paralyzed, unable to budge her door, as if it were locked from outside. Vinnie was shaken by her suffering. Her repugnance toward her sister-in-law mounted: "Sue, with her pride, her indifference," she thought, "will be Emily's death." Alone, Emily sought rescue from words which, anchored in the mind, blocked the outlet of sorrow. Sue's appearance had dissolved, and the constant thought of her made the loss greater. She thought, what if Sue were ill; what if she died shut within the house? Anguish wrenched her heart, and for hours she remained immobilized by the window. Sue's house was still and sealed. Emily expressed her pain in letters to Sue, who – somewhat slow in responding – finally wrote her a letter, the only one surviving Vinnie's mania. (She burned Sue's letters immediately after Emily's death.)

> Private
>
> I have intended to write you Emily to-day but the quiet has not been mine. I send you this, lest I should seem to have turned away from a kiss –If you have suffered this past summer I am sorry I Emily bear a sorrow that I never uncover – – If a nightingale sings with her breast against a thorn, why not we [!] When I can, I shall write – Sue –

"Oh yes – she loves me!" Emily exalted. "And her sharing my pain helps me bear my burden!"

Distorting Mirrors of Loneliness

Emily was lost – tortured by pangs of desire. Like a thirsting tiger in the desert she pled for water to slake her thirst ("A Dying Tiger – moaned for drink" – #566). She imagined the squeaking of doors opening and closing in Evergreens. The delightful, barely discernible noise was stirring, as she envisioned Sue emerging from Evergreens, taking the path to the Homestead . . . padding up the stairs . . . entering her room . . . taking her hands . . . leaning close . . . tenderly kissing her. Then thoughts of fulfilled passion like refreshing water surged through her heart (#211):

Come slowly – Eden!
Lips unused to Thee –
Bashful – sip thy Jessamines –
As the fainting Bee –

Reaching late his flower,
Round her chamber hums –

Counts his nectars –
Enters – and is lost in Balms.

She longed for the beloved in the house opposite; she missed Benjamin, her friend lost for years; she dwelt on Humphrey's intellect and enthusiasm; she reveled in the imagined erotic embrace of Bowles; and how could her thoughts not repeatedly swing to Wadsworth, among the most energizing souls she had ever encountered?

She yearned to see them once more – to be plucked from the grip of death – but she was frozen in her room. Also, she realized that paradoxically she might not be able to endure anyone's touch – except that of Sue, her other self: "The Woman my favorite . . . Here is Celebration – If I ever cut off my fingers, in their place Sue's fingers would grow." Thus she wrote as she reached out her hands toward Evergreens to link with Sue, so that hand-in-hand they could live passion at the core of their being.

Her frame ached with the demand for contact. Hearing the churning of desire in her body, she shuddered, yet she was unable to open the door, to rush down and out across the yard and seek the beloved arms. The terrible pain – descending from the head along the spine down to the soles of her feet – filled her with fear and panic. As an iron crown crushed her head, and manacles clamped her wrists and ankles, she collapsed strengthless onto her bed. The emptiness of death seemed to enclose her, yet in her heart and mind she knew that if she could touch Sue, nothingness would withdraw. Oh that laying her head on Sue's sacred breast, she might experience that most splendid of all solaces! "Of all the Souls that stand create – / I have elected – One" (#664).

She strove, however, to retrieve the path of logic – to find relief from the tyranny of self, to root out yearning for earthly fulfillment, to be liberated from longing, to surrender to curative inspiration. As the angels of creativity summoned all her powers, she arduously turned from the physical to the mental sphere, shaping words to save herself (#642):

Me from Myself – to banish –
Had I Art –
Impregnable my Fortress
Unto All Heart –

But since Myself – assault Me –
How have I peace
Except by subjugating
Consciousness?

And since We're Mutual Monarch
How this be
Except by Abdication –
Me – of Me?

But the self, remorselessly demanding, insisted on its searing claims (#601):

A still – Volcano – Life –
That flickered in the night –
When it was dark enough to do
Without erasing sight –

A quiet – Earthquake Style –
Too subtle to suspect
By natures this side Naples –
The North cannot detect

The Solemn – Torrid – Symbol –
The lips can never lie –
Whose hissing Corals part – and shut –
And Cities – ooze away –

She recognized her state and shuddered beholding the murderous waters threatening to engulf her: "Adrift! A little boat adrift! / And night is coming down! / Will *no* one guide a little boat / Unto the nearest town?" (#30)

Wild waves of emotion thrust her toward oblivion. As she wrote in a letter to a friend, "I feel that I am sailing upon the brink of an awful precipice from which I cannot escape and over which I fear my tiny boat will soon glide if I do not receive help from above." She held with all her might to the lifeline of work. She perceived the swells of the mind washing her into savage tempests, and with insistent efforts she strove to save herself because she knew that she could be thrown into a treacherous course far from the harbor of sanity (#556):

The Brain, within its Groove
Runs evenly – and true –
But let a splinter swerve –
'Twere easier for You –

To put a Current back –
When Floods have slit the Hills –
And scooped a Turnpike for Themselves –
And trodden out the Mills –

The groove of terror was treacherous, slippery – and she slid into alien territory. The reassuring words of her family could not reach her. She experienced existential chaos, the horrendous realm of spiritual blankness which Kafka wrote about a century later (#761):

From Blank to Blank –
A Threadless Way
I pushed Mechanic feet –
To stop – or perish – or advance –
Alike indifferent –
If end I gained
It ends beyond
Indefinite disclosed –
I shut my eyes – and groped as well
'Twas lighter – to be Blind –

The fall continued. It reached the deep unconscious, "so wild a place we are soon dismayed." With enormous efforts she fought back up to the surface, gripped the hands of the spirit, and swung herself into the shrine of Beauty. Agony, pain, panic, fear of death, the tyranny of love, jealousy, and the struggle for life sent out to poetry a cry for salvation. For her, poetry alone could provide both direction and spiritual strength. She transcended her self, took hold of knowledge solid and entire, shaping her lines to express the essence we all strive to discover in the depths of our spirit when darkness threatens annihilation. She examined pain threatening the powers of regeneration (#561):

I measure every Grief I meet
With narrow, probing, Eyes. . .

She experienced the near obliteration of her being (#599) . . .

There is a pain – so utter –
It swallows substance up –
Then covers the Abyss with Trance –
So Memory can step

Around – across – upon it –
As one within a Swoon –
Goes safely – where an open eye –
Would drop Him – Bone by Bone.

She studied the drop into nothingness (#650):

Pain – has an Element of Blank –
It cannot recollect
When it begun or if there were
A time when it was not –

When pain finally passes, there comes a persistent state of spiritual numb-ness, which she describes with enormous power (#341):

After great pain, a formal feeling comes –
The Nerves sit ceremonious, like Tombs –
The stiff Heart questions was it He, that bore,
And Yesterday, or Centuries before?

The Feet, mechanical, go round –
Of Ground, or Air, or Ought –
A Wooden way
Regardless grown,
A Quartz contentment, like a stone –

This is the Hour of Lead –
Remembered if outlived,
As Freezing persons, recollect the Snow –
First – Chill – then Stupor – then the letting go –

The Soul At Its Limits

She weighed her anguish and put it in its place like the unruly body: "I measure every pain I meet, [but] I am not concerned with the body. I love the timid soul which hides because it fears the bold, meddlesome flesh." So agony of dark nights came to haunt Emily's days, and she wondered if this might be insanity (#410):

The first Day's Night had come –
And grateful that a thing
So terrible – had been endured –
I told my Soul to sing –

She said her Strings were snapt –
Her Bow – to Atoms blown –
And so to mend her – gave me work
Until another Morn –

And then – a Day as huge
As Yesterdays in pairs,
Unrolled its horrors in my face –
Until it blocked my eyes –

My Brain – begun to laugh –
I mumbled – like a fool –
And tho' 'tis Years ago – that Day –
My Brain keeps giggling – still.

And Something's odd – within –
That person that I was –
And this One – do not feel the same –
Could it be Madness – this?

Emily Dickinson: Goddess of the Volcano

The field of her consciousness was accordingly transformed when loneliness planted the fear of death at the center of her thought and her body succumbed to its iron grip. She lay down, and as her eyes fixed on her inert body, she spoke of her own death:

I heard a Fly buzz – when I died –
The Stillness in the Room
Was like the Stillness in the Air –
Between the Heaves of Storm – . . .
(#465)

***

I felt a Funeral, in my Brain,
And Mourners to and fro
Kept treading – treading – till it seemed
That Sense was breaking through –
(#280)

***

It was not Death, for I stood up,
And all the Dead, lie down –
It was not Night, for all the Bells
Put out their Tongues, for Noon.
(#510)

With the wisdom she had gained, she did not give in to the fear of death, but analyzed her feelings, concluding (#335):

'Tis not that Dying hurts us so –
'Tis Living – hurts us more –
But Dying – is a different way –
A Kind behind the Door –

Incredible as it may seem, the mind gradually came to accept death – familiarized itself with its reality. If death was nature's dictate, she had to prepare for it (#412):

I read my sentence – steadily –
Reviewed it with my eyes,
To see that I made no mistake
In its extremest clause –
The Date, and manner, of the shame –
And then the Pious Form
That "God have mercy" on the Soul
The Jury voted Him –
I made my soul familiar – with her extremity –
That at the last, it should not be a novel Agony –
But she, and Death, acquainted –
Met tranquilly, as friends –
Salute, and pass, without a Hint –
And there, the Matter ends –

Whether she was thinking of death itself, or the fading of happiness in this life, she had seen both of these forms of loss, and she had discovered that the spirit can transcend them. Thus, her soul leapt from the body and followed its own path – that of poetry (#351):

I felt my life with both my hands
To see if it was there –
I held my spirit to the Glass,
To prove it possibler –

The buffets of experience had threatened to debilitate her, but she strove to support herself joyfully with powers that dispersed the cloud of annihilation. She perceived that "the sheer sense of living is joy enough." As she thought, the words, overwhelming, relieved her. Vinnie, too, was a saving presence beside her – her voice a soothing, tender caress. Through creativity and spiritual fellowship, Emily could encounter the miracle of change. "I will enter new channels of experience," she decided. "I will be re-baptized. I will name my way of living. I will cease to belong" to ordinary channels of salvation:

I'm ceded – I've stopped being Theirs –
The name They dropped upon my face
With water, in the country church
Is finished using, now,
(#508)

She had dared to immerse in the secret, obscure world of the self; she had reached the extreme depths of melancholy, examining them in the distorted mirror of loneliness, and she had been dragged into savage emotions, but she was determined to retrieve her spiritual direction. She knew that when she was on society's paths, she felt wounded and powerless, but when she fought the waves of personal suffering alone, then inspiration seized her like the breath of life, leading the spirit into ecstatic moments. As she wrote, she called up every sensation she had experienced, unimpeded and complete. Thus, each poem dealt with pain and sang out the joyous adventure of change in creativity. Then she reached the truth about herself: "The shore is safer but I love to buffet the sea. I can count the little wrecks in friendly waters and hear the whispering of the wind; but Ah, danger enthralls me!"

"Life holds the most delightful secret!" she later wrote with a shrewd smile, reaching into her pocket where she always had poems written on slips of paper. The words leapt up bleeding but alive. They breathed thought and passion. Her heart surged – her mind exalted, finding herself among the supreme creative spirits of all time. It was not egotistic self-indulgence, but simply a reality granted to her. She would take a poem at random, read and reread it. She liked its strangeness – as if she had not written it herself. She chose another – a third, and a fourth. She read them all, and all were blooming. Joy flooded within her. She had aimed at uniqueness, and it seemed that she was on the right road. "Yes, I am a poet! – perhaps even a master poet!"

An impulse made her laugh and taste a joy that made her body shiver. She spread the poems on her bed. The white coverlet was filled with colors. She gazed at them, stroked them a long time, and a deep impulse came upon her. She removed her clothing and shoes, and – calmly and softly – she stretched out on the live papers. They trembled, pressed against her naked flesh, warmed, and caressed her; and this strange contact brought her primal serenity. She stayed there for a long time.

She arose, dressed, took the poems one-by-one and touched them to her lips. That rare moment, Emily confirmed that no person or event could offer her the ecstasy of supreme art. She had absorbed the touch of words on her soul and body, and she had experienced satisfaction as a gift without arrogance; it was simply pure arousal, as if she were not treading on earth but flying with ethereal movements. She herself had become art. Her space was not her room but an exotic precinct, as if some matchless sovereign had guided her there, had seated her on an honorary throne, had bestowed a crown on her head, and proclaimed her queen. "If I should be a queen tomorrow!" The thrill of creativity swept her away. Now she knew what her withdrawal from the world meant. It was the basis of the enormous task of innovative creativity. She was bringing something new into the world! She also realized that withdrawal included never fully revealing her poetry to people, lest its magic be contaminated, its form be compromised, and the miracle of creativity be cancelled.

A triumphant laugh burst out of her as she placed poems in the drawer. The sound of rushing footsteps on the stairs made her laugh even louder. With gaping, startled eyes, Vinnie rushed into the room. Emily, still laughing, thrust her hands into her pocket for a few poems not yet in the drawer.

"Yes!" she cried, "Yes, yes, yes!"

"Oh, Emily, how wonderful . . . to see you happy!" Vinnie spoke stumblingly – terrified.

"Oh, I am, Vinnie! I am very happy! Do you want me to read you a poem?"

Vinnie nodded, reaching out a hand to calm her sister. "Yes, read me a poem, Emily!"

Emily plucked a poem out of her pocket. She read the lines in her clear, melodious voice, and Vinnie responded self-consciously, "I don't . . . I don't get most of it, Emily – but, goodness me, how much I like it! Read me more!"

Emily read another, and yet another, and Vinnie, laughing, kept wiping her eyes.

"Don't cry, Vinnie dear. I'm well – I'm very well indeed!" Emily exclaimed, and sweeping her hand around the room she added, "Home means paradise, Vinnie, and paradise means poetry. We are in paradise!"

Vinnie threw open her wide embrace, Emily nestled close, and the two understood that Emily's depression had subsided and even more important, the path of madness had been transformed to the highroad of creative exuberance.

They opened the door and descended – Vinnie to the kitchen and Emily to the garden. Her flowers lifted their little heads to look at her and their leaves moved as if touched by her coming. The birds flitted from branch to branch celebrating her presence, and she turned to take the path to Sue, her steadfast link to the outer world.

The path of her solitude had led to a highway of discovery. Creativity was "Ecstasy, the gift of the gods at the center of the poet's own being." Immortality was waiting for her around the turn of the bend!

Take all away from me, but leave me Ecstasy,
And I am richer then than all my Fellow Men –
Ill it becometh me to dwell so wealthily
When at my very Door are those possessing more,
In abject poverty –
(#1640)

Take all away –
The only thing worth larceny
Is left – the Immortality –
(#1365)

The moments when the psyche was bleeding and had to be "bandaged" had become few. Her blood had found its natural rhythm. When the angry waves now and then hurled her upon the jagged rocks of solitude, she sought calm ports for refuge. When the tides of depression threatened, she wrote to Sue, "Do not cease, Sister. Should I turn in my long night I should murmur Sue." Hugging her, Sue would say, "My precious, Emily, do not surrender to the waves of the mind; for I fear that then they may sweep me away with you into the deep and we both will drown."

"Sue," Emily breathed, "you are my universe."

John Graves

The Soul achieves - Herself

The number of fascicles in the drawer mounted yearly, but every year also brought events in family life that were unforeseen and difficult. The letter arriving from Boston the first week of April, 1860, was addressed to Emily's mother. She held it in her hands with joy, without the least premonition of the sad news it contained. Smilingly she stepped to the kitchen table by the window, put on her glasses, broke the seal, and began to read. It was a message of one paragraph filled with agony and pain that she was expected to bear. It was from Loring, husband of Emily Norcross Dickinson's sister Lavinia, who must have written it with a trembling hand, for the letters were confused and broken, the lines running askew on the page. "My dear Emily, your little sister, my beloved Lavinia, fallen sick unto death. Send Vinnie to care for her. I am afraid, Emily – oh, Lord, I am so afraid."

The letter dropped from Emily Norcross's hands, and a long-drawn "ah – ah –ah ahhh" broke the silence of the house. The sisters swiftly arrived in the kitchen, and Vinnie picked up the letter. "I will leave at once," she announced; "I can take the afternoon train. Take heart; I will bring her back to health." She rushed upstairs to pack her suitcase, looking back to reassure them: "You will see. You will see. All will be well!" Emily went into the garden with trembling heart and gathered flowers to send to her beloved aunt.

One letter followed the other. In each Vinnie pledged her aunt's recovery. Improvement was terribly slow, but she was sure that auntie would be up and around before long. "And to tell you pleasant news: I will bring her to

Amherst. . .". Thus she promised, and Emily dreamed, longing for the moment of Vinnie's return, auntie by her side.

Three weeks later came the final word, laden with grief. "Our aunt departed willingly to meet her Lord." Forlorn, Vinnie returned and held first her sister's and then her mother's hand, comforting them with the picture of her aunt's last hours filled with courage and longing for the imminent meeting with her savior. As mother gripped her head in grief, Emily was struck by the birds in the garden, still singing and celebrating the summer, the season treasured by her aunt. She would not live it again. She would not hear their warbling again. So why did they go on singing?

Fifty-one years of age, Aunt Lavinia died of the same disease that struck down so many Norcrosses, and Emily wrote her dearest cousins, the daughters of Aunt Lavinia: "Since I cannot pray for my aunt, let me sing."

Fall arrived and death struck once more. The pastor's wife, who had been motherly to Emily, had departed from Amherst just a few months before, and now she had moved once more. She had gone to meet her Lord, and indeed had done so with great Christian willingness. Emily felt the pain as if she had lost two mothers, and amidst her grief came word of renewed fear. Dear Sue was pregnant. Everyone in both houses was numb with agony. The thought of Maria, Sue's sister, brought indelible fear. In summer of 1861, everyone anxiously awaited the successful outcome of Sue's pregnancy.

Perspiring, with tense hands, Emily sat by the window observing what was taking place in the house opposite. Hours without water, without a bite to eat, she watched the sun climb the sky's stair with the ease of an adolescent; it reached the peak, then bent softly on the other side, at first carefully, and by the end of the day dived headlong and disappeared. The town was blanketed in darkness, the streets deserted except for an occasional carriage moving by. Blankness and silence reigned. Only the two houses with their lamp light bore witness to the agonizing event. Emily anxiously followed the movement of the lamplight in the house opposite. Sue's birth pains had begun in the morning and had sharply mounted through the day. The doctor was by her side.

Soon after the doctor, Harriet and Mattie had arrived. Austin kept a steady vigil. Vinnie had been there from very early and Maggie hurried back and forth between the two houses. Emily was at her window viewing faces, movements. The night had fallen, and standing at the same spot she was waiting breathlessly, and the moment the sun began to break – sending repeated ribbons of light from far below, painting delicate red hues on the horizon, timidly touching the tops of trees and throwing faded yellow that turned to white – Emily caught sight of Vinnie. She was running – laughing, skipping, as if she was dancing – along the path. Looking up at the window she excitedly waved both hands towards Emily, who opened the window and called,

"Are they alive – do they breathe? Tell me!"

"It's a boy! It's a boy!" Vinnie shouted joyful but exhausted.

Emily sighed deeply in relief but jealousy raised its head and affirmed, "Sue will give her all for the baby and her love for me will fade." Then joy surged in her heart – "But dear Sue is well!" – and in a few days she wrote Sue a poem (#218):

Is it true, dear Sue?
Are there two?
I shouldn't like to come
For fear of joggling Him!
If I could shut him up
In a Coffee Cup,
Or tie him to a pin
Till I got in –
Or make him fast
To "Toby's" fist –
Hist! Whist! I'd come!

Toby: Vinnie's cat.

Austin was in bliss, as was Edward, with the arrival of the boy. Indeed, Austin and Sue had written the elder Dickinson a letter requesting the honor of naming the child after him. Everything was so beautiful with life's new gift, and there was no hint of Ned's developmental problems, which were unseen on the far horizon.

In 1861, the months passed with Emily's soul on fire and her body on ice. Her production of poems was steadily increasing, and she was able to confirm that "The Soul achieves – Herself" – that her spirit could stand on its own, above loneliness, within the confines of her father's house: "A Prison gets to be a friend" (#652). Her isolation intensified as the waves of her spirit and thought surged down the pages. Vinnie was steadfast by her side, caring for her; and when signs of anguish appeared on Emily's face, Emily reassured her, "Vinnie, don't worry. We grow accustomed to any agony or pain," and she read her a poem (#419):

We grow accustomed to the Dark –
When Light is put away –
As when the Neighbor holds the Lamp
To witness her Goodbye –

A Moment – We uncertain step
For newness of the night –
Then – fit our Vision to the Dark –
And meet the Road – erect –

And so of larger – Darknesses –
Those Evenings of the Brain –
When not a Moon disclose a sign –
Or Star – come out – within –

The Bravest – grope a little –
And sometimes hit a Tree
Directly in the Forehead –
But as they learn to see –

Either the Darkness alters –
Or something in the sight
Adjusts itself to Midnight –
And Life steps almost straight.

And, becoming cynical, she shared more bitter lines:

I reason, Earth is short
And Anguish – absolute –
And many hurt,
But, what of that?

I reason, we could die –
The best Vitality
Cannot excel Decay,
But, what of that?

I reason that in Heaven –
Somehow, it will be even –
Some new Equation, given –
But, what of that? (#301)

Still, she could endure her trials, solid in her spiritual independence and fellowship with a few kindred spirits. Her perceptions and feelings would arise in a world of her own making (#303):

The Soul selects her own Society
Then – shuts the Door –
To her divine Majority –
Present no more –

Unmoved – she notes the Chariots – pausing –
At her low Gate –
Unmoved – an Emperor be kneeling
Upon her Mat –

I've know her – from an ample nation –
Choose One –
Then – close the Valves of her attention –
Like Stone –

By 1862 the number of poems had reached three hundred and thirty-one. Emily was living life as she had chosen. Her answer to the brevity of existence was: Life is short – creativity eternal.

An Incredible Argument

In 1862 the weather was difficult, but human folly made life even more trying. It all began one blustery Sunday at Sue's. Samuel and Maria Bowles had come to spend the day and stay overnight. Evergreens, with its splendid hospitality, could have been the perfect environment for the diversion of Maria Bowles, whose time was exhausted by housekeeping and child care, but the truth was that she was hardly enamored with the company of Sue Dickinson, whom she did not trust; and Sue, in turn, could not stand seeing the gallant Bowles imprisoned in a marriage with – in her eyes – such a brainless woman, who had the audacity to advise Sue as a young mother regarding the care of the new-born child.

It was soon after supper when between the two women, one word led to another. Sue raised her voice, and the husbands, eyes bulging, found their wives exchanging epithets in shrill voices. Maria, outraged by Sue's insults, strode to the door, flung it open, and shouted back to her husband: "Bring the suitcases at once – we are going home!"

It was bitterly cold, with steady freezing rain. Wrapped in blankets, mute and glum, the Bowleses set out to cover a distance of many miles; and as if that was not enough, midway the journey was interrupted when a wheel sank in the mud. Bowles hastily pulled the blanket over his head and with enormous effort wedged a plank under the imprisoned wheel. He pushed with all his strength as the steady, freezing rain soaked him. The carriage moved, and he climbed back in the driver's seat, threw off the damp blanket, and felt the cold assail him from his frozen feet to his shivering back. As he took the reins he began to cough.

Exhausted, continually coughing, in bed, Bowles saw a trip to Europe as the sole therapy for his mental and physical condition. Making plans for the trip was his only relief in his alarming condition. His health had always been fragile due to the exhausting hours of work in the newspaper, plus many activities in social life. This crisis, however, was unprecedented, as he underwent a relapse into coughing and weakness for days on end. He went, as usual, to Northampton hospital for treatment, but to no avail. Thus the transatlantic retreat, far from family and professional pressures, was indeed imperative. Accordingly, he departed for a long sojourn abroad, taking Maria Whitney along regardless of gossipers' whispering. After all he had need for a trusted person who could aid him in the event of an emergency. Following the trip, he was often to visit Evergreens, especially valuing his friendship with Austin with whom he pledged an eternal bond.

Following the incident at Evergreens, Maria Bowles's anger settled into fixed aversion to Sue. Sue regretted that the row had taken place, albeit she believed it was not her fault. In any case, she told herself, she had never sought the friendship of that woman who did nothing but bear children, most of them stillborn. She had no reason to apologize. Let the Bowles woman never set foot in Evergreens again!

Through her window, Emily observed the lives of her friends from afar. "Human beings," she mused sadly, "all have their own centrifugal force which determines their course ."

The centrifugal force swept friends not only a great distance from others but from themselves as well, and Emily looked on, never judging the reasons for their actions. She missed Bowles during his stay on the continent, and she missed Sue, who had spent some time with the child visiting her aunt in Geneva, New York. Left alone, Austin took his meals at the Homestead. His expression was always vacant and sad. "What is going on in his life?" Emily wondered. "From the moment Austin left for his wedding, we began to miss him, and now that he comes every day we miss him more than ever."

Enigma in White

A Spider sewed at Night
Without a Light
Upon an Arc of White.
(#1138)

In the train bound for Amherst, Edward Dickinson sat comfortably on the velvet pillow custom-fitted for him. A faint smile played on his lips as his breast filled with pride toward his significant part in bringing this modern means of transportation to his town. Everyone, conductors, engineers and station masters, as well as many travelers he met along the route, recognized this as his personal contribution and expressed gratitude. With difficulty he masked his pride in the accomplishment. With the advent of the railroad connection, travel to Amherst had become swift and comfortable, greatly benefiting both business and cultural affairs.

He was returning home. After the long trip from Washington through New York and Boston, Edward was at last entering the countryside around Amherst. In a few minutes the train would reach the town, and his eagerness to see his family intensified. After weeks in the capital, he greatly missed them, and one of their letters had troubled him. His anxiety regarding Emily increased as he neared the station.

He slowly stepped down and assumed a placid manner, nodding to townspeople and railway officials. He quickened his steps on Main Street as he approached the Homestead. Lamps glowing in the windows, the house seemed to reach out to him. His heart began to throb almost violently. He wondered how the family was. In spite of his wife's tendency to self-absorption, she was considerate and soft-spoken toward him, and he had recently noticed that when she was with Amherst friends she had become more outgoing. However, his daughter, his beloved Emily, what had happened to her in recent years? She had closeted herself in her room, and she spoke little. Her voice was calm, but sometimes so low as to be barely audible. And that new white dress of hers – why did she wear it daily and why had they written to him about it? What did her behavior mean? He wished she would be as she had been as a young student, lively, happy, and talkative.

Such were his thoughts on the short stroll from the station. As he approached the kitchen door by the back porch, the delightful aroma of baking bread soothed his tension. His face lit up. It was a sure sign that his gifted daughter might well have overcome her troubles – Emily was preparing for him the bread he loved so much; and would that she would be playing the piano as before!

Although his apprehension had mounted so high that he could barely breathe, he sighed with a measure of relief and opened the door to find them all gathered in the kitchen. The entire family was there – attired in their Sunday best, their arms wide for an affectionate embrace. In her long white dress, Emily lovingly greeted him with a carefree smile. He was home! His heart soared. *What a delight life was with such a wonderful family!*

As the burden of concern receded, he responded to the welcome with spirited hugs and kisses. The days went by with familiar activities and conversations. To be sure, Emily did not come downstairs for bible readings. She did not appear in the morning or afternoon, but she did join the family for dinner and pleasant talk. Nonetheless, Edward's heart constricted when their eyes met. He found something odd etched in her gaze, in her vague gestures, in the hushed manner of her speech. He lost heart. Doubts and conjectures once more multiplied. As the days passed, it became increasingly evident that things were not as he wished. The atmosphere seemed to be submerged in murky waters – nothing came out clearly, as if the circumstances were covered by a heavy cloak, which parted only on rare occasions to reveal fleeting glimpses of strange regions and inexplicable developments. Intense feelings threw him into shifting moods. This man, puritan discipline personified, who maintained strict family rule, who always confidently came to grips with difficulties and dealt with the strongest challenges, found above all in his elder daughter an overwhelming impasse. What he feared – and had repeatedly confirmed – was that she had not taken the road he had laid down for his three offspring. This was unspeakably painful – humiliating. Vinnie, always affable and obedient, of radiant countenance, had a life utterly devoid of anxiety and questioning. Placid, flexible, eager, she steadily responded to the needs of others; she never provoked anger or displayed pride, precisely like his son. Hard-working, obedient, married, with a child of his own, Austin never caused difficulties or disturbances. But the other one, Emily; in her presence, he felt a strange uneasiness, but also – amazingly – awe. From infancy, she had stirred confusion in his soul. The spark of genius was in her eye, but she was subject to disruptive moods and raised explosive issues about life, death, and even the existence of God. No one knew how to react to her questioning. In essence, from the outset this child had not traveled the family path – or the road of people in general. Her questions were endless and strange, her vocabulary baffling and ambiguous, her talk formerly as endless as her present silence.

After her school years, her problems had increased: she withdrew from the church, her friends, and the people of the town. And now – was she withdrawing from the rest of the family? Alone in her room, what was she doing? Reading? Lying in bed? He did not know what to think or conjecture. For him she was the great question mark – her ways brought anguish, distress, anger, fear, and an odd feeling of respect. So many contradictory thoughts and feelings baffled him; he had no way to react. And all these difficulties were his alone. His wife seemed oblivious to Emily's peculiarities, and Vinnie showed no concern at all. Once when he had elicited her thoughts about her sister, her eyes had glittered with pride as she announced: "She is a great poetess!" "Poetry – hogwash!" was his reaction, and he spoke with Austin. "You amaze me, father! Don't you know your own daughter?" was the reply. "It's a pose. She's playing the poet," he added coolly, without a trace of anxiety.

Edward had tried to be calm and to view the situation as others did, but difficulties increased in the Dickinson household. It wasn't Emily alone; there was also the little boy – his grandson. He could not erase from his mind the first morning after his return. He had gone to his daughter-in-law for coffee. The boy was with her – little Ned, who seemed to be perfectly well. Smiling and reaching out to give the boy a hug, he met the child's eyes. His little eyes stood inert in his face. He would never forget those eyes – empty of feeling, empty of awareness. There was an appalling vacancy there, and he was powerless to master the panic that seized him. Sensing the mood, the mother caught the child in her arms and spoke in a gentle but serious tone: "It's grandpa, Ned"; and the child seemed to recover, but it took time. And thus another anxiety mounted. A vague suspicion of something that was not right caused Edward to quake. He had a different feeling of strangeness about his daughter. Many times as she sat down at the dinner table in her white dress, he was overcome by the feeling that an airy sprite was among them. She took her dinner in silence, and only when she was addressed did she speak enigmatically. Looking at her with admiration, Vinnie acted as if she completely understood what Emily was saying – it was quite proper and correct; while her mother's gaze jumped awkwardly around the table, a question in her eyes, her mouth open, but silent, as if to query Emily's every word. He had looked at Emily, seeing her as an increasingly remote image of his memory of her – not a presence here and now. Each day that passed in the Homestead deepened his anxiety. He did not know precisely what troubled him, and why he did not speak out. But what would he ask her? He feared the reply – ambiguous, mysterious, yet totally plausible, somehow. What, then, would be his rejoinder – and, worse – what if she broke out in rage? Yet just to sit back and do nothing was wrong. He was a responsible father. He had to seek the aid of someone wise in the ways of the human soul.

The names of individuals within or outside his circle passed through his mind, and he pondered which one was suited to render a verdict. His choice fell upon pastor Jonathan Jenkins. He was not only the family minister but a long-time friend. He esteemed the Reverend Jenkins for his profound learning and loved him for his concern for the congregation. He trusted his sincerity, discretion, and deep sensitivity.

The pastor dropped by early in the afternoon, his bible under his arm and the Lord by his side. The moment he arrived, Edward felt relieved. Yes, he was the one person in the world who would be able to help. He would provide counsel, and together they would determine the appropriate therapy and – if necessary – physician.

Emily came down the steps with a smile to consult with the beloved minister and family friend. She had always been preoccupied with the divine. She had many questions to which the pastor she admired could suggest answers. The two of them conversed confidentially for an hour in the sitting room, and then the Reverend Jenkins appeared in the hall. His eyes radiant, his step joyous, his face held a smile that was like sacred light. He raised the bible and waved it above his head, and before leaving by the front door, he exclaimed to

Edward, who was anxiously waiting for a diagnosis: "Sound, my dear friend – sound!"

Deeply inspired, Reverend Jenkins did not wish to speak to anyone, especially Edward Dickinson. Besides, he had nothing to add. Edward's dark eyes glowed as he viewed the face of his minister. Hearing the word *sound*, this man, who never in his life laughed, and had rarely smiled, felt immense relief. As the door closed, a burst of laughter erupted, which he controlled and covered with a cough. When Vinnie, who knew every detail of the family's thoughts and feelings, heard that sound from her father's lips, she also laughed out loud, while Edward's wife looked at him in surprise from the kitchen doorway.

Rev. Thomas
Wentworth
Higginson

CHAPTER III

The Step Into The Outside World

Thomas Wentworth Higginson

As if I asked common Alms,
And in my wondering hand
A Stranger pressed a Kingdom . . .
(#323)

Softly singing, spring was coming. Melting snow from the hilltops flowed down in humming streams that refreshed the slopes and valleys, which responded with foliage and flowers. Emily – a vision in white – stepped into her garden, and their handyman, Joseph, hastened to bring the little pillow on which she knelt. She smiled and gave him heartfelt thanks. She took a deep breath that was like communion, and with awe greeted the arrival of the season. In their unique tones, the little souls around her, spectacular in their natural beauty, warbled in their varied language the joy that filled their hearts. Bluebirds, cardinals, robins, spritely sparrows, and her beloved bobolinks all exchanged notes as they hopped from branch to branch. Delicate, brightly colored butterflies brushed the petals of flowers; Emily's beloved bees buzzed as they sipped nectar. Nature held her in its embrace. Her soul found peace. She breathed deeply the blend of scents and ecstatically beckoned to the world: "Prithee, come into my garden!"

Her mind returned to the theme that had preoccupied her for days: Would she take the great step of inviting the world into the garden of her poetry? Would she answer Mr. Thomas Wentworth Higginson's invitation? It was a great question – a crucial decision.

A week ago she had, as usual, enjoyed perusing the *Atlantic Monthly*. As she focused on a section that was popular among poets, an article sprang to her attention. It presented a challenge that applied to her. Should she indeed respond?

Higginson's piece, which was written in plain language – simple phrasing laced with elegant literary touches – caused her to smile; nonetheless, fate, combined with deep impulses, determines our actions, and thus Emily felt the need to write to the author, seeking his advice about her poetry. His article, "Letter to a Young Contributor," offered practical advice for poets of both sexes concerning the writing and publication of verse. Having touched on basics ("Always use black ink, white paper, and neat script"), the author went on to points of substance: "Work hard. The practice of writing leads to its perfection." The crafting of the poem was not neglected: "Push language to its limits. A word can be charged with years of suffering, and half a lifetime can be contained in a single sentence. A single word can be a window through which one can view the entire universe." And there were also observations that made a great impression on Emily, stimulating her creative drive: "Literature is an attar of roses, one distilled drop from a million blossoms." The conclusion was inspiring: "Carry the form of poetry into Life."

These words played through Emily's thoughts as she worked in her garden. She touched the delicate roots of plants and felt their longing to stand tall in the sun. Observing nature celebrating the coming of spring, she was deeply inspired by the resurgence of life. Escaping from the restrictions of her room, she spread the wings of her imagination and delivered herself to the great calling of producing poetry for the world.

Yes, the time had come. She would open herself to the lovers of language through contact with that romantic writer of the article who was sensitive to the poetic word and who honored and loved nature as she did. If she would send him poems, he might well become her advisor and thus her work would reach individuals who were critically aware and attuned to innovative techniques.

As she knelt in the paradise of her garden enjoying the presence of her personal friends, butterflies, bees, and birds, who without fear circled around her, she composed in her mind the first letter she would send him, which began:

Mr. Higginson,

Are you too deeply occupied to say if my Verse is alive?

She visualized his receiving her appeal and smiled. Thomas Wentworth Higginson was nationally famous. She read his columns regularly in the *Atlantic* and in her dear friend Bowles's *Springfield Republican*. She appreciated the directness of Higginson's style and recognized his romantic sensibility, especially when he penned poems about gleaming lakes with many-hued lilies. She admired him, not so much as a poet, but as a forceful progressive activist. Though he was not, perhaps, among those thinkers who penetrated the utmost depths of the mind and spirit, his insight and awareness did strike sensitive chords in his readers' hearts. As she read him, Emily esteemed his steadfast stand against social injustice in New England and elsewhere. The issues of women's rights, slavery, the need for changes in the educational system, religion without dogma – all these themes were given fiery treatment in his articles. If president Abraham Lincoln shook the hand of Harriet Beecher Stowe, author of *Uncle Tom's Cabin*, calling her "the little lady who created this great war," he could have pressed with equal enthusiasm the hand of Thomas Wentworth

Higginson, who literally contributed to arms for the first uprising in the south by visionary John Brown, his sons, and son-in-law, who were in the vanguard presaging the civil war. Higginson also contributed to the development of the famous Underground Railroad. He worked to overthrow certain laws of New England that theoretically forbade slavery but did not affect regulations regarding the rights of private ownership. Slaves escaping to the north were arrested and returned to the south, where they were cruelly whipped under the laws of the region. The case of a fifteen-year-old slave named Sims brought tears to people of conscience and cynical smiles to the face of the indifferent.

Young Sims, starving, arrived by walking and swimming at Boston, the first major stop on the road to freedom, but he had no opportunity to find a safe haven. He was taken into custody by the authorities in spite of the avid support of Higginson and his group. The judgment of the court weighed heavily on the heart of the public. Sims was ordered to return to Louisiana, and upon arrival he was whipped, as was the practice, all the way from the border of the state to the plantation. He was turned over to his owner dripping with blood as the accompanying officers from Boston stood by, forbidden by law to intervene.

In another case – that of the twenty-year-old slave, Anthony Burns – Higginson conjured up a plan whereby the Boston court's decision could be circumvented: After the judge's ruling, Burns would be taken by Higginson's abolitionist agents out of the second floor window of the court house. The prisoner would slip away from the guards and jump from the window into a carriage waiting directly below that would spirit him away. The day before the planned escape, Higginson discovered with consternation that bars had been installed around the windows and that there was a possibility of betrayal by parties involved in his plan. Nonetheless, this event did not terminate his efforts. His next action was bolder. Realizing that "the abolitionist cause demands aggressive action," Higginson planned to inspire people from his lecture audiences to break into the courthouse and liberate the prisoner. The plan proceeded as a large group approached the door, but they were fired on and began to scatter. Higginson ordered them to hold fast, accusing them of cowardice, but they fled, abandoning him and a few supporters, who managed to break down the door, but were unable to reach Burns. Guards awaited them, pushing them off. No one was injured or jailed. This greatly distressed their leader since arrest, in accordance with Thoreau's concept of civil disobedience, was part of the plan. Higginson had hoped that arrest would arouse the press in favor of his cause – an event that he would publicize in a series of articles promoting judicial reform. As for the young slave, his trial was completed – the ruling, his return to the south. All along the route to Boston harbor, a crowd of five thousand applauded Burns who, well dressed with head held high, took the cruel, unjust road of his fate. The day of the event at the courthouse, Higginson received an injury under his chin – a badge of his participation in the movement against the national shame of slavery, which so appalled him.

It was April 15, 1862, and Emily, having completed her gardening, hurried to her room to set her letter to Higginson down on paper. Vinnie hastily took the letter to the post office, and Emily's eyes stayed glued to the window in expectation of the postman bringing a reply. Would a reply from the busy editor indeed be forthcoming, and what would it say?

Higginson was at work on yet another article concerning the necessity of a war declared in the cause of abolition. He was troubled by the position of President Lincoln, who declared war, not against slavery, but for the preservation of the union. For Higginson the president should have focused on the key issue of human rights. A great nation like the United States should be a center of civilization, establishing liberty and justice for all of its citizens of every race and creed.

After all, it was for such rights that his ancestors in 1629 had arrived at the land of milk and honey with their six goats and their seven children – the eighth having died in the crossing. They had foreseen freedom of worship and liberation from all forms of oppression. Their crossing paid for, they established themselves on 1,500 acres, with the support of 30 pounds per year and only one obligation – the conversion of the natives, which they pursued with zeal, leading to unique situations.

Higginson's pilgrim forebears established their colony at the town of Naumkeag, which they renamed Salem. As head of the colony, the first Higginson was involved in exiling a mother and son "unfaithful" to the church, leading to their demise at the hands of Indians – according to the righteous, evidence of divine favor of the trials. When the first Higginson died, his son took over the community and under him the first hanging of alleged witches took place in 1692. The persecution of accused witches continued to the day that it reached the door of Pastor Higginson himself. His daughter was accused of witchcraft. The pastor at once reversed his stance and with great efforts brought the witch-hunt to an end. To his credit, as set down in records, he deeply repented his participation in such unjust and cruel puritan acts, the only such incidents that took place in the new world.

These were the first pilgrim forefathers of Thomas Wentworth Higginson. Immediately thereafter, his family members became entrepreneurs and sea captains who amassed great wealth. However, his father, Stephen Higginson, a Harvard professor, had a deplorable capacity to squander his sizeable inheritance. He was so generous that people quipped he would willingly give away his wife and children. He did not have time to fulfill the comment, as his wife passed away, leaving him with five children. He speedily married their governess, Louisa Storrow, who was from a respected family and had served in the household from the age of eleven. During the nineteen years of their marriage, she bore ten additional children, of whom six survived. Thomas Wentworth Storrow Higginson was the youngest child. His mother would say that he was "the star that gilds the evening of my days and he must shine bright and clear or my path would be darkened."

Higginson adored his mother and acknowledged that she was the only woman who influenced him regarding the many causes to which he committed himself, though at the age of nineteen, he married a liberated young lady, Maria. His mother did not approve of her, as she always had to have the last word on any subject. Not long after his marriage, his wife was struck by a disease, perhaps multiple sclerosis, which left her increasingly overwrought and helpless. Higginson was greatly distressed by her malady and the fact that she was unable to bear children, whom he adored, as shown by his frequently inviting his brothers' children to his home.

Higginson grew up in an environment that was wealthy but declined somewhat over the years. His surroundings were intellectually rich. His father's Harvard colleagues often visited. They brought books to his attractive aunt, his mother's sister who lived with them; and they encouraged the lad's presence during endless complex debates and discussions. Innovative ideas under the rubric "Newness" had sprung up in Boston, especially around the great university, and they spread like wildfire throughout the New England area and beyond. Significant universities and colleges were established at the time and increased in number to this day. Intellectual developments in the areas of music, theology, literature, philosophy, and poetry were furthered by writers and thinkers such as Nathaniel Hawthorne, Herman Melville, W.H. Channing, Henry David Thoreau, Ralph Waldo Emerson, feminists Margaret Fuller and Elizabeth Peabody, and the brilliant James family – philosopher Henry James, Sr., novelist Henry James, and psychologist William James. In poetry, this movement, the American Renaissance, came to a peak in the work of Walt Whitman and (with posthumous recognition) Emily Dickinson.

Thomas Wentworth Higginson grew up in this intellectual milieu. From the age of four, he read assiduously, immersed himself in poetry, and studied at Harvard. He received a degree at Harvard Divinity School and briefly served in the ministry, but he resigned, as he opposed dogmatism, supporting the ideals of love and brotherhood. The abolition of slavery became the main force of his existence. His convictions were expressed by his decision to become colonel of the 1st South Carolina Volunteers, the pioneering regiment of Afro-American soldiers. He was, however, wounded and forced to leave the service. Higginson studied ancient Greek throughout his life, and after the war he translated the Stoic philosopher Epictetus, a former slave who taught that all souls are equal and free. Devouring the books in his father's library, he especially admired devotees of divine beauty, including his favorite thinkers who became his close friends – Emerson and Thoreau. A novelist and poet, he was also a tireless editor and prolific writer of articles literary and political. He and fellow abolitionists were condemned by moderates as "foggy headed dreamers," and hard-core reactionaries maintained that their antislavery stance was a veiled attack against the church, the Bible, and Christianity in general. Conservatives attacked them, not so much for their anti-slavery position, as for their intense critique of fundamentalist beliefs.

Higginson favored unbridled devotion to one's cause, stating, "Without a little madness a man cannot do his duty in his times." (Emily agreed, elaborating: "Assent – and you are sane – / Demure – you're straightway dangerous –/ And handled with a chain.")

His pursuit of his ideals was driving and sincere. His many activities, however, weakened his literary effectiveness. With Mabel Loomis Todd he was editor of selections of Emily Dickinson's poems, but, as he later recognized, his work was faulty, permitting his collaborator to take license with the texts, a fact that Higginson recalled with great distress at the end of his life.

Is My Verse Alive?

Early in the morning, Thomas Wentworth Higginson arrived at his office as literary editor of *The Atlantic*, and his breath was cut by the sight of his desk piled high with letters from readers. He sighed, knowing that his day would be burdened by reading missives and poems that would often evoke his sarcastic, disappointed, or angry response, though perhaps there might be a poem or two worthy of publication. This was another day that showed the results of his article challenging aspiring poets, many of whom – especially women – zealously replied.

Taking off his coat and rolling up his sleeves, Higginson attacked the stack of letters, and it must have been around noon when he opened one from Amherst. He was shocked. The letter began with a blunt inquiry. It was not written in black ink, nor were the letters clear and rounded, but elongated, as if hurriedly put down. Furthermore, there was no signature. He read the page in a single glance and reread it slowly, carefully.

15 April 1862

Mr. Higginson,

> Are you too deeply occupied to say if my Verse is alive?
>
> The Mind is so near itself – it cannot see, distinctly – and I have none to ask –
>
> Should you think it breathed – and had you the leisure to tell me, I should feel quick gratitude –
>
> If I make the mistake – that you dared to tell me – would give me sincerer honor – toward you –
>
> I enclose my name – asking you – if you please – Sir – to tell me what is true?
>
> That you will not betray me – it is needless to ask – since Honor is it's [sic] own pawn –

He took a deep breath and, gently placing the letter on his desk, he took the little envelope enclosed, which held the poet's card and signature, together with four poems. Looking at the poet's name, he wondered about her identity. Of course, he knew of Edward Dickinson, but there were many Dickinsons in Amherst, and he doubted that the writer was a relative of the famous politician. Women of good families were not publicly involved in writing poetry. It was not proper for one of such high social standing and such a conservative family. Who this woman was, with her idiosyncratic letter, he had no idea.

He glanced at the first poem, moved uncomfortably in his chair, and reread it carefully: "I'll tell you how the Sun rose / A ribbon at a time" (#318). He turned to the second, which struck him like a bolt of lightning ("Safe in their Alabaster Chambers" – #216). Was this a poet who dared to treat the idea of the resurrection in a paradoxical way? Next came, "We play at Paste – Till qualified, for Pearl" (#320). With amazement, Higginson thought, "What I wrote in my advice to young poets, she makes a powerful poem!" Finally, he perused "The nearest Dream recedes – unrealized" (#319). Here was yet another strange lyric. He experienced the powerful feeling evoked in the reader by deep thought presented in intriguing language – in this case the image of a bewildered boy "homesick for the steadfast Honey" of transcendence.

It was as if the poet were sending Higginson the image of existence in four acts: Life, Death, Loss, Creativity. He was so stunned that thirty years *later* he recalled every facet of his reaction: "Unique poetry! It did not conform to any category of verse or possibility of criticism!" Higginson, of course, had no crystal ball. How could he foretell that this poetry, along with Whitman's, was the most powerful and innovative of its time, anticipating twentieth- century Modernism and Imagism? How could he have imagined that in her Amherst room alone, Emily Dickinson foreshadowed advanced critical theories of the coming century (like those of Bloom and Derrida)?

Higginson was understandably baffled by the poems, yet the poet was seeking *his* critical appraisal! Yes, he realized, this verse had something unique about it, but the question arose: "Was this, in terms he understood, poetry?" This poet did not observe traditional stanza structure, or consistent meter or regular rhyme. Higginson recognized that there was (to his knowledge) no precedent for this type of verse – with its irregular and half-rhyme, together with odd and obtuse imagery. Had Higginson known the work of Donne and the metaphysical poets, he would have been prepared for Dickinson's poems, but the vogue of the metaphysical poets was not to occur until the twentieth century. In turn, there were hints in Emily's poems of ballad meter, but the rhythms were irregular, and speech sounds were injected through the poet's tone and unorthodox punctuation with dashes. The metaphors were arcane but superb. The meaning was inexhaustible – and expressed in succinct, obscure phrasing. The subtle melody and wording, ambiguous and complex, thrilled him. Her words had the power to suggest significance at the profoundest level, involving the reader in active interpretation. These were elements that attracted and enticed him but confused and stymied him as a critic. How could he find language to engage in analysis or justify involvement with such peculiar verse?

He got up, took a drink of water, and returned to his desk. He gathered all the other letters and put them in a drawer as if he had finished reading for the day. Picking up the Amherst letter and poems, he looked at them for a long time. Surely, they had nothing in common with the poets of the age. This poet did not treat the standard themes of the time; she had nothing in common, for example, with the most popular American poet of the century, Longfellow. She did not treat social issues in a familiar manner. She dealt with the mind and spirit from unusual angles, avoiding traditional language. She did not directly introduce the woman's movement or the issue of slavery. Who had ever come up with an astonishing line like "Safe in their Alabaster Chambers" (#216)? Was the meaning ironic or cynical, or did it express religious insight? In the poem about the sun (#318), the poet stated that she knew how it rises but not how it sets. Would readers comprehend that she meant life and death? Who had ever likened the refining of a poem in the mind to the creation of a pearl by a grain of sand in the oyster's shell (#320)? Who could this woman poet be? What was her education? How old was she? Would her appearance be as unique as her verse?

Higginson arose from his desk, strolled the crowded streets of Worcester, breathed the atmosphere of the normal scene, and felt better. He returned to his office and, thinking of his mother, he wrote to her a letter and also penned a letter to his wife. His wife's reply raises unanswerable questions about what he wrote. What did he say in his letter that led her to the negative remark "all the cracked ones answer your challenges"?

Higginson repeatedly reread the poems, confirming again and again their virtues but also their deviation from traditional form. Holding his feelings in check and concentrating on his response to the correspondent's poetic oddities, he answered Emily's letter, striving to be delicate and polite. Because she had asked his advice and indeed urged him to speak frankly, since "honor was its own pawn," he would do precisely that. He would advise her how poetry is to be written, urge her to be patient, to work hard, and not yet to expect publication.

Emily anxiously waited by the window, and several days later saw the postman bringing a letter to the house. She dashed down the stairs, leapt to the front door, and profusely thanked the postman.

With the letter in her pocket, Emily smilingly returned to her room. She sat down and opened the letter with a steady hand. Scanning the words in a single glance, she smiled at the correspondent's tone as if it were precisely what she expected – polite, hesitant, controlled. She was gratified by the restraint of Higginson's remarks and felt his deep need to know more about her and the sources of her poetry. She was pleased. The letter demanded her immediate response. Indeed, she had not been mistaken in her choice of a poetic advisor. He was a gracious gentleman, and with her return letter she would enclose additional verses.

She stood up and looked out on her hills. Their green slopes offered their open arms to her – their trees a resting place for birds carefully constructing their nests. Higginson's response to her letter would build the nest she sought to hold her future fame. She would entrust her thoughts to him, her family secrets, details about her life – all that would be preserved and one day would be known to the world. She had chosen the right person. He would examine her work closely – which Bowles, a close friend – and his collaborator Holland had not done. Although they had requested her poetry, they did not publish it without intervention in wording and form, and they never commented on her philosophic qualities or her subtleties as a poet.

Yes, she would reply at once to Higginson's letter, but she had to be very circumspect. Her responses would be innocent (after all, she was from a good family), intelligent (she was a poet), but ambiguous (she was Emily Dickinson). She read and smiled; she wrote and laughed. She knew her correspondent's every thought, doubt, and hesitation. He was an honorable man, without pride and arrogance. He valued her poetry but did not know a category in which to place it. She forgave him for that, and she smiled at his efforts to nudge her toward the conventions of verse, which were the very traps she wished to avoid.

Emily wrote precisely what she felt: "Mr. Higginson, Thank you for your surgery – it was not so painful as I supposed." She continued her letter in regard to the proper form of poetry, which he said she did not possess, sending him the poem "I cannot dance upon my toes" (#326). What the poem demonstrates, of course, is precisely the poet's capacity to dance upon the toes of her own unique verse:

I cannot dance upon my Toes –
No Man instructed me –
But oftentimes, among my mind,
A Glee possesseth me,

That had I Ballet knowledge –
Would put itself abroad
In Pirouette to blanch a Troupe –
Or lay a Prima, mad,

And though I had no Gown of Gauze –
No Ringlet, to my Hair,
Nor hopped to Audiences – like Birds,
One Claw upon the Air,

Nor tossed my shape in Eider Balls,
Nor rolled on wheels of snow
Till I was out of sight, in sound,
The House encore me so –

Nor any know I know the Art
I mention – easy – Here –
Nor any Placard boast me –
It's full as Opera –

The second poem sent Higginson a powerful message regarding inspiration. He had, in essence, counseled that she had to conform to conventions. In the reply, which was to become famous, she chastised him with a poem about burning inspiration related to the "finer forge" of spiritual discovery. Hers was a poetry wrought at the "white heat" of transcendence (#365):

Dare you see a Soul at the White Heat?
Then crouch within the door –
Red – is the Fire's common tint –
But when the vivid Ore
Has vanquished Flame's conditions,
It quivers from the Forge
Without a color, but the light
Of unanointed Blaze.
Least Village has its Blacksmith
Whose Anvil's even ring
Stands symbol for the finer Forge
That soundless tugs – within –
Refining these impatient Ores
With Hammer, and with Blaze
Until the Designated Light
Repudiate the Forge –

If Higginson were capable of grasping Dickinson's originality, he would perceive the telling implications of the first line, which spoke to his intellectual timidity ("dare you") and to her spiritual passion ("White Heat").

The Step Into The Outside World

To Higginson's question about her appearance, requesting a picture, she answered with heart-stopping delicacy and power:

> Could you believe me now – without? I had no portrait, now, but am small, like the Wren, and my Hair is bold, like the Chestnut Bur – and my eyes, like the Sherry in the Glass. . . .

Concerning her studies, tragic personal experience, daily life, and family relationships, she wrote:

> I went to school – but in your manner of the phrase – had no education. When a little Girl, I had a friend, who taught me Immortality – but venturing too near, himself – he never returned – Soon after, my Tutor, died – and for several years, my Lexicon – was my only companion – Then I found one more – but he was not contented I be his scholar – so he left the Land.
>
> You ask of my Companions Hills – Sir – and the Sundown – and a Dog – large as myself . . . They are better than Beings – because they know – but do not tell. . . . My Mother does not care for thought – and Father, too busy with his Briefs – to notice what we do – He buys me many Books – but begs me not to read them – because he fears they joggle the Mind. They are religious – except me . . .

As for influences, she told Higginson:

> You inquire my Books – For Poets – I have
> Keats – and Mr and Mrs Browning.
> For Prose – Mr Ruskin – Sir Thomas Browne – and the Revelations . . . .

adding later,

You speak of Mr Whitman – I never read his Book – but was told that he was disgraceful.

Finally, in their initial exchange of letters, Emily speaks to the issue of publication, and she also mentions Higginson's challenge to her metrical propriety (without, of course, accepting his judgment):

Dear Friend, 7 June 1862

I smile when you suggest that I delay "to publish" that being foreign to my thought, as Firmament to Fin. . . .

You think my gait "spasmodic" – I am in danger – Sir –

You think me "uncontrolled" – I have no Tribunal.

Emily Dickinson corresponded with Thomas Wentworth Higginson to the end of her lifetime, and every letter revealed insights into her life, beliefs, and questions about poetics. Concerning her mother, she repeated the familiar phase, "I never had a mother," adding, "My mother never cared about thought." As for her creed, which was the great question of her life, she narrated an episode: "When I was young I attended a funeral which I know now was a strange sadness, and the pastor posed the question, 'Did God's arm shorten so he was unable to offer salvation?' I misinterpreted his phrasing as a doubt about immortality, and not daring to ask, I am still confused . . . In any case, I never cease to address God. 'Thank you, Father, for these strange thoughts. They attract me against you.'"

When Higginson inquired why she never went out, she replied: "In such a porcelain life, one likes to be sure that all is well, lest one stumble upon one's hopes in a pile of broken crockery." She sincerely expressed how much she honored their friendship and understanding: "In the hand you extended I placed my own," and in the same letter she offered a poem, adding, "Of our greatest acts we are in ignorance. You were not aware that you saved my life."

As if I asked a common Alms,

And in my wondering hand

A Stranger pressed a Kingdom,
And I, bewildered, stand –
As if I asked the Orient
Had it for me a Morn –
And it should lift its purple Dikes,
And shatter me with Dawn!
(#323)

The correspondence continued, and during its course Emily complained when Higginson was late in replying:

Did I displease you, Mr. Higginson?

But won't you tell me How?

Your friend,

E. Dickinson

She had not realized that the social activist had become a soldier. He was the colonel in charge of an Afro-American regiment. Only when Higginson was wounded and was forced to leave the service, did she learn what had occurred.

A Fiery Fog

Four years after the end of the Civil War (11 May, 1869) Emily received word from Higginson that he wanted to come and see her. Seven years had passed from the day that their correspondence had begun. How many events had occurred in the meantime! She recalled the panic one morning in April, 1864, when she had awakened with severe pain in her eyes and could not make out letters on the page. Fearing blindness, she was terrified that loss of eyesight would cause her to lose contact with the world of letters. The thought that "there are so few real books, I could easily find someone to read them all," was of no comfort. She was faced with the immediate ordeal of an obligatory visit to the ophthalmological clinic in distant Boston. The walk from the house to the railroad station was the first great challenge. What if she met townspeople? Often, as she was hiding behind the curtains in her bedroom, she watched them stumble because they were looking up at her window. What would happen if she met someone who wished to greet her by taking her hand?

"Maggie and I will be by your side," Vinnie reassured her. "I promise you, Emily, we will meet no one, and if people appear we will not let them come too close."

Thus, they set off one morning to consult with Boston's leading ophthalmologist. "All will be well," Vinnie soothed, and indeed it was. The physician informed Emily that her problem would be resolved. Hers was a condition of "hysterical blindness" due to psychological causes resulting in hypersensitivity to light. Her cure would be not to tire her eyes for extended periods of time, resting in semi-darkness. Emily and Vinnie went from the clinic to the home where Aunt Lavinia had lived and their two cousins were delighted to see them. Her residence in Boston for three months for treatment was pleasant and the cure was complete, but her return to Amherst was bliss. The following year she again took the train to Boston for a follow-up visit with the doctor. This was the last time she visited a doctor and the last time she went out of her house.

Higginson's letter, expressing the desire to see her, deeply moved Emily, and her heart dwelt on the tie established through their correspondence. Beneath the stream of their mutual respect ran an undercurrent of tenderness, and Higginson was continually a presence in her life. She perused the letter with deep feelings. Her friend confided:

Ms. Dickinson

I often take out your letters and your poems, my dear friend, and I feel their strange power. It is no wonder that I find it very difficult to write you. . . . I have a burning need to see you, to take you by the hand and be someone for you, but you surround yourself with a fiery fog and I cannot reach you . . . . Every year I try to find ways to be able to go to Amherst to see you . . . .

Your eternal friend,

Higginson

Emily's mentor, advisor to many literary people of the age, had the capacity to humble himself before her and, at the same time, to express his perception with the precise image "fiery fog," as he characterized features of her letters, poems, and her life itself. Emily smiled with delight. From childhood, she had adored the unknown, the mysterious, the enigmatic. Once, while attending the Academy, she had written to Sue: "In a world where everything is obvious, you and I could not live"; and to Higginson years later, she had expressed the same thought: "It is true that the unknown is the great need of the mind, although no one thinks of thanking God." This is also her advice to the "young man of Athens" (#1768):

Lad of Athens, faithful be
To Thyself,
And Mystery –
All the rest is Perjury –

In Higginson's letter, the most important point was that the extremely busy man of letters wished to travel to Amherst. The letter provided the most important reason for the visit: "To get to know one another by touching one another." This shook her. He truly wanted to come close to her, and she could not refuse his request. However, visitors – few and rare – frightened her. For days before and after the event she slept badly, lost the flow of her writing, and wandered distractedly around the house. Her state became psychologically exhausting, not only for her, but for everyone around her. Nevertheless, Higginson was her trusted friend. She wished to see him and had often said so in letters, yet she had felt relieved that before he had been too busy to visit. But now he had asked – and had expressed the need to touch her!

Stepping to her desk, she affectionately felt her copy of Higginson's last novel, *Malbone*. Her hand trembled and her heart pounded irregularly. Higginson's heroine Emilia – the object of the passion of the dashing hero, her stepsister's betrothed – most certainly was modeled on the poet of Amherst. The heroine was a priestess of art, an ethereal figure with the melodious voice of a delicate creature but with a wild streak, passionately occupied with the arcane choice of words. Such heroines of the period had a tragic fate. Higginson's Emilia was drowned one stormy summer night, leaving the hero inconsolable.

The extended correspondence of Emily Dickinson and Thomas Wentworth Higginson was outwardly based on literary concerns but the letters were also punctuated with overtones of subliminal eroticism. In his novel, however, Higgins had freedom of expression; he could project his desires through the experiences and words of his hero.

Who, then, desired the meeting in Amherst – the novelist or his protagonist? And who would be meeting him – Emily or Emilia?

There was a knock at the door, and the hearts of the three women skipped a beat. For weeks now – with thrilling thoughts, racing pulses, and imagined scenes, they had awaited the coming of Mr. Higginson. Maggie would receive him, and Vinnie would be by Emily's side as she waited to go down to greet the visitor. As the day had approached, Emily had been distressingly silent.

Maggie, attired in a new black dress, a white embroidered apron, and little cap, stepped trembling to the front door. Before she opened, she took a deep breath, fixed a smile on her lips, and, opening, she spoke the words she had memorized, "Miss Emily is expecting you."

Returning the greeting with a faint smile, Higginson removed his hat and stepped into the hall. Maggie took his hat, led him into the living room, and asked him to be seated. From the couch he scanned the titles of the volumes in the small bookcase. Feeling that he was in a familiar intellectual environment, he grew calm. His novels, essays, and poems, as well as works by his favorite writers, were there. The only thing that put him off in the room was its austere Puritan ambience. It was strange that such a famous citizen, representative Edward Dickinson, lived in such an aesthetically austere environment. Spare furniture – the couch, two chairs, the bookcase – did not offer comfort or harmony of colors; only the piano opposite suggested feelings of pleasure.

There was a faint knock at the door, and Edward Dickinson stepped into the room. Tall and thin, with reddish hair graying at the temples, he extended his hand and remarked on the pleasure of meeting the distinguished guest. With a few words about the mild weather, unusual for the season, he politely took his leave.

Pleased by this brief but warm-hearted reception, Higginson once more glanced at the decor, and at that moment he heard "a step like a pattering child's in entry," as he later remarked in his journal, continuing, "in glided a little plain woman with two smooth bands of reddish hair . . . in a plain & exquisitely clean white pique & blue net worsted shawl [who] came to me with two day lilies which she put in a sort of childlike way into my hand & said 'These are my introduction' in a soft frightened breathless childlike voice – & added under her breath 'Forgive me if I am frightened; I never see strangers & hardly know what I say'. . . ." Soon, however, a flood of words poured from her and he could not easily break in.

And then – in no time at all, it seemed – it was all over. His hat in his hand, Higginson found himself outside in the road. Emily had slumped to her bed, exhausted by the meeting, feeling the warmth of his hands, his searching eyes, his friendly smile. . . . His words . . . No – she did not remember what he said, what she said, how long they were together. She only remembered her reply when he promised her that he would come again sometime. "No," she corrected him. "Say in a long time – that will be nearer. *Some time* is nothing."

Higginson descended the stoop seriously and formally, but the moment he stepped into the street he departed from the Homestead as swiftly as he could. In the square, he pulled up, breathed deeply, and, releasing a sigh of relief, he proceeded to the stable where he had left his carriage. He settled into the seat, took the reins, and set off on the trip back to Worcester. In the evening he found himself seated at his desk and with a blank sheet of paper before him he brought to mind the strange and fascinating encounter with Emily Dickinson. Yes – having initially informed him of her awkwardness before strangers and her difficulty in conversing, she had launched explosively and eloquently into her philosophic views as well as incidents of everyday life – a high level of communication in an energetic mode of expression that eschewed the ordinary discourse of the time, bringing the listener to the brink of spiritual infinity; his only choice that of listening. Higginson jotted down several memorable statements of the poet:

> I find ecstasy in living – the mere sense of living is joy enough.
> How do most people live without any thoughts?
> Gratitude is the only feeling that is inexpressible.
> Truth is such a *rare* thing it is delightful to tell it.
> Say the truth but say it slant.
> To multiply the lakes does not lessen the sea.

Higginson felt once more the exhaustion of his effort to comprehend the meaning of her words as she spoke to him with such intensity and authority. He sighed and surrendered to emotional depletion. Emily's person once more appeared before him. Studying it, he concluded that while the poet's appearance might in many respects appear to be rather plain, her presence was overwhelming. He noted in his journal that he had never met anyone "who drained my nerve power so much." He wondered how such an emotional draining could have come without her having literally touched him at all. Fortunately, he noted, "I am glad I do not live near her." Suddenly his wife's statement about "cracked women" passed through his mind. He smiled and corrected the statement to "the partially cracked poetess of Amherst." Opening his drawer, he took a sheet of paper and with a warm feeling in his heart wrote her a letter.

From the living room window Vinnie watched Higginson walk swiftly away. "A handsome man!" she thought smiling. "You never know. His wife is sickly – and he is so suited to Emily!" That moment Emily, in her room, was writing to Sue, using her favorite nickname from Shakespeare: "Egypt, thou knew'st too well." She did not need to specify the allusion, for Sue knew the magical lines from *Antony and Cleopatra*:

Egypt, thou knew'st too well
My heart was to thy rudder tied by th' strings,
And thou should'st tow me after.
(III.xi)

Four years later, in 1873, Higginson paid a second and final visit. At this time he anxiously raised the question that had tortured him: "How do you pass the time without anything to do?" he inquired hesitantly. This was undoubtedly among the most gigantic *faux pas* in literary history – a blunder into the realm of absurd comedy. Emily serenely responded with a poem inspired by Higginson's description of birds: "The Birds begun at Four o'clock" (#783). Years later, after her death – when her poetry had matured in his mind – he remembered his blunder, recalling something else she had whispered to him: "The memory is a strange bell – of great celebration and mourning reverberation."

Little Ned

With the force lent by nature, the earth swirled on its axis, and as its face rested, now in light and now in darkness, its inhabitants found themselves at times in joy and at times in sorrow. Over the globe hung a cloud of inevitability. In the light everything was glowing but when earth's face was turned to blackness, bitterness and anguish prevailed.

Sue awakened in raw darkness. There was a strange sound, magnified by the midnight hour. It came from right above her head on the second floor where her little boy slept. The noise shocked her out of her sleep. Her body shuddered and a terrible fear stole her breath.

"Austin!" she shook him and he bolted upright.

They rushed upstairs with pounding hearts. Austin threw open the door and they found themselves facing a horrendous sight. Little Ned's body was jerking with terrible spasms. His eyelids were open; his eye-balls rolled back; his lips covered with foam. Unaware of what was happening, he was shaking for some time until the fit gradually subsided and he returned to deep, motionless sleep. The spasms disappeared as if nothing had happened, but the parents' hearts continued to quake inconsolably.

Attempting to control themselves, Austin and Sue gently placed the boy in the middle of the bed, tenderly covered him with the blanket, and stayed there weeping by the bedside the rest of the night. They were grateful that their two-year-old daughter, Martha, nicknamed Mattie, had slept undisturbed in the next room. She had not been wakened – had not heard a thing. In the all-night vigil over the little fellow, the parents were shaken by anguished thoughts. As dawn broke and light filled the room, their eyes were still fixed on the face of the child, who – opening his eyes – saw them, did not question their presence, and jumped into their arms with a placid smile. Wordlessly they kissed him and tenderly stroked his head.

"It's epilepsy," the doctor murmured sadly, and Sue threw herself onto the bed, wishing death would release her from the nightmare.

Emily embraced her wordlessly, and with sobs, Sue confessed, "I did not want a child. . . . I feared giving birth. Emily, I feared having a child . . . and when I became pregnant, I wanted the pregnancy to end, but the child held fast in the womb; it refused to fall. I had terrible fears. I didn't want to give birth, and you see what happened? . . . . Oh, how I adore Ned! The other day he put his little arm around my shoulder and pressed his little face against mine, saying 'I love you mommy . . . I love you!'... My poor little boy – I put a curse on you before you were born. . . ."

Emily strove to comfort her with a tender touch as Sue's thoughts dwelt on her guilty feelings.

With time they came to live with the burden of the malady; they adjusted, seeing light once more surround the child, as he grew up responsive and tender toward his parents and aunts – especially Aunt Emily. He loved Aunt Emily's letters about Aunt Vinnie's cats and the poor birds that did not come out in the rain because they had no umbrellas. Little Ned laughed and laughed and loved everything his eyes touched – people, kitties, horses, grandpa and grandma. Only school he did not love as befitted a Dickinson. Sue and Emily adored him. Looking upon him, Austin, however, could not be proud. A wave of anger toward Sue would wash over him. "I married her above all to bear strong children," he later confessed to his mistress Mabel. "I never loved her," he went on, "I adore you!"

Disturbing sounds from the bedroom above them kept recurring. Sue, sensitized, could even hear the sound of her little boy's breathing. Any variation terrified her, and when spasms came, she wakened Austin and she waited outside Ned's door, praying he would return to natural sleep. Only when Ned recovered did Sue enter his room, wipe away the perspiration, cover him gently, and kiss him as she begged forgiveness in her heart.

The parents explained Ned's condition to him only when he grew up. Now, as a child, he was not fully conscious during the crisis, and exhausted could not go to school the next day. The parents suffered during the crisis night. The bitterness between them increased, and their arguing voices could be heard to the end of the block.

The neighbors outside Sue's circle heard their voices raised in argument and were pleased that her pride was being punished. The little children in the house were horrified, and Emily turned her eyes in anguish away from Evergreens toward the other window facing the hills. Vinnie whispered to Maggie, "Austin has finally understood what sort of woman his wife is!" and Maggie set down the scenes in her mind, for she had a lot to tell her sister on Sunday.

The Sudden Death of Edward Dickinson

Each that we lose takes part of us . . .
   (#1605)

The emergency telegram from the state legislature arrived in Amherst. Austin was notified; Emily Norcross Dickinson buried her head in her hands, so she could not see or hear; Vinnie stood tensely by the window, trying to hold back the news. Emily – pale and trembling – descended to the kitchen. Sue, beside her, held her hand, bending every so often to whisper a word in her ear, though Emily's face suggested that she could not grasp the meaning of the phrases. Pounding her breast, Maggie wordlessly swayed in anguish. Austin spoke a few calm words of reassurance. With Vinnie by his side, he hurried to the station to catch the train to Boston. On the kitchen table, the telegram stated: *REPRESENTATIVE EDWARD DICKINSON GRAVELY ILL.* The daughters and wife of beloved Edward numbly awaited good news

The afternoon of the next day – after what seemed an eternity of waiting – the women saw Austin and Vinnie approaching the kitchen door. Darkness cast over them, they froze in the doorway, seemingly unable to bring themselves to cross the threshold. Emily knew the terrible words before they were uttered in Austin's heavy, hoarse voice:

"It is over . . . his heart. "

"His heart was pure and terrible and I think no other like it exists." The words flashed in Emily's mind. No one uttered a syllable. Not even a sigh came from their lips. As the news sank slowly, heavily, in their hearts, they blindly hoped that words of emendation might somehow emerge from Austin's mouth, but he continued his explanation in the same strange voice. "As he was addressing the state house of representatives, he suddenly felt ill, and he went to the hotel to rest. Believing it was simply exhaustion – it was cruelly hot – the doctor administered morphine. At three in the afternoon his heart stopped, the doctor recorded. The house curtailed the session by unanimous consent. Word of his death spread rapidly through the press: "Representative Edward Dickinson Dead from Heart Failure."

Emily's thoughts continued: "I joy that there is Immortality – but I would prefer to taste it myself before entrusting him to it."

The same day the casket arrived with due ceremony, and the tears flowed with all the pain of the loss of a father. Austin leaned over the coffin and placed a kiss. "There, father – what I have wished to do since I was a little child," he murmured and burst into tears. Emily Norcross collapsed to the floor. Vinnie knelt by her mother's side and helped her to her bed, while Maggie foresaw each movement that would reinforce her strength. She gently massaged Vinnie's back, brought her water and whispered the name of each visitor, attuned to her every need. Sue, dry-eyed, attended closely to Emily, and when people arrived, she followed her up to her room. She brought Samuel Bowles there – and Judge Otis Lord, with his wife – the only visitors whom Emily received among the many that came to offer condolences. Maggie stayed with Emily in her room the day of the funeral and interment.

Emily struggled to put her heart in order, being "cut off from that vital space called Father." She wrote Higginson as her dearest friend about "the last afternoon my Father lived, though with no premonition," and she recalled an incident that took place a few days before his last departure for the legislature.

She had come down from her room to take a book from the library. Edward, sitting alone in the kitchen, was thinking of her that very moment. He wanted so much to talk with her that his thoughts had virtually summoned her. She was sitting on the sofa with the book open, and, taking a deep breath, he approached.

"Oh, Emily," he whispered. He was so moved that he sat next to her as if his legs could not support him.

"Mother and Vinnie were napping. Father and I talked, our voices quiet and tender. The sun was setting, the light faded, and we had so much to say to one another. There was so much tenderness in his eyes that it embarrassed me, and that moment Austin came in and I suggested the two of them go for a walk. Father hesitantly arose – probably he followed Austin for my sake. He proceeded toward the door and stopped there. He turned toward me, deeply moved or sad? He looked at me. He didn't want to go. 'I wish that this afternoon would never end,' he said. They left the living room and went for a stroll. The next morning I woke him to catch the train and never saw him again."

At the funeral eulogies were reverently delivered. It was clear that now everyone had nothing but love for the Honorable Representative of Amherst. Everyone dwelt on his accomplishments, and the anecdotes were endless. Once a little boy walking around Amherst College campus with his father asked, "Whose college is it, father – whose?" and the father impatiently replied, "Why, Edward Dickinson's! Be quiet now, young whippersnapper!" Another favorite story: One Sunday afternoon after church, Edward entered a store to purchase a bottle of spirits, and the proprietor respectfully informed him that sale of alcohol was prohibited on the Sabbath. "According to the law, sir!" the proprietor solemnly added. "But I sponsored that law, and I can tell you – it doesn't apply to me!" Edward announced loudly.

Old inhabitants of Amherst remembered themselves as students drinking on campus and the great rumpus they created in the town; and everyone agreed that young Edward had been the wildest of the rowdies – a gift for relaxation unfortunately not inherited by his son.

Everyone also remembered his inspiring speeches on Independence Day, but there were those who did not forget his initial position on slavery. At first he recommended moderation – after all, slaves were private property; but later his sentiments changed, and he spoke fine words in favor of liberation.

No matter what people thought or said about him, the fact was that Amherst's most distinguished citizen had departed forever, leaving behind the most significant features of the town: the new railroad line and station as well as the ever-expanding College, glowing demonstrations of his achievement. Few, if any – however – had the least hint of his most magnificent contribution, not only to the town, but to the world of poetic art, his daughter Emily!

The curtains of the Homestead were drawn shut, leaden silence reigned, voices were hushed, footsteps were measured, and doors rarely opened. The life of the family had withered. As the days passed spiritless and dark, the loss of the main pillar of its support became increasingly clear to all. Emily Norcross Dickinson rose from bed only at meal time to eat "like a bird" as Maggie said, working quietly around the house with Vinnie, who kept close watch on her mother and Emily. Gravely weighed down by mourning, Emily's poems on the theme of death increased, as did references to sadness in letters to friends (#1300):

From his slim Palace in the Dust
He regulates the Realm,
More loyal for the exody
That has befallen him.

Sue's visits were frequent, but Emily remained clouded in withdrawal, deeply shaken by the unforeseen event. In the past, how often she had thought of Sue's visits – how often she had longed for them. Many times she had wished that she would be feeling poorly, and Sue would come to sit by her bedside, reading poetry and murmuring affectionately to her. She always cherished the memory of one afternoon when she was confined to bed. As Sue was reading to her scenes from Jane Austen, one moment she had closed her eyes and, believing she had fallen asleep, Sue leaned over and touched her lips. Yes, she had kissed her tenderly, as she had stayed absolutely still. Not a syllable passed from their lips. She had simply wished that moment would endure the rest of her life. But now? Now Sue's words of comfort, her affectionate embraces, did not touch the wound in her soul brought by the loss of her father. The wound hemorrhaged from regret and repentance for everything she had once said and laughingly written to Austin. Her mocking words became daggers in her heart. She recalled the great celebration of 1852 when the first train arrived at Amherst station. What joy and pride of all the townspeople who, in their finest suits and hats, gathered around the station! Bands played bouncing marches, flags fluttered in the breeze, and Edward, at the center of local officials, proudly addressed friends and supporters. It was a great celebration, incredibly joyous. From her window, watching her father triumphantly stride off toward the station, Emily had laughed sarcastically and she had written Austin ironically – "Father is really *sober* from excessive satisfaction, and bears his honors with a most becoming air. He is marching around town with New London at his heels like some old Roman General, upon a Triumph Day." Youthful irony toward her parents had been for Emily a daily routine, and now it was too late to reach out, tenderly touch father, and utter the words she felt deep in her heart. Life's motion had ceased; time had stopped. There was no going back. Father was out of reach, and her only outlet for expression was blank paper. Poetry was her sole means of spiritual contact.

During the week of Edward's death, an Amherst woman nineteen years of age, of a good family, the newspaper said, took her life as atonement for her great shame. She had been in love, thoughtlessly given herself, and in nine months her "great sin" was exposed to the small community, which was appalled by the fact, while the little boy was born in blooming health, as if he had the right to live – not as the fruit of a forbidden deed, but as the proof of love. The young woman, however, cringing before the puritan outcry, could not bear it. She saved her child but died by her own hand. Everyone spoke of her being condemned to hell. She was Satan's own, while Edward trod the paths of paradise.

Emily, confronted by emptiness, asked, "Sue, where is Father? Where do you think he has gone?" Sue humbly replied, "I went to the cemetery and placed flowers on his grave"; and Emily wrote (#1393):

Lay the Laurel on the One
Too intrinsic for Renown –
Laurel – veil your deathless tree –
Him you chasten, that is He!

Time passed, but the event continued to cast a shadow on Amherst, and people repeatedly recalled unforeseen deaths. Emily pondered mortality, concluding it was the darkest mystery of humanity. For Vinnie, however, death was a matter of fact, for she was occupied with the necessities of day-to-day life. In life, Edward Dickinson had been in charge of financial responsibilities, which were now undertaken by Austin.

The widow, with pains in her legs and fears in her heart, was a shadow in the big house; Maggie was Vinnie's shadow; Emily was the shadow of her own thoughts; Vinnie was the only creature of flesh and blood, who attended to everyone. Austin was simply a visitor with the monthly income in hand. As the family attempted to retrieve the thread of their lives, Emily realized, "You can get used to anything except death."

Earth continued to move in the shadow of ominous, trying events. Precisely a year to the day of father's passing, mother collapsed to the floor. The doctor confirmed – paralysis. When the silent, ever gentle sharer of others' pains, baker of sweets, became permanently bedridden in her room on the second floor, her elder daughter stayed at her side for the seven years remaining. She was grateful that she could be by her mother's side. Thus, time passed reading to her, fanning her in the hot days of summer, preparing heated bricks for her comfort in winter, and seeing to all the necessities of her daily life.

One month after paralysis struck Emily Norcross Dickinson and thirteen months after the loss of Edward Dickinson, a beam of light shone into the family's world – a little boy was added to the clan.

A Joyful Event

Austin knelt before his wife, whispering, "Oh, Sue, bless you – thank you!" He took the infant in his arms and gazed upon it. "God be praised!" he sang out, "Sue, the babe smiled at me!" He tenderly kissed the child and placed it in Sue's arms.

"Silly," Sue smiled, "You know very well that the newly born don't smile. It's a response from gas!"

"He's such a handsome boy," Austin returned, "and when I say he smiled, I speak true!"

"Of course you do, my love!" Sue returned, and Austin looked at her with infinite love. "'My love'! how many years," he thought, it has been since I have heard that word from her lips!"

"I want a favor," she said quietly. "I want to name the child Gilbert."

He looked at her in confusion. "Gilbert. You mean *his* name?" He went to say 'the drunkard' but fortunately he caught himself. "Your father's," he added.

"Yes, Austin! Yes. He has been on my mind for some time. I forgive him, or rather, I understand what drove him to drink. He tried to be a good father; but, think of it: he was younger than we are now, a widower in his forties, with six children to bring up. He never remarried because of his love for my mother. He always had her in his heart, and he drank in hope of forgetting."

"And what will we call the little boy – Gilbert?"

"Gib!" she smiled.

"Gib!" Austin echoed. "Thomas Gilbert Dickinson – nicknamed Gib. I like it, Sue! Thank you, my dearest!"

A few days later, as she climbed the stairs to Emily's room with the babe in her arms, Sue eagerly called her name. Emily opened her door, and they looked at each other silently, simply exchanging glances with deep feeling. They had not seen one another for a long time. Emily took Sue by the hand and drew her into the room. Sue placed the baby in Emily's arms, and Emily rocked him, murmuring a lullaby. Tears overflowed and fell on the infant's face. She dried them with kisses. Sue put her arms around Emily.

"Sue – the wonderful little boy!" Emily murmured.

"Yes, Emily – he will be mine and yours!"

"Will he truly be ours?"

"Yes, yes, yes!" Their heads touched tenderly as they bowed to kiss the child.

Eyes glued to the west window of her room, Emily watched Gib growing up. Her heart throbbed as she watched Sue push the baby carriage, followed by Carlo, Emily's dog, and, further back, Vinnie's cat. What a wonderful sight it was to see the little fellow coming out of the door of Evergreens. At work on poems, she watched Gib romping in the yard, ever lively, energetic. He and his friends played tag and climbed trees, making Emily fearful that he may fall. On Sundays she would watch the young lads, Ned and Gib, going to church in handsome suits, sporting canes, as was the fashion. Neighbors invited them for tea and biscuits, but the little boy would not touch them. "My aunt's are my favorites!" he would say, and he and his friends would eagerly run to Emily's window, waiting for her to lower them cookies in a basket.

A Visit

The noted writer and poet Helen Hunt, known as H.H., who had lived for years away from Amherst, heard the excellent news from Thomas Wentworth Higginson, when he recited poems by Emily.

"You must know Emily Dickinson," Higginson told her. "You are the same age and from the same town."

"Of course I know her," Hunt announced. "We attended Amherst Academy together. I remember a slim, bashful girl, accompanied by her plump little sister." She continued enthusiastically, "I didn't know she writes poetry. The poems you recited are superb. They must be published."

Helen Hunt.

A week later she knocked at the door of the Homestead.

"We are out," Maggie stated, resorting to the habitual formula.

"No, Maggie, you are in, and I must see the significant lady of the house at once!" Hunt answered sharply, taking a step to enter, but Maggie blocked her way.

The visitor smiled, looked at Maggie insistently, opened her handbag, took a handkerchief, shook it, spread it on the upper stoop step, sat down, and gravely declared, "Tell Emily that Helen Hunt will not budge until she sees her."

Maggie returned at once. "Come in," she said, leading the famous writer to the living room.

"You are a great poet," Hunt told Emily, "and it is wrong that you will not sing aloud!" She pressed Emily's hands, which were trembling with excitement. Emily smiled with delight.

"I love your poetry!" she sincerely announced to Helen.

"Emily, I know all the publishers in Boston. If they like my poetry, imagine how much they would like yours. Grant them the pleasure of reading your work."

Emily's heart skipped a beat as she thought of the bundles of poetry in her drawer. If she took a few poems, if she gave them this moment? A sharp pain went though her, as if a portion of her body had been cut off.

"No, Helen, I cannot!" Her voice – clear, sharp – declared her irrevocable decision. But Helen refused to acquiesce. She would not leave Amherst without at least one poem from Emily; and she achieved her goal. Emily handed her "Success is counted sweetest" (# 67), which would be published anonymously in a contest the following month.

Success is counted sweetest
By those who ne'er succeed.
To comprehend a nectar
Requires sorest need.

Not one of all the purple Host
Who took the Flag today
Can tell the definition
So clear of Victory

As he defeated – dying –
On whose forbidden ear
The distant strains of triumph
Burst agonized and clear!

The judges accepted the amazing poem, which they attributed to Emerson! It was published, and Emily was delighted. She did not disclose her authorship, but Bowles did, by suggestion, in his paper. Emily just whispered to Sue: "If I could make you and Austin proud some time – but a long time later – I would jump for joy." Nevertheless, she continued to shy from publication, and seeing her reluctance, Helen Hunt wrote a letter begging forgiveness, but still expressing the desire that Emily's verse see the light of day:

... Your hand felt like such a wisp in mine that you frightened me.
I felt like a great ox talking to a white moth....
You say you find great pleasure in reading my verses. Let somebody somewhere whom you do not know have the same pleasure in reading yours....

Their correspondence continued, and Hunt begged her: "Leave your poetry with me as your executor lest the great event – which others call death – happens first to you...".

Emily did not answer, but she wept bitterly when she learned of Hunt's "great event." Helen Hunt had lived to the full all the joys and bitterness of life. Her drive to publish never abandoned her. She lived to write. Nothing could stop her, not even the death of her husband, a distinguished officer whom Emily admired for his courage. Not even the death of her only son held Hunt back. She married again, went to Colorado, where she wrote novels, poems, and letters to Emily, all of which were cut off when Death in the guise of cancer of the stomach, pitiless and demanding, commanded her to relinquish her pen.

Emily was embittered, but she did not write to a spiritual advisor of Helen Hunt, inquiring if she had gone willingly to meet the Lord. She knew very well there was no such person in the life of H. H., who had had never stepped through the door of a church.

The Departure of Samuel Bowles

We outgrow love, like other things
And put it in the Drawer –
(#887)

Pale-faced, Sue climbed the stairs with difficulty and sat mutely on the edge of the bed, staring at the floor. Emily took her by the chin and raised her head.

"Sue," she said, "what has happened! Tell me! I am like a reed – I bend but do not break! Speak to me!"

"Bowles . . ." came the choked whisper.

Sitting down beside her cherished friend, Emily put her arm around Sue's shoulders and gazed out at the hills.

"Yesterday . . . Yesterday morning. . . ."

Emily remained silent, her eyes fixed on the hillsides. It seemed that, *in memoriam*, tons of snow had crushed the limbs of trees and bushes.

Rising, Sue stood a moment in the doorway. "I'm not attending the memorial service . . . I can't bear it. I can't." She broke down in tears.

Emily heard Sue descend the stairs. It seemed that she stopped a moment in the kitchen. Then the door slammed. That moment heavy flakes began to fall on the frozen white drifts, absorbing sounds, magnifying the silence.

Seated as yet on the edge of the bed, Emily again heard footsteps on the stairs. The door opened and Vinnie came to her, gently touching her shoulder. "I will go with Austin, dear. I will go. . . . The service is on Monday." She gravely withdrew and shut the door quietly.

Closing her eyes, Emily whispered to herself, "Five months! In five months three friends are gone, as if the plague struck beginning with father's death. In September, dignified Maria Higginson died." "With sadness upon the death of your happiness," she wrote Higginson. "The wilderness is new for you, Master – let me be your guide"; and in the second letter she stressed, "Perhaps she has not gone so far away as you, who remain, think." And but three months had not passed when Judge Lord's wife departed. "Mrs. Lord is gone, and poor Judge Lord is all alone," she thought, choked in pain. The Lords were very close family friends who visited the Dickinsons often. Mrs. Lord had passed away suddenly, without forewarning. Emily felt a stab of passionate feeling for that dignified judge of the Massachusetts Supreme Court. She had experienced traces of infatuation for Otis Lord from the day she had heard him speak at Amherst College. Then seventeen, she was at the onset of sensual awakening, and she felt a surge of attraction toward this man with gray side burns. The decisive tones of his speech always stayed with her. At the time of her father's death, the Lords had stayed with them to offer comfort. Emily thought of that moment of her anguish when she had nestled in his arms – that feeling of security, love, and safety that lodged in her heart. Now, without his companion, Lord lived with his sister-in-law and her daughter. Emily had to write him a letter of condolence, but she had not as yet done so when she learned Bowles was gone.

Emily's tears flowed uncontrollably. The word *gone* – the thought *vanished* – brought such pain that it activated a site in the mind where overpowering memories reside. The door that locked out memories through daily routine burst open, and, one-by-one, reminiscences poured out before her eyes with all the aching sensations of joy and sorrow they contained. Radiant moments filled her breast with feeling, and it was as if she were reliving experiences that moment. As one memory fled, it invited another, and time, like life, rushed down hill toward its terminus. "Life is a brief fleeting moment between the past and the future," she sighed, and added, "And yet the terrific event has not taken place in my life." Everything she desired crowded within her mind – there were too many things yet to be lived, and time was so short. Her thoughts turned to Samuel Bowles, who had accomplished so much yet felt unfulfilled. He had passed, gone, disappeared forever, in the prime of his life at the age of fifty-two. She would miss him terribly. Though she had refused to see him the last twelve years, she would miss him as much as the others. For Austin he was brother and friend. For Sue, a fancied lover. That was the innocent game that she and Sue played. For Vinnie, he was a great personage – friend of the family. And for Emily, he was, moreover, the romantic hero of the novel, as he rose aristocratic and vital, from Charlotte Bronte's pages. He was Rochester and she was Jane Eyre – what a marvelous game of love, this matchless fantasy!

She had fallen in love with Bowles at the age of twenty-five. Amorous feelings ruled at that age, and he was an extraordinarily handsome, keen intellectual! His figure was athletic; his mien Apollo's – eyes like the sun. His erotic energy lighted fires in both houses, and both Sue and she were wildly excited by him.

Her heart beat strongly again as she heard that desirable question: "Would you send me poems for publication?" If they had only honored my style, the great event would have been fulfilled, she thought. At the time hope, "a thing with feathers," nested in her and for years she had sent him poems, hoping that he would understand and correctly publish them. It was then that she fell deeply in love with him. She could recall the precise moment, and she relived herself in Evergreen's hall as a young girl with joy her entire being. She remembered the scene in detail, reliving the delight once more. "That was the moment of love," she thought, "when I was jolted with jealousy."

One Sunday early in the afternoon, seeing Bowles's carriage outside Austin's house, she rushed down the path to Evergreens. She entered by the kitchen door and stepped down the hall to the living room. The two of them, Sue and Bowles, were alone – sitting side-by-side and laughing. Austin, a church elder, was still at a church meeting, and the pair were enjoying their delightful rapport. Radiant, Sue was laughing with that familiar resonance that Emily believed was reserved for her. Reading poetry together and holding hands, their feelings would reach a pitch of spiritual intensity. Sue would lean her head on Emily's shoulder and laugh, and that laughter was so delightful that Emily would kiss her with an intensity that left her limp. Now Emily heard similar laughter on Sue's lips. She saw the pair and froze. They were sitting very close. They did not press against one another; but her hand was in his. He whispered something to her, and, giggling, she leaned toward him, seeking his shoulder. Thunderstruck, Emily stared at them.

Sensing someone was looking at them, the pair looked up. Facing her, they shot to their feet nervously asking, "What is it, Emily?"

She wished to turn her back and flee to her room; but she didn't have time. Bowles took her by the hand, drew her to the couch and seated her beside him. Slipping his arm around her, he asked her in the tender voice of an older brother, "Is our girl well?" His hand moved from her shoulders to her head. He stroked her hair and then her cheek. His eyes as yet aroused, he looked at her with infinite love; and, melting, she saw fully for the first time how handsome he was – how considerate, gentle, and, above all, aristocratic. Yes, he was Rochester – the hero of the novel she had read and reread so often. He was so dashing and noble. Transformed into the little heroine-governess, Emily felt love flood her heart.

"I am well, Mr. Roches –. . . – Mr. Bowles. I am very well, thank you," she breathed.

Seated on the edge of her bed, at the time of Bowles's death, Emily let images swell, bringing old feelings one after another. She remembered the desire that his muscular body gave her, his handsome face, his laughter – at times carefree, at times ironic, at times weighty. Memory was a dream without beginning or end. She thought of Bowles in language she had also applied to Sue: "Mr. Bowles, you are the beloved of my imagination!" A wave of gratitude set her heart soaring. "My friends are my wealth. Each of them in a special way wraps my soul in precious feelings. How many loves I have had for you, Mr. Bowles! How you were transformed each time I looked at your face. What inspirations from you have gone into my writing. I have sent you fifty poems to express the love and joy which flood me with the thought of you." Emily sighed, drying her eyes. "The three letters I call 'Letters to the Master' were for you. I received your smile and your warm arm around my shoulder that brought a shiver of desire. 'That, I believe, is as close to Paradise as we can reach in life,' you said, and I was thinking that it was you who bore us to Paradise – me, Austin, Sue, and even Vinnie."

"In my letters I wrote to you not as Emily but as Jane Eyre, a woman, in love with the higher divinity of passion. Yes, I would think of you on cold winter nights when the fire went down to embers and the chill crept rudely into the room. The blanket pulled over my head, I waited. . . . I was trembling. . . . The stairs would creak as you ascended, the door silently opened, and the mattress sank as you lay down by me. You embraced me, and oh – what took place then! Mr. Bowles, the imagination of the poet is bolder, more vital, than what is called reality. The poet's flames illuminate the profoundest depths, so that inspiration is born and ecstasy follows. But do not imagine that I would have given myself to you. No – never doubt my snow, Mr. Bowles. I have had no body for anyone. I have sacrificed you – and my life as a whole – to imagination. Yet, albeit for a moment, I knew what it was to be a woman. You have granted Me the title of wife."

I'm "wife" – I've finished that –
That other state –
I'm Czar – I'm "Woman" now –
It's safer so –
(#199)

Emily Dickinson: Goddess of the Volcano

Emily continued her thoughts with powerful feelings. "I awaited your call as women do. You were the master of my body and soul. You were my god."

He found my Being – set it up –
Adjusted it to place –
Then carved his name – upon it –
And bade it to the East

Be faithful – in his absence –
And he would come again –
With Equipage of Amber –
That time – to take it Home.
(#603)

"When you fell ill, it was terror for all of us. I thought of how I would cure you, and I sent you this poem" (#691):

Would you like summer? Taste of ours.
Spices? Buy here!
Ill! We have berries, for the parching!
Weary! Furloughs of down!
Perplexed! Estates of Violet trouble ne'er looked on!
Captive! We bring reprieve of roses!
Fainting! Flasks of air!
Even for Death, a fairy medicine.
But, which is it, sir?

"Your illness was our daily agony," she thought, "and when you got better we lost you to Europe. Time is catalytic. It smothered the flame that burned in me . . . it quelled the tide that drowned me . . . and finally my love for you retreated. Love was replaced by another emotion that made me suffer as much as the love I had for you. Of the many poems I sent you, you published only five, and they were changed to serve the reader – not to present the form of the creator. It was then that I decided not to publish anything . . . not one more poem."

Her mind was flooded with reminiscences, sometimes bitter and sometimes splendid, according to the image that arose before her. She heard once again his "You rascal, come down!" He alone could make *rascal* resound like a compliment. That was his gift. He possessed the charisma to enchant the people around him. "Perhaps that is what I loved – his personal magnetism." The word *love* smote her. 'Truly,' she asked herself, 'did I love him?' Now – this moment – I don't feel it was passion. We get over love, like anything else. I miss him, I feel pain – he left life so early. But I don't feel passion. Was it, then, ever love? Was it love or an intense search for excitement, inspiration, the fulfillment of youthful longing?

She thought, pondered, decided. "Forgive me, Mr. Bowles. I believe I exploited you. Now it is all in the past. I confess without shame or remorse that I drew on your charismatic intellectual and physical power for the sake of my creativity. You inspired so many poems and so many letters. I thank you, dear friend. Thank you – I send you my blessing wherever you are, Mr. Bowles." A smile appeared on her face that was like a grimace. "Till we meet again!" She wiped her eyes, and her gaze went through the western window to Sue's house across the way.

The curtains of Evergreens were all drawn – silence of sadness absolute.

Sue was mourning. Again Emily experienced the feeling of jealousy. Both of them had fallen in love with him. She had given up her place, distanced herself from his presence. It had indeed been difficult, but beloved Sue was happy, that was the goal. Sue had continued to love him, simultaneously keeping her eye on Emily's window or climbing the stairs to give her a great hug or kiss. When everyone complained of her withdrawal, Emily wrote Bowles: "They do not realize that I gave up my claim; as always, the prophet is not heard in his own country. My heart directed the rest."

From the window she thought she saw Sue gazing toward the Homestead. "Sue, there will always be the two of us, without competition or jealousy." Her soul was serene. "Volcanos bide their time"; she smiled, "but dormant they stoically await the moment of renewed eruption." That moment Sue, opposite, raised her hand in greeting. "Vesuvius at home," Emily whispered (#1705):

> *Volcanoes be in Sicily*
> *And South America*
> *I judge from my Geography –*
> *Volcanoes never here*
> *A Lava step at any time*
> *Am I inclined to climb –*
> *A Crater I may contemplate*
> *Vesuvius at Home.*

She sat down at her desk and wrote a letter of condolence to Maria Bowles, praising the beautiful spirit and personality of her beloved friend: "I often think of you after the darkness – although the one cannot help the other in the night of the other. . . . I hope that you have found comfort in the thought that he has received the Immortality with which he so conversed."

The Last Eruption of Love

Yet, tenderness has not a date –
It comes and overwhelms.
    E. D.

Snow fell gently, covering the past, cooling the crater of the volcano, yet the coals sustained the fire within them, ready for a revived explosion – its name, Judge Otis PhillipsLord.

Sue sent Emily the message. Otis Lord Phillips and his niece would be staying for several days at Evergreens. "He is coming for you, of course, but he does not consider proper now that Father is gone for him to stay with four women. Take care not to let yourself go." Emily smiled with deep anticipation. Such visits would be small seismic events. They would heat the interior lava of poetry, which had been in a condition of relative inactivity from the time that mother had broken her hip.

Now both she and Otis were free from former ties and influences, and time was shrinking. The moment, however, remained – the precious now – and her heart, still young and free, gave itself to the man she had begun to desire as a girl. "My dear friend from Salem," she whispered, and Maggie, who had brought the message and awaited a note in reply, understood Emily's glowing smile.

"All is well, Miss Emily?"

"Truly well – truly well!" came the reply.

"The Judge is coming," Maggie chirped. "I want to help you bake bread."

"I'll bake the bread alone," came the spirited answer, and Maggie cheerfully descended the stairs. When Miss Emily was happy, so was the house as a whole – especially mother.

The renowned judge was esteemed for the strict standards and unfailing eye for error that set him apart from the other members of the court. His colleagues characterized him as "dynamite" and considered him an authority on the human spirit. And that was his goal as a judge: "The one who possesses absolute knowledge of the human spirit and passions has achieved a greater triumph than the one who has discovered a planet," he said, fixing his eye on Emily. And Emily responded with her own warm eye and the words which she put down daily. Otis was her last celebration of love, as both of them recognized. When he lost his wife, he awakened in forty-eight-year old Emily the fiery eroticism that endlessly nourished her heart. For seven years of endless labor at the side of her bedridden mother, she had few occasions for ecstasy of feelings. His coming was a stirring of the soul that broke the monotony of the Homestead. He would be here tomorrow! She smiled at the thought of him, and that moment she heard hasty steps on the stairs. Opening the door, she found Maggie breathless and upset.

"Miss Emily, there's a gentleman who insists you must see him. . . . I showed him to the living room," she said trembling.

"Maggie, didn't you say we are not at home?" Emily asked in alarm, her heart beating quickly.

"Naturally I said so, Miss Emily, but he would not listen. It's terribly urgent! I'm afraid you must receive him." She lowered her head and whispered, "I think it is that man with the deep voice, as Miss Vinnie puts it."

"My spiritual counselor?" Emily asked, trembling.

Maggie nodded her head. Emily reached out and Maggie took her hand but remained with head bent. She was not willing to accompany her downstairs.

"Stay with mother, then," Emily returned, attempting to get a grip on herself. Touching her hair and her dress, she hesitantly pushed open the door. Yes, she had seized on his acquaintance, had greatly admired him, and in her imagination had raised him to the heavens. In the famous preacher she had found a blessed companion. They had passionately shared thoughts about Divinity, Death, Poetry, Immortality. He had inspired her to write marriage poems like this one (#1072):

Title divine – is mine!
The Wife – without the Sign!
Acute Degree – conferred on me –
Empress of Calvary!
Royal – all but the Crown!
Betrothed – without the swoon
God sends us Women –
When you – hold – Garnet to Garnet –
Gold – to Gold –
Born – Bridalled – Shrouded –
In a Day –
Tri Victory
"My Husband" – women say –
Stroking the Melody –
Is this – the way?

"My beloved friends bring me the gift of passion for the sake of my poems," she thought as she slowly descended the stairs, feeling in her breast the shadow of her former longing. Charles Wadsworth – "the friend of my heart" as she called him – was seated on the living room sofa. Now bent and frail, he was wearing a voluminous black overcoat, and she at once observed dark circles around his eyes. Arising wearily, he reached out, gently took her hands, and searched her face with profound feeling. Her visage was like parchment but as yet held a glow of vitality. Her hair, dark brown with red highlights, reflected, as always, her intense sensibility – her eyes, her razor-keen intellect. He lifted her hands to his lips as if a magnificent butterfly were cupped in her palms. He touched his dry lips to her fingers, and it felt like balsam for his soul.

"Emily, my dear, I have come to say good-bye," he whispered. "I am dying . . . and I came to see you for the last time." Trembling, they stood holding one another's hands. Wadsworth touched his lips to her fingertips, bathing her tender palms with tears. Overcome, Emily placed a kiss on his forehead. For both, the visit swiftly came to an end. With head lowered, Wadsworth descended the Homestead stoop, left Amherst, and two years later departed from this life.

In a warm corner of her heart, Charles Wadsworth had remained a significant friend and spiritual counselor; and when he was cut off from life, she found comfort through corresponding with his spiritual advisor, Bishop Clark of Northampton, wishing to glean details about the life and death of "my dear friend from Philadelphia." She asked how he met his death – was he calm at the time of departing? And she inquired regarding his family – the number of his children, brothers and sisters – as well as the publication of his sermons. Bishop Clark promptly responded to all her letters and sent her the recently published collection of Reverend Wadsworth's sermons. Their correspondence continued up to the time of his death.

Emily was overwhelmed with sadness, but rays of hope began to return as she moved toward the kitchen to prepare bread for her special visitor, Judge Otis Lord.

Mabel Loomis Todd

David Peck
Todd

CHAPTER IV

Temptation Arrives in Amherst

On August 31, 1881, David and Mabel Todd reached Amherst. Mabel was above all relieved that on that starlit night there was no one in the streets to witness the couple's weariness and bedraggled appearance. At this juncture, Mabel was not in her habitual attractive, well-groomed form. Her dress was mussed, her hair unkempt, her lip-rouge dull and patchy. In sum, her appearance failed to display her characteristic vitality and fashionable, cosmopolitan background. She was from the nation's capital, a product of the finest schools, pianist, singer, and dabbler in painting. These, she unshakably believed – along with her flamboyant good looks – made her distinguished, as did her handsome young spouse. Professor, astronomer, he was an accomplished stargazer. The post at Amherst was above all important to him because this small academic community offered him a showcase for his talent, a stepping-stone to more prestigious American universities. David Todd's ambition, to distinguish himself in his field and rise to the status of astronomer-of-the century, was unreservedly shared by his wife.

The young couple dragged their suitcases with heavy hearts because it was evident, in spite of the darkness, that the town in which they found themselves was a backwater. Mabel's heart sank with the thought that perhaps this was not the proper ground for her to trumpet her gifts and receive the accolades she deserved. Entering Main Street, they came upon the imposing Homestead with its handsome white fence and, immediately after, equally impressive Evergreens. They jealously admired these structures, hardly imagining that these residences literally embodied their own fate.

Just down the street was the boarding house where they had secured accommodations. Their rooms had large windows facing a garden with tall trees. The first was a small sitting room with a miserable couch and two rickety armchairs, which they hoped would last through the time of their search for a decent place to live. The second was the bedroom with a double bed, whose mattress appeared – in their exhausted condition – the most comfortable they had ever seen. As Mabel had barely enough time to think that a set of curtains they had brought along would work in their temporary abode, deep sleep and a strange dream came upon her: In a huge house with many dark, narrow halls, she was frantically searching to find her room. All the doors were closed and locked. Nevertheless, the excitement of the new environment made her race through the halls with elation. David had an equally bizarre and traumatic dream. He saw the stars he studied going out, and he hopelessly scrambled for a way to turn the lamps of heaven back on. He ran to and fro frantically, futilely searching for the switch, and he awoke soaked with sweat, the stars as yet snuffed out. In the morning the couple opened their eyes slowly, fixing their gaze on the ceiling and trying to recall where they were.

That morning Sue awoke with body aching and spirit depressed – a condition that had occurred frequently following the death of Samuel Bowles. Moreover, she was upset by a terrible dream. It involved looking for a place to live and finding it in a cemetery. As a matter of fact, the one she came on wasn't even the familiar one in the neighborhood but was in a distant location by the sea. Sitting by a tombstone, which was like the stoop of a house, she looked out on the open sea. A ship had gone down, and statues from its hold were floating in the surf, which was not foam but white balls of yarn tangled with one another. Sue found herself amidst the balls of yarn, which stuck painfully on her body like suction cups. Pulling them off one-by-one, she decided to save herself by holding on to a statue. She found one that remained intact. It was the bust of a woman. Hanging on, she reached the beach, and then, when she stood up, she discovered that the bust, too, was made of hollow composite paper. As it, too, began to dissolve, she woke up. "Where does all this come from, and what does it mean?" she asked herself, nauseated and upset. Whatever it meant, it boded no good. Hearing Austin preparing to go to the office, she was, as always, irritated by his fastidious morning routine. "Over an hour to bathe, trim his beard, and don his fancy clothes!" she sighed. "Not even an actor would take so long in the dressing room!"

Finishing his preparations, Austin appeared at the bedroom door with a cup of coffee in his hand.

"Where is your cup?" he asked. "I thought you had one. Take this, and I'll go for another."

"Can't you see I'm still in bed? Anyhow – don't bother!" she angrily returned.

Austin gazed at her. She was even more irritable than usual. He didn't say a word, but with a grimace he gulped his coffee, set the cup and saucer on the dresser, and – eyes averted – slammed the door and left the house. As he walked past the boarding house on his way to his office, he caught sight of a comely young woman seated on the porch looking around as if she were viewing the town for the first time. Austin tipped his hat to her as his discerning eye brought a complacent smile to his face. The young woman of twenty-seven made a little bow in return, exposing her décolleté. A pair of smooth, pert breasts rose above her bodice. With a smile answering his, she turned, flustered, and withdrew into her room.

"David!" she shook her husband who was about to return to sleep. "Wake up! Your boss just walked by. He's a true-blue aristocrat!"

"What about me?" He threw her on the bed and began to kiss her fervently. "Of course," she giggled, "he can't hold a candle to you, darling!" Her laughter had an ironic ring, but her husband paid no heed.

Finishing his stroll to work, Austin retained the image of the young woman, especially the fetching outline of her bosom. "Who can she be?" he wondered, and a strange excitement possessed him. "That must be Mrs. Todd, the wife of Todd, the new Astronomy professor!" he concluded, and with great satisfaction he quickened his pace and entered his office ready for a productive day.

That moment the wheel of fate held an ironic smile as it was set in rapid motion.

Still in bed, Sue thought about her life. "So dry and desolate after the death of my dear friend!" The figure of Bowles – his sparkling eyes, alert expression, and warm hands – appeared once more before her, expressing the pain of his departure. "That is death – eternal absence!" she sighed, and tears would have flowed had little Gib not appeared. She lifted the covers and the little boy with arms outstretched snuggled up against her. His little feet tapped against her stomach and legs as he wrapped his arms around her neck. "This is bliss!" her heart sang as she hugged him and filled his face with kisses.

Word of the new couple's recent arrival rapidly spread through town. The astronomer would be giving exciting lectures; his vivacious wife would be singing and playing the piano in the church; and the couple would in every way make a refreshing contribution to life in Amherst. They had to hasten to establish social contacts before meeting Sue Dickinson, for everyone knew about her tendency to monopolize the friendship of people of her choice.

In her room, Mabel wrote her first letter from Amherst to her mother and grandmother in Washington, D.C., who were caring for her little daughter, Millicent. Mable filled them in on details of town life, with emphasis on the sister of the college treasurer, whom Mabel dubbed "the myth of Amherst."

Sue got word of the young couple at supper on the day of their arrival.

"Mom," twenty-year-old Ned asked, "has dad told you about the new professor of Astronomy?"

"The Todds just arrived," Austin said, looking up from his plate and continuing casually. "They're staying nearby. I met David Todd this morning at my office, and he apologized for not making the opening meeting of faculty and student body. Apparently, it was a matter of a cold. He begins teaching next week."

"Mrs. Todd is beautiful!" Ned burst out.

"I'll have them for tea tomorrow," Sue said. "I want to meet Mrs. Todd at once. Hopefully they will be new blood in our circle, so we won't stay stuck with the same old dull faces and conversations."

The children continued their talk about Mattie's lessons and Ned's work as an assistant librarian at the college. Gib bubbled over with questions and demands. The couple did not address one another during the meal. At its conclusion, Austin withdrew into his office with a cup of tea in his hand, Gib hanging on his legs. He lifted him up and carried him in his arms. In the living room, Sue and Mattie continued to discuss her school work. Ned went to his room, waiting to play games with his brother after Gib's time with his dad.

Before going to bed, Ned hugged his mother and whispered in her ear.

"Can I take the invitation to Mrs. Todd?"

"Of course, my boy," Sue smiled. "By all means, you should be the one to take the invitation to the Todds."

Thus, simply and decisively tragedy began – the prelude, a year of pleasant social contact.

"Emily – listen to this! You won't believe it! Ned is in puppy-love with Mabel Todd!" Sue said, she and Emily laughing in delight. Always lively, in spite of his mental challenges, Ned was very communicative and sociable, and his contact with Mrs. Todd would be harmless. Sue expanded her complimentary comments about Mabel Todd – her cosmopolitan air, her feminine charms, and, something more important, the strong influence she had on young fifteen-year-old Mattie, as well as the wonderful piano lessons she was giving both children. Enchanted by the vibrant teacher, they practiced avidly.

For a year the relationship of the Dickinsons and the Todds was idyllic, including the gentlemanly David aiding Vinnie, who gratefully took advantage of his help in little chores around the Homestead. Both Dickinson homes profited from the relationship. On one point only Sue had reservations. She did not want the young faculty wife to cultivate a relationship with Emily. She advised Mabel that neither she nor her husband should visit the Homestead, since the two sisters did not have strict ethical standards. However, she read Mabel poems by Emily, and the young woman, enthusiastic, desired to meet the mysterious recluse.

Vinnie, hungry for new friends, repeatedly invited Mabel, and when she was received at the Homestead, Vinnie asked her to sing for her mother who was bedridden in her room on the second floor. Emily's door would be open, for she always enjoyed beautiful music. Mabel, with little gifts for the poet, willingly passed many afternoons singing, and the poet always responded with a flower, a poem, or even a pleasant – though obscure – note. The word *trap* always occurred in these brief letters, but the ambitious singer always overlooked any suspect implications and continued her visits with gifts and music. Emily, consistent with her dictum, *The Soul selects her own society*, never consented to meeting this woman whose affair with her brother was to disrupt her peace and shorten her life, though after her death Mabel was to undertake the significant task of preserving her poetry for posterity.

Was the coming of Mabel Todd to Amherst a matter of chance? Or was it fate, loving ironic games, that brought her to the town a few years before the death of the great poet? In any case, Austin and Sue's contact with the young couple was at first as enjoyable an experience as they could have dreamed of. The lamps of Evergreens burnt late into the night as the friends shared special dinners, refined conversations, and the reading of Emily's poems. In short, a deep rapport and mutual admiration was for a time shared by all. What they did not glimpse was the impending fire of Mabel and Austin's relationship that seared virtually everyone involved, yet left one party ostensibly unscathed – Mabel Loomis Todd.

Temptation Arrives in Amherst

Sue watched the teacher seated close to Ned on the piano bench. Her side innocently brushed against his and her fingers gently touched his, arranging their proper position above the keyboard – a manner of teaching suitable to the special needs of Ned, who smiled in response. Ned, whose habits were based on the life of his contemporaries, would dress up in his best and take frequent walks by Mabel's house. His most delightful moments were when Mattie played the piano as his teacher and he waltzed around the room. Sue watched Ned draw his attractive dancing partner close. He certainly was a flourishing twenty-year-old, capable of a charming and flirtatious attitude. Something which Sue did not know was that when Mabel's husband was absent Ned liked to hang about his teacher's door-step warbling serenades. Sue simply watched the development of her son with special needs and shared her happiness with Emily.

Sue's melancholy was diminishing as picnics, suppers, and conversations with her friends multiplied. Her need for an intellectual outlet had found its proper object, as it had in the case of Bowles, and the young professor's wife eagerly absorbed each word which fell from the lips of her superb hostess. The months of their association swelled into a year, and it all seemed wholly satisfactory, even when Sue's young friend left Amherst on visits to her parents, whereupon she filled in the gap of her absence with letters full of love and gratitude.

At the beginning of September the following year, Mabel suddenly departed on a trip to Washington, D.C. The Dickinsons were upset, particularly Ned, who was eager to accompany Mabel to Boston on the first leg of her journey. Two days later, Ned returned, but he was no longer his smiling, carefree self. Traces of discontent formed on his face, in his words and actions. He neglected his appearance, stayed hours shut up in his room, and – particularly distressing – he curtailed his habit of playing with beloved little Gib.

Sue had to discover what, precisely, was going on with Ned. It seemed, of course, that Mabel's departure was involved. Certainly the young wife would have corrected the lad in the case that something untoward had occurred. Ned would have to conform to the severe Dickinson code, and not permit his youthful feelings to take the upper hand. She would counsel him, and everything would be in order once more.

Thus, she summoned her son, tenderly took his hand, and spoke in the voice of reason, but the response of the unruly young man was incomprehensible.

"Mama, you don't see what I mean. Things are not the way you say. Mrs. Todd does not want to see me again. She does not want me ever to come near her house." Ned almost burst into tears.

"But that's quite correct, my boy," Sue answered as gently as she could. "She is a proper married woman!"

"Mama, listen to what I'm telling you! It's not me she's thinking about. She doesn't want me around because papa's there. Do you understand now . . . ?"

His words were cut off by the sight of his mother's face. Her features were transformed into something strange and wild. Growing pale, she let his hand drop and slumped back on the sofa. Ned hurried to bring a glass of water, but she could not swallow. All she knew was that a voice in her head kept pounding, "Austin, oh, Austin, why were you at Mabel's? How many times? What on earth is going on? My husband – a man in his position!"

Of course, when he was at home at the time of Ned's lessons, Austin would graciously accompany Ned's teacher on her return to her residence. Sue's memory turned to such occasions, focusing on her husband's words and compliments to the young woman in phrases he had not used with Sue for years. How gallantly he offered her his arm, took interest in the College's supporting the Todds building a house near Evergreens, recognizing the contributions of the young Astronomer. These words became suspect now to Sue. Yet, were her suspicions well founded? Did not Mabel love her husband, who was supposedly there when Austin went to their house?

"What about Mr. Todd?" Sue asked, attempting to speak in natural, casual tones.

"He doesn't mind," Ned spontaneously replied. "He just doesn't enter their conversations, and often he goes for a walk."

"Is that so!" Sue exclaimed, wishing to draw some clear hints from her son.

"Mr. Todd likes to stroll around town, meet students, and take them to the observatory." As he saw his mother's eyes bulge, he tried to explain.

"Students from Smith College come just to meet Professor Todd. They want to learn about Astronomy using the telescope, and he shows them the constellations."

A leaden silence descended on mother and son. Ned wanted to reassure his mother, but he could not find words, and there was a terrible weight in his breast. Sue saw that Ned was experiencing a profound crisis. She controlled herself as much as possible, patted his cheek, and stated, hoping beyond hope,

"When Mrs. Todd comes back from Washington, I'm sure everything will be as it once was."

Sue was stricken. Things were extremely grave. Seated alone on the living room couch, she felt that the light coming through the window could not pierce the darkness closing in upon her. She could not evade the mounting extremity of her situation. Her mind's eye focused on her everyday relationship with Austin – their harsh words, their verbal clashes, and then the sudden silence followed by the explosion of the door slamming behind him. What above all shattered her was his virtual absence from her life. He was increasingly away from home, and when at home, they were both busy at their own tasks. She found herself forgetting his features. They seldom talked, gazing into the distance even when they exchanged retorts and curses.

She recalled the last time they made love. When little Gib came so magically into their life, everything was so delightful and tender. Yes, at that time they made love. Then Bowles's death – the devastation of his loss. Then love making and communication between them ceased. The lack of communication frightened her more than his possible flirtation with Mabel, toward which she continued to be in denial. Her despair was the crumbling marital relationship, which she perceived fully for the first time.

Fate had brought her to this pass, and of course she attributed the faults involved not to herself but to Austin. Austin was a failed human being. She had to convey that to him, to make him understand, change his behavior, and become useful in their small community. He had to succeed! His income was sufficient, but that was not enough. His involvement in the beautification of the town, the planting of trees, the building of the church opposite their home, his speeches at college events, and the planning of the new cemetery were not enough. These were an imitation of his father and grandfather. At the age of fifty-three, how could it be that he was still merely imitating others? He had not as yet realized his own identity. Sue had to stress all this with him – for his own good. And something of paramount importance: She had to put that baggage in her place! That would go a long way toward setting things in order.

Nevertheless, the strife continued to build to Homeric proportions, without Sue probing the key issue, for how could she imagine that Austin would enter in his diary on 11 September 1882 the word RUBICON, indicating a point of no return in his life. As for herself, she was determined the pattern of relations would change the moment that hussy returned from Washington. Then Sir Austin would learn about life on the battlefield!

Upset and confused, Mabel stood on the stoop of Evergreens. Opposite her, Sue – an ominous, menacing figure – blocked her entrance. Shocked, she begged an explanation. Severe, cool, decisive, Sue replied, "My dear, I fear that our relationship of old cannot be restored!" She added a few choice words and slammed the door in Mabel's astonished face.

The Rubicon

Mabel did not pause to hear further insults through the sealed door, but turned her back, descended from the stoop, and with watery knees and shaking heart made her way toward the boarding house. In a nearby grove she paused, attempting to find comfort in the warnings of neighbors, which flashed into her mind: "Beware!" they said, "As gracious as Sue Dickinson is to new friends, she is eventually bitter toward them. She will throw you out of her house!" Obviously, Mabel thought, townspeople were right. How shameful for Sue to say such things to a gentlewoman like herself! Her poor husband, Austin – so gallant, considerate, romantic, sensitive, and prominent, married to such a mean, trivial, vulgar, foul-mouthed hag!" Her quick mind raced to summon appropriate labels as her heart filled with pity toward poor Austin. Austin! Suddenly the man was right there before her! As he stepped from behind a tree and fondly spread his arms, her legs gave way and she collapsed upon his breast. He tenderly held her steady, and she found her eyes overflowing and her heart shaking uncontrollably. He held her close stroking her hair and whispering, "There, there! Banish tears and suffering. You will see – all will be well." That moment reaching through a gap in leaves and branches, moonlight fell upon them, and they were overcome. "Ah, Ah!" she moaned. Her lips parted and Austin, trembling, pressed his lips to hers. The kiss – buried in his heart all these years of marriage, hungry and deprived – was released, fiery and long in an embrace full of pulsing desire, shouting *yes! yes!* in the silent contact of the bodies. Their flesh trembled in impatient need, silently shouting for swift, passionate union. How sustained that kiss held in a timeless moment! Only when she finally began to pull away, did Austin come back to the world. Their lips separated, their arms fell limp, and he stepped back, turned toward the street, and was lost in the trees.

Hidden from her eyes, he began to bound through the field behind Evergreens and crossed to the rear of the Homestead. He strode through the garden and lunged through the kitchen door. Vinnie, Emily – and Maggie as well – scrambled to their feet and stared in amazement. No one uttered a word. Emily approached her brother, took him by the hand, and led him to her room. She sat on the edge of her bed and gestured toward the chair by her little desk.

He stood before her, a faint smile forming amidst his disturbed, tear-stained features.

Wiping his tears with the back of his hand, he said, "Emily, my precious . . . Emily, tonight I am a new being. Tonight I am reborn, Emily. I exist! Look at me! I am myself – master of my soul!" Overcome, he collapsed into the chair and exploded in tears. Emily went to him and threw her arms around him.

"It's my Rubicon! My Rubicon – do you see!" he exclaimed. "I have crossed and there's no going back, nor desire to return to what was! I am born in the cradle of love!" He gazed at his sister and her calm reassured him.

"Emily, do not judge me," he implored. Emily kissed his brow, and he hugged her. "What relief you have granted my soul," he breathed.

Wordlessly Emily released an extended sigh. Her mind dwelt with pain on Sue. That moment as the preamble to the affair began, no one foresaw the tragic dimensions that Rubicon would take in all their lives. Emily accompanied Austin back to the kitchen. Vinnie looked him straight in the eye, and Maggie turned her head toward the evening meal simmering on the stove. Austin murmured goodnight and closed the door behind him. They heard him humming a pleasant tune as he turned toward Evergreens. The three women exchanged not a word, but they all thought of Sue – as yet in the dark.

Darkness Descends on the Family

When the ravenous heart feeds upon desire, intellect and judgment go by the board, and a profound fall is inevitable. Under the new circumstances of Austin's impending affair, currents in the two Dickinson homes shifted. Planted in the feelings and minds of the families, malaise took root. It flowered in anger, rage, and overwhelming despair. From Evergreens sounds of raised voices drifted over to the Homestead. Vinnie broke out in recriminations toward Sue, Maggie nodded her head in anguish, and Emily closed her mother's door, raising the volume of her reading to mask the disturbance.

In Evergreens, Ned had epileptic seizures, Mattie sobbed herself to sleep every night, and at the first sound of an outbreak, little Gib scrambled to the kitchen and took refuge under the table. All this was the result of the impending break. For a time, however, the Dickinsons and the Todds kept sporadic social contact with fragile smiles and sterile compliments.

Christmas of 1882 was approaching. Snow fell steadily, and Mabel prepared for another trip to Washington. Her absence would be felt in the restlessness of Ned and Austin, particularly of the latter. With her finger on the trigger, Sue looked for signs that her fears were based on reality, not suspicion, and this was confirmed when Mabel returned from the capital. She did not come back at once to Amherst, but remained for several days shopping in Boston. David went for two days to be with her in Boston, and immediately after his return Sue discovered with horror that Austin was preparing to go to Boston "on an urgent matter."

Sue did not dare to challenge him, but immediately on his return she surprised him with a direct inquiry: "Did you see Mabel in Boston?" and the return came abruptly: "Of course; it was for her I went."

Now the skirmishes became full-blown battles.

Regarding the erotic agreement between the lovers, Mabel's tactics as a liberated sophisticate had set the non-negotiable terms: first the husband and then the lover. Both accepted the arrangement.

The family was divided into two camps – Austin gained the support of little Gib, and the two older children sided with Sue. The alliances were signed in their minds, and the war lasted unbelievably long – to the end of their lives and beyond.

The claims of personal freedom and the satisfaction of the couple's erotic demands cancelled all logic, ethics, social norms, and any impediment whatsoever to infinite fulfillment of desire. To the thrust of Eros were added another motive equally intense: Mabel's envy and disdain toward Sue. Her initial feeling of admiration toward Sue's cultivation in the arts and her taste in décor, appearance, dress and accessories was overturned by a compulsive need for her eradication; and Mabel spread this venom in all her contacts and actions.

Sue's well being – indeed her very survival, Mabel left to the mercy of God alone. After all, to her Sue was – in the final analysis – merely the spawn of a drunkard and publican with no place among the elite Dickinsons.

She promoted this constant theme with her spouse, her lover, and her circle in Amherst. She always let it be known that such a lofty social position as Sue's by rights belonged to her – the one possessing the requisite background, intellect, and accomplishments. In every respect the unworthy spouse had to be marginalized, and to that end she enlisted the aid not only of David and Austin but also of a "righteous God" to whom she assiduously appealed.

Sue had to defend her position and that of the children. The family was under siege, and she had to repel the assault at all costs. So, Sue in her fifty-second year – along with Ned, twenty, and Mattie, fifteen – undertook the regular surveillance of the head of the household. Every hour, every minute, of the day they had to be certain where and with whom the husband and father was.

The lovers battled stubbornly, devising machinations for their meetings and correspondence. Their great ally was Mabel's husband David, who had much to gain from the affair. First, his wife would turn a blind eye to his own repeated extramarital dallying; moreover, the satisfied college official would take all the necessary actions to further David's career. And indeed David's anticipations proved correct. During the thirteen years of the fiery affair, as a key college administrator, Austin offered his mistress's husband much. He appointed him director of the newly constructed observatory, he arranged for a significant boost in his salary, and he secured world-wide travel grants for the professor's observation of solar eclipses, which enhanced Todd's reputation (though he was unfortunately unable to secure documentation through photographs). Furthermore, when Mabel was away on trips, he assisted David in household chores. Everything worked as David planned and Mabel arranged. What a pity, however: one detail escaped David – the side effects on his own psyche.

Temptation Arrives in Amherst

Warfare at Evergreens made a continuous rumble. At first just echoes were heard at the Homestead, but soon everyone in the two homes was affected. Even Emily in her fortress of isolation was fated to be involved. The family conflict devastatingly penetrated into her room and mortally battered her. The "beloved of Salem," Judge Otis Lord, was her last tender support in the face of coming misery.

Judge
Otis Phillip Lord

The Abyss - Ascent and Redescent

Judge Otis Phillips Lord

"My lovely Salem smiles at me, I seek his face so often – But I have done with guises. I confess that I love him – I rejoice that I love him – exaltation floods me – I cannot find my channel. The Creek turns Sea at the thought of thee . . . I incarcerate me in yourself. . . ."

(E.D. in a letter)

Otis Lord was the great delight, the serene harbor, the retreat from barbaric events as well as the link to life and happiness. For the first time in relationship to a man, Emily lived in a world of reality rather than imagination. With him, she drew on down to earth possibilities. Cerebral poetry did not mediate between them – only the eloquent letters, which they exchanged frequently. Copies of these erotic missives were found in a file after Emily's death. With trembling hands Austin had delivered the file to Mabel, with the command that the letters be carefully hidden, and years later Mabel gave the letters to her daughter. In her last little book, *Emily Dickinson: A Revelation*, Millicent Todd Bingham states that the file was never opened or taken from the apocryphal closet in which it was placed by her mother. Eager scholars have avidly, futilely, sought this folder.

The powerful judge and family friend was not merely a figure in Emily's girlhood memories but a flesh-and-blood male who made her tremble with desire. "I will not wash my hand," she wrote him, "so your touch will not be lost." Their correspondence was florid, continuous, bold. She foresaw marriage in their future – for the first time a workable, developing relationship with a man; and her pen poured this out on paper. She delighted in the visits of her friend from Salem, to the great alarm of Sue, who chanced on a sudden visit to interrupt them in an avid embrace. Her concern was clear when, overcome by jealousy, she counseled Mabel at the time of their great friendship that she should not visit the homestead because the sisters lacked ethical standards. Sue was jealous indeed.

As to the marriage of Emily Dickinson and Judge Otis Lord – in spite of their promises, plans, and desires – it was not to be. The poet's destiny was shaken whenever she was enticed by worldly happiness. Her sole destination was eternity.

In September, 1883, Austin was celebrating the first anniversary of his "lofty" bond with Mabel which "base" folk could not fathom. Only his mistress's husband could understand, pleased with the sight of his wife sharing ecstatic moments with the leading citizen of Amherst. The "vulgar" town folk were disturbed, casting hidden glances and lewd smiles on the couple (as Austin and Mabel stated, common people were incapable of elevated feelings). Worst of all were the parents of the beloved mistress, who were wholly lacking in refined sentiment. They visited Mabel and David in their spacious rented house, which Mabel's parents judged beyond a college professor's means. Furthermore, how could the couple fund a house warming for three hundred guests served wine, canapés, chicken salad, and dessert? Dismayed, they asked, "Where did you find the money?" Receiving no reply, they had their suspicions. Mabel's father castigated his son-in-law, and her mother pointed a finger at Austin Dickinson, who penned a letter demanding that they withdraw their insinuations and thus avoid a suit for slander. The parents packed their things and fled to Washington, never to return to Amherst, but they left behind their grandchild, Millicent, to witness the events when the time for testimony arrived.

Vinnie entered Emily's room with her eager smile, and Emily understood that she would request something beyond her powers.

"I beg you, Emily. Accept it for Austin's sake and my own. I pity him. He's on fire! He needs to see her!"

Emily shut her eyes against unavoidable circumstances. All she could do was sigh and suffer what she was about to hear.

"He's not asking much – simply to see her here. You love music. You will hear her playing in the living room. She plays and sings so beautifully."

Thus, Mabel came to the Homestead, sang and played, and brought a painting of flowers for Emily; and Emily listened to the music through her door ajar, sending Mabel thank-you notes, which were cool yet moved Mabel to tears because they implied the poet's understanding of the lovers' feelings. So Mabel visited the Homestead, free of Sue's spies and the presence of her little daughter, while Sue, hurt and angry with Emily, took her distance from her friend.

From high at her bedroom window, Emily mournfully followed the tragicomic deviations of the people she loved so dearly.

Spring was in the air – the month of March – but the folk of Amherst did not trust the promise of melting snow, bringing the emergence of pleasant days and delightful walks in the countryside. The month was known as 'capricious', one day following another with variable temperatures, showers, and even snow. Over the years, the poet produced poems on the theme of March according to her feelings of the moment: areas lately covered with snow (#736); March's purple shoes (spring flowers) (#1213); "dear March" (#1320); and "the month of Expectation" (#1404). In 1881, she could not imagine that in this month would come the first blow to her last love. Although she hoped for good weather for Otis's visit, cold smote weary travelers. Judge Lord, seventy years of age, weary and exhausted after a difficult legal proceeding in Springfield, did not drop by at Amherst but went home to Salem, where he arrived late at night. He first experienced symptoms of a cold, but before dawn fell into apoplexy. The judge's niece notified Sue. Dismayed as they were by his illness, she and Sue were relieved that plans for the marriage could not go forward. What would people say about such a marriage? Moreover, both women were personally motivated to oppose the match. Lord's niece was his sole beneficiary, and Emily was Sue's sole love.

That week, clutching a newspaper, Vinnie went to Emily's room, where she was writing her letter of the day.

"Emily, have you seen today's paper?" Vinnie asked. Her trembling voice foretold the bad news. The pen fell from Emily's hand.

"Otis is ill," Vinnie murmured, with lowered eyes, placing the paper on Emily's desk.

"No . . . No. . . It can't be true," Emily breathed. "I received a letter from him yesterday, and I'm writing him this moment." Pointing to the paper on her desk, she raised her voice as if the statement could cancel events.

They fearfully awaited news of the judge's health. A month and two days later Emily received a letter from him. He had recovered and was coming on a visit to Evergreens. Emily broke down in tears of joy.

Farewell to Emily Norcross Dickinson
(November 14, 1882)

Past midnight Emily Norcross Dickinson awoke. She felt completely well and ready to travel. Yes, she would go to Monson and visit her family! It was the first time she felt so deeply the need to see her parents and siblings. She was sure that the large carriage was already waiting for her in the street, and she was embarrassed that she was still in bed. Her family should not be kept waiting. She had to dress quickly and leave the confines of her closed, dark room.

She threw off her blanket and hopped to her feet by her bedside. She could not see without a candle, but her clothes had to be on the chair where she had laid them in preparation for departure. She reached out, put on each item of her attire, and carefully smoothed her hair. Suddenly words flowed from her lips like a beautiful melody. A song filled her room whose words were not distinct but nonetheless articulated one-by-one the syllables that were in her heart, and these became music that overflowed her room, spread through the house, and poured out through the street of Amherst, into the woods, across the streams, over the meadows, and all the way to the farm at Monson, the country house of her childhood; and, pushing the door, she found herself in the spacious dining room. With large windows, it was so full of light, vivid colors, and familiar smells that bore pleasant memories. Everyone was there at the table. She hugged mother first, then her little sister Lavinia, and then William Austin, her big brother. How handsome he was! How much he looked like the other Austin, her boy! How much she had missed everyone who was looking at her with admiration and infinite love – with so much love that like a gentle breeze refreshed her face, her limbs, her body; and she was carried to a land of dreams. Her spirit soared, and she kept singing a song that was a pledge – that she would never again depart from the home of her birth at Monson. She would stay there forever! She felt a bliss that had been missing so long; and the thought came to her: Why had she deserted her family? Why had she gone to live so far away? How many years had she been so far from home? How could she endure not seeing them all that time, not being near them? She was smothered in sadness. The feeling swept her away, and suddenly it was dark. The light in the dining room was gone, and she could no longer see her loved ones. Turning her eyes to the doorway, she was shaken as she beheld the figure of Edward Dickinson. It was he who exuded the darkness that engulfed her loved ones. Her heart could not endure it, and she sank into silence.

In bed – immobile, terrified – she surrendered to the silent darkness. Her mouth attempted to form the song, but all that remained in her chest was a tiny bit of warm air without melody – a wisp of breath like a sigh.

Emily entered the room with a tray holding flowers from her garden, a glass of warm milk, a boiled egg, and buttered toast spread with honey. As always, she would awaken mother with a few quiet words – "How did you sleep?" Thus she would not jolt her with disappointment in leaving behind a comforting dream. She would reassure her that they were together, that she would give her a nice bath, wrap her in a fresh wool blanket, and read to her from her favorite book.

"Mother . . ." she breathed. "Look what I've brought you. . . . Look at the beautiful colors – how delicate they are! Mother, feel the petals . . . mother . . . mother."

There was no reply, and Emily feared that her mother was awaking in a sad mood. Perhaps her eyes were filled with tears. She set the tray on the bedside table, walked to the window, and opened the curtains. The dull winter morning brought slight illumination into the room. She gently approached the bedside and touched her mother's forehead. It was so cold! A fearful sound came from her lips with a whispered complaint: "Why, mother? Oh, why?"

Sitting on the edge of the bed, she took her mother's hand and wondered: Had she ever told her mother *I love you.* She could not recall. For seven years she had performed that strange role – the daughter as her mother's mother. She was always tender, comforting, caring at her bedside, never thinking that the end would come.

"Mother," she whispered, "you know I love you!"

She arose, took the tray, and with slow steps descended to the kitchen.

The two practical mistresses of the house, Vinnie and Maggie, were occupied. They did not turn for some time to view the tray untouched and Emily sitting on the edge of the chair.

Emily lowered her eyes and said, "Mother flew," and she continued filled with wonder: "Who could have imagined it!"

"Oh, dear Emily!" Vinnie said, and motioning to Maggie to stay by Emily's side, she climbed the stairs.

It was November, 14, 1882, and after seven years bed-ridden, mother took flight to heaven.

"Who could have believed that mother, who could not walk, today flew?" With those words Emily announced the death to her friends, as suddenly she discovered, "To have a mother – what a wonderful thing! Now the days are so sad without our dear mother." And added, "There was never closeness between us at the time of my childhood but when she became our child, what a transformation it was!"

With deep sadness, Emily wrote in her mother's memory (#1573):

To the bright east she flies,
Brothers of Paradise
Remit her home,
Without a change of wings,
Or Love's convenient things,
Enticed to come.

Fashioning what she is,
Fathoming what she was,
We deem we dream –
And that dissolves the days
Through which existence strays
Homeless at home.

Heartsick, Vinnie ceaselessly sang her mother's praise to Maggie, who always had something to add that pictured the lady of the house in the loftiest spiritual realm. She repeatedly recalled Mrs. Dickinson's great revolutionary act, which always brought surprised smiles. As a young housewife she had dared to oppose the wishes of her commanding husband.

She was carrying Emily at the time she visited a local shop displaying new styles of wallpaper. How she loved the gentle shades of bedroom wallpaper, and how she begged her Puritanical husband, but he would not hear of a purchase involving such useless decoration. Nevertheless she dared to place an order and indeed finished the improvement the day of Emily's birth. What a symbolic date! Because of the event Edward could not, of course, utter a single word of opposition.

The death of Emily Norcross came as a shock not only to Emily but to both camps at Evergreens (Austin and Mabel, who attended the funeral, and Sue and the children). The parties observed a brief armistice to shed tears for the quiet life that had slipped away in the night, adding to the distress of the family. Marital strife resumed immediately after the funeral, placing psychological and economic pressures on the two sisters, while the period of coolness in the relationship of Sue and Emily continued.

Otis Lord's visits resumed, providing relief from the bitterness that endlessly flowed from Evergreens. However, illness hovered over him, and Emily expressed her deep fears in the sole poem she dedicated to her beloved (#1633):

Still own thee – still thou art
What Surgeons call alive –
Though slipping – slipping I perceive
To thy reportless Grave –

Which question shall I clutch –
What answer wrest from thee
Before thou dost exude away
In the recallless [sic] sea?

Again it was summer and once more it was the time, in 1883, for Dickinson families, uncles and aunts from neighboring states, to visit Amherst, as was done beginning in Edward's era. Arriving in Amherst, Uncle William conceived the idea that the remains of his father and mother should be removed from the family plot of Edward Dickinson to their own cemetery. His thought was that the family burial site was for Edward, his spouse, and his parents. His original assumption was that Edward's daughters would marry and have their own family plots. But by 1883 the time had passed for their marriage, and the resting place for daughters Emily and Lavinia would be by their parents. Thus, William transferred the remains of his parents to their own burial plots. What a pity, however, for the empty ground remained to be occupied, at least for a short time – not by its owners – but by the little boy of the clan, the beloved child of both families cherished by everyone in Amherst – little Gib.

Illuminate the House

For each ecstatic instant
We must an anguish pay
In keen and quivering ratio
To the ecstasy.

For each beloved hour
Sharp pittances of years –
Bitter contested farthings –
And Coffers heaped with Tears!
(#125)

Emily awoke with the feeling of enormous loss. Her life felt infinitely empty, and she was falling ever deeper into the gulf. She tried to reach out to the members of her family, to familiar objects in her environment, but she could not identify the people around her; everybody had changed. She felt alone and lost. Austin was in a world of his own. He had returned to a younger age as shown in his manner of dressing, behaving, laughing. It was a laughter that exploded from his mouth, and when he spoke each word was an abysmal affront to Emily's beloved Sue and his children. Sue, too, had changed. Her spirit had hardened through feelings of self-righteousness, meanness, and spite. Her daughter, Mattie, was swept into the region of disdain and superiority in opposition to her fallen father. At night she tossed in her bed with thoughts of triumphantly catching him in a compromising situation, so from early in the morning she positioned herself outside Mabel's house, her father's office, the court house, or the observatory – wherever she might trap him in incriminating circumstances. Even mild Ned had become aggressive, caught between love of his mother and residual respect for his father. The situation in the home had also touched little Gib. It seemed that the boy had lost his spontaneity. He cried frequently and often his eyes betrayed a trauma to his fragile soul, as if he had seen something terrible that he could neither understand nor forget.

Gilbert Dickinson

At the Homestead Vinnie spoke with Maggie of nothing but Sue's getting what she deserved. Vinnie did not conceal her satisfaction and held on to her friendship with the Todds. David was her trusty helper around the Homestead and his wife Mabel her sophisticated friend. She could even tolerate the little child, Millicent.

As for Emily, with her discerning eye turned toward Evergreens, she felt the pain of every exchange in word and thought between her loved ones – her brother and his wife – and the mere awareness of their situation sufficed to thrust her ever deeper into her aching heart, bringing blight to her body and spirit. There were moments of absolute despair when the only salvation was withdrawal, and life took on the stain of alienation, finding itself in an inescapable dead-end.

Emily evaded despair through the frequent visits of Otis Lord, which brought intimate conversations and soothing tenderness to her heart. Only then did she laugh, savor existence, and feel her loved ones' troubles recede. Her sadness was also dispersed by her relationship with little Gib.

Oh, Gib!

Every morning, the little boy brought her first dose of joy – therapy for loneliness and emptiness. She stood by the western window to drink in the presence of "the little man" neatly dressed, briefcase in hand, ready to go to school. What a marvelous sight! And in the afternoon, hair flying, he would dash down the path between the two homes shouting, "What have you got for me, Aunt Emily?" Near the window, she would be waiting. It was the time of their special game. Gib would come dashing down the path, and she would approach the window, affecting surprise and call down to him, "Let's see, do I have anything today?" Then she would lower the little basket, and he would excitedly lift away the napkin to reveal auntie's gift of the day – was it cookies, flowers, a pretty sketch, or a book? His little hand would snatch it up as he looked up and beamed at Aunt Emily. "Thank you, Aunt Emily!" he warbled and dashed off to meet his friends.

"A wonderful little boy – what more can life offer! How generously nature grants us beauty! The very essence of delight is a beautiful child!" Emily thought, and in the afternoon she ecstatically observed little Gib returning and entering his house, his image dancing in the eye and mind. She sighed and felt gratitude in her heart that life had granted her the great gift of love. "My work is to love!" she sang in her heart.

Open the Door . . . Open the Door . . .

It was the fall of 1883, and from day to day, the first rays of sunrise appeared more beautiful than ever before. The trees, still full of leaves, were clad in the deep red of autumn, the flowers stretched out their last petals, and the garden rows paid their final farewell to summer. God's sole task was to lend light to the eyes of those who could perceive the daily appearance and variety of radiant things around them. Calm as the peaceful autumn day, Emily resisted dark thoughts and savored the change of seasons: "To live is a sacred gift!" She looked at the house opposite and mourned for those who no longer had eyes for the simple substance of life.

The morning of Thursday, September 27, Emily awoke, as always, to enjoy each day of the season's end and to witness the most notable daily event – Gib going off to school as she delighted in the dazzling course of his life. She observed the lad in his school blazer, smiling, scrubbed and groomed, setting off to class. The other two children, Ned and Mattie, were already at their posts, keeping an eye on the culprit of the family.

That afternoon, the precious lad was late returning home, and Emily waited anxiously by the window to lower him his basket of treats. She stood by the window, her eyes darting up and down the street until he reached Evergreen's front door. Soaked and dirty, he appeared tired as the door opened and a hand hastily pulled him inside to whisk him to a bath. Gib had been playing with a friend in muddy water, as Maggie explained to Emily, who simply smiled at the picture of the mischievous lad without giving the matter further thought. She simply took the cookies from the basket and placed them in a canister in antic-ipation of his smiling face the following day.

That evening with a slight fever Gib went to bed without supper. His father read to him longer than usual, while his mother frequently came to his room and bent to touch her lips to his hot forehead. The boy fell asleep, but when he awoke at midnight his parents, still by his bedside, anxiously followed his rapidly rising temperature. Their hearts were beating with mounting agony as they sensed that this was no ordinary fever. As Sue pressed her lips to Gib's now burning brow, Austin read in her eyes the shocking word that had also come to his mind, and – paralyzed with fear – he raced to fetch the family physician.

Breathlessly Sue and Austin watched the doctor bending over the child. His features dark, he could barely bring himself to pronounce the diagnosis. "Typhoid Fever." His voice broke and the parents crumbled in despair. "There are cases of recovery," he was hasty to add. "We must absolutely avoid dehydra-tion," he added without conviction.

The days savage, the nights sluggish, Austin and Sue – with dry eyes and burning prayers – kept terrified vigil, striving to sustain Gib's life. Emily – close to the window speechless and exhausted – followed the movements of the lamp at night, attempting to grasp the situation; and during the day, in the words of Vinnie and Maggie – who went back and forth to Sue's house – she discerned the darkness falling ever more heavily on both houses.

Thursday night a week later, past midnight, Emily descended to Maggie's room and awakened her. "Come," she said; and with lantern in hand Maggie guided trembling Emily along the beloved path she had not trod for years to the house opposite, and the instant she entered, the smell of antiseptics made her dizzy and nauseous. She entered the room to find her little prince flaming with sweat on the white sheet. Upon her entrance he attempted to sit up and with his small hand pointed toward the door. "Open the door . . . Open the door . . . They are waiting. . ." he cried, weary and panting.

"Agony opened the door and our little one ran to the grave, to the feet of his grandfather. Is there anything more than Love and Death? If there is, tell me its name!" wrote Emily in anguish.

She returned to the Homestead and collapsed on the bed. From there she heard Gib depart. He passed below her window but she could not rise to see his little hands touching her fence. She remained prostrate at the time of his death, the day of his funeral, and the endless days of mourning. On Friday, October 5, only nine days after the stroke of the sickness, the church bell mournfully tolled as on the awful days of young soldiers' funerals during the Civil War. Just as they mourned the boys unjustly lost in war, now they grieved over beloved little Gib. Everyone in Amherst was in the streets dressed in mourning, and all the shops were closed. Only Emily and Sue – shut in their rooms, their heads covered – did not go outside to participate in the funeral. No – it was not a spectacle for the tender mothers' eyes. They numbly heard the death knell tolling through the town, and in that sound Emily also caught the reverberation of her own approaching demise.

The hour was quarter to five the afternoon of Friday 5 October 1883. Sue collapsed by the lifeless body of her son; she kissed and embraced him, rocked him calling to him to awake. She understood that the world was lost, and frenzied by grief shut herself in her room, wrapped herself in black, and for days did not open the door, even when Ned, weeping, begged her to come out and take a little food and water.

Exhausted, Austin took hold of himself to make the necessary arrangements: the funeral service, the burial, and meeting everyone who supported them in their hour of need. Then he returned home and fell on his bed sick unto death. Alone, he tossed, trembled, and wept. His temperature shot up, and he ached inside and out. Malaria, which had not recurred in years, struck him like a lightning bolt. He desired only for death to come . . . for death to come . . . for death to come. He moaned and begged and prayed that he might close his eyes, enter his final sleep; that he might think no more, escape his endless pain, and evade the Furies that encompassed him, robbed him of breath, and assailed his ears with hellish taunts.

Lavinia Norcross Dickinson

Once again it was Vinnie's hour. She summoned Maggie to Emily's sickbed, and with her sleeves rolled up she entered the house opposite, which frightened her and she rarely visited. By her beloved brother's bedside, she vowed that she would not leave him in Death's hands.

Lavinia Norcross Dickinson was ever present and ready to help everyone in the family. She always said, "Father believes, and mother loves. Emily must think; she is the only one among us who must do that. Austin cares for Amherst (the railroad station, the college, town development), and I care for my family." Six weeks later, though her heart was stricken with the loss of Gib, but with the certainty that she had saved Austin, she brought him to the Homestead. Yes, she had done it! Through her care and patience, he had evaded death's onslaught against him. He had opened his eyes and taken sips of water and some tea, and one morning had managed to rise to his feet. Barely able to walk, he put himself in the hands of Vinnie, who held him around the waist and took him to see sunlight and Emily. That short walk was the best medicine. Vinnie was smiling happily. Pale and crazed, with tears behind his eyelids ready to burst out, Austin realized that Death had disdained to claim him. He heaved a sigh as Vinnie led him along the path which he had walked so many times brimming with feelings of love, joy, pride, and even anger; but now he was empty, puny, worthless, with legs that barely held him up. It was Vinnie who was carrying him, and he mechanically dragged his feet as the tears rolled down his cheeks; the tall trees of the grove as a matter of course swayed and bowed as he passed, and the air by nature stroked his face, though he was but a scarecrow, orphaned in the most awful way possible – by the death of his child. Oh, when would he die, to leave this pain behind? Vinnie led him to the back door of his father's house, where once upon a time he was king. Vinnie opened, and they entered the kitchen.

There in the center stood an angel with wings spread in affectionate, powerful welcome. She engulfed him and he felt the breath of life flow over him in waves. It was a magical warmth. Never had he experienced such comfort. He gave himself to the angel's embrace as she raised on the tips of her toes to reach him, to cover his face with kisses; and between the kisses her voice came from on high – far, far on high – but he could hear what she was saying: "My love, my love . . . I will comfort you. I will heal your calamity, your woe," and her tender kisses on his lips and cheeks dried his tears, warmed his body and heart. Vitalized, he held Mabel – dressed in white – tightly in his arms. This angel, he now knew, would bring him back to life. Yes, with her he would live and be once more the Patrician, the attorney with weighty legal concerns, the bursar of the college; and in memory of his little son, he would line the streets with flowering trees. Yes, Amherst would become the handsomest town in the country in the name of his little boy. For Thomas Gilbert Dickinson's sake. Thomas Gilbert Dickinson, just eight years old.

Vinnie sighed in relief. Austin was saved. Suddenly she felt totally exhausted. Her legs were buckling, and, holding onto the banister, she dragged herself up the stairs; Maggie rushed, put her arm around her waist, and lifting her softly, led her to her bed. Without speaking, she undressed her, pulled up the covers, and stroked her cheek.

"There, there, our lady of the house. There, there, my dear, good lady," she whispered tenderly. Vinnie gazed at Maggie with half-open eyes, as tears of gratitude coursed down her cheeks.

"Total exhaustion!" the doctor pronounced.

"It will pass," Vinnie thought, sinking into deep sleep.

Straits of Suffering

Through the straight pass of suffering –
The Martyrs – even – trod.
(#792)

Slow, mournful, mute, the rhythm of both houses. Emily underwent the pain of death. She realized that death has many faces – each distinct. Indelibly it casts its pall on the spirit and flesh – "Each that we lose takes part of us" (#1605). But now came a new discovery: one kind of death takes more than a part of life; it sweeps away the whole like a total eclipse:

Each that we lose takes part of us;
A crescent still abides,
Which like the moon, some turbid night,
Is summoned by tides.

The Homestead and Evergreens remained dark and deserted – with not a hint of activity. The days moved in a fog like an eerie dream, as if all the residents had died and been transported to Purgatory where, voiceless, they awaited expiation before they might resume life and articulate a human word.

October brought the usual changes in the landscape – the face of the town – but the two residences remained inert. Amidst the immense sorrow dates did not exist, for on October 5, 1883, the awful mass of an enormous rock had crushed the houses.

Emily lay prostrate in her room; her gaze fixed on the ceiling. Her spirit with Sue, she added her beloved's anguish to her own. She was confronted with a loss that claimed no less than all. It was a stroke beyond human endurance. It had to be reduced. Something had to mediate. The heart demanded a wondrous event, another dimension of being. Only that could relieve such anguish. Her spirit turned to the miracle of transcendence, and the comforting thought of that countered the weight of despair. The joy of life had been covered by dust, but she resorted to a regenerative, luminous road.

Toward the end of October, Emily wrote a letter to Sue about the child they had lost. In her words the charismatic qualities of the boy, embodied in radiant images of his being, manifested that comforting light. His life was transformed into a star. Their little hero lived on high, soaring through the universe. He existed – he lived most fully and gloriously. He taught them of Eternity – the mystic goal of the soul. Emily's hymn to Gib is among her most touching moments of exaltation:

October, 1883
Dear Sue,

The Vision of Immortal Life has been fulfilled –
How simply at the last the Fathom comes! The Passenger and not the
Sea, we find surprises us –
Gilbert rejoiced in Secrets –
His life was panting with them – With what menace of Light he cried
"Don't tell, Aunt Emily!" Now my ascended Playmate must instruct me.
Show us, prattling Preceptor, but the way to thee!
He knew no niggard moment – His Life was full of Boon – The Playthings
of the Dervish were not so wild as his –
No Crescent was this Creature – he travelled from the Full –
Such soar, but never set –
I see him in the Star, and meet his sweet velocity in everything that flies –
His Life was like the Bugle, which winds itself away, his Elegy an echo – his
Requiem ecstasy –
Dawn and Meridian in one.
Wherefore would he wait, wronged only of Night, which he left for us –

Emily Dickinson: Goddess of the Volcano

Without a speculation, our little Ajax spans the whole –

Pass to thy Rendezvous of Light,
Pangless except for us –
Who slowly ford the Mystery
Which thou hast leaped across!

The picture of the child on the journey to Eternity, the thought of Immortality – the child lives and exists! – became with time the breath of life for Emily. Recent images became engraved on her mind – Gib on his death bed, feverishly demanding with trembling voice, "Open the door!" And Emily asked, "What door? Who invited the child? Someone summoned him!"

The Heart has many Doors –
I can but knock –
For any sweet "Come In"
Impelled to hark –
Not saddened by repulse,
Repast to me
That somewhere, there exists,
Supremacy –
(#1567)

Time's Tortured Path

Time smothers all earthly things

Austin surrendered to Mabel's downy embrace.
Sue mourned, sealed in her little boy's bedroom,
Vinnie hovered over Emily day and night.
Emily – grief's dam broken – lamented like anguished Lear.

T'was comfort in her Dying Room
To hear the living Clock –
A short relief to have the wind
Walk boldly up and knock –
Diversion from the Dying Theme
To hear the children play –
But wrong the more
That these could live
And this of ours must die. *(#1703)*

***

Mabel's Tangled Course

The Beggar at the Door for Fame
Were easily supplied
But Bread is that Diviner thing
Disclosed to be denied
(#1240)

Mabel edged up to the window whispering her daily prayer, "Oh, Lord – may no one be spying on me today!" Though for weeks now she had not been under surveillance, the prayer had become a fixed habit. Each morning she carefully approached the window, and shrinking behind the curtains, peeped into the street, behind trees, near the church opposite, to confirm that as yet another day she was unwatched. Relieved that once more no one was there, she opened the curtains to admit the morning light.

After Gib's death, Sue's agents, Mattie and Ned, no longer frequented the area around Mabel's house, but she continued to think of them with irritation and rage – those worthless brats! Once she had actually been fond of them as their eager piano instructor for a year. But they had proved unworthy of her concern. As for Ned, she would gladly wring his neck. She had been gracious toward his handicap and they had even danced together again and again! Yet those two had fumblingly played sleuth, reporting what she did and where she went, even what she was wearing, to their mother. The boy had been infatuated with her, but truly it had not been her fault. Admittedly, she had flirted a little – any spirited woman would – but not so as to invite love and a confession of passion! A dignified married woman like herself having to listen to the avow-als of a pipsqueak so far beneath her! When such a splendid father showed signs of interest, who would pay heed to the flawed son? She refused to expend a single thought on self-justification. Her superiority determined her options, and a man like Austin Dickinson had always been her dream. She sighed with irritation at the thought of Ned. He was out of line in every respect. He had betrayed his father without hesitation. He had blabbed details to his mother – anything that came into his head!

Shrugging her shoulders, Mabel turned from the window and crossed to the little table on which lay her diary and the house plans. Her heart's king had left the blueprints there the night before. Fondling them complacently, she eyed them with awe. Indeed she was worthy of such a home! She simply had to wait a while for the two sisters to sign over full ownership of the lot to Austin. Then work would immediately begin. Austin was confident that his sisters would inscribe their signatures the moment he introduced the subject, and Mabel had no doubts, seeing how they loved him and respected her. Vinnie was always thoughtful to her, offering her tea and cakes when she came to the Homestead. When Austin would arrive, Vinnie would apologize for having work to do and exit, leaving them alone. That was Vinnie's routine the three times per week she went to the Homestead to be with her lover. And the other sister, the poet, admired her greatly. She had sent her three notes, a flower, and one time a glass of liqueur. Perhaps she made it herself and sent it because she was fond of her playing and singing. Of course, she didn't understand Emily's notes completely, including the word "trap," but Austin assured her that the poet's missives required decoding. Someday she would get around to that, but in the meantime she and her love could meet freely in the house, Vinnie with her errands, Emily closeted in her room, and Maggie the guardian angel keeping watch at the door.

Mabel checked the time. She had to prepare the dress with the white lapel, for in the afternoon after her tryst she had to go to church for choir prac- tice. She was the soprano soloist, and the congregation adored her, eagerly awaiting her performances. She opened her wardrobe to get the dress – it was overflowing. Her patrician could not offer his "queen" too much. The least mention of an item of jewelry, a dress, a recent publication, and it was in her hands the next day. That was Austin! It was the same with the house. "It will be your castle," he announced. It would go up on the lot behind his and would have a hidden door for him to enter or leave by, should he wish to escape in the event of an undesirable visitor. Austin thought of everything – like David's whistling a certain tune on the way back from the observatory. He would walk at a snail's pace. Even when it rained or snowed, he would whistle slowly along, gazing up at the sky. That way Austin would avoid the awkwardness of David's finding him there when Mabel met him at the door with a welcome-home kiss. Not that there were any problems in Austin and David's relationship. They were the best of friends, but the hidden door opening on the grove between the houses was a brilliant idea. That was Austin. One could depend on him absolutely.

Time was slipping by. She had to put on the finishing touches, to make herself pleasing and beautiful but modest, as befitted an afternoon of choir practice in the sanctuary. As soprano soloist, she had to be there on time prepared to give her best. Amherst respected her for all her qualities. She was flawless in everything she did. She had, for example, made sure her daughter was in good hands – those of her mother, father, and grandmother – though they had recently cancelled the arrangement, not understanding the burden of her social commitments and ambitions in her new situation. Her daughter had gone to the best schools and had a governess, though – poor thing – she wasn't truly attractive; she lacked her mother's striking good looks. But that didn't mean, for goodness' sake, she didn't love her. All was well, especially with her husband, David. She would never offend him by comparing him with Austin, as she confided to her diary. She jotted an entry for each tryst, scoring Austin with stars for erotic peaks. Several times they had reached splendid heights – so high did they soar – that she awarded him five stars, while David had received around two, at the most three, for months now. In any case, her conjugal duties were always fulfilled.

For a moment her thoughts remained with David. She smiled. She thought of the hours they had spent as he attempted to convince her that sleeping with someone else, as he did, didn't mean anything at all. It was an experience, a pleasant moment confined to the duration of the act. How wrong he was! Hers was a sacred relationship. She worshipped Austin – he was her King, her Lord.

"And who am I?" David would ask as his hands wandered over her choice parts. "Why, my excellent husband!" she would answer, slipping by his side. They often made love on the floor and she recorded it in her diary but without exclamation marks. The love she made in the Homestead before the fireplace on the tiger rug she marked with the top score. Truly, all those years with David, they had never – emphatically never! – achieved such sensual bliss. Not that she had ever complained. She did not want to humiliate poor David, but the fact that for him love making with other women was nothing more than a moment's act was understandable. His partners were inferior creatures, whereas she chose a nobleman, a man among men.

Once she even had praise for Sue, Austin's wife – had admired her, loved her, but later Sue's attitude upset and confused her. No, she could endure her no longer. She wanted her wholly out of the picture. The way things were going, she was beginning to fear Sue because she knew the power she possessed. All she had to do was give you that *look*. When she was cool, she could give you pneumonia – so chilly were her eyes and voice. Mabel's feelings were so confused regarding Sue that the mere thought of her was disturbing. "Why should Sue be alive?" For Mabel that was the ultimate mystery of things. She kept telling Austin how happy she would be if Sue no longer existed – if she had disappeared, vanished, passed away. Why not? That was her complaint to God. Why had He not taken her for her own good – so she could escape the unbearable pain of her little boy's loss? Why should that Black Mongol – that sable-clad hag, go on living, locked in her castle like a gothic recluse, never receiving anyone, never setting foot in the town? Why, she had even quit sending out her ridiculous private investigators! Anyhow, no one could say Mabel Todd was at fault. She had not broken the Dickinsons' marital tie, for indeed, they had none! Of that she was certain. How many complaints Sue's splendid husband had! She had asked him to put them down in black and white so that one day the world would learn the truth directly from him, not only from her diary. The world would know, for example, that he felt entirely alone at his wedding with Susan Gilbert, as if he were going to his execution. He only went because his sisters insisted and because he believed that at least Sue had a sturdy constitution that would provide hardy offspring. But she did not want children and who knows what she did when she was carrying Ned! And what she had made of Evergreens! She had turned it into a tavern like her drunkard father's! All her guests – though they called themselves intellectuals – only came to Evergreens for food and drink!

Austin had not precluded setting down his grievances in his diary, but he never did. He never recorded his complaints, and if she had any grievance it was that . . . and one more. He had not left his house. Though he could have moved in with his sisters, he stayed at Evergreens, cared for his family, and took them on outings. She was thinking that she should not forgive him on the last count – yet she loved him, that's why she compromised!

With his bold red locks and a sparkle in his eye, Austin vividly flashed in her mind. In a few minutes, the handsome mansion – the Homestead or family home, call it what you will – would reverberate with erotic sighs, moans, and bursts of delight. As she made her way there, she prayed once again. "Lord, make this the day that I meet Emily!" Unfortunately for her such a day never dawned.

Toward five, Austin kissed her tenderly, wishing her a fine choir practice. With a wink he pointed to the pocket of his jacket hanging in the hall. "Today, they are signing!" he breathed. "How lovely, Austin!" she murmured, kissing him adieu once more.

Austin waited patiently for Vinnie's return and for Emily to come down. Then in a formal tone, he said,

"Your signatures go right here."

Ned Dickinson

"Yes, Austin, where exactly?" said Vinnie, taking the pen.

"And what, precisely, are we signing, dear brother?" Emily inquired, not waiting for him to respond. With a single word that rang decisively: "Never!" she ascended the stairs. Austin heard the key turn in the lock and knew that no one and nothing could change the force of that word.

Ned

Lightning had struck very near, for the walls of Evergreens shook, the windows rattled, and Ned awoke to a terrific storm that steadily buffeted the house. He sat up in bed and a chill made his hair stand on end. Looking out of the window, his gaze could not penetrate the pall of mist and rain.

He rose hesitantly and his feet located his slippers. He did not find his robe but in a flash of lightning he caught sight of his jacket on a chair. Throwing it over his shoulders, he dragged his steps along the hall. Darkness everywhere, and the house freezing. He stopped at Gib's room, where his mother had moved. Standing before the locked door, he heard her groping around without light. "Dear mommy!" he said to himself, caressing the door, and he wondered, "Did the thunder wake her up, or her terrible grief?" He descended to the first floor where daddy slept. He pressed his ear to the door and heard his father's regular breathing in deep sleep – the sleep of the just. He leaned his head against the door and burst out in sobs. He could not help himself – tears just welled from his eyes. He missed his father so much, as if he were off on a long trip. He had been away so long! Memories of loving moments revived. He remembered how, when he was, his father would hug him laughing – "Come! Let us two men go sleighing!"

How wonderful winter was then! One time a snowstorm broke out. It was freezing cold, and wrapped snugly in a heavy wool blanket, he sat close to father as he guided the sleigh over the snow and ice! And snow from tree limbs and drifts blew over them as the wind whistled around their heads! They weren't cold, and they weren't afraid. Instead, his father cracked the whip over the horses' heads, shouting for them to go faster! They laughed! How they laughed! And as father wrapped him with his powerful arm, how he loved him! How much he loved him! Everything was so significant in his life; everything was so natural, right, and beautiful. Even when he was older and had fits in his sleep, he wasn't afraid. It was just something natural and acceptable in him. Mother and father weren't at all afraid and didn't send him away to a special school – they wanted him with them. And how happy he was when his little brother arrived! He didn't feel he'd lost his privileges because he was no longer the only little man in the house. Rather, his heart gained a love for his little brother that grew day by day. He adored little Gib, and it was natural that all of them – his parents and Mattie – would be even more delighted in little Gib's games than in his. How much the little boy loved him, copied the way he walked and talked, and wanted a walking stick like his. Everything had been so wonderful in their lives. How delighted they had been when he began to work as an assistant in the college library. The time arrived when he was working at the college like father! It wasn't a big job, of course; but still he had responsibility and made enough money to rent a carriage and take a friend for an outing. When he asked Mabel to go for a ride, she sat beside him in his fine rented carriage dressed in her Sunday best. It was marvelous to nod to people as they rode along. One time they drove to Northampton, and along the way father came up behind them. Signaling to him, he had stepped down from his carriage and said, "Ned, you take my carriage home, and I'll take yours." He enjoyed driving father's carriage, but why had he interrupted his drive with Mabel? At first he didn't understand, but then the thought came to him that father wanted to talk warmly to Mabel as he himself had the week before. She had been angry with him, saying that wasn't proper – but what about father? What did she say to him?

That had been the end of outings with Mabel. He told mother about it, and the change – the great change – in their life began. His parents would begin an argument that went on forever. For days they would not speak to one another anything but nastiness. They did not eat together, and at bedtime went to separate rooms. There would be shouting and slamming of doors. Then, the moment they began to speak once more, the arguments would return with even greater fury.

Still leaning on father's door and wiping his eyes, he shivered from the cold. The chill on the ground floor was enormous, and be began to shake. As he touched the door with spread palms it was like patting father's back. "Why did you change, daddy, why?" he moaned. The scene he had witnessed before the death of little Gib flashed in his mind and smote his heart. Mother was kneeling by the couch before father, who was rigidly staring away from her across the room. She was sobbing and whispering to him, but he did not look at her. She had placed her hands on his knee saying, "Forgive me if I caused you pain. I love you!" but he shoved her hands away with anger and disgust, as if he could not stand her touch, screaming at her, "It's over between us, Sue – finished! Get that into your head once and for all!" Jumping up, he rushed from the house as if he hated them all, and with her hands covering her face mother collapsed on the empty couch sobbing – sobbing so hard that Ned feared to approach. If he had touched her in that moment of great humiliation he feared she would shatter, so he just sat at a distance immobile, knowing in his heart that the family was no longer a family and he was no longer a son. His father no longer loved him. He was a pitiable epileptic; he was not a true man of the family but a handicapped creature who would never become a librarian, only a stupid assistant. He would never have a place in life; and nothing mattered any longer – not the suits hanging in the wardrobe, or the silk foulards, or his cane with a silver handle. His world was obliterated.

"I am a scarecrow without a real body. The name Dickinson does not belong to me, it's not mine," he whispered to himself.

His hands, dropping from the door where they had rested for some time, fell slack by his side. The pounding rain accompanied his tears. Fearing his mounting sobs would wake his father, he backed down the hall not knowing where he was going. The truth was he did not want to go anywhere; he did not know where he could go. All he knew was, he did not wish to exist. Ned was not Ned – that was why. Father had abandoned him; mother could not see him through the tears or take care of him; Mattie had gone off to college; and Gib . . . Gib had gone to heaven, leaving him *here*, which had become *nowhere.* He was like a ghost, and if he left the house, no one would miss him. He was alone, empty, nothing. If he would disappear from the house – if he would die – what did it matter? No one loved him; no one would miss him, he thought as he crept down the freezing hall into the library. A bolt of lightning drew his attention outside the window – to the absolute darkness of the garden. As the flash subsided, followed by the noise of thunder, in the house opposite, on the second floor, a small candle was burning – the utterly clear light of Aunt Emily. Aunt Emily! Yes, Aunt Emily was not asleep. . . . She was thinking of him. She loved him, writing him letters from the time of his childhood. "To Ned," she wrote on the envelope. *To Ned!* he thought, sitting down on the armchair exactly where mother sat to wave to Aunt Emily. He was so moved that his heart began to throb warmly. He felt that, after all, he did not have epilepsy. It was as if things had a double existence – two sides to view. It was the interpretation that mattered, as in his favorite poem by Aunt Emily, dedicated to him (#1545):

The Bible is an antique Volume –
Written by faded Men
At the suggestion of Holy Spectres –
Subjects – Bethlehem –
Eden – the ancient Homestead –
Satan – the Brigadier –
Judas – the Great Defaulter –
David – the Troubadour –
Sin – a distinguished Precipice

Others must resist –
Boys that "believe" are very lonesome –
Other Boys are "lost" –
Had but the Tale of warbling Teller –
All the Boys would come –
Orpheus' Sermon captivated –
It did not condemn –

The poem reflected his own humor. Mother, who believed in scripture, did not laugh, but he had memorized it because Aunt Emily had special love in her heart for him. It did not lessen with the arrival of Gib. She loved them equally, and what grief she had when Gib died! His poor aunt fell terribly ill. What if he also died? How much grief he would add! She might become even sicker because of him! No, he would not be the cause of such terrific suffering!

He focused his gaze on his aunt's window. The little candle was agleam, casting light into his darkened soul. He tried to wipe away his tears. They kept welling, but now they were not bitter – they were pleasant tears of relief. He had decided. He was Ned, the first born – the elder son. He would not die; he would live and be the man in the family who would care first for his mother and then for his two aunts. And if his father came to love him once more, how he would adore him!

He mounted the stairs. His feet steadily guided him through the dark. The cold had abated somewhat and he no longer trembled. After all, he was a man. He entered his bedroom and softly closed the door. Lying down, he listened to the raging wind cut by chill rain and thought, "It's winter now, but it will come to an end. The snow will melt, and not that alone – it will water the ground, which will flower again for us!"

The Yawning Chasm

A World made penniless by that departure...
(#1623)

March arrived and the heavy snow of Amherst melted to uncover the fresh greenery springing from the soil. The world gleamed with beauty, and the townspeople poked their noses out of doors to take pleasant walks, to gather wild flowers in the meadows, and to receive distinguished visitors to the college, where students eagerly flocked to the lecture halls.

Emily's heart awoke from winter sleep, lifted up, and passionately sought ecstasy, the great jewel of life. The rhythm of her being joined with the pulse of spring, and the large patch of her spirit wounded by the loss of Gib was swathed in bandages with soothing salves, reviving thoughts of her beloved Otis. She reread the letters of proposal he had written in the winter, and her heart was stirred as she replied to him. She was more and more inclined to accept, though she was saddened by the prospect of leaving the Homestead, Vinnie, and Sue.

How could she part from Sue, the woman she adored, the most cherished dream of her life? No, that was impossible, though she would have to give up Judge Lord. He was "the glass from which she imbibed ecstasy" – life's magic liquor, but Sue had been her soul's delight from the time she was a girl. With the meeting of Sue at the age of sixteen time had come to a stop for her. That was the most glorious period of her life. She was with her parents, Austin, and Vinnie, and in the afternoon when the sun washed the horizon with scarlet, as it slipped smoothly over the far side of the world, Sue would be coming down the street. Just the two of them would sit together on the stoop. Their sides touched and feelings stirred for the first time. Oh – how could she leave Sue? Yet, again, how significant Lord was in her spirit! He represented the image of a perfect life, though she knew that in human existence there was no total fulfillment. Only creativity approached the ultimate.

She walked to the window hoping to see Sue. She looked for her silhouette behind the glass of the library window where she sat so as to be seen, but her figure wasn't there. The house called Evergreens was silent, empty, negated. The depth of winter had smitten the souls of those residing there, the house forlorn in their spiritual absence.

Sighing, she sat down at her desk. Remembering words she had sent Sue, she murmured them again: "Sue, help me expel the shadows which swiftly surround me. I love you so tenderly." The response she then received from Sue filled her with such joy! Her letter had continued: "I cannot fill my cup with such happiness for fear the thirsty angels will drink of it. Sue, I nest in your warm heart, and never again will I hear the wind blow and the storm strike – never again." Now everything had changed. The torment brewed in fiery cauldrons of suffering had smitten their hearts, and memory alone held an echo of their first secret dreams.

Memory, intact, came again to caress her heart. "I will forever be faithful to memory," she thought, and continued, "I never see a Rose in the Boat, without beholding you, and were you only at the Helm, it would be supreme." She dried the tears of recollection and wrote to Sue:

Show me eternity and I will show you memory
Be Sue – while I am Emily –
Be next – what you have ever been, infinitely.

She arose from her desk, moved to the window, and there was darling Sue! She was sitting in the armchair looking toward the Homestead. Emily, by the window with her palms on the glass, stood in her sight. Every so often Sue raised a brocade handkerchief to wipe her eyes, and Emily high up in the window leaned down as if she were brushing Sue's lips with hers, whispering "Sue, you are my All." She felt a throb of doubt again possess her. Marriage with Otis Lord seemed increasingly problematic.

She went out into the hall and, descending the stairs, heard Vinnie's announcement: "Emily, a letter from Otis!" Taking the envelope, she returned to her room, broke the seal, and opened it carefully. Her heart stopped before the virtual blankness of the page on which only three words were inscribed: "A caller comes." What did he mean? She wanted to write him – but to say what? What clarification would she seek? She bit her lip and waited.

The Death of Otis Lord

The next day, 13 March 1884, was cloudy, and the little newspaper boy was in a hurry. He aimed the folded paper at the porch and it hit the center of the door with a thump.

Hearing the sound, Emily was jolted, but she set aside her agonized thoughts. She would be baking bread for her dear Otis. She pictured the aroma reaching across the many miles between Amherst and Salem, bringing her precious companion to her as quickly as possible. Yes, spring would come! She rolled up her sleeves and checked the ingredients set on the kitchen table. They were all there, ready to be combined. Kelly tapped on the door and entered the kitchen with his cap in hand. Relatives of Maggie's, he and Joseph were permanent workmen for both homes. Emily bid Kelly a warm "good day," pleased by his gentle smile. He responded, eyes cast to the floor and turning his cap in his hands, "Top o' the morning, Miss Emily!"

Emily was putting on her apron so she would not soil her dress, and Kelly – his head still bent – kept smiling with the pleasure of seeing Miss Emily. Vinnie entered the kitchen – pale as if blood had drained from her face, with eyes wide in terror and knotted words in her throat; the newspaper drooping from her hands showing the headline "The World Poorer for His Loss."

With broken syllables Vinnie painfully breathed, "Emily . . . It's Lord . . . It's our dear Otis. . ." and Emily heard the shattering of the last remaining vessel of happiness. She took a step, her knees collapsed, and Kelley swiftly spread his arm to support her.

Vinnie continued to gasp, "Oh, our beloved Otis."

"No . . . No . . ." Emily spoke faintly, her tears falling on Kelly's sleeve as her head sank on his arm.

He held her softly and spoke brokenly,

"No, no – don't cry, Miss Emily. I can't bear it!"

Drying his tears with his cap, he guided her tenderly to the nearest chair. She let her sobs take their course, the futile expression of acute pain. "The Abyss has no biography," she thought. "That is the fate of one's seeking ecstasy in life, where there is no permanent source. Suffering always finds its way to the center of my Soul. Those few most beloved are my many."

She sent her last love a lyric farewell (#1638):

Go thy great way!
The Stars thou meetst
Are even as Thyself –
For what are Stars but Asterisks
To point a human Life?

Precious Encounters

Though the day was God's smile upon the earth – a spring to lift one high with aromas, colors, sounds, and fantastic images, I, at my desk, felt death's frozen blast strike my spine and numb the core of my soul.

Emily's end was rapidly approaching.

I arose, exited my study, and left behind the bookshelves lined with volumes containing the poems, correspondence, and studies probing her every inspiration, action, thought, torment, and anguish. I needed the volumes no longer. They had nothing more to tell me.

I was bent on finding the road that would take me back to Amherst. An urgent need I could not evade was driving me to reach the Homestead at once – before the enormous event – to meet not only Emily but Sue, those two women who for months mounting to years, or my whole life, had been with me, no matter where I was or what I did. They were the center of my universe. They were my dearest companions, my closest relatives. They were my spiritual family. They were with me when I went to bed, when I got up, when I ate, drank, cried, and laughed. We were bound by a spiritual affinity that we alone recognized. We felt it at the core of our minds and hearts, cultivated it in our thoughts and conversations, and cherished it as an inestimable treasure. There were no secrets among us. Shame, egotism, antagonism, jealousy – whatever distances people from one another – played no part in our relationship. There were no incomplete feelings. Our spirits and minds were one. We shared every particle of our lives: every thought, desire, delight – every tear that fell from a slight irritation or great trauma. I knew details of their every act and activity – what time they went to bed and got up; what they were delighted by; who repulsed them. I knew whom they loved and for how long.

I also knew what preoccupied the town gossips and what many scholars wrote – that Emily suffered from a nervous condition, agoraphobia, or even epilepsy – but I don't believe a word of it. She consciously chose the style of life suited to her creative passion and followed it rigorously. She achieved enlightenment, viewing humanity from that perspective. She loved people. "Let us love better, it's most that's left to do" she wrote to her cousins. Nevertheless, she was embarrassed by people's pettiness. Their words were shameful; they sullied her mood. She did not care about their thoughts, their habitual words, their mundane pursuits. Having shrunk their lives into empty trivialities, to her amazement they cut themselves off from thought – "How can they live without thinking?" She saw that people began and ended life in continuous sleep. That was why she avoided them – lest she interrupt their sleep. "We're out!" she taught Maggie to say – a little phrase that summed up her attitude about the mundane human world. She shocked herself, writing, "Had I a mighty gun / I'd think I shoot the human race / And then to glory run" (# 118).

When she met someone who was energized by unique perception, she experienced the deep feeling of *eros.* These few were her many – the ones who sufficed for her – her "divine majority." As for the church, or any institution, she could not endure preaching and dogmatism. Life cannot bear dogma. She was moved by a sermon only one time, and she rushed to tell Austin with whom she shared youthful experiences. There had been just that one instance aside from Reverend Wadsworth's words. Of course she had stopped going to church, but she had always pondered the divine. Contact with universal being does not derive from words or dogma. She came to understand that "When the time comes," to face ultimate things, "I will know."

The time came and I knew I must meet her!

My knowing her through her poetry, through critical studies, though cherished thoughts, became a passion to meet her. I was seized by the need first to find Emily, then Sue, as if it could naturally and readily be done. I knew the road whatever means of transportation I chose. I could go by car from wherever I was in the United States; I could take the train and get off two steps from Emily's house, stopping by the little snack shop opposite the property to have homemade soup and bread as I gazed at the fence around the Homestead.

Or I could take Olympic Airlines across the Atlantic!

I could even take my path of blue. Shutting my eyes under my blue coverlet, I would reach her garden instantly. It wasn't difficult. Whatever route I would take, I'd get there – but I could not delay. Time was shrinking. In a month Emily would sink into a coma. Heartbroken, I set off with a poem whirling madly in my mind (#1603):

The going from a world we know
To one a wonder still
Is like child's adversity

Whose vista is a hill,
Behind the hill is sorcery
And everything unknown,
But will the secret compensate
For climbing it alone?

Determined to arrive in time, I reached Emily's garden. The great weight of mortality once more shrouded the Homestead. The house stood before me silent, proud, unique. Would it receive me? At the back door, I heard a noise and knocked. The door opened and Maggie recognized me at once.

"Ah, it's you," she said abruptly. "What are you doing here?" "Come, come, Maggie," I returned, "You very well know why I've come. I need – I absolutely need – to see her. Will you take me up, or shall I go by myself?" I spoke firmly to convince her, and she looked at me with an ironic smile. Then she grew serious. "Wait here," she motioned me to the chair in which Samuel had sat, then Edward, and – more significantly – Emily. I sat in obedience to the great rule of research – "Patience and Expectation." In a few moments Vinnie appeared.

Vinnie was, as always, overworked, but she was ever helpful, especially when it was for the good of the family. Nothing deterred her. The great love that ruled in her was the shield of the entire clan. Emily's genius did not awe or overwhelm her. Emily was simply one way; she another. It sufficed that she was by her sister's side to love and aid her, exactly as she had always been with her mother, father, and Austin. She did not bear the weight of regrets – she had no time for remorse. She stood by the side of anyone in the family who needed her; she would support them all to her final breath. That was the mission on earth she understood and chose.

Vinnie bustled into the kitchen with her orange cat in her arms. Resting her head on her mistress's shoulder, the cat was enjoying affectionate caresses. I observed Vinnie's precisely combed hair and pristine attire. Well-groomed, unpretentious, she carried a shield for Emily. Woe to the person who dared to say or think anything amiss. She looked at me with a searching eye, about to ask who I was – what I wanted. Lowering the tabby carefully, she went to say something, but I interrupted her. I assumed an imposing tone, smiled broadly, and rising from the chair I greeted her with a phrase from a poem of Emily's.

"Vinnie, you are a Soldier and Angel with drawn sword at the gate of paradise, and I, as an angel, bow before you." I warmly pressed her hand.

"You and I are angels! What do you mean?" she responded with a shrewd gleam in her eyes.

She motioned for me to be seated opposite her, and I was prepared to speak of Angels and Eden, poetry and creativity, but these were not "life" for Vinnie, as her father put it. She stopped me with an extended hand and in a severe voice announced,

"If you want to learn why Emily withdrew from Amherst society, the answer is straightforward: it just happened. It was simple and inevitable, which is to say . . . ."

"Say no more," I injected; "I know that's the way it was."

"Who are you and what do you want? What can I do for you?"

Then I launched my appeal. I continued, admittedly with a flourish, "I am the humblest angel of paradise, and my work is contributing to Emily's immortality."

"What does that mean, precisely?" Her face glowed in delight. Naturally I knew that only if I impressed her would she pay heed and aid me in my purposes.

"You see, I do little chores in the Paradise of her poems, and before I submit my work I have to check with Emily to see that it's to her liking. I've got to see her!"

Pleasure first appeared in Vinnie's eyes and then spread over her face.

She looked at Maggie, who all his time had been at the stove cooking. Maggie did not turn, but continued to stir the pot with quick, deft movements.

Vinnie appeared satisfied, "Sorry, it cannot be done," and then she addressed Maggie. "We must not forget tonight to lock the door!" she said, leaving the kitchen.

"Yes, certainly," Maggie laughed, and I knew that I would be able to enter by that very door.

I got up at once, gave dear Maggie a smile of thanks, which she returned, and went out into the garden to talk with Vinnie. She was nowhere to be seen, but since I was sure of entering the house that night, I turned my attention to Sue.

I had to express my feelings to Sue. I was wounded by what people said of her – that she was angry, arrogant, sharp tongued, and merciless. True, she was proud and blunt. Even Emily said of her in a poem, "her beautiful words are blades. ..." Yes, I admit she was that way – but why she was that way I wanted to learn directly from her. I respected her. I knew Susie, I think, better than I knew myself. Oh, she was angry all right – who would not have been in her situation? Only one caught between two searing flames could understand. Sue was caught between the love of great art and the incapacity to produce it. Sue wrote. She penned poems, and articles with humor and insight, but she never entered the domain of greatness. Nonetheless, in her day, Sue could have become a recognized poet or woman of letters (as her daughter later did), and she had a number of publications, while Emily had published only seven poems. But it was not publication that Sue cared about. She did not aspire to it. Like Emily, she understood that the pleasure of art is the process of creation itself. Every time she received a letter or poem from Emily, she felt a thrill of inspiration run through her. Each poem, each word, penetrated to her core. She would trace the words ever so gently with her finger tips and bring the letter tenderly to her lips. Coming directly from Emily's hands, the poem went straight to her heart, moving her spiritually and erotically. The words pierced her with a thrill but they also aroused pain and anger. The higher Emily's work lifted her to ecstasy, the more Sue felt her own sterility. She adored Emily with the same intensity she envied her uniqueness. She recognized original technique but did not have the creative power to conceive and sustain it. What a tragic fate it was to be so close to one of the creative giants of the ages! But could she stand being at a distance?

She read each piece of Emily's writing, letter or poem, so many times that she learned it by heart. Fastening it on her lapel with a pin, she would unpin, study it, and re-pin it, keeping it with her throughout the day. At night, when she went to bed, she would whisper the lines to herself like a prayer before putting the letter in a chest along with the rest of her precious treasure. I saw with my own eyes the pin pricks made on the letters, and it hurt me when I saw them. They looked like the little wounds of her relationship with Emily, and I recognized their relationship: the passion of creation was expressed in the erotic passion of their exchange. Emily possessed it and generously offered it to Sue, and Sue responded with reservations so as not to violate her boundaries. The contrast between them was an affliction for her. She avoided an expression of her feelings which she would later regret. Love and art formed a complex clash of feelings that baffled and maddened her. Her fate was marriage to Emily's brother. The church approved that relationship just as it cancelled the other relationship with black ink.

I walked to the back of Evergreens and entered from the washroom door, which was always open. In fact thieves one time had slipped in that way and stripped the upper floor of valuables the moment that delicacies were being served in the dining room. It was the period of the great famine in Ireland, and according to natural law, when people are hungry, they pour into every corner of the globe, taking what they can get. Austin's house was game for break-ins, whereas the house opposite offered nothing for immediate profit.

I took the stairs to the second floor and Gib's room, which Sue had made her own. Sue was a dark shape slumped in a chair. When she turned to look at me, I saw her eyes. They had lost the human glow. I remembered that once I had seen the eyes of an abandoned horse, sickly, at death's door. It was overwhelmed by the knowledge of death, which was inscribed in its eyes. Thus was Sue. She indifferently turned her gaze upon me with no sign of interest.

"Sue . . ." I whispered, kneeling. As I took her hands lying slack on her lap, I noticed the letter she was holding.

"I know why you are here," she whispered faintly. "You have come to ask me about Emily." Her mournful eyes weighed upon me. "I've been expecting you from day before yesterday when I dreamed about you."

"Oh Sue," I burst out, "I also had a dream about you that night! Is that possible?" I was thrilled by the thought.

She continued in the same even tone. "Why, should it not be possible? I recognize you. In my dream you entered by the back door. . . ."

"Yes, I saw your maid, Claire, at the door. . . ."

"She ignored you," she interrupted. "That is the way my servants behave – they pay no attention to visitors."

"Yes," I whispered, trembling, "but then Joseph came from across the lawn," I continued.

"I didn't see him," she said, "but you entered my bedroom where I was asleep, and your presence awakened me."

"You sat up in bed," I said.

"And I answered your question, 'Sue', you asked, 'if you lived your life over, would you have lived with Emily? Would you not have married and had children, but have been by Emily's side, sharing one another's life?'"

"Yes," I continued, "I remember the dream very well. You looked at me and said. . . ."

"I said no," Sue continued. "I would not have stayed with Emily, because that would not be life but an exquisite moment – of delirious happiness!"

"Yes, that was precisely the word you used . . . exquisite . . . and I wondered. . . ."

She raised her hand with the letter. "I want to read you this," she said, putting on the spectacles she took from her pocket. I was still pondering the word *exquisite* that she had stressed in the dream, and the word had moved me so much that I woke up. I immediately checked the dictionary to find the word in Greek: *thespesia.* If I had stayed in the dream, she would have read the letter to me. Who can fathom the labyrinth of human communication? She interrupted my thoughts:

Emily Dickinson: Goddess of the Volcano

"I want to read you the letter," said Sue, "for you to see the paradox – what a sacred communion Emily and I had in loneliness. What she wrote in the letter I was living. I thought of putting it into writing but I didn't have the courage to set it down, nor the power to describe the *loneness* . . . ."

She began to read, pausing only now and then to wipe away the tears.

> Susie – it is a little thing to say how lone it is – anyone can do it, but to wear the loneness next your heart for weeks, when you sleep, and when you wake, ever missing something, this, all cannot say, and it baffles me.
>
> I could paint a portrait which would bring the tears, had I canvas for it, and the scene should be solitude, and the figures – solitude – the lights and shades, each a solitude.
>
> I could fill a chamber with landscapes so lone, men should pause and weep there; then haste grateful home, for a loved one left. . . .
>
> In all I number you. I want to think of you each hour in the day. What you are saying – doing – I want to walk with you, as seeing yet unseen .

Sue's tears continued. "She wrote that, and I lived it. The feeling was mine; the thoughts were mine, but the words! – the style was hers!" She fell into silent thought. Then she looked at me with infinite sadness. "Once I dreamed of her, and it was so real – the reality of my life, my fate. She came up and stood before me dressed in a fine white dress covered with bright dangling ribbons. She was laughing; her eyes glowed; and filled with admiration and love, I spread my arms. I wanted to hold her tight, but she stepped back and began to dance on her toes. And as she spun the ribbons floated and rose up high, becoming branches of a tree blooming with many-colored flowers and loaded with fruit. I yearned to touch her, to breathe her scent, but I could not reach her. I had become like a tiny child at the roots of the tree. I could reach nothing – not one single blossom or fruit, so small was I, and suddenly I began to hurt. My body was weighed down by the dense shadow cast by the tree. The shadow blackened and flattened me – I could not breathe."

As Sue continued to sob, the clock struck midnight, and my heart beat chaotically. The time had come to meet Emily before she departed from this life. I said, "I will be back again, Sue. I will come one more time before we part forever, but now I must go."

She said nothing. Whether she heard me or not, I did not know, but I quickly arose, opened the door, and took the path back to the Homestead. Sue had deeply shaken me. I ached from the loneness she felt, but nothing could be done to change her fate. All that concerned me that moment was to see Emily.

On the path I looked upward. I had not seen such a crystal clear sky in many years. I remember being in the countryside far from the glow of city lights and beholding such a sky. It glittered with dazzling stars, which shone upon me and protected me. As a child I felt such joy as I felt now by Emily's kitchen door. I stood with eyes raised, and once more, as I did then, I experienced wonder. Without analysis, I felt instantly and completely the immensity of nature. Her beauty was immeasurable. I smiled, thanked the world for its splendor, and took hold of the door knob. As I expected, the door was open.

I entered the totally dark house. I had counted on Vinnie's leaving a lamp lighted, but no matter – I knew the space as well as my own home. I crossed the kitchen and entered the hall. With outstretched hand I readily found the banister and, with no impediment, flew up the stairs. Not far from the top of the stairs I found a lighted candle by Emily's door – open a crack; and suddenly there I was – where I had wanted to be for years.

By the door was a little pillow placed for me to sit – or to kneel? 'Thank you, Vinnie,' I thought and knelt facing Emily's door. Cold sweat ran down my neck as I heard the creaking of the bed. Had she heard me and was rising? Then came the swish of feet as she approached the door. That moment I realized my great boldness. Would the door instantly open wide? I began to tremble. Then, as I heard her step to the threshold, I came to my senses. If she suddenly appeared before me, what would I say to her? How would I greet her – how even open my mouth to utter a syllable? I could not recall what I wanted to say to her. I did not bring notes, my head was totally empty, and my limbs were shaking. I was voiceless, and I knew my eyes overflowed with panic. What was I doing there? What exchange could I have with this woman of the ages? Perhaps she could help me understand fully how she changed my life – what she had added or erased. All my questions – about life, death, God, cosmic truth, nature's splendor, the human spectacle – seemed to be inscribed in Emily's white dress. I had gleaned all of this; it was etched in my heart. My heart accepted the course of life to death, and with the knowledge my mind developed, I imbibed the ecstasy contained in the distance between the two. These insights came at the time of reading and writing. Now, meeting the wondrous person who was their wellspring, what words would I find to express myself?

Waiting breathless before the door ajar, viewing the slender, transparent fingers about to open it, and the sleeve of the white dress, I remained kneeling, frozen on the pillow. As she peeked through the gap and gazed at me, I looked into her face. Her glowing aura filled me with awe and struck my heart. She smiled in expectation. I had to speak.

"My . . . the pages – my manuscript . . ." I whispered, searching the floor for the sheets, which of course I had not brought with me.

"Thank you for coming," she said, "and what do your pages say?" she asked politely.

"They say . . . they say. . . that Immortality exists . . . because its Messengers exist! They bring the message of light. They lead us on the path to the glory of the Cosmos – they elevate us and confirm that we are a portion of the Universe. The Messengers bear the communion chalice and go before us to partake of Immortality – they offer holy communion with the oneness surrounding us. For that sacred communion I am here to give you thanks . . . and to wish you well in whatever form you find yourself!" I said this rapidly, spontaneously, without calculation, in a single breath.

Then the door instantly fell away, and Emily appeared before me, dazzling as a goddess, clothed in glowing white, smiling peacefully. Her countenance was radiant and serene, her being fulfilled.

CHAPTER V

Images of Light - Adieu

Images of Light, Adieu –
Thanks for the interview–
So long – so short –
Preceptor of the whole –
Coeval Cardinal –
Impart – Depart –
(#1556)

Emily was confined to bed, gravely ill. Deeply anxious, Vinnie once again strove to save her sister.

"We must bring a doctor!" she exclaimed to Austin, but Emily would only receive the physician at a distance, through the door ajar. He appeared and delivered his diagnosis: Bright's Disease. Day by day the malady intensified, and Emily felt her strength diminishing.

Vinnie hoped that summer, Emily's beloved season, reviving her powers, would bring recovery. Indeed, summer arrived triumphantly, bringing with it all the gifts of the sun – flowers, birds, bees, and butterflies; and Emily came down to go out and sit in the garden, observing nature's grandeur without being able to take an active part. Then, one morning as she came down to the kitchen prepared to go outside, she swooned. A week later she wrote to Mrs. Holland:

> I saw a great darkness coming and knew no more until late at night. I woke to find Austin and Vinnie and a strange physician bending over me, and I supposed I was dying, or had died, all was so kind and hallowed. I had fainted and lain unconscious for the first time in my life. The doctor calls it "revenge of the nerves" but who but Death wronged them?

Summer passed, bringing in fall, and – before people knew it – it was again the depth of winter. The days and weeks dragged on, weighed down by rain, snow, and ice, and the citizens of Amherst stayed shut in, longing for the weather to invite them out-of-doors.

Emily spent the days in bed or by the window. From November, 1885, one cold after another did not permit her to stand up, and when she managed, she went to her desk to write mainly letters to friends and acquaintances. She even wrote to people she had never met, congratulating them on their contribution to the arts.

Physical weakness appeared ever more clearly in her body. Vinnie was losing heart, but Maggie assured her that the moment spring came all would be well once more. And beloved spring came as it always does, but Emily found it too hard to leave her room. She remained sad and weak in her room, writing her last notes.

To Sue
Remember, Dear, an unfaltering Yes is my only
reply to your utmost question –
With constancy
Emily.

To her beloved Cousins:
Little Cousins,
Called Back,
Emily

She smiled at Vinnie – "My work, Vinnie – my work!" – and it was as if for her people and the world were no more.

13 May 1886. With weak limbs, Emily came slowly and carefully down to the kitchen, smiled at Maggie, and asked to bake bread.

"Whatever pleases Miss Emily!" Maggie responded with evident pleasure, fetching the ingredients. Emily was about to reach out and knead the dough, when a white fog enclosed her like a dream. An absolute silence fell upon her frail body and the world with a soft swish moved into the distance. The channels of the mind were empty, still; the body sank into a deep sleep.

Paralyzed by a trembling heart, Vinnie could not breathe or touch her sister. Her wide eyes, the twisting of the face, said the words that her mouth could not utter. Maggie furiously plunged through the door and dashed to the house opposite. Panting before Sue, she mutely waved her arms toward the Homestead. Sue gasping for air turned to her son and screamed, "Ned, run – bring your father!" and pushing Maggie aside, rushed down the path, entered the kitchen, and hearing whispers, she rushed into the living room. She found Joseph lowering Emily's body, seemingly light as a feather, to the couch. "Run for the doctor!" she addressed him, and gently touching Emily's face, she leaned over and pressed her ear over her heart. The body was absolutely still, but Sue discerned faint heart beats as the blood flowed haltingly. Emily's life, surrounding her frame like an aura, awaited the ultimate hour – her spirit had turned toward the journey of immortality.

Toward evening, the breathing increased in difficulty and became a rattle. Hands over her ears, Vinnie was on her knees praying in a whisper. Maggie was by her side. Nearby, trembling Austin, hearing the harsh breath, the bugle call of death, rushed off sobbing. His tears wetted the diary as he recorded, "Emily will awake on the other side of life." Two days later, on 15 May 1886, Austin added in black ink: "It was an awful day. She stopped that terrible breathing just before the vespers bell."

May evening! The many-colored earthly light faded gently as the radiance of eternity shone. The earth in exultation spread the lush grass and the wild flowers celebrated in a rich variety of colors and scents. In the trees crickets and birds hailed the rebirth of nature. On such a splendid day, Emily Dickinson, fifty-five years of age, embarked for the sun, precisely as she described it (#150):

She died, – this was the way she died.
And when her breath was done
Took up her single wardrobe
And started for the sun.
Her little figure at the gate
The Angels must have spied,
Since I could never find her
Upon the mortal side.

It was Wednesday, 15 May 1886, shortly before six in the evening and on the other side of the cosmos called Paradise, there was a great festival.

Sue's Lament

Seeming to hear the slam of the Homestead kitchen door across the way, Sue sprang to her feet. Through the window of Evergreens she saw the sickly yellow light of sunset penetrate through the leaves of the tall trees, but she paid no heed. Her gaze intensely scanned the path between the houses. It was empty. An enormously sad sigh escaped her lips. She tried to get hold of herself. No – it was not the sound of the kitchen door that had disturbed her but her own anxiety. Her feet drew her through the house, which had become so small you would think it had shrunk. With slow steps she crept through the hall and up the steps to the little one's room. It was freshly swept, his tricycle in one corner, his infant cradle in another. She touched the coverlet of his bed, smoothed it, and caressed it. Her eyes were large and dry. She no longer shed tears. Her aching breast sought relief in sighs. The sound of the door came again, and she rushed toward the stairs. Ordinarily, she would have thought even a door slamming was impossible to hear from that distance, but her agony had shortened the distance, had sharpened her hearing. For two days now she had even heard each breath of Emily's along with every strange sound that occurred in the Homestead. Yes, her senses were functioning. She heard the Homestead's kitchen door open with a creak and close with a slam that was real. With her heart in her mouth she dragged her feet along the hall, looking at the path outside. It was empty. She breathed a sigh of relief. The path was still empty. "Everything is fine," she thought, and suddenly she heard a knock at her kitchen door. She opened and found Maggie staring at her. She raced once again to Gib's room, got a small package, and swiftly came back downstairs. "After this, I will not cross that path again," she thought. "My life, as I knew it, is over. It is finished. . . . All is loss . . ." she thought, "great loss . . . great loss."

"Loss . . . loss. . . ." she repeated, and walked firmly and quickly to the Homestead. In the kitchen, she said nothing to Vinnie – she had nothing to say. She climbed the stairs. "These stairs, this house, the residents are nothing to me. This moment everything is over. My entire life as I knew it this instant is finished."

She opened the door. On the bed was Emily's lifeless form, illuminated by an aura of peace, of which the last portion she had within her had overflowed onto her countenance. Sue quietly sat down by the bedside, and Maggie appeared at the door.

"Mrs. Sue," she sighed, "Emily's request was that you prepare her for burial."

"Water and vinegar," Sue breathed, and she rose to wait by the door.

Maggie swiftly returned, in one hand a tray with enamel basins of water and vinegar, and in the other a lighted lantern, which she placed on the desk. Sue asked her to leave, and softly closed the door behind her. The time had come to be alone with her beloved. She stood by the head of the bed and held her a long

411

time within her gaze. "Priceless, wondrous Emily, we endured our fate," she whispered, and spoke the lines (#458) –

Like Eyes that looked on Wastes –
Incredulous of Ought
But Blank – and steady Wilderness –
Diversified by Night –

Just Infinities of Nought –
As far as it could see –
So looked the face I looked upon –
So looked itself – on Me –

I offered it no Help –
Because the Cause was Mine –
The Misery a Compact
As hopeless – as divine –

Neither would be absolved –
Neither would be a Queen
Without the Other – Therefore –
We perish tho' We reign –

"Yes, my love," Sue said, "your lines express with wisdom and pain the love we lived. It was Wilderness and Loss, but at the same time our existence was queenly, though we could not taste the felicity that was alive in what might have been."

With delicate movements, she removed the clothing. The body, white as rare porcelain, she washed with tears. It seemed a priceless work of art, and with utmost care she dried her salty tears, and then passed a soft sponge over the skin in movements like a fine caress. She unwrapped the package – soft, white flannel, the burial dress she had sewed herself. She tenderly clad Emily in the dress, all the while speaking gently as she wiped her eyes.

"Do you remember the Aurora Borealis we watched from the stoop? You and I! We were in a world of our own – just the two of us, showered by heavenly light. What superb colors! What a variety of hues, what powerful light! Mesmerized, we held hands. The light seared us and we trembled with excitement. The colored lights fell dancing on your face and arms; they transformed your face into what you were within – a holy creature! And you began to speak – your syllables rays of light! You said, 'Poetry must be written in awe and provoke surprise!' –which was exactly what you were to me: awe and surprise! That light and your words charged my entire life! Light, Love, Logos. Fearfully I held back. . . ." She paused, and with a devout kiss resumed. "Magic – the light. And the great difference. You gathered it within you and gave it back to the world. I looked for the light of others to guide my raw steps. You illumined your nightmares, making them birds caroling anguish and ecstasy, and they gave you Immorality.

"I denied my nightmares, and the emptiness in me swallowed me. I listened to the word of others. It was deafening. . . . I silenced it with another noise to fill the loss of your word. I could not hear you, I could not hear me, and I kept falling. . . . The abyss, Emily, has no bottom. You were further and further away, and I sank deeper in the world of others looking for you. You were to be found nowhere – and in no one. Horror your loss. Whatever memory I touch slashes me like a knife.

"My dearest one, love is an exotic journey of the soul. Motionless I journeyed when I sat at the window and saw you gazing upon me from a distance. My heart, free, tenderly sang my love of you. The hour of joy. Now the hour of sorrow. Your letters and poems my bandages. Salve for my wounds. Amulets for my barren soul. I will read them and let their voice sink deep inside me. I will reach out to touch your essence, radiant as moonlight. I will caress your face, royal velvet. I will place your words of wisdom in my mind and soften the anguish. Your natural grace will be my delight, your laugh my breath, the fragrance of your form the sacred aura enclosing me!

"I did not lose you after all, Emily, as I did not lose little Gib. My wondrous Emily and my beautiful little boy, you both were and are mine. I hold you in my arms. I am the mother of that charismatic boy, and I am Susan Huntington Gilbert, the beloved of Emily Dickinson."

She lay down, put her arms around her, and rested her head on her neck, dampening it with tears. The light of dawn crept into the room, and Sue arose.

"Emily," she whispered, "I am going to arrange the place you will rest. It will be a temple for the pilgrimage of poetry lovers through the centuries. I was the first to make my pilgrimage to you as poetess of the ages! Eternal Thanks, Emily Dickinson."

She kissed her tenderly, arose, descended, not looking into the living room where people had already begun to gather, and crossed to Evergreens, never again to return to the Homestead. She went to the forest and gathered aromatic boughs to strew at the bottom of the grave. She locked herself in her little boy's room and did not attend the funeral service. Everything was over. All that remained was to write the obituary which appeared on May 18th in the *Springfield Republican*, the newspaper of Samuel Bowles, the son of their dear friend.

With enormous effort Vinnie controlled herself, so she would not crumble, scream, tear her hair, but remain the proper, dignified head of the house leading the guests to the library, opening the small white coffin with sacred respect to reveal its sealed treasure. Emily was in white, with a crown of flowers, a necklace of violets, and strewn pansies and wild flowers Vinnie had picked from the garden. She opened the door with care not to let in the bees that buzzed in pain in the garden. A few had entered the house and buzzed around the crown as if they heard once more the sacred invitation, "Prithee, brothers, into my garden come." And I – deep in my writing – from afar, prayed, "In the name of the Bee – And of the Butterfly – And of the Breeze – Amen!"

Higginson arrived. For the third time he appeared before his friend Emily. Three days before he had received lines that complained, "I am sick . . . deprived of writing and thought," but death had not come into his mind. The day before the funeral, the notice arrived. Naturally he would go. The invitation was from Emily, who had left instructions with Vinnie concerning guests and the simple funeral service. Emily's friend and teacher, as she called him, had not seen her for thirteen years. He stood a long time before the open casket viewing her beautiful face – more beautiful than he had ever seen it. It was tranquil, smooth – without wrinkles – the red hair with but a few streaks of white, as if she had not been subject to time. "So many singular people have passed from life!" He painfully recalled bidding farewell to Helen Hunt Jackson, Ralph Waldo Emerson, Henry David Thoreau, and this moment he was standing before the casket of Emily Elizabeth Dickinson. He stood for a long time. Clearing his throat to call the attention of the guests, he recited lines by Emily Bronte:

No coward soul is mine
No trembler in the world's storm-troubled sphere:
I see Heaven's glories shine,
And faith shines equal, arming me from fear.

The time had come for the goddess to ascend from the world she had blessed. Placing two heliotrope blossoms in her hands, Vinnie whispered, "For Otis Lord, Emily. . . ." The casket was sealed, and professors of Amherst bore it outside, where four workman from the Homestead waited, attired in their old wedding suits. Sorrowful and awkward, they took the light casket and moved slowly through the Dickinsons' aromatic garden with birds in a flurry behind. The pall arrived at the Amherst cemetery by the house where she lived as a child. The interment would take place in a plot by her parents' graves. All the way, Joseph and Kelly trudged weeping, and the people of Amherst followed in awe and sadness.

Two Lonely Women

How empty can a large house become, its curtains drawn – its rooms dark and hushed? The light, hesitant footsteps of Vinnie – who had become quite frail from mourning – were not audible, nor were the awkward movements of Maggie. Without Emily, the two women, lacking a core for existence, became elderly and mute from the age of fifty. The house was haunted. On the upper floor they caught fleeting glimpses of a white dress where her spirit tiptoed, making them tremble with longing for her.

Silently they went up and down the stairway to her room to inquire regarding her needs. Finding it vacant, they would resume the lament. Vinnie would snip flowers from the garden to arrange in the vase on the precious desk. Reaching to smooth the white counterpane of her bed, she would rest her face on the pillow as if it were dear Emily's beloved countenance. She spoke to her, asked questions, and awaited a reply. When it did not come, she overflowed with tears.

In the anguish of their loss, the relationship of the two women changed. Vinnie was no longer the Lady, Maggie the maid. Pain united them, though at first they maintained certain social forms. For a time Vinnie remained alone at the long dining room table served by Maggie, while Maggie took her supper at a small table behind Vinnie. Thus, the two women dined together and conversed, not so much about present daily affairs as about scenes of former life. With Emily the center, their hearts found peace. It was but a few weeks after Emily's departure when Maggie left her separate table with her plate and sat down by Vinnie.

"People are talking!" Her expression was angry, indignant.

Resting her fork on her plate, Vinnie responded with the same irritation. "Tell me their names, and I'll fix their wagon!"

"They're saying Emily became a recluse because she was in love with a married man." She paused, livid with rage. "And they say the postal clerk kept his eye out for Emily's letters."

Vinnie was unable to continue eating. "People don't have anything better to do than watch what others are doing and say whatever they like! Their lives are so miserable!"

Vinnie, Emily's guardian angel, had to guide the direction of rumors about such an important figure as her sister. "Emily thinks." she would say, growing taller. Vinnie had to protect her sister from gossip about the man in her life, for – as people believed – every action of a woman relates to a man. For Emily to withdraw from society, people would think she must have suffered from the loss of a great love. Who, then, was the man? Could it be the married pastor, Charles Wadsworth, known throughout the country, or could it be Samuel Bowles – he, too, famous and married? The secret might be found in Emily's correspondence.

Amherst's skinny young postal clerk, terribly nosey, kept notes on how often and with whom important townspeople corresponded, and he was particularly curious about Emily, since all of Amherst thirsted for hints of her mysterious life. Folk wondered, naturally enough, to whom a woman sequestered within four walls would be writing. The clerk kept tabs and in the evening he mentioned names to his wife, the neighborhood gossip. In turn, he responded to the avid questions of townspeople with vague snippets of information, becoming a favorite guest in Amherst homes. Vinnie, the worldly wise member of the family, had warned her sister not to write Wadsworth directly, but to enclose sealed correspondence in letters to Mrs. Holland – a practice that had reduced the number of invitations to the clerk from families in town. After Emily's death, however, gossip once more swelled, and the clerk dredged his memory for clues to the mystery from the past.

Vinnie's notion was that people's thoughts should be diverted to a young bachelor, a proper object of Emily's attention in the eyes of the Puritan community. To this end she thought of taking advantage of a visit to Mrs. Aurelia Davis, whom townspeople called "saintly." (The Davises had an attractive daughter with whom Ned had been flirting, warned by Sue, "Not yet Ned. . . .Wait a while."). That evening, after time was consumed by voluminous talk accompanied by tea and cookies, standing by the door, about to say good night, Vinnie spoke:

"I want to confide in you, Aurelia. I know you would never breathe a word to anyone!"

"God forbid, my dear," she answered, trembling with curiosity.

"You know how strict father was. He never allowed us even a single step outside the house, and you know how sensitive Emily was. However, she naturally had her interests."

"Of course . . . a charming young woman would!" Vinnie's friend eagerly agreed, awaiting the revelation.

"You remember the young minister, George Gould, who clerked in the deacon's shop when he was a student?"

"I didn't know him as a student, but as a pastor. Oh, what a devout young man – and so handsome! He was my pastor for a time, before he went off to Mexico. Was he the man in Emily's life?"

"Oh, he was her heart-throb!" Vinnie sighed. "But father would not hear of it because young Gould was poor as a church mouse! Emily was so stricken she never wanted anyone else. At first she stayed in her room in a pique, but it became permanent. She never went out. That's what happened . . . ".

"Tsk! Tsk!" Aurelia shook her head. "What a shame! He was such a fine minister! His words of faith lodged in my heart!"

Repressing a smile at Aurelia's quaint ways, bidding her good night, Vinnie emphasized that the mystery of Emily's love was not for the world's ears.

In the morning all of Amherst came to know that George Gould was Emily Dickinson's great passion. Her heart was tragically devoted to that youth, not to the famous married minister, or the prominent newspaper editor, as it was whispered about.

Anyhow, "She did not want to meet another person, nor to go outside the house. At first she stayed inside because of disappointment; then it became a habit," Vinnie emphasized. This story was later refuted by Mattie Dickinson, who favored Emily in love with the Reverend Charles Wadsworth, and this view was perpetuated in many later studies.

Having spread the word about Emily's "beloved," George Gould, Vinnie also had to look into the drawers containing Emily's correspondence. The very thought of this was distressing. She did not feel up to the task, but duty obliged her.

"Maggie! Maggie!" She was heard all over the house, her voice brimming with excitement. Maggie, uncertain why the tone was so urgent, hurried up the stairs to Emily's room. She found Vinnie standing with her arms overflowing with papers. The bed was covered with them, and there were heaps on the floor.

"Look, Maggie – poems! So many poems!"

Maggie looked, wide-eyed, and spoke hesitantly. "Miss Vinnie, I have some, too. Miss Emily gave them to me to store in my trunk." She lowered her head. "I'd forgotten about them."

Vinnie was shedding tears of joy and laughing in delight. She placed the papers she was holding on the bed, and some of them slipped to the floor. She wiped her eyes, and then she dried her hands on her apron in order to touch the poems, stroke them, and open them to read. As she read lines, her tears flowed afresh.

"Listen to this . . . listen, Maggie!" She read a passage at random and fixed her gaze in admiration. "I should throw open the window and trumpet these poems to the world. We would see who would grasp their meaning! These lines vie even with Shakespeare!" Maggie looked on with amazement, wishing to ask who Shakespeare was. "Folks who babble about 'crazy' and 'neurotic' must hear these poems. They must read them. Then we will see what they say!" Her voice became plaintive. "Maggie," she said, "why are people so narrow-minded – so eager to denigrate others?"

"Don't fret, dear lady! Don't worry your head about people. Some of them are slow to learn, but one day everyone, shedding a tear, will say, 'Ah, Miss Emily, Miss Emily,' and they will weep bitterly."

"Do you think so, Maggie? Do you believe it will come to pass?"

"Yes, Miss Vinnie, yes! You just wait and see!"

Vinnie calmed herself and fell into thought. "The poems must be published so they are available to everyone!" Her face glowed – her life had a great purpose! "The poems must be put in order. I'll begin tomorrow. Tomorrow very early."

At once she set to work. She gathered all the papers, poems and letters to be found in the room. From the floor, the desk, and all around the bed, she tenderly set them at the center of the bed and stretched the coverlet over them. Among the papers were many sets of poems sewn like little books. "Look at these small volumes, forty in number!" Vinnie said. "This week," Vinnie told Maggie, "I'll see where everything goes. Now let's have some tea and reminisce about Emily." They left the room, carefully locking the door. Placing the key deep in her pocket, Vinnie squeezed it with a radiant smile. Vinnie took some sets of poems to her room, and with the sense of Emily being with them, the friends descended the stairs to the first floor.

The next morning Vinnie awoke before sunrise, her mind focused on whom she would find to make a fair copy of the poems so they could immediately be sent to Higginson. He knew publishers, was close to major literary figures, and worshipped Emily, as shown in his moving recitation of poetry at her funeral. Vinnie wiped her eyes. "The poems will be published immediately," she thought. The copying of the poems would begin with those sewn in booklets. Who would do it? Austin would be of no help. She would have to forget about him. He was in a different world. From the time construction had begun on Mabel's house, he had thoughts about nothing else. Sue was the most likely one to be of aid. She was familiar with Emily's handwriting and poetry, she loved Emily, and wanted to see the poems in print.

Yes, Sue – only Sue. She sighed deep in her heart. How would she find the courage to go to Evergreens, to see her face-to-face, to talk with her – to speak to one whose sharp tongue made her tremble. Well, it was six in the morning, and she would have to wait at least two hours. She heard bustling downstairs in the kitchen; Maggie had already begun morning chores. She hurried down to drink tea with her and discuss matters. Listening attentively, Maggie agreed with her thoughts. Sue would support publication, and eight o'clock was the right time to pay a visit and inform her about the amazing find. Vinnie went to her room, changed into an appropriate dress, and carefully combed her hair. Then, carrying a box, she descended once more and crossed over to Evergreens. Ned opened the door. "Aunt Vinnie!" he said and embraced her warmly. Hearing the door open, Mattie looked down on the visitor from the top of the stairs and disappeared into her room.

"Come, Aunt Vinnie, come." Ned led Vinnie into the library. "Sit down;" he said tenderly, "I'll call mother."

Sue – in nightgown and slippers; uncombed and with no sign of pleasure appeared before Vinnie.

"Sue, look!" she said trembling. She held out the box holding little sewn booklets. "There are forty of them – over eight hundred poems! Isn't it amazing – Emily's poetry!"

Sue's eyes glittered. She glanced with wonder at several of the booklets, running her fingers over the contents of the box.

"And there are more!" Vinnie exclaimed, "I have hundreds more separate in my room, and Maggie also has a stack in her trunk! I'll bring them for you to see! Sue, they've got to be copied clearly and sent to Mr. Higginson as soon as possible. Will you copy them?" Vinnie said it all in a rush. Sue's eyes were fastened on the little booklets, and she seemed not to be listening to the words of Vinnie, who was expecting an excited response. Sue, her eyes glazed, was clutching the poems against her breast.

"What do you say, Sue? What do you say?"

Without releasing the booklets, Sue took Vinnie by the arm and guided her outside to the rear of the house from which Mabel's home, called the Dell, could now be seen. The imposing new structure made Vinnie ask:

"When did building begin? When did they have time to do so much?"

"When you signed over the land!" Sue answered severely, leaving Vinnie and rushing back into the house, closing the door behind her.

In the kitchen of the Homestead trembling from head to foot, Vinnie broke into sobs. Maggie half-heartedly offered comfort:

"Don't worry, Miss Vinnie," she said. "She'll get over it – everything will be all right," she repeated without believing it.

Angrily mounting the stairs, Vinnie went to her room to arrange the letters. Wiping her eyes, she spat harsh words about Sue, and whenever she came upon Emily's correspondence with her sister-in-law, she threw the letters to the floor. She would burn them at once. Finding others – to Gould, Wadsworth, Bowles, and even Higginson, she slid them into her pocket and later turned them to ashes in the kitchen stove. Few items of correspondence escaped Vinnie's wrath – innocent letters of close friends like Lou and Francis, and Mrs. Holland. She also retrieved poems and letters from Maggie's trunk, adding the poems to the list for copying. Thus the world would know what a sister she had! Probably Sue's anger would soon pass, and she would do her part to arrange the copying of the poems. The book of Emily's poetry would be published! She took an oath that it would be her life's purpose. Then, what a joy the world would know!

Panting, Sue ascended the stairs to Gib's room, set the box of booklets on the bed, and began to peruse the poems closely. Ned and Mattie knocked on the door hourly only to hear the same words, "Not now. Let me alone for a while." Sue studied the lines, read aloud, wept, laughed. "Masterpieces!" The word escaped her lips now and then as she was drawn ever deeper into the verses. She was baffled by certain phrases and images. These were not poems of the age. They were extraordinarily different. What readers of her time would fathom them? Readers would not be prepared to receive them. As she wrote in the obituary: "Her talk and her writing were like no one else's. . . . A Damascus blade gleaming and glancing in the sun was her wit. Her swift poetic rapture was like the long glistening note of a bird one hears in the June woods at high noon, but can never see. Like a magician she caught the shadowy apparitions of her brain and tossed them in startling picturesqueness." Sue sighed as she touched the papers. "This is poetry;" she told herself, "it will be raised to the heavens! But who will understand it?" Then a thought shook her. "If these poems are published, and readers are prepared – if they recognize the quality of this work, what will become of the Dickinson name? Everything will come to light – our family's shame, draped in black robes of adultery, will become the satirical story of the time. No!" she concluded, "the poems should not be published – not for the present!"

Vinnie waited, burning. "I will die before the book is published; I will never know what readers say! Oh, why is Sue so slow? She will be the death of me!" she told Maggie again and again. She went sleepless thinking of who could do this job best – simply copying the poems. She would send the poems to Higginson, paying if money were needed. Thus the publication would be secured. She could expect no help from Austin. She was sure he would say "Women of good families do not publish, Vinnie!"

The Adulteress and the Poet

Irony is the centrifugal force that overturns the order of life. No one is capable of escaping the trap of the all-powerful goddess of Irony – even the creator, who is said to have shaped man in his own image.

The sun was not up when Mabel arose from bed brimming with life and fervor. She would be overseeing housecleaning in her little nest – a thirteen-room residence at the top of the Dickinson property named the Dell, which she considered the pride of Amherst. This day in particular, her enthusiasm was not limited to care for the new house but included a feeling welling up from the depths of her soul – a divine revelation that the work of her life lay before her, that it was rapidly approaching. She would achieve a success that would make her both rich and famous. The *challenge,* the dream, was right around the corner. She would seize it and fame would be hers.

Clearly, her life was linked to the Dickinson name. Of course, if the good Lord had listened to her prayers, Sue would have vanished, and she not only would live happily ever after with Austin but would set the name Dickinson by her other two names. That is, she would be known as Mabel Loomis Todd Dickinson, because she would never be divorced from David. He was her husband. She would simply add Austin's name, since the two men held such a high place in her heart. "I know what one is – I know what the other is, and two entirely separate sides of my nature go out to them," she wrote in her diary with joyful pride. Naturally, she had her complaints about both of them. David,

425

for example, went with women of classes inferior to theirs. How often had she warned him to be more cautious in his choices, but while he agreed with her, he kept failing in judgment, as if he could not distinguish the marks of inferiority. Austin made a different mistake: he could not oppose his family's pride, and although he was in love with her, he did nothing about Sue's evil tongue, which could blemish Mabel's good name throughout the town. In any case, Mabel forgave the two men. Her life was good, her personality perfection itself, and all would go smoothly with God's blessing.

The house was superb – the furnishings her own, brought from her parents' home, in certain cases in spite of their objections. What was she to do – the things were hers, bought by them at the time of her wedding, not brought to Amherst because they had been living in boarding houses. Now she needed them, having her own house with three floors, indeed in a short time, and on a professor's salary! Everything was hers! David and the child – Millicent – were on the first floor. For Mabel, motherhood was not a first priority, since she was an intellectual, an artist, and that was the primary role for her in life. Millicent could have remained in her parents' care. In any case, she was here now, and Mabel with her "king" – who visited in the afternoon – had her cozy nest on the top level in front of a roaring fire.

One could say that everything was perfect, but Mabel did not use the word, for the situation was not quite that. What if someone would build a house nearby her recently constructed castle, blocking her view? That would be atrocious! If, however, she could have a small portion of the Dickinson lot, which ran from the upper road by her property, that would be happiness indeed! Austin understood her point. He would speak with Vinnie. She was not to worry, since Vinnie loved her and would be willing to sign an agreement that could even go into effect in the event of his death.

Poor Vinnie was all alone. Of course Mabel felt as if she were Vinnie's sister. Dressed in black at Emily's funereal, Mabel cried so much that she became hoarse and could not perform in church services. She and Vinnie were like sisters, and she did not care what was whispered about Austin and her. Mabel felt secure in Vinnie's affection; she did whatever she could in her behalf, and Vinnie would reciprocate. They would meet that afternoon. Two years had already passed from the time that Sue had taken the poems but had done nothing toward publication.

"Two years wasted, isn't that so, dear," she emphasized sorrowfully. Then she added gracefully, playfully, "I forgot to tell you, Vinnie. I'm learning to type. Do you want to see one poem of Emily's typed?"

Vinnie thought, "Would I like to see *one* or *two*? Why not *ten*, a *hundred* – why not *two hundred*. And if she did that many – why not *all of them*?"

"Yes, yes! Of course yes!" she exclaimed, and that was the beginning.

Mabel got to work. In the evening, as soon as night fell, hidden from Sue, Vinnie took the path from the back door to Mabel's house with a box of poems and letters, and Mabel, with David's help, worked into the night editing and typing the texts.

"Emily's poetry is wonderful," Mabel thought, "but it needs correction." Thus, she changed stanza structure, revised words to suit rhyme, and introduced other changes that made the poems more understandable, she thought, for readers. She did her best for Emily's sake.

Mabel Loomis Todd began typing on 30 November 1887 and by 11 March 1888 had prepared the typescript of the first selection of Emily Dickinson's poetry which, with the help of Thomas Wentworth Higginson, was published in 1890.

Vinnie lay down on Emily's bed plunged deep in thought.

It was already three months from the day that the selected edition had appeared in bookstores in Boston and New York, and Vinnie, her heart in her mouth, awaited readers' reactions.

It had rained throughout the night, but the clouds had not been dispersed by the downpour, which was as heavy as Vinnie's tears. "Can it be that four years have passed since the day she ceased to breathe in this room, yet my tears have not ceased to flow?" she thought as she wiped her eyes with a damp handkerchief.

There was a hesitant knock at the door and Maggie entered without waiting for a reply.

"Mistress!" she said urgently, and then, seeing her red eyes, she said more softly, "My good Mistress, someone is asking for you. A young woman wants to see you." Disturbed, Vinnie jumped to her feet. "Where, Maggie? Is she still outside with so much rain?"

"No, I asked her to step inside."

Upset, Vinnie hastily went down, smoothing her dress and hair so as to appear presentable. By the door, her coat soaked and a little pool of water at her feet, stood a young lady wearing a humble smile.

"Pardon me for bothering you, Miss Dickinson," she said in a warm voice filled with emotion. "Yesterday I bought this at the bookstore." She extended her hand and Vinnie saw the title: *Emily Dickinson: Poems.*

"I read all night . . . and at sunrise I took my father's carriage and came. . . . I wanted to see her house . . . her room . . . where she breathed . . . the place she wrote. . . ." Her voice broke and she fell silent, tears rolling down her damp cheeks.

Vinnie spread her arms and the girl nestled in her embrace.

Vinnie, weeping, was saying,

"Here. . . . This is her home. . . . Thank you . . . Thank you. . . . I will show you her room. . . . I am her sister . . . her sister. . . ." On the other side of the hallway, Maggie watched and blew her nose loudly.

The first pilgrim had arrived, having just read the poems, not suspecting that her spontaneous visit would forever be followed by a stream of pilgrims from around the globe.

As enthusiastic reviews by poets and ordinary readers from America and Europe poured in, the battle between the Homestead and Evergreens broke out once more. Sue and Mattie ceased to talk with Vinnie, who had dared – secretly to be sure – give poems to *that woman*. Vinnie was fearful of Sue. She was caught, moreover, in a labyrinth of feelings. She was joyful in the publication but she was also troubled that the name Mabel Loomis Todd appeared below the name Emily Dickinson on the title page. In her excitement about the publication, Vinnie had not realized that the name of the editor would appear so prominently. In the meantime the success of the book sharpened Mabel's ambition, as it made her name known in intellectual circles and, furthermore, increased her income from talks and discussions throughout New England, where she presented the poet as a friend. This was untrue, as Emily had never met her, nor had desired to meet her. Mabel had seen the poet's face for the first and last time at the funeral. In the meantime, Mabel was preparing a second edition with the same violations of the texts, and – something more, which promised renewed battles – she foresaw a third publication, selected letters. Thus, while Mabel was gaining money and fame, Vinnie had nothing – only confused feelings. As for Sue, she had no time for sighs but in rage wrote Higginson, who futilely asked Mabel to honor the integrity of the poems.

Every attempt of Sue's to intervene in order to preserve the authenticity of the texts led nowhere, to the great delight of Mabel, whose arrogance and assumed intellectual capacity not only demanded changes but overcame Higginson who, in the midst of Vinnie, Mabel, and Sue, caved in to the pressure from fearless, young Mabel.

This fact cost him dearly later in life as the recognition of Emily's writing spread throughout the United States and Europe. It was the irony of his fate that the most significant event in his intellectual experience was transformed into his most immense sadness. Up to the time of her death, Emily had sent him around one hundred poems, but at that time the historical issue of the liberation of the slaves concerned him more than poetry. After her death and the publication of the first selection of poems, her recognition through the eyes of readers led him to understand his great error – not to be the one to promote her poetry during her lifetime, and not to oppose the young lady whose intervention in Dickinson's texts blemished his reputation as a literary man of the time.

Though it was too late to be of assistance to Emily or to facilitate a correct first selection of her works, Higginson now devoted his life to supporting her work, to speaking at Harvard, and writing newspaper and magazine articles. He also created a circle of prominent scholars and thinkers devoted to the greatness of Dickinson's work and appreciation of her genius, a term he applied exclusively to her.

In the meantime, Mabel was in her glory days. As the women's rights movement grew, invitations to her increased, and she read poems in her warm, melodious voice, spoke of the idiosyncratic life of Emily Dickinson, magnetized audiences, and developed the reputation of a capable speaker. Her income increased along with her trips to many areas of the country. Her reputation reinforced her opinions, confirmed her editorial interventions, and silenced not only Higginson, but Austin as well – on whom she imposed the condition that the name *Sue* be erased from the poems and dedications, that in certain poems the word *she* be replaced with *he* – and one more little matter – that the little strip of land by her property be signed over to her name. Austin agreed.

Vinnie – faced with Mabel as the protagonist in the new developments – was overcome with rage, and the "little strip" of Dickinson property was the drop that made the glass of bitterness overflow.

Death – the Consistent

The torrent of Time rages in our veins and sweeps us away. . . .

What mystery pervades a well!
That water lives so far –
A neighbor from another world

Residing in a jar
Whose limit none have ever seen,
But just a lid of glass –
Like looking every time you please
In an abyss's face!
(#1400)

William Austin Dickinson

A hesitant knock on his office door interrupted Austin's thoughts. Before him were important legal documents, but he was not up to the task. Although he was attempting to revise them carefully, pinpoint precedents, and so forth, a whirl of worries and bitterness assailed him.

William Austin Dickinson in 1890

He felt an abyss of emptiness. Throughout life, feelings of "profound darkness" had haunted him. He had been plagued by melancholy, "blue moods", and now the loss of his little son threatened to plunge him into utter oblivion. Mabel had held him back from the brink. But now, with her away lecturing, he was beginning to slip over the precipice once more. In youth, he had Emily to shield him with her love and admiration, and in maturity he had replaced Emily with Sue. Now both of them were distant. His soul had fallen into emptiness when he had lost the most precious portion of his self – the child. But though he was lost in the darkness, he was pulled upward by passion for life in the person of the beautiful girl. Yes, through her he rediscovered the beginning. She would bestow on him ongoing life, and the dream would be fulfilled through a child by her. Mabel was young, while Sue had passed the age of conception; and Mabel adored him – she called him her prince, her king, and passion carried him like a storm to heights unknown to the norms of love.

Though he had begun the day's professional work with the best intentions, he was getting nowhere, and now there was another interruption! Someone was insistently pounding on the office door. As the pounding became more intense, he could no longer ignore it. Pushing his weighty thoughts side, he lifted his head.

"Come in!"

At once the neighborhood minister stepped in. His countenance was grave; it contained no hint of a friendly attitude or even civility. With a forced smile, Austin arose, extending his hand. "What can I do for you, sir?" he inquired.

The visitor, without accepting the handshake, announced in severe tones: "You can do nothing for me, sir. I come to do something for you. We must talk."

"With pleasure," the lawyer replied. "Please give me a moment to complete something I'm writing."

The clergyman took a seat in front of the desk, as Austin perused the documents, inserted a word now and then, and consulted tomes on bookshelves. All the while, the visitor attempted to draw attention with a discreet cough.

Austin turned not a single time to look up, and as time wore on the minister acknowledged the situation to himself, wordlessly arose, and walked out the door.

"May no one dare bandy words about a pure love relationship!" Austin told himself exultantly. Before succumbing once again to mental confusion, he experienced a moment of serenity and exaltation. He suddenly shoved the legal papers into a drawer, abandoned the law books, and turned his mind back to the beginning. What had happened in his life? How had the years passed! When did it all begin, and where would it go? It all seemed a shifting dream, a recurrent nightmare; and he unsteadily formed visions of the future. The future! When would the future come? And when it came, what would it be like? Where was he going and with whom? Once, it was Emily! Yes, she had been close to him in childhood, while the rest were somewhere else, and later Sue, who had replaced Emily's role as sister and mother. She became his wife-mother; but what role had he played in her life? His serving her had never succeeded, try as he might. Then came Mabel with her incredible vitality. That surge of life was suddenly severed with the death of the child, but his dearest had soon succeeded once more in sweeping him to relief and exultation. Mabel's arms were an oasis for existence – therapy for the soul, though the abyss remained a threat. When she held him in her embrace, he was in Eden – he was not threatened; Sue's accusations faded. Life spread grandly before him as it had when he was young. He was young again. They would go west! Westward, Ho! The past would be erased, and they would begin all over again! The west was his future! Mabel would follow his lead! All they needed was a plan of escape. Nebraska awaited the coming of the expert man of the law, and beautiful, gifted Mabel would bear him a son! Yes – there would be succession of perfect Dickinsons. The western land spread vast as Mabel's embrace, and the child with red hair frolicked about the farm with cows, chickens, horses, and the eternal promise of the Dickinson name.

But suddenly the dream faded. Nature refused him a child by Mabel. Mabel made every effort, and he passionately made love to fulfill his purpose, but to no avail. And now came another impediment to his plans. He was devastated. The publication of Emily's poetry brought her name in capital letters before the entire New England intelligentsia – an event he wished to avoid. Emily, his younger sister who he thought "posed" as a poet suddenly became *the* poet of the nation; and Mabel – whom he needed above all else – was repeatedly away lecturing on Emily, while their very future was being lost in the clouds!

All he could do was be patient and wait. David, he, and Millicent awaited the return of his beloved like a whirlwind to slake their desires; but no sooner did Mabel return than she was off to Boston again. David did not appear to be greatly bothered, nor did the child; only he sharply felt her absence. He missed her – how much he missed her, but she – a lady of a good family – was out there somewhere, admired and applauded by audiences. These things should not have been! Such ill had befallen him recently, thrusting him down, down, down into the abyss. On top of that, there was Vinnie insisting, "Austin, you must read Emily's correspondence to decide what will be published and what must be burned!" And they read and burned . . . read and burned. There was no end of it.

Austin realized he had not risen from his chair all day, had not taken a drink of water or a bite of food, yet he had not arrived at a solution for his predicament. He asked himself if he was at fault for the morass in which he found himself.

Darkness was crowding him, narrowing his space, and he insisted on piercing through the murk. It was past midnight. He did not light a lamp, but in the deep blackness of the office suddenly an insight appeared like the flickering of a candle. He groped in the shadows, and it seemed he touched a truth about his life. A sharp pain pierced his heart – the swelling of a discovery. On his twisted features was etched the knowledge of what in fact had taken place: For a lifetime his face had been turned toward the others, and he had followed their expectations. Others had written the play, and he had performed the role. Life had been laid down by others and he had taken that path. He had borrowed life from other people's dreams and desires, and life mercilessly demanded that he live his own! He gave in to the enormous sadness of total, comfortless remorse, without words to console him.

Time raced on.

A year later, in 1895, at the age of sixty-six, weary, spiritless and profoundly sad, William Austin Dickinson – Edward's pride, deeply loved by the noted poet, a person of vast potential – was an old man who surrendered to the journey to the other side, the object of Vinnie's deep sorrow and Sue's unremitting wrath. It was a clear evening in the month of August, with a gentle sky and placid sunset. At 7:20 his mournful heart stopped without bidding goodbye to Mabel and David, who were away on a trip.

Beside his father's coffin, Ned wept for his unfulfilled need of his father's love, Mattie gazed at the deceased as a stranger who filled her with outrage, and Sue, stiff and cool, was planning the plaque over Austin's grave and its position. It would be at a distance from the graves of the other family members, and it would be inscribed only with his initials. She could think of nothing to quote as a creed on the plaque, for she had never received a hint of such a thing in Austin's heart.

Vinnie, thinking of all the suffering of her family, was sobbing painfully. In the extreme weakness of her body, she relented, gave in to Mabel's pressure, and accepted honoring her brother's memory by signing over the 'small strip' of property to Mabel.

Soon, however, Vinnie felt the Furies striking on all sides. For the first time she realized precisely what had been whispered about Amherst: this young woman had thrust herself into the Dickinsons' life like a leech for purposes of profit and self-aggrandizement.

Vinnie deeply regretted giving Mabel Emily's letters and poems, and worse, caving in to her pressure to sign over the strip of land that rightfully belonged to the Dickinson children. She was overcome by grief and suffered for months to find a way to cancel the latter transaction. She filed a law suit against Mabel. "I did not know what I was signing," testified shrewd Vinnie. "No one explained it to me – neither Mabel, nor even the notary. They came one evening to see the family silverware, and brought with them papers for me to sign." Thus the trial began.

Mabel held that the land was compensation for her work of many months as editor of the poems, but Vinnie was ahead of her. Maggie came to her aid, testifying to the erotic tie between Mabel and Austin. Maggie's testimony was taken at the Homestead, not at the courthouse, for no one wished to blemish the memory of Austin Dickinson. Maggie (who was supposedly ill and scheduled for treatment in Boston) straightforwardly and honestly bore witness to the couple's coming to the Homestead when Emily was in her room and Vinnie was away from home on chores. She spoke simply without personal feeling, and the facts were apparent. Thus, Mabel's attorneys were faced with the great dilemma of the Puritan age between the law and social norms. If they undertook the support of an adulteress, it would be the end of their careers. Thus, they resigned on ethical grounds, and the suit ended in the nullification of the transaction.

Ned and Mattie, present daily in the packed courtroom, stood by their aunt's side. Vinnie in her yellow shoes, plain blue dress and black shawl of mourning, appeared to be a deceived elderly woman confused by the matters put forward by Mabel's attorneys. They maintained that the endless hours of Mabel's work could not be repaid merely by intellectual endeavor but should be materially compensated. Vinnie held to her line of ignorance. She could not understand them because that was "business" – a domain foreign to her. No one was fooled by Vinnie's theatrics, but the people of the little town especially revered the Dickinson family, and the judge did not permit an outsider to receive such a portion of the patrician's estate.

The Dickinsons did not have time to celebrate the defeat of Mabel, who was threatening to appeal the decision to a higher court (which eventually ruled against her and levied a fine). This was their second victory, but a Pyrrhic one. It claimed its price.

Ned, exhausted by the heat and the daily contentions in court, died of heart failure (1898). Sue's heart was torn to pieces. She could not forgive Vinnie. It was her fault that her son paid with his life due to the tension in the legal proceedings. Vinnie, deeply sorrowful, followed Ned a few months later, 31 August in 1899, to the great pain of Maggie.

Vinnie's rights to the poetry and correspondence went to the heiress, Mattie Dickinson, and a new conflict arose. The battle between Sue and Mabel was over, and the strife between descendents Millicent Todd Bingham and Martha Dickinson Bianchi had begun.

David and Mabel

Depression attacks smooth faces, bright eyes, and smiling lips. Mabel, seated across from David, studied his features and saw the stark shadow that enveloped him. He had become alien and indifferent to existence. Nobody – nothing – could break his dark silence. He never spoke or laughed.

Mabel touched him gently. "David," she whispered, "tell me what is happening to you?" Lowering his eyes, he whispered, "Adultery. . . adultery." His illusions and blinders removed, he was hurled into a hellish region that was his alone. It was a place blank and arid, with a lurid stain in the midst that was swelling enormously over the years. Now that the stain had a name he cringed immobile in the house of their dreams endlessly whispering: "Adultery is evil. . . evil. . . Adultery is evil . . .". Within a few months Mabel confined him in a Boston clinic where he died intoning the same refrain.

In her bitterness of defeat in the trial, Mabel added to her life yet another hate. The hate which she had nursed for Sue, she transferred to the person of Vinnie. Her only hope for vindication was that her daughter – a respected scholar – would review every detail of the trial and cast on her a favorable light.

On 13 May 1913, Mabel hid her satisfaction behind the brief statement set down in her diary: "Poor Sue died."

Sue had spent the remaining years of her life in frequent trips to Boston and Europe. Letters and poems by Emily were always in her pockets. Her face glowing in joy, she read the poetry of her friend at frequent cultural events. In turn, she wrote articles and verse published in young Samuel Bowles's newspaper. She died at the age of eighty-three.

Mabel insisted on living alone in Amherst. One day not long after Sue's death, amidst an insufferable heart wave, she ventured out for a swim in the college pool. As she was crossing the street, a black shadow loomed before her. A carriage was careening toward her, its black-clad driver flaying the white stallion with a riding crop. Mabel only had time to scream and lift a futile arm before she was hurled to the road.

She came to in her bed, her neighbors and her physician standing over her. "You had a sun-stroke, Mrs. Todd," they told her, and she furiously corrected them:

"It was Sue Dickinson! I saw her! She came at me with her horse and buggy!"

The doctor repeated his statement, explaining that Sue was deceased and that Mrs. Todd had suffered a sun-stroke, but she angrily insisted, "The witch ran over me! I saw her steely eyes!"

A few days later, she suffered a stroke that left her left side paralyzed. She walked with difficulty, could not play the piano or write, could not speak properly, and thus could not continue her lectures. She moved to Florida with a new man, who unfortunately was her inferior.

Millicent was now her only salvation. Mabel bestowed on her a mother's commands and blessings, and Millicent – a serious Dickinson scholar – took up poems and letters as the baton was passed. She was a witness to the lives of those in the circle in three valuable books.

Mabel did not live to see the books in print. She died on October 19, 1932. This ambitious, hard working woman, who loved to be in the Amherst spotlight, has become a focus of interest for all who delight in reading Emily Dickinson. No matter how they view her behavior, they honor her contribution and acknowl-edge her importance in saving the poems.

To Millicent's three books, Martha Dickinson Bianchi reacted stubbornly and angrily, defending her mother's name and describing the friendship of her aunt and mother. (Bianchi is Martha Dickinson's name by marriage to a Russian cavalry officer – handsome and pleasant, but careless in practical affairs – who vanished one morning leaving debts but no offspring.)

Mattie remained at Evergreens, transforming the library into the Emily Dickinson Room. Emily's furniture, books, and dress were brought from the Homestead for a permanent exhibit at Evergreens. As the sole inheritor, she sued the Todd family for property rights. She continued to write novels and poetry until her death in 1943. Her property and literary rights she left to her secretary. He left the literary rights to Harvard and to Amherst College the two residences – timeless monuments to the life and spirit of Emily Dickinson.

Martha Dickinson Bianchi

Epilogue

'Twas my one Glory –
Let it be
Remembered
I was owned of Thee –
(#1028)

The story is told, and it is time to gather up notes, books, knowledge, and feelings – and whatever else has accumulated from the years of study and the task of writing. It is the hour of departure, and I must find a way to say good-by to the friends whom I loved and admired with all my heart.

My farewell is more difficult than the adventure of research and writing. The weave of my feelings is so overpowering that it does not let me freely and painlessly bid them farewell. I lived with them the events of life great and small; I participated in pain, love, death; I probed their experiences. I learned about secrets of life that inspire thought and analysis. I loved them without reservation, and I admired them for what they offered to my mind and heart. I suffered with them in all the dead-ends of feelings that entrapped them, their prejudices, and the neuroses in which they were caught. I lived with Emily the incredible flowering of her poetic voice, the exercise of her critical powers, her enduring drive to live and work. I witnessed the loves of her bountiful heart.

Walking around the properties, I deeply felt the Dickinsons' absence. The Homestead and Evergreens were closed – everything frozen in snow and emptiness. Serene the Dickinson grounds. The two houses uninhabited, yet they bore witness that here dwelt, in the one house, a goddess of art and thought, and in the other, the two closest witnesses and most dearly beloved in her life.

Vital, imposing, the two residences await the coming of other scholars and admirers – to enter with passionate devotion. Yes, I felt such a flame, though my heart is stricken now, and my eyes testify to my sadness. Like a psalm whispered the letter Emily wrote to Sue when they were as yet young girls:

> I miss you, mourn for you, and walk the Streets alone – often at night, beside, I fall asleep in tears, for your dear face, yet not one word comes back to me from that silent West. If it is finished, tell me, and I will raise the lid to my box of Phantoms, and lay one more love in; but if it lives and beats still, still lives and beats for me, then say me so, and I will strike the strings to one more strain of happiness before I die.

I tried to bring young Emily and Sue to mind, but unfortunately I had just put up my papers and books, and my imagination had faded. Suddenly everything was lost without the promise of renewal. It was as if it all had been removed to some distant planet. I would not see them again, although I had promised Sue to drop by one more time. Now, however, with notes filed and volumes tightly shelved, the possibility of renewed contact was remote.

And yet the exaltation of the encounters and the tenderness of the friendships endured. Four years held in the exotic garden of Emily's verse had left inexhaustible the distillation of her thoughts and feelings. I had heard the call of her voice – "Prithee come to my Garden. . ." – and I had gently given myself to her Paradise of metaphors and images. *Like an inebriated Bee I sucked from the jasmine of her syllables. I immersed in the balsam of her thoughts. Together we traversed the straits of human anguish, and she instilled the strength required to scale the heights before me, expelling the shadows that rush to encircle me. I was like the figure in her poem (#1587) who was transformed, my soul infinitely nourished by a book of verse:*

He ate and drank the precious Words –
His Spirit grew robust –
He knew no more that he was poor,
Nor that his frame was Dust –

He danced along the dingy Days
And this Bequest of Wings
Was but a Book – What Liberty
A loosened spirit brings –

True, the Spirit leads to Cosmic Consciousness – the path to the Ecstasy of Transcendent awareness, the most precious gift of the universe, which all too often seems to have been abandoned and forgotten. There the great secret dwells: the Divine and the Self are One.

I looked up to her bedroom window and I seemed to glimpse her aura. She was on the balcony of God, elevated by the glory of her gifts to art, the human spirit, the poetry of the world.

I entered the path toward Evergreens, the home of Sue – it, too, like the Homestead, sealed and dark. Yet it was as familiar as the house of my birth. It had taken so long – so long – to get there, but I had arrived!

Tho' I get home how late – how late –
So I get home – 'twill compensate –
Better will be the Ecstasy
That they have done expecting me –
When Night – descending – dumb – and dark –
They hear my unexpected knock –

Transporting must the moment be –
Brewed from decades of Agony !

To think just how the fire will burn –
Just how long-cheated eyes will turn –
To wonder what myself will say,
And what itself, will say to me –
Beguiles the Centuries of way!
(#207)

My sad steps led from the grounds of the Homestead. I stepped into Main Street, and by the fence awaited my life companion. He took me tenderly by the hand.

"Well," he smiled, "tell me about the great journey of writing! Was it beautiful?" I felt the intensity of his warm embrace and replied, deeply moved,

"Beautiful beyond description – like the journey of our lives. Thank you!"

Contents

CHAPTER II

Contents

CHAPTER III

CHAPTER IV

CHAPTER V

POEMS QUOTED

Bibliography

Anderson, Charles. *Emily Dickinson's Poetry: Stairway of Surprise.* New York: Rinehart and Winston, 1960.

Bianchi, Martha Dickinson. *Emily Dickinson Face to Face: Unpublished Letters with Notes and Reminiscences.* Boston: Houghton Mifflin, 1932.

_____. *The Life and Letters of Emily Dickinson.* New York: Houghton Mifflin, 1924.

Bingham, Millicent Todd. *Ancestor's Brocades: The Literary Discovery of Emily Dickinson.* New York: Harper, 1955.

_____. *Bolts of Melody: New Poems of Emily Dickinson.* New York: Harper, 1945.

_____. *Emily Dickinson: A Revelation.* New York: Harper, 1954.

Cody, John. *After Great Pain: The Inner Life of Emily Dickinson.* Cambridge: Harvard University Press, 1971. Farr, Judith. *The Passion of Emily Dickinson.* Cambridge: Harvard University Press, 1992.

_____. *The Gardens of Emily Dickinson.* Cambridge: Harvard University Press, 2004.

Gordon, Lyndall. *Lives Like Loaded Guns: Emily Dickinson and her Family's Frauds.* New York: Viking, 2004.

Hart, Ellen and Martha Nell Smith. *Open Me Carefully: Emily Dickinson's Intimate Letters to Susan Huntington Dickinson.* Ashfield, Massachusetts: Paris Press, 2010.

Higginson, Thomas Wentworth. "Letter to a Young Contributor." *Atlantic Monthly IX*, 401-411.

Hitchcock, Edward. *Mary Lyon.* Northampton, Massachusetts, 1851.

Johnson, Thomas H. (ed.). *The Complete Poems of Emily Dickinson.* New York: Little, Brown, 1957.

_____. *Emily Dickinson: An Interpretive Biography.* Cambridge: Harvard University Press, 1963.

Leyda, Jay. *The Years and Hours of Emily Dickinson*, 2 volumes. New Haven: Yale University Press, 1960.

Longworth, Polly. *Austin and Mabel: The Amherst Affair and Love Letters of Austin Dickinson and Mabel Loomis Todd.* New York: Farrar, Straus, Giroux, 1984.

Patterson, Rebecca. *The Riddle of Emily Dickinson.* Boston: Houghton Mifflin, 1951.

Pollak, Vivian R. *A Poet's Parents: The Courtship Letters of Emily Norcross and Edward Dickinson.* Chapel Hill: U North Carolina Press,1988.

Sewell, Richard B. *The Life of Emily Dickinson.* Cambridge: Harvard University Press, 1974.

_____. *The Lyman Letters: New Light on Emily Dickinson and her Family.* Amherst: University of Massachusetts Press, 1946.

Sherwood, W. Robert. *Circumference and Circumstance: Stages in the Mind and Art of Emily Dickinson.* New York: Columbia University Press, 1968.

Schultz, Liana Sakelliou (ed.). *Ralph Waldo Emerson: Dokimia* (Essays, 2 vols.). Athens: Gutenburg, 1994.

Synadinou, Elli. *Emily Dickinson: To anexantlyta Symainon* [91 poems]. Athens: Ideogramma, 2006.

Sophras, Errikos. *Emily Dickinson: 44 Poiimata kai 3 Grammata.* Athens: To Rodakio, 2005.

Shurr, William H. *The Marriage of Emily Dickinson.* New York: University Press of America, 1992.

Bibliography

Taggard, Genevieve. *The Life and Mind of Emily Dickinson.* New York: Knopf, 1930.

Todd, Mabel Loomis (ed.), *Letter of Emily Dickinson.* Boston Roberts Brothers, 1894. Kessinger Legacy Reprints.

Ward, Theodora Van Wagenen. *The Capsule of the Mind: Chapters in the Mind of Emily Dickinson.* Cambridge: Harvard University Press, 1961.

Whicher, George. *This Was a Poet: A Critical Biography of Emily Dickinson.* New York: Scribner's, 1938.

Wineapple, Brenda. *White Heat: The Friendship of Emily Dickinson and Thomas Wentworth Higginson.* New York: Knopf, 2008.

Wolff, Cynthia Griffin. *Emily Dickinson.* Reading, Massachusetts: Perseus Press, 1998.

The Author

Despina Lala Crist, born in Athens, Greece, came to the United States in 1956 to pursue literary studies. As an English-History major, she met professor Robert Crist; they married in 1960, thenceforth residing in both countries.

Despina Lala Crist is a renowned novelist in Greece. She has written a number of books for children and young adults, short stories, and critical articles, as well as producing a study of the famous innovative writer, Giorgos Heimonas. In her five novels, which alternate in settings between Greece and the United States, her style is marked by the unique way in which she interacts with her characters. Her novels in translation include *Nostos*, trans. Robert Crist (2001) and (upcoming) *The Writer's Secret*.

The Translator

Robert Crist – Haverford College (B.A.), the University of Chicago (M.A., Ph.D.) – is Professor Emeritus of the University of Athens. Among his translations of poetry, prose, and fiction are works by Aris Alexandrou, Katerina Anghelaki-Rooke, Nikos Kyriazis, and Despina Lala Crist, as well as Constantine J. Vamvacas's The Founders of Western Thought – The Presocratics (Springer: Boston Studies in the Philosophy of Science, 2009). Soon to appear: Giorgos Heimonas, Graphimata – The Collected Writings (Seaburn).

Art Work

Ave George Ionnides, of Greek descent, was born in Russia, lives in Greece, and studies in the Fine Arts Department, University of Western Macedonia, Greece.

Made in the USA
Columbia, SC
18 August 2018